"LOVE YOU .... SEE YOU SOON !"

INTRODUCTION

A coming of age Love Story as Dave and Sandra meet, fall in Love and plan to build their lives together. Based in and around the Yorkshire Moors, where two secrets from the past will impact massively, but differently on their lives, each one with devastatingly different results.

Intermingled with family, friends and work, as well as humorous episodes in their lives, the story is told over 14 years from 1981 to 1995, as they find each other physically, and emotionally, and their plans are working perfectly from the night they sealed their love for each other, to when their daughter Caroline is born.

As they develop their lives together the impact of greed collides with their plans, leading up to the moment their lives are changed forever, and one is left to deal with the result of the untold secrets, which remain secrets until they meet the truth.

Chapter 1 - Winter - 1981

Dave Baxter had come into the picture in the winter of 1981, as their paths crossed at work where Sandra Robertson worked in the Administration Support Department. The Council Christmas party which for some reason was in the first week of December was where it started, and could have ended, as Daniel Bruce having grown some airs and graces as he found his feet at the Council made a bee line for Sandra as she was at the bar getting two halves of lager and lime for her and Marion from the Administration Support Department.

"I'll get these!" she heard from behind her and recognising Daniel's voice turned around to the sound of "These ladies are with us" as Dave and Sid arrived at the bar at the same time, Sid holding a £5 note for the barman to see. "Sorry didn't realise" said Daniel as he looked at Sid, who stood some 6 inches taller at 6ft 3in than Daniel, walking away with a disappointed backward look at Sandra as Sid said "No problem" as he ordered their drinks. "Two pints of Lager and two halves of Lager and Lime looking at Sandra for confirmation and having been served took his pint of Lager and Marion's half of Lager and Lime and they headed back into the party which was finally starting to liven up as the DJ had found a groove with David Bowie's Let's Dance.

"Hi" said Dave now they were on their own as Sandra sipped her drink, "Looks like I saved you from Daniel's clutches"

Blushing slightly, which she hoped Dave wouldn't notice Sandra took another sip of the over sweet lager and lime. "Where have Sid and Marion gone to?"

"Don't worry about them they'll be all over each other by

now, I just used Sid to cut off Daniel and get you to myself"

"Oh you did, did you" she said blushing even more "Well that was very presumptuous of you"

"Sandra, I should tell you I have fancied you for ages, ever since you joined the Council. Did the smiles and hellos not get through" said Dave hoping this wasn't going to end like his last attempt to get a girlfriend, with a slap and a strangled laugh.

Seeing Daniel in the background hovering, Sandra made a decision and said pointing towards the table near the stage "Shall we join Sid, and Marion over there", where the amorous couple were oblivious to everyone else as they became one body joined at the mouth.

Moving past Daniel on their way to join Sid and Marion, Sandra could see him mouth something but couldn't hear for the music which was now getting everyone to do the YMCA, but she was sure it was "You'll regret that!" before he turned away and left.

The evening according to Sid and Marion was a Blast! But Dave couldn't really remember much about the party, other than drinking too much, but the slow walk home holding Sandra's hand was imprinted on his memory forever. They got to Sandra's home at 01.30 and neither of them could seem to place what had happened on what should have been a 20 minute walk from the party which ended at 12.00. The longest, short walk he had ever taken he thought, having kissed Sandra for what seemed the 100th time before letting her go as the lights went on upstairs in her house and Sandra said she had to go in as her mum would be down to see where she was as she worried about her. Taking a short cut across the fields from Sandra's house to his home through the light snow that had just arrived, it was one happy 'Romeo' Dave who went to bed looking forward to the future, and time with his new girlfriend Sandra Robertson.

Over the next few weeks Dave and Sandra began to see each other not just at work where a stolen kiss a break times, was a regular interlude in the dreary Council routine for both of them, but most nights they would meet up for a walk or to go to one of the many local pubs, if the weather which was now bitterly cold having picked up an Arctic blast drove them indoors but just being together meant the most to both of them. With Christmas almost upon them Dave had no idea what to buy Sandra, his first real girlfriend, so asking Sid over a pint on Wednesday 23rd December at the Malt Shovel where they usually met, always avoiding joining in the regular Quiz Night which was in the Wednesday night 'Entertainment slot', he was a bit shocked when Sid said as a matter of fact "Knickers! Then she gets a present, and so do you!" Spitting the froth off his newly ordered pint Dave gave Sid a withering look of 'What planet do you come from?'Before breaking into a roaring laugh at the honesty of the comment it was no wonder Sid was so popular with the ladies, has two girlfriends on the go the last he had heard.

"Really do you think of nothing else Sid?"

"Nope" was the factual retort.

"You're head over heels, aren't you" Sid continued before returning to his pint without looking at Dave.

"Nah" said Dave hoping his nose wasn't growing and picking up his pint downed it and nodded to Ian the barman for two more with a two finger rabbit ears gesture using the time to change the subject.

Finishing the night with a game of pool, which they had had to wait for, hence the extra couple of pints, well that was their excuse, the now somewhat intoxicated pair headed home, parting at the end of the estate to go their separate ways with Dave somewhat melancholy and looking forward to seeing Sandra tomorrow at work when he had some big questions to ask, and hopefully some big answers.

Crossing the road to reach the Alley that took him to the back of his home with his coat pulled close against the freezing wind that had been coming for the last few days he wished he had brought a hat and turning into the Alley, Dave didn't see the figure behind the hedge leading to the Alley, only felt the blow on his head that continued onto his shoulder that knocked him down onto his knees, and then a second blow that sent him down onto his back to look at the stars above the broken street light when he heard a voice from above saying "Stay ...!" and then a third blow that sent him down into a cold, dark abyss, alone, no longer seeing or hearing anything.

◆ ◆ ◆

Chapter Two

"No Dave Baxter" said Barbara, PA to Eric Normanton the Chief Surveyor at the Council Property Department as she looked at the clock and 08.30 passed. Dave Baxter hadn't appeared for work as usual at 08.00 which was odd.

"Give his mum, I think it's Diane, a ring, it's not like Dave to be ill" said Eric as he finished off the first of his usual 8 cups of tea a day, looking at the files containing the workload he had on his desk. Without Dave he would have to move things about a bit but he had high hopes for Dave, true he wasn't a fast track candidate like Daniel Bruce, but with time he would be a good right hand man with some mentoring, so not to be here on a Thursday was not like Dave.

Eric could hear Barbara on the phone as he opened the top folder and started on his plans for today without looking up when he heard Barbara put the receiver down and she turned to Eric with a hand in the air and a concerned look on her face.

"Eric, Dave Baxter is in hospital at the Infirmary, he's in a coma, he was mugged last night says his mum"

"Jesus Christ" said Eric forgetting he had been told numerous times by his wife Jane not to take the Lord's name in vain! "Anything we can do" he replied.

"They say there is nothing they can say until he comes out of the coma"

Taking onboard Barbara's comment Eric didn't correct her using 'if he comes out of the coma' but taking a few minutes before getting back to workload he wondered who on earth would get mugged on a Wednesday night in Kirkdale, beggars belief! What is going on in this town he thought!

Sandra found out about Dave from Barbara later that morning, as she usually didn't see him on a Thursday as Eric Normanton usually took him out on site, and they would meet up to walk home at the end of the day. She knew there was something wrong when Barbara came up to her in the corridor and wrapped her arms around her with a whispered.

"I'm so sorry"

"What" said Sandra as she disentangled herself and saw Barbara's eyes were tearful and red with rubbing.

"What are you on about Barbara" Sandra restated.

"Dave, Dave Baxter has been mugged and is in hospital" replied Barbara

"But, but, but" Sandra tried to say but got no further than one word.

"He's in a coma according to his mum" replied Barbara. Then the flood gates opened and Sandra's tears now flowing down her cheeks, hugged Barbara as the pair held each other to save saying anything else before parting, and Barbara going back to the Property Department and Sandra rushing off to see her Manager to try and get the rest of the day off to go to the Infirmary. She hadn't been seeing Dave for more than a few weeks since the Council Christmas Party, but the way he looked at her and the things he said on their walks home, about the future and how he was going to get on in the Property Department and would be a good catch for someone, with a sly wink to Sandra. She was sure that this relationship would be so much better than the pressure she felt when she went out with Daniel Bruce in the summer. It was a shame it had ended but Daniel was such a controlling boyfriend that she felt she was always at his beck and call. When he wanted to take her to his house, as his parents were away for the weekend to celebrate their Wedding Anniversary that Saturday, they broke up, she was sure he was planning on more than a little 'us time' and had even heard a few of his friends whisper comments at work along the lines of, 'packed your Negligee Sandra? You won't need it! playing mummies and daddies this weekend Sandra ! With her mind wandering Sandra was on the way down the corridor to the Administration Support Department to see her Manager when saw Daniel coming her way and trying to cover up her red eyes, looked to one side as they got closer so he wouldn't see her distress, but when they were close she heard Daniel say in a vicious almost theatrical way "Bad news Sandra?" and without breaking step he carried on without looking back, as if he already knew the answer to his question.

Sandra carried onto the Administration Support Department, not sure what to make of Daniel's comment and seeing her Manager at her desk it was obvious Barbara had phoned ahead as Janice stood up as she approached and opened her arms to envelope Sandra and whispered "He'll be alright, you'll see, get yourself off to the Infirmary and we will see you tomorrow, Beverly can cover your work." Picking up her handbag Sandra headed back where she had come from and hoping not to see Daniel again, took the stairs to the Main Entrance and waved at Alice the Receptionist as she left the building, crossed the road to the Bus Station and started working out which bus to get to the Infirmary. Taking her purse out of the handbag Sandra took out some coins to get a ticket for the Number 9 circular which she could also get back as it was on the route home from the Infirmary. As she paid for her ticket and sat next to an old woman who had obviously been shopping in the market, judging by the bulging bag she had balanced between her feet with a large Cauliflower sitting proud at the top, she realised putting her change back into her purse, that tonight was when the late Christmas opening for the shops all across the Town took place and she had been planning to buy Dave's present. She had chosen a Flat cap, partly as

a bit of a joke and they hadn't been going out long enough for anything too serious, and because he was such an old man at times with his plans for this and plans for that! Besides what else would a Yorkshireman want when he already had the best Christmas present ...her! It would have to wait.

The constant start and stopping of the bus had made Sandra fall into a light stupor, she only regained her senses when the old lady gave her a nudge as this was her stop, looking around she realised they were at the Infirmary stop and got up quickly so they both could get off before the bus had a chance to set off but being not quite with it, she realised stepping onto the pavement that the bus would be waiting for the passengers to board so would be here for a few minutes. Get yourself together she thought as she looked at the signs pointing to the various wards at the Infirmary. Not sure where to go she headed for Reception and asked where she should go to find Dave Baxter. The uniformed Receptionist said "Just a moment while I look him up" without looking up from the computer and then precisely stated "ICU, second floor, lift's on your right!"

Sandra almost asked her to repeat it as it was given in such a staccato way but deciding not to she turned on her heel, and making a squeaky sound set off for the lifts. There was a queue for the lift with two wheelchairs so she decided to take the stairs as it was only on the second floor and having counted 48 steps, she opened the stairwell door to see the sign for ICU on the left and headed towards the main door to the Ward when she saw Sid dressed in his work boiler suit that has seen better days, coming out, not looking at her but at the floor as if all the answers were wrapped up in the lino pattern.

"Sid, what brings you here?" she said before realising her mouth had beaten her brain again.

"Sorry Sid, how is he" she corrected

"Not good Sandra he's still in a coma, and added "So will the

guy be who did it if I ever get hold of him" before giving Sandra a hug and saying Dave's mum was with him as his Dad was at work.

"We were only out together last night at the Malt Shovel. Having a laugh, had a few too many but never thought I would be visiting him in here today!"

"Me neither" replied Sandra wondering what more she could say as Sid was Dave's best friend but they were poles apart in behaviour and she hardly knew Dave never mind Sid.

"I'll head off" he said and started for the stairs before turning around and coming back to give her another hug and whispering "He'll be alright. Not like the other guy when I find him" and letting go Sid disappeared through the door to the stairs and was gone.

Taking a moment to compose herself and check her look in her pocket compact mirror, she wanted to look her best for Dave, Sandra went through the Ward doors and seeing the nurse's station approached the desk to ask after Dave. Bed 3 love, said the nurse without looking up from what seemed a small mountain of paperwork, just like she herself had left back at the Council. Approaching the bed where Dave lay motionless and surrounded by all kinds of equipment she took a short breathe before touching Dave's mum Mary's shoulder and she turned with a look that all mothers have had at some time 'Why my boy!' Standing up she stood for a second before giving Sandra a hug which seemed to be the going rate for the day.

"He's not changed since he came in" Mary said almost like an automaton before letting go of Sandra and sitting back down to return to her vigil at Dave's side lost in her own world of memories.

Pulling a nearby spare chair next to Mary, Sandra sat down feeling so out of place, but at the same time glad that she had

managed to get time off and get to see Dave, she really did think they would be good together and she took his hand that wasn't connected to all the tubes and machines and squeezed gently, subconsciously hoping he would know it was her, as they had after all held hands all the time since the party where they had got together for the first time. Sitting there completely out of her depth she looked again at Mary and wondered if she was thinking the same, who would do a thing like this?

◆ ◆ ◆

Chapter 3

Christmas soon came around with all the street decorations hanging from the lampposts and large Christmas Tree in the Town Square provided by the Council with pomp and circumstance in the local paper, together with a 'Celebrity Christmas light switching on' ceremony but paid for by the people of Kirkdale through their Council Tax.

Dave was still in hospital but was now out of ICU but still described as 'poorly but no longer in danger' and the Consultant had told Mary and Alan Baxter that he wouldn't be home for Christmas but he was hopeful that Dave would be able to go home before the New Year. With no recollection of the attack he was sleeping a lot but when Sandra visited he always seemed to cheer up and his welcoming smile when she came into the Ward told her all she needed to know that his feelings for her hadn't been diminished by the mugging and subsequent operation.

'Hello gorgeous' Dave would say before pointing to his lips with his middle finger for his reward for rejoining the living. With visiting hours limited now he was back on a normal Ward they would chat about nothing in particular but it was important to both of them that they created some kind of normality between them.

"Sorry I haven't got you a Christmas present, but there isn't much choice in here" said Dave as Sandra was getting up to leave, at which she took his hand and replied "Having you in my life ......is my Christmas present" and kissing him with more passion than usual, said she would see him on Boxing Day as his parents would be visiting on Christmas Day as she was spending the day with her own parents. "See you Amica"

said Dave as she was leaving the Ward with a smile, and a question of what Amica meant, then a feeling of regret that she never got the Flat cap she was going to get him for Christmas, she just managed to get the Number 9 bus into town as the queue for last minute shoppers had delayed it by a few precious seconds and standing up, as there were no empty seats she resolved to get that Flat cap just so she could see Dave's face on Boxing Day light up, she hoped like Blackpool Illuminations.

Sandra bumped into Peggy and Sharon from the Administration Support Department in town as she came out of 'Greenwoods the Menswear Outfitters' with the must get Flat cap for Dave, and after asking how Dave was, Peggy asked what Sandra was doing tonight as they and a few other girlfriends were going out into Town and she was definitely welcome to join them. "You can't stay in on Christmas Eve with your parents" said Sharon, adding "Nice as Jim and Diane are" Looking decidedly not sure they screamed in perfect harmony "It's Chr....ist....mas!" in their best Noddy Holder mimicry, at which Sandra knew she had no choice and would join the 'Barmy Army' out on the Town, despite an underlying feeling that it was unfair on Dave who would be going nowhere but he had encouraged her to go out with her friends as they would make up for it with a mischievous grin, when he got out of Stalag 9!

Going into town on what had become through time an annual pilgrimage for the appropriately named 'Barmy Army' consisting of Council staff from all over the area with the aim of visiting as many public houses as you could until either you gave up and went home or for the single people managed to fine a fellow single lost soul, or in some cases not single but available and intoxicated. Diane had tea ready for her when she got home and as they sat down for tea of toad in the hole sausage, mash and gravy, the general consensus was that she should go to town and Jim would give her a lift as they were only staying in and watching a film, and her brother Tony would be going out straight from work so if Sandra saw him tell him not to get too drunk, but they all knew that would probably be a waste of breath. Having finished her tea and knowing her Dad would want to have his evening by the TV, Sandra set of to her bedroom to get ready for Christmas Eve, her last Christmas alone she hoped. Caught between going all glam for Christmas Eve and trying not to look too available as she was now with Dave, Sandra tried on three outfits until a call from downstairs from her Dad asking "You ready yet Sandra" focussed her thinking and putting on a black pencil skirt with an oversized silver belt and vanilla spotted blouse she finished brushing and putting her shoulder length black hair into place and checking one last time in the full length wardrobe mirror she called out "Just coming" in a delayed response to her Dad who she knew would already have his coat on and would be checking himself in the hall mirror even though he was only going to be sitting in a car, 'Doesn't hurt to have a few standards' he always reminded her.

"You look nice darling" her mum said adding "Enjoy yourself and I'll see you in the morning as I suppose you will be late" at which Sandra rolled her eyes in that age old generational "For goodness sake, really Mum". Kissing her Mum on the cheek she followed her Dad out to the car and settling into the passenger seat the "Don't forget your seatbelt Sandra" comment hit her ears just as she clicked the belt, "Done Dad, shall we go?" Dropping Sandra off in Town outside the George pub where she had arranged to meet Peggy and Sharon, Jim said "Enjoy yourself, see you tomorrow" always stating the obvious she thought and replying with "Will do see you" she heading into what was by now at 7.40 a very busy pub as she looked for the 'Barmy Army'.

Over by the bar she spotted Sharon's bright blonde hair, which to be fair, a few of the men in here had obviously also noticed as she seemed to have a gang of men around her while Peggy was attempting to get served at the bar, oblivious or should it be acclimatised, to the attention her workmate was getting. Seeing Sandra through the throng she waved and shouted hoping Sandra would hear or see her as she was trying to get served, but moments later she felt a tug at her elbow and Sandra had managed to get to her in a roundabout way pushing her way through several gangs of people who definitely were enjoying the Christmas spirit, some of whom she doubted would make midnight.

"What you drinking" Peggy said having finally attracted the overworked barman. "Lager and lime please" she said thinking to herself that only a few days ago Dave had asked exactly the same question. He'll be all on his own tonight she thought, and wondering if it was a good thing that she was out enjoying herself, well that has yet to be decide, she was lost in her thoughts when a splash of Lager and Black, Sharon's drink of choice splashed on her face. "Sorry about that" she heard Peggy say as she struggled to hand over the drinks she had bought for them all, "Some people have no manners!" she said to anyone within earshot, which no one heard over the pounding sound system which seemed to be on Christmas only records tonight. "Glad you could come" she carried on at the same time as Mandy and Jo from the Administration Support Department joined them from the first of many visits to 'Powder their nose'. Linda, Maggie and Ann from the Personnel Department joined them, having been round the back bar and once the hugs, and drowned by the music chats about nothing had taken their course a loud "Come on Barmy Army" shout rose above a lull in the music from Sharon and gathering together the 'Barmy Army' including now several other Council staff headed off to the next pub on the circuit, The Line, with Sharon, her blond hair blowing in the wind leading the way as ever, leaving behind broken dreams, as ever.

The next couple of hours followed a well worn path of chatting to workmates and occasional random strangers who swore they knew you but who you knew you had never seen before but where was the harm it's Christmas! After five more pubs and having managed to avoid the various spilt drinks that had ruined Peggy's, 'Why always me', yellow shirt with Sharon's Lager and Black the 'Barmy Army' had dispersed somewhat with boyfriends to meet and lifts to parties or home to get, so the remaining now 'Gang of Four' of Sandra, Sharon, a damp Peggy and Jo were heading to the Cross Keys next, which had a late licence until 1.00 am, where they could be at midnight and it would be mayhem but in a good way as the Landlord Nigel was quite strict and had even asked Sandra for her ID until a few months ago. Walking down the street they avoided the numerous mini-conga's and stumbling couples and solo grinning drunks of both sexes, who had either been barred from, or had had enough of the various pubs in the Town. I hope I don't look that bad Sandra thought to herself as they reached the Cross Keys and made their way through the throng to the bar. As she eased past Sharon to get to the toilets Sandra realised she must have had seven, or was that eight drinks and was feeling a bit unsteady, a visit to the loo was definitely in need after the walk from the Shears in the cold. Satisfied looking in the toilet mirror, that while she didn't look like a recovering alcoholic she did have a slight blush about her and applying a bit of 'lippy' she returned to the bar where the ever reliable Peggy was once again, but somewhat louder than at the start of the evening trying to get served. "Lager and lime Sandra" she heard above the music, "No can I have a Vodka and Coke please, I'm full of Lager" she requested hoping Peggy would hear. Struggling to see the others through the sea of bodies, Sandra felt Peggy next to her, and taking her Vodka and Coke and Jo's glass of Cider they headed towards the small dance floor where Sharon was doing her best to fend off the attention of a couple of lads who had obviously seen Saturday Night Fever as their arms were in the air but their feet had the ability and grace of a drunken kangaroo. As the music changed Sharon came to join them and downing half of her Lager and Black in one, she smiled a wicked berry stained smile "Come and join me so I can get rid of Dozey and Dopey you lot" and grabbing Peggy by the left hand giving her just enough time to hand her drink to Jo, they set off to the morass that was now the dance floor. "You can't stop her when she's on one" said Jo to which Sandra just nodded having only just caught her comment over the music.

With only a few minutes left before Christmas and feeling the alcohol and heat taking its toll the 'Gang of Four' managed to find a table to sit at near the window, and laughing at the sight through the window of a couple trying to cross the road towards the Cross Keys in a straight line but impersonating a couple of snails, Sharon held her glass out and said "Here's to us!" and with that, finished her drink and headed to the bar for a refill. Peggy followed her with a weary look back at Sandra and Jo, who had moved to sit next to Sandra, now that Sharon had gone to the bar. "I haven't had a chance to say how sorry I was to hear about Dave" said Jo now they were on their own "I hear you two are all loved up!" Sandra blushed at Jo's comment and without the words to respond just nodded and took a hefty swig of her drink. Regaining her composure she replied "It's early days yet". Seeing Sharon and Peggy returning from the bar with more drinks, Peggy even remembered her change to Vodka and Coke, the DJ announced it would be countdown to Christmas after the next record which was greeted with a scream from Sharon and a loud "Come on you lot" as the opening bars of 'Come on Eileen' by Dexy's Midnight Runners, pumped out of the speakers and the dance floor was crammed with would a myriad of colours and arms and legs all seemingly joined together, until the chorus when the arms had a life of their own and friends, strangers and lovers were all a teeming mass of humanity enjoying the moment.

As the DJ led the countdown the girls stayed on the dance floor and tried to out sing or rather out shout, everyone else and although not a competition Sharon was sure she had been heard mainly because she closest to the DJ's microphone. The thudding guitar of Slade's 'Merry Christmas Everyone' started and lifted the already enthusiastic crowd to new heights and with hands joined like Maypole Dancers, the girls saw in Christmas as a slightly wobbly 'Gang of Four' with smiles, glistening cheeks and all to hope for until the DJ decided to quieten down things and played 'Truly' by Lionel Ritchie, for all the World's lovers, and the girls returned to their table trusting that no one had taken their drinks that they had only bought two records ago. "Well here's to us!" said Sharon, obviously not remembering she had already held that particular toast, holding her drink up and then finishing it before even looking at the others followed by "Whose round is it?" at which Jo grabbed Sandra's hand and said "My turn, come on" as they headed to the bar which had relented from its earlier three deep in customers, and finding a gap between a couple who seemed bereft of Christmas spirit but full of alcohol spirit, managed to catch the attention of one of the bar staff and ordered their 4 drinks, 'and one for yourself' added as a last minute gesture of good will, or just for serving them before anyone else. Returning to their table where Sharon and Peggy had company from a couple of guys looking for an early Christmas present. With nowhere to sit Jo put the two drinks on the table and turned to Sandra who had their drinks and said "I see you have an admirer!" at which Sandra turned round and spotted Daniel Bruce staring straight at her, with his friend Steve who had their arms around each other like long lost friends, albeit more than a little drunk long lost friends!

Taking a few seconds to pluck up some courage Sandra waved at Daniel and turned away almost immediately to talk to Jo, but in what seemed like light speed Daniel and Steve had made their way over to where they were standing. "Hello Sandra, Jo" said Daniel with a hefty slur, at which Steve chirped in with "Girls" as if remembering two names was beyond him. "Having a good time Jo?" said Steve suddenly remembering that Daniel and Sandra used to date and that Jo was his target. "Not as good as you two" responded Jo with a bit of sarcasm, but not too much as Steve was definitely good looking despite the dodgy haircut and boyfriend material to boot, and she so wanted a boyfriend, before taking a sip of her Cider and giving him a smile that said, try harder. The hint in her smile managed to pass through the alcohol he had consumed and as Steve caught the beginning of 'Don't you want me Baby', by the Human League he held out a hand to Jo and eyes meeting hers, pointed his head to the dance floor at which Jo gave Sandra her drink and headed off to whatever fate would have in store.

Daniel looked at Sandra and without giving her a chance to reply said "I've really missed you. You look great! I thought we might meet up before now, but what with work and the extra courses I have been on there doesn't a moment to spare. Do you still work in the Administration Support Department? Stupid of course you do as you're out with Jo. How are you?" Taking a sip of her drink and gaining a few moments to think Sandra was just about to answer Daniel, when noticing she had both hands full with her own and Jo's drink, he leaned forward and put his arms around her and just as he said 'Happy Christmas' kissed her so suddenly that she was unprepared to rebuff his advances, and before she had a chance to react found herself in a full blown festive snogg! Maybe because they had been together in the Summer, or because she was more than a little drunk, or maybe because she wanted someone to hold her tonight she found herself responding to his kiss and it wasn't until Jo and Steve returned from the dance floor that they broke apart.

"Wow, I really have missed you!" said Daniel delighted at the success of his initiative, as Jo and Steve returned holding hands from the dance floor. Jo must have seen Daniel and Sandra kissing as she gave her a knowing but quizzical look and proceeded to squeeze Steve's hand. "Hey you two" said Steve looking at Daniel and Sandra as if they had been away for hours

"Jo and I are starving so we're going to go for something to eat do you want to join us?" "Sure" said Daniel on behalf of both of them without asking her, and taking Sandra's hand in his, just like the old times, started to follow Jo and Steve out of the Cross Keys, when Peggy who had just returned from the toilet put out her hand to Sandra and said "You okay Sandra?" knowing the previous history between them and the fact that Sandra and Brian were now supposed to be an item. Sandra nodded a reply which gave Peggy no confidence in what was happening knowing how much they had all had to drink and she was just about to say something when Sharon's voice cut through her thoughts. "C'mon Peggy it's your round, go get them in, and two pints for these god's gifts!" as she had a habit of calling blokes who came onto her, which was often. As she turned back to see if there was any further comment from Sandra, the door was closing and they were gone into the night.

◆ ◆ ◆

Chapter 4

Christmas Day at the Robertson house was always a set for-
mula. Dinner at three with all the trimmings, Roast Pork, not
that dry tasteless Turkey, as Jim said every year when Diane
offered her usual doomed question of 'Shall we have a change
this year Jim ?'. The family usually congregated in the kitchen
in the morning reacting to the smell of bacon under the grill
which Jim always said Diane could get a job in a Cafe if she
wanted they were that good! Presents were always opened before Dinner and after clearing up the wrappers from the 'You
shouldn't have, thanks very much, just what I wanted' presents Dinner was served.

Following Christmas Pudding which Jim always said he
couldn't fit it, but always managed after adding custard they
would 'retire' to the Lounge to argue over what to watch on
TV before agreeing on a film they had already seen, but which
Jim had never seen the end as he was always ended up having
40 winks, and Tony dozed off to rather than watch this rub-
bish and catch up on the sleep he had missed leaving Diane
and Sandra to dissect the plot and avoid the washing up for another hour or two.

But this Christmas Day was different.

By midday neither Tony nor Sandra had made it downstairs,
and knowing Tony's habit of sleeping off whatever he had
consumed the night before Diane expected he would make an
appearance at lunchtime when his hunger overwhelmed the
alcohol in his system. Sandra usually would have been down
for a bacon butty before now, it was unlike her, but she must
have been home late as she hadn't heard her come home, unlike Tony who whose slamming of the door after 03.00 let her

know he was home, as if the Taxi dropping him off hadn't already woken her .

Having been up since just after 8am, when she had come downstairs to make a cup of tea for her and Jim, while he was in the shower. Diane had prepped all the vegetables and potatoes for their Christmas dinner and putting the Leg of Pork in the oven to slowly roast until they all sat down in a few hours checking the time and noticing it was nearly midday, she made a another cup of tea this time for Diane and heading upstairs could hear the shower running so going into Sandra's bedroom put the cup down on the bedside cabinet and turning to leave bumped into Tony who she hadn't heard was up and was now back from the stupor he must have been in. "Any bacon left" he said knowing that there wouldn't be but hoping his mum had saved some. "Sure, I put some aside thinking you might be hungry "she said, adding "Dinner is at three in case you didn't know" "No problem, as soon as Sandra has made herself presentable I'll be down" he said looking at the locked bathroom door and turning went back to his room wishing they had two bathrooms so he could ease his by now nearly full bladder. 'What on earth had they drank last night' he pondered although that was a question that could only be answered tomorrow when the lads all got together again to watch the footie on Boxing Day in the pub. A few minutes later hearing Sandra come out of the bathroom he quickly set off out of his room to alleviate his bladder and before he could say "Morning Sis" she had returned to her room but when she slammed her door shut, which was most unlike her he thought to himself 'This is going to be a fun day".

"Happy Christmas darling" said Diane, as Sandra entered the kitchen just after midday and relying automatically responded "and you mum" giving her a hug, before turning to her Dad who was putting the kettle on "Happy Christmas Dad" she said approaching him for what she knew would be a squeeze rather than a hug, "Happy Christmas Sandra" he mumbled in her ear as he wrapped his arms around her and after releasing her, went back to making a pot of tea, picking up a third cup for Sandra. From the hallway a tired "Any chance of cuppa" was heard just before Tony entered the kitchen at which Jim sighed, and getting another cup from the tree mug thing that Diane had bought but he couldn't remember seeing until it seemed it had always been there, he set about making them all a brew as he called it, as Diane finished microwaving Tony's bacon to go in a roll which he liberally doused with brown sauce and devoured before picking up his tea and taking a few sips said to no one in particular "Happy Christmas everyone".

"You were late in last night, or should I say this morning" said Diane remembering the taxi waking her up, to Tony as he put his hands behind his head and stretched as if that could cure his hangover which had definitely kicked in by now. "Was I" he responded trying to cut off his mum before she started asking questions as she always did, but this time he was saved by "And what time did you get home Sandra?" as Diane changed her attention to her daughter who she hadn't heard come home and more to the point never stayed out late unlike her brother. The "I don't feel well mum" reply came swiftly and in tandem as Sandra left the table and headed back to her bedroom clutching her cup of tea. "Lightweight" called Tony after her, regretting it almost immediately as the brown sauce overkill on his bacon roll attacked his senses. "Leave her alone, you're no great shining example" he heard from the kitchen corner where Jim had been quietly enjoying his tea, and deciding to cut his Dad off before he could build up a head of steam to go down the well trod road of 'You're wasting your life away in the pub' he picked up his tea and without a look at either parent set off for the Lounge with a mumbled 'Yeah right'.

With the Christmas Dinner nearing the complexity of everything being ready at the same time, Diane went into the

Lounge and said to the 'men of the house' that dinner would be in 10 and shouted up the stairs as she returned to the kitchen "Sandra, dinner in 10" before heading into the kitchen to get the last leg of her 'military operation' started as she had just realised she had forgotten the Broccoli, but there was some in the freezer so the day wasn't lost. Putting a pan on the back gas ring she surveyed her 'military operation. Roast Leg of Pork with stuffing - in the oven, Roast potatoes - in the oven, pigs in blankets and parsnips - in the oven, peas, carrot and turnip mash – in the pan, cabbage – in the pan, gravy to do when the joint comes out, oh and of course Broccoli – in the pan. All on target and with a contended exhale of breath she felt Jim's arms around her "Smells gorgeous as ever" adding "Just like you!" for good measure at which Diane replied "For that, you have to have Broccoli!" before turning round to give him a kiss on the cheek and an aside of "Jim the Joint will be done, do the honours, while I get everything else sorted" and with that, the final preparations came together with the 'best cutlery and glasses from the cupboard' appearing on the table next to ser-viettes and place settings which for the rest of the year never made an appearance, even at Birthdays.

Diane loved to cook but even she said she might have over-done it this year when she couldn't find room on the table for the Broccoli, which she already knew no one but her would touch. Just as Diane started putting the dishes of vegetables onto the table leaving a space for the 'piece de resistance' as Jim would have it of the Roast Leg of Pork, crackling, stuffing and pigs in blankets on the biggest oval plate which was a pre-sent for 'Jim and Diane's Wedding' all those years ago, they had laid out everything like a feast for Henry the Eight, Sandra ar-rived in the kitchen with a "Can I help" question that she knew would be rejected, and was. With Jim and Diane in full flow Sandra asked her brother where he had been last night which she expected would be 'oh just the pub or several pubs' when he said "Went to the George to start with, then the Sportsman followed the Cross Keys but there was a bloody disco on, so me and Paul and a few others went on a crawl through town and ended up at the Old Cock which had a band on. Not your cup of tea Sis, Blade something I think they were called, they were great, no Christmas songs at all!" and blushing slightly thankful that her brother hated Disco, and so had moved on from the Cross Keys and hadn't seen her, she took a drink of the wine, awaiting the obvious question to come, that they always had for some reason with Christmas Dinner but never at any other meals. "What about you?" came at her like a bullet even though she was expecting it "Oh, I met the girls from work, and we went round a few pubs before ending up at the Cross Keys for midnight which was great despite what you think about Disco!" the three years between them really showed up at times but having started went on "Sharon and Peggy got chatted up by two real odd bods but that's Christmas for you!" she said thankful that she was interrupted as the full Christmas Dinner was completed and the table disappeared under the festive fayre, and Jim, pleased with his carving skills on the Roast Leg of Pork which now sat in a circular tower awaiting the first hungry diner to stab and devour said "Dig in everyone" beating everyone to the first slices of pork and picking up some crackling with his spare hand, popping it straight into his mouth and as a second thought adding roast potatoes, carrots and parsnips and gravy to his plate and avoiding the Broccoli set about seeing if he was a hungry as he felt. Diane said to Tony "Help yourself, you probably need it after last night" at the same time sneaking a sideways look at Sandra to let her know she had still to find out about her own evening.

With the silence that seems to come with any assembly that has a full plate and an appetite to match there was little talk for the next few minutes before Sandra broke the peace with "This is gorgeous mum" before adding belatedly "and dad" at which Tony, having just added a whole roast potato into his mouth merely grunted 'Mmmm' at which Diane said " I do, do a good Christmas Dinner even if I may say so myself "and popping a piece of Broccoli onto her fork waved it towards Jim and popped it into her mouth as if to say 'I haven't forgotten and you had better not!'

As the circular tower of pork now resembled a battlefield, Tony stabbed another slice and adding a few more roast potatoes and parsnips together with a river of gravy, looked across at Sandra who had barely managed half of her meal and said "Late night Sis?" Taking a moment to finish chewing the 'pigs in blankets' that she loved she responded with "Not as late as you Tony!" hoping her sharp put down would cut his flow but immediately he said "Says who?" and with a look at her mother that said 'Help' she returned to her dinner ignoring his comment and thankful for the "That's enough Tony" from her mother who she was sure would return to the question later. When Jim started rubbing his left hand over his now somewhat tighter shirt, Diane got up and putting the custard to warm through, got the Christmas Pudding out of the oven and returning to the table took the plates away from everyone including Sandra's half eaten attempt, before returning with four bowls of steaming Christmas Pudding and the gravy boat now and full of custard. "Eat up!" she said knowing that despite the groans she, Jim and Tony would finish it off but she wasn't so sure about Sandra today who for some reason wasn't herself today and she didn't think it was all about the amount of alcohol she drank last night as Sandra wasn't like her brother, thank God! No there was something up with Sandra she thought and annoyed at herself for not hearing her come in this morning she decided to wait until later when the 'women of the family' could have a chat without interference from the men folk.

"Beer Tony?" said Jim heading towards the fridge and expecting only one answer in the affirmative, after they had both demolished their Christmas Pudding and Custard and were about to 'retire to the Lounge' "Sure why not" came the expected answer at which Diane responded with "We'll do the dishes, no equality in this house!" which was as she expected replied with a joined Neanderthal grunt from the direction of the Lounge.

"Give us a hand darling" said Diane adding "and you can tell me about your night, did you have a good time?" Picking up the bowl with a spoonful of Christmas Pudding, Sandra scraped the remnants into the bin and handing her mother the bowl, returned for what would be a further ten trips to the table then to the bin before the table was finally cleared of all evidence of the feast that had taken most of the morning, which she had missed, to prepare. Having replied to her mother's initial question Sandra had been fairly scant on her recollection of the evening just saying she had a good time and how it was funny how Sharon always attracted the male attention and Peggy would just go along with her no matter that the limelight was always on Sharon. Diane could hear that Sandra was being somewhat economical with the outline of her evening but decided to let it pass as she was at least coming round a bit from this morning which hadn't been the Sandra she knew.

The Oval Plate disappeared to the back of the cupboard for another year as Diane said "Well thank goodness that's all done, do you want a cup of tea and then we can join those two and get the presents open" adding with a degree of sarcasm" as you two missed the morning". Once the kettle had boiled and the pot of tea made, Sandra headed into to the Lounge with two cups as her mother held back "Just got to get something" she said disappearing upstairs without embellishing her comment. "Hello you two, didn't expect to see you still awake " she said as she entered the Lounge putting down her mother's tea by her usual comfy seat by the fire and turning round joined Tony on the sofa where sleep wasn't so very far away. Getting no response she heard her mother come down the stairs and with a slightly jovial smile on her face as she entered the Lounge with a resounding "Present time" at which Tony knew he would not be able to drop off just yet, but was only putting off the inevitable.

"Tony, here's yours from your Dad and me, hope you like it" said Diane and with an attempt to look interested Tony picked up the gaudy coloured wrapped envelope that he couldn't help but shake, as everyone seems to do. Not working out what was inside he took to ripping the paper off with no thought for the artistic effort or cost Tony was actually appearing to enjoy himself destroying the outer wrapping until he got to the envelope that was the present itself. "Wow, Thanks" he said genuinely pleased as he opened the envelope that was inside the now destroyed outer wrapper "Two tickets for The Jam at Exhibition Hall in Leeds! In April Wow!" he reiterated, before seeing that it was on the 1st of April 1983, 'April Fool's Day' at which he took a hard look at his Dad and asked, hoping it wasn't true "Dad, you didn't did you?" knowing that Jim worked at a printers that had the capability to do tickets and almost reluctantly looked again at the tickets when Jim said "Think I would waste my time on that noisy lot!" as parents throughout the years would no doubt echo." Genuine tickets son, enjoy, from your Mother and me!" at which, knowing how hard The Jam tickets were to come by, Tony, now stuck in mode said "Wow!" and took the last swig of his beer and holding it out to his now highly thought of Dad added "Another" at which a swift downward confirmation nod from an amused Jim sent Tony off to the kitchen fridge for replenishments.

Diane, in her role as Christmas present guide, picked up the next shiny present and passing it to Sandra who took it with a mouthed 'Thanks' watched a she slowly and carefully pulled at the tape and slowly the present unravelled and seeing that there was another layer of wrapping took a swift look at her mother with a 'do you have to' raise of her eyes and seeing where the folds were undid the second lot of tape to reveal a pink Kashmir scarf that she had seen when they went to Meadow Hall Shopping Centre before Christmas. How had her mother managed to get it she wondered before coming out with "It's beautiful just what I wanted, thanks mum...and dad"

Tony returned with two beers and the present pile gradually went down with dad 'Very pleased' with his book on 'How to play better Golf' by 'Seve Ballesteros', even though work curtailed his desire to play more golf, 'One day' he would often say. Jim gave Diane a look that she knew was trouble as he gave her his present. Opening the box that he had obviously wrapped at work, as it was covered in brown paper, she ripped at the paper following the Tony method of opening presents, and seeing the edge of what she knew she had been dropping hints about for the last three months she finished opening the box to look at the Pallet of Oil Paints that she had so set her heart upon and looked at Jim before going over to him and giving him a hug with a "So you do listen to what I say!" as an afterthought. Before returning to her seat to examine the brushes and paints she had so wanted she passed close by Sandra and surreptitiously dropping a small neatly wrapped box on her lap, with a wink that Sandra just caught from her mother as the box landed on her unexpectedly. "From an admirer" she caught as her mother sat down and then watch intently as a puzzled and slightly apprehensive Sandra started to open the surprise present. Having dispensed with the wrapping paper she lifted the lid of the box to reveal a silver necklace and plaque which had 'Amica' inscribed. "Where, how" Sandra started her sentence before her mother saved her any more words. "Dave came round, before his accident and asked me to give it to you on Christmas Day as he knew he wouldn't see you"

Dropping the box and necklace from her lap, Sandra seemed to be already crying before she had fully stood up, and trying not to look at her mother for help through what was now a flood of tears she ran out of the Lounge to her bedroom where the sound of the door slamming broke the silence. "Don't love" said Jim to Diane as she started to get out of her chair, "Give her some time on her own" and turning to the TV saw it was halfway through a movie he had yet and probably never would see although he had a feeling he wouldn't be dozing off today.

It was an hour later and Jim had finally seen the end of the movie that had, as he had expected been a waste of an hour of his life when Diane offered to make a cup of tea "or do you want another beer Jim?" at which a quick look at the now fast asleep Tony made his mind up "Tea would be lovely" and without really waiting for Jim's reply Diane was already half way to the kitchen and her ulterior motive of taking a cup of tea upstairs to Sandra to see why she had reacted so oddly to Dave's present. He had seemed a really nice young man when he had been introduced last week by Sandra after they had been out and he had walked her home. Polite, called her Mrs Robertson and had even bought her some flowers, albeit they were obviously from the petrol station on the main road, but the thought counted, she had said to Sandra after he had left. What on earth had he done she wondered as the kettle slowly came to a boil and shut itself off with a click that brought her back to matters in hand. Filling the three cups and taking one into Jim she indicated with the two remaining cups that she was going upstairs at which Jim raised his eyebrows and with his eyes fixed on the steaming hot cup of tea mouth 'okay' before returning to watch the news that was now on the TV.

Gently tapping on the door to Sandra's bedroom Diane quietly entered while at the same time adding "I've brought you a cup of tea" meaning us but hoping her daughter hadn't noticed. "Thanks mum" came the reply from a now recovered but still very red eyed Sandra, and taking the cup of tea but immediately putting it down on the bedside cabinet, she held out her arms for her mother to give her a hug, and gain a few more precious seconds before she would have to answer the question that would inevitably be coming. After coming together and not saying anything Diane finally eased away from Sandra and asked the dreaded question. "What wrong darling, I didn't expect that reaction to Dave's present!" At which Sandra turned away from the mother and looking out of the bedroom window towards the moorland on the horizon she offloaded the events of Christmas Eve.

After they had left the Cross Keys with Daniel holding her hand as they walked towards the Punjab Star for something to eat, Jo and Steve, arms around each other and talking gibberish between the kisses. Sandra was concentrating on walking in a straight line although being led somewhat by Daniel, as the fresh air hit the alcohol in her system. How many had she had she thought to herself four or five lagers and then three or four vodka's, no wonder she was struggling to walk at which time Daniel put his arm around her and said "I've missed you, have you missed me" which she didn't respond to but which he didn't seem to notice as they reached the Punjab Star and holding the door open Steve offered "Ladies first, not you Daniel!" which Jo thought was funny for some reason and giggling she and Steve followed the waiter, who was now used to the entire clientele being drunk or worse, hoping they would all have enough money left to pay their bills, and with a smile that said he would rather be anywhere else, led them to one of the two remaining tables with Daniel and Sandra lagging behind as Daniel once again held Sandra's hand. As Jo and Steve carried on their overtly romantic alcohol induced tryst, Daniel and Sandra were finding the going somewhat harder despite Daniel's best endeavours to rekindle their relationship from the summer. Having managed to order in between conversations which she couldn't remember anything about, the starters finally arrived with Jo so drunk by now that she thought her comment about the Sheekh kebab Steve had ordered being like a turd, was so funny she had trouble calming down enough to eat he Chicken Tikka and when he put a bit of the kebab in his mouth she immediately said "Turd eater, you're a turd eater" and thinking it was the funniest thing ever she leaned back eyes shut and promptly fell back-wards off her chair grabbing the tablecloth as she fell with all their starters inevitably following with it as she landed still laughing on the floor. As the carnage of Christmas Eve was not unexpected in the Punjab Star several waiters appeared swiftly at their table and with a professional "Are you okay? Let me help you" but with a combined look of disdain, the table contents which were now on the floor were being swiftly cleared and cleaned up ready for the next drunken clients. With Jo holding onto Steve like he was a telegraph post, Daniel took charge and going towards the reception asked for their main courses to be made into takeaways and can they phone for two taxis adding as an matter of politeness, please. Cer-tainly Sir said the 'Seen it all it before' Manager snidely adding "I hope you enjoyed your meal Sir" After a few minutes their takeaways were handed to the Manager and with an overly pleasant "Your taxis are outside Sir, Merry Christmas" and holding the door open watched them get into the taxis as an-other group of 'Festive' customers headed for his door. Jo and Steve were oblivious to everything and everyone around as they tried to speak and kiss at the same time before the taxi driver eventually gleaned that they wanted to go to the Cliff Estate, Church Close. Daniel and Sandra got into the second taxi and without a second thought Daniel said 52, Greenwood Street to the driver. As Daniel put his arm around Sandra to pull her closer in the back of the taxi and gave her a long kiss that she had to push him away as she was feeling woozy as the alcohol really started taking effect. Leaving his arm around her Daniel said "God that was funny when Jo fell over!" and laughing at his own memory of the sliding tablecloth heading towards Jo her face shocked at the impending disaster he added " We do have good times together Sandra" before clos-ing in for another kiss at what was now a more than slightly drunk Sandra.

Arriving at Daniel's house he helped her out of the taxi giving the driver a fiver and a backhanded cheers mate, Happy Christmas! Leading Sandra with an arm across her shoulders towards the Front door he found his key and let them both in and with only the hall light on it was obvious his parents were still at the Kirkdale Social Club with Pete and Mary from down the road. Opening the door to the Lounge and putting the light on, before quickly turning the dimmer switch down to low, he guided Sandra towards the sofa and as she sat down almost asleep he took off his jacket and joined her on the sofa where she leaned into him as he sat down as his weight being more than hers unbalanced the cushions, and before she knew it she had twisted and she was halfway across his lap looking up through her drunken haze as he looked directly down at her face and he was stroking her long dark hair. "God I've missed you" he said kissing her passionately as she was now directly underneath him. Lacking the motivation or ability as a result of the alcohol to say no, Sandra closed her eyes and remembering the good times of their summer romance returning his kisses. Coming out of the fog of memories she felt his right hand move down and over between her breasts which were now exposed as her blouse was open to her naval and her bra had been pushed up over her breasts. Suddenly she was all too aware of the reason they had split up when Daniel used to pressure her to go to the next base, as he liked to call it, but which she had determinedly said no to on several occasions. Squirming to get out of the position directly under Daniel she tried to straighten up but he lent further over her leaving his hand where it was. "Come on Sandra" he said adding "It's Christmas" to justify his actions and moving his left hand further down towards her belt he bent his head down to kiss her exposed breasts while stroking her hair with his right hand. Feeling his left hand undo her belt and skirt button, and feeling her zip release and a hand start to push her skirt down she pushed out with her stomach to try make it more difficult, but she felt her skirt around her knees in seconds, and deciding now was the time to try to get out of this situation before she was pinned down, she twisted her hips towards the floor and managed to get extricate herself from Daniel's lap and onto the floor. Suddenly realising what Daniel had ultimately in mind she managed to stand and pulling her skirt up she pushed her bra down to cover her breasts that Daniel had been kissing a moment ago. Looking directly at Daniel like he was a different person to the one that she knew from the summer she started to do up the first button on her spotted blouse when she saw it was missing, looking even harder at Daniel before going onto the next button just as he said "C'mon Sandra you know you want to, we should have done it in summer and we would still be together" before adding "You can't keep your virginity forever!" and standing up he started to undo his belt, but fell backwards with a huge grin on his face "Oopsy" he said before trying to get up again, now with a more determined look on his face. Just as Sandra had finished doing up her blouse and with Daniel still halfway towards standing up she knew what was coming next if she didn't take action. Taking a step back she kicked out her right foot with what strength she had before losing her footing as it connected and landed on her back on the floor as her left leg gave way. Lying on her back on the floor she took a second to get her breath back and as Daniel hadn't landed on top of her she looked in the direction of the sofa where a rolled up Daniel was holding his hands around the subject of Sandra's right foot. Confident that Daniel had lost his amour Sandra got up, put on her shoes that she couldn't remember taking off and hearing a groaning Daniel muttering 'Bitch, Bitch, Bitch' she looked around for her jacket then realised she hadn't worn one tonight. Turning to leave she stopped to look back at Daniel who was now muttering into a cushion. "Daniel" she spat out. "If you mention this to anyone, ever, I'll tell everyone you tried to rape me! You Bastard!" and leaving the Lounge she headed out through the Front door slamming it with as much anger as she had left, just as Daniel's parents arrived home from the club in a taxi. Despite a "Merry

Christmas Sandra" from an inebriated and slightly confused Mary Bruce getting out of the taxi, Sandra didn't respond and turning away wrapping her arms around herself to keep warm on a very chilly Christmas Eve, subconsciously wishing she has brought her jacket, and set off for what would be a long two mile walk home in the freezing weather, a stroll compared to the last few hours. "Merry Christmas, Good will to all men" she muttered between chattering teeth, "Ill will to all women" and with her resolve set at full speed, she headed for home, and safety.

"Oh Sandra darling" Diane finally said having taken in Sandra's story of Christmas Eve before approaching her daughter for a physical connection that in some way she hoped would go some way to conveying the emotion she felt. Wrapping her arms around each other they stayed wrapped up in the moment between mother and daughter until Sandra broke the moment by saying quietly "I wish I had never gone out now, it was a stupid decision", before correcting herself "Stupid Daniel!" and sitting down on the bed looked at her mother standing above her and patting her left hand over the bed cover for Diane to sit and join her they held hands and sat both contemplating what to do now. Sandra broke the silence "I'm not going to tell Dave, I've thought it over and over and although it was horrible he's had a bad enough Christmas without finding out his girlfriend spent Christmas Eve with another boy. I've decided to just say I went out with the girls and leave it at that. He'll never get to know as only me, and Daniel know what happened and he's hardly likely to brag about it, I hope! I feel such a fool especially so when you gave me his Christmas present, it was just like him he's such a romantic, not like Daniel!"

Diane gave her daughter another hug and whispered "It's your decision, for what it's worth I think you are doing the right thing darling, just stay away from Daniel, put it all out of your mind and let's go and join them downstairs, they'll be wondering where we are, or they will both be asleep!" she ended trying to lighten the mood. It was no surprise to see the TV still on but both Jim and Tony fast asleep when they entered the Lounge. "Let's have a cup of tea, tidy up the kitchen and then we'll wake up the 'sleeping beauties' Diane said as they headed for the kitchen holding hands.

The rest of Christmas Day slumbered onwards with no further mention of Sandra's outburst, as the law laid down by Diane to Jim and especially Tony, when Sandra wasn't in the room had left the right impression ie. No means No. With the third film of the day out of the way Tony decided to add to his already impressive 10 hours of sleep, 3 of which were on the sofa and headed to bed. As the news finished, Jim stretched the stretch of a man who has eaten and drank too much and standing up said he was 'Done' and off to bed. Diane said she would be up in a moment and passing Sandra, Jim quietly said despite being told not to "Glad you're feeling better love, I hope he's worth it" getting completely the wrong side of what had happened, at which a look from Diane sent him off to bed like a 5 year old and turning back to Sandra she smiled and added "Men!" raising her eyebrows to the ceiling to emphasise her comment.

Left alone downstairs now that the 'lightweights' had gone to bed Diane went to the kitchen and returning with two glasses of wine, she handed one to Sandra without saying a word, and settling into her 'mum's chair' a mutual silence overtook them both as a Hollywood romance started. With neither of them ready for sleep and the thoughts that would undoubtedly come and stay with them conscious or unconscious, the film fulfilled its criteria of twists and turns and boy gets girl at the end and the world is a wonderful place, which if anyone ever asked them, they would never remember the title but that didn't really matter as it was after all only a film not real life. 'If only life were a film and there was a happy ending' she thought as Diane turned off the TV and offering her left hand pointing in the direction of the hall let Sandra go upstairs first before saying at the top of the stairs. "Try to put it all out of your mind and get a good night's sleep" which as she said it, she realised it would probably bring back the memories rather than bury them and finishing with "Sorry darling" and headed into their bedroom where she saw a fast asleep Jim had pulled all the duvet around him 'Men' she thought pulling the duvet across to her side and undressing, slipped into her nightie and into bed to what she hoped, but doubted would be a good night's sleep. Sandra took her time cleaning her teeth, and after closing the door to her bedroom sat at the end of the bed. Convinced that keeping the details of Christmas Eve events to herself, and of course her mother, she decided in the cold analysis of what happened, it could have been much worse if Daniel had managed to have his way, or she had passed out, like she had but only for a few moments, after all when they dated in summer she had let him undo her bra and caress, more like squash and mould her breasts, which he took as a sign that they would go further but she wasn't ready for that next step despite Daniel's attempts to cajole her into going to 3rd base or whatever language that was, that boys used. There was a mile and some, between liking someone and going out with them, and loving someone where you give your trust and in return trust them. If only she hadn't had so much to drink she would have been more in control when Daniel turned up at the Cross Keys catching her unawares with that kiss and everything that followed. Enough she thought, before pulling the duvet to one side and getting underneath what was in effect a large comfort blanket tonight.

◆ ◆ ◆

Chapter 5

Boxing Day arrived with a slam as Tony left to join his 'mates' in the pub to before going to the George with Pete and the rest of his mates. The noise was heard above the sound of the shower as Sandra washed the sleep and memories out of her system with liberal doses of Alberto Balsam until she was tingling with the heat of the shower and al the conditioner was out of her hair. Wrapping a bath towel around herself and another around her head she knew that she safe from view now that Tony had gone as he always teased her, as she went back to her bedroom closing the door she looked in the full length mirror in the wardrobe. Taking the towel around her head she dried her hair as best she wanted, before she would use the hairdryer and shaking her long black hair she thought for one second about just leaving it then decided that was such a silly idea and picked up a large toothed comb and straightened her hair before turning to get her hairdryer. Pleased with her look after a few minutes of styling her hair she let the bath towel fall to her bare feet and looking straight at herself in the mirror said to herself 'I'll decide when someone gets to have this!' and turning to choose what to wear she picked up the blouse she had worn on Christmas Eve and which was now lying half under her bed she picked it up and threw it in the bin saying quietly "Let that be an end to it!"

Having decided on a white T shirt and her tight blue jeans she picked up the pink Kashmir scarf she has been given for Christmas and heading downstairs heard her mother in the kitchen making a pot of tea and entering the kitchen she said "Good morning" just as her mother finished pouring the tea into the three mugs in front of her. "I was going to bring you one up but here you are, I'll just take your Dad this one as he's having a lie in." She was returned in a minute "He's fallen back to sleep!" she said incredulously upon returning "Anyway it doesn't matter it's Boxing Day, so not much going on today. Your Dad was going to give you a lift to the Infirmary, but I'll do it instead as I'm up and it's horrible outside. "Thanks mum" she said sipping her mug of tea and adding "I heard Tony go out the door, is he gone for the day?"I expect so, he needs a girl that boy!" at which she looked at Sandra "Will Dave be getting out soon?" "Don't really know should have some news today I hope" Sandra quickly replied, hoping there would be positive news. Standing up, she put on her scarf and jacket and started blushing as her mum commented "He's a lucky boy, and I don't mean recovering from the attack!" while she rearranged her scarf so her hair fell over, rather than under the material. Delighted at her minor amendment Diane reiterated"Lucky boy!" before they headed out to the car and the 10 minute trip to the Infirmary. "I'll wait for you" said Diane as they neared the Infirmary, despite Sandra saying she could catch the bus home her mother said she wouldn't hear of it in this weather and besides what else was she to do with Jim still in bed.

Following the signs to the Ward where Dave had been moved a few days ago Sandra could see Dave in the third bed on the right where he had been before and seeing that he was reading a large book which presumably was a Christmas present from his parents he caught her walk out of the corner of his eye and putting the book down put an arm out to welcome her. As she got closer to him he extended his other arm as she reached the bed, and fell with a huge amount of relief into his arms where they were locked for a while, before he eased her slightly away and kissed her passionately as her as her mouth came into contact with his lips. "You look gorgeous, I've missed you" he said as they parted, both of them smiling and getting their breath back "Mum and dad have been great but well, you know, they're not you! Did you get my present.....Amica?" "Oh it's beautiful Dave" she said giving him another hug and holding on for longer than she had intended so she could regain her composure thankful that she hadn't actually cried , but it was a close thing. Then she remembered Dave's present in her jacket pocket which was squashing against the bed and asking him to close his eyes and hold out his hands, she placed what she was now in her own mind sure was a somewhat debatable present. Barely was the present in his hands and Dave's eyes were open before she could say he could open them. "What have we here......socks?" he said before ripping with as much enthusiasm as he could, the wrapping paper Sandra had so carefully chosen with little Christmas presents on it. Having disposed of the wrapping paper he immediately put the cap on his head and with a huge smile said to the entire Ward "Sandra, I absolutely love it. They'll never doubt me being a Yorkshireman now!" and holding out his arms she fell into another hug that she knew wouldn't be the last ....not by a long way if she had anything to do about it.

As visiting time was coming to an end Dave and Sandra were sat holding hands, her on the visitors chair and him on the bed discussing what they both got for Christmas, and if they should plan something for New Years Eve when he said out of the blue "Don't bother coming tomorrow Sandra" in a dead pan tone looking down at her, with his flat cap on and a serious face, unable to read him and not knowing what to say she started crying at which he got down from the bed and holding her close as the tears ran down her face he whispered into her ear "You are such a softy, I am going to have to take really good care of you. I meant, don't come tomorrow as they are letting me go home if the Consultant says so after he had done his rounds. I'm sorry it sounded so harsh it's just my sense of humour!" At this she slapped him on top of his head knocking off his cap which flew under the bed."You'll have to understand that I'm poorly" he said watching his present come to a halt under the bottom of the bed."Call yourself a Yorkshireman, fancy losing your cap in less than 5 minutes" she retorted standing up, at which he went to the end of the bed and picked up his cap and placing it back on his head, walked back to where Sandra was standing and putting his right hand under her chin moved in for a kiss that he knew she wouldn't resist......and she didn't.

Returning to where her mother was waiting Sandra pulled open the door of the car to the sound of the radio playing an inevitable Christmas record, getting in before the rain got to her she said without looking at her mother "Home please driver" at which Diane made no comment just delighted that her daughter had had a weight of emotion lifted, and was back to the Sandra she has lost over the last two days, without even a cursory glance at Sandra to ask what had made the change, she drove out of the Infirmary car park taking a quick look in the mirror and headed home already knowing the answer.

The following day was such a damp squib it was perfectly matched by the weather but that hadn't stopped Sandra and Diane from going to the Sales in town. When the phone rang at lunchtime just as Tony was passing he picked it up and with the attention span of a child listened as Dave related the news that he would be allowed home tomorrow and could he let Sandra know, "Sure" said Tony putting the phone down, as he put his coat on he wondered if the weather would ease off before he got to the pub and headed out to meet Pete to put the world to rights over several games of pool and accompanying pints. 'Wish I had a hat' he thought to himself as the rain came off the moors and slowly started to dampen his demeanour, all thoughts of the phone call already gone.

Jim got home from work just as Diane and Sandra were getting off the bus down the road, and putting the kettle on set about making a pot of tea for them all. 'Why he had to go into work today was beyond him' he thought waiting for the kettle to finish, as all the urgent work had been for Christmas and he could have done with another day off as he was feeling a bit lethargic after his long lie in yesterday. Pouring out the tea as the door opened, and quickly slammed shut by the wind a few seconds later, the kitchen table soon filled up with 'Sale bargains' and as Jim looked at Diane handing her a mug of tea she cut him off with "We thought we would treat ourselves, and besides they were less than half price!" which basically meant don't bother arguing you've already lost and taking the high ground, he headed for the sanctuary of the Lounge leaving the kitchen as he heard the words "Such a bargain" for the third time in the last few minutes and settling into 'his chair' turned the TV on to check out the news, of which there wouldn't be much if it was like his day at work, and there wasn't.

After tea which was by now running somewhat late, they sat in the Lounge and after watching 'Coronation Street' and with nothing much else of interest on the TV Diane suggested watching a film and got up and put a VHS cassette in the machine. "Love this film" she said as she returned to 'her chair' at which Jim thought 'so why are we watching it again?' before taking the sensible option and keeping quiet, as the machine loaded what he now realised was 'The Big Sleep' which he actually liked and kicking off his shoes settled down to watch the classic 'film noir' as Diane called it, already knowing he would probably fall asleep and miss the end which is exactly what happened, and only Tony returning from the pub just as the film ended, saved him from the usual 'Enjoy that Jim' snide comment. Putting his soaked coat on the hook Tony stuck his head round the door and using minimal use of the English vocabulary stated "Tea" and headed for the kitchen without waiting for an answer. As the kettle clicked off and Tony set up the mugs like soldiers Diane appeared at his shoulder and handing him a towel said "I'll finish off, you need to get dry, it must be horrible outside" at which Tony, now thoroughly drying his hair, grunted a reply lost to all and having finished handed the towel to Diane who put it on the radiator to dry. Suddenly the motion of the rough hair drying pulled a thought from deep down and as Sandra joined them in the kitchen the light bulb moment hit Tony and without a shred of guilt about not leaving a note said "Sis, Dave rang earlier to say he would be home tomorrow" at which Diane quickly responded, before Sandra could say anything "So when was this he called? Didn't you think to leave a note? Your sister had been worried sick all day, not having heard anything thinking the worst!" taken aback he replied "Calm down mum, she knows now" adding as he wrapping his arms around himself in a hug, and pouting his lips "So she can dream about him tonight" at which the damp towel landed on his head thrown from the other side of the kitchen by a slightly blushing but definitely happy Sandra.

◆ ◆ ◆

Chapter 6

Alan Baxter had taken part of the morning of the 28th December off work at Dysert and Co Accountants where he was a Senior Auditor, so he could pick up David from the Infirmary, but he had to pick up Mary on the way as she insisted on coming and besides she didn't drive yet having failed her test twice. "Next time dear" he had said after her last failure in September since which time she hadn't even had a lesson "Maybe in the New Year" she had quickly replied her confidence dented, but time would heal. As he sat outside their house watching Mary lock the door with one hand and with a box in the other, he wondered for the first time what had happened on the 23rd when David had been attacked. There had to be a reason, Dave's wallet wasn't taken and he still had his watch from his birthday so why, and what was the background. Trying to analyse what had happened before, his thoughts were put to one side as Mary opened the door and placing the box, which he now saw was a box of chocolates from their somewhat lonely Christmas on the back seat "Just a little something for the nurses" Mary said closing the door and putting on her seatbelt and they set of for the Infirmary for what they hoped would be the last time ...ever.

On entering the Ward Mary made a bee line for the Ward Sister and apologising for the present with "Just a little something to say thank you for all you have done for David" as she handed it over the Ward Sister gracefully responded with "Much appreciated, he's ready for home. He's got some tablets for the next fortnight that should help with the headaches he has been getting, but they should ease over the next few days, so he's ready to go" and letting Alan and Mary know she was finished with an outstretched arm in the direction of his bed, they headed towards David who was proudly putting on his flat cap which got a look of disdain from Mary, but a smirk from Alan, as the Ward Sister went back to the paperwork she had been plodding through for the last hour between calls.

The journey home was uneventful and small talk was kept to a minimum as it always was as liked to concentrate on the road and Mary was still scared enough of it to not put him off. So it was some 10 minutes later that they disembarked from the Datsun Bluebird that was his father's pride and joy, and entering the kitchen to the smell of cooking Mary said "I've done some vegetable soup and bread to make you feel at home" which it certainly did and as they settled back into the Baxter family routine Mary gave David's arm a squeeze saying "Glad you're home" not expecting a reply but the "Me too" reply made Mary smile at Alan, who reciprocated and returned to his half eaten soup saying nothing.

After lunch with a sense of normality resumed, Alan went back to work and Mary and David made their way into the Front room to relax for the afternoon with a cup of coffee each, Mary carrying a plate of biscuits which he figured would be from the Christmas Day he had missed."Are you feeling okay" she said setting down the plate of biscuits on the coffee table by the TV "It was such a shock when the policeman knocked on the door and told us the news. The trip to the Infirmary seemed to take ages despite your Dad speeding, which you know he never does. Then seeing you all bandaged up and connected to tubes and pipes. Well I must say we both feared the worst. I don't think I've ever seen you Dad so angry in all my life. What he wasn't going to do to the person who did this to David. Well you can imagine!" and having got all the last 5 days off her mind she offered the plate of biscuits and as he took a 'Nice' biscuit, Mary without waiting for a response to her outburst, picked up her book and settled down, picking up the bookmark and re-entered the world of 'Maeve Binchy' where she had left it.

After attempting to match his mother's reading ability it really wasn't happening and realising he had read the same page three times, and seeing the weather was windy but not wet, he got up and touched his mother on the arm and said he was going for a walk and would be back for tea, as he had been cooped up like a battery hen for the last 5 days, at which she just nodded and went back to her book, wherever it was taking her. Putting his winter jacket on followed swiftly by the now irreplaceable flat cap, he checked he had a key and set off heading out of the street and automatically found himself in the alleyway where he had been attacked, a lifetime ago. Noticing that the streetlight hadn't been repaired, he wondered if it had been working on the night he was attacked would he have been able to recognise his attacker. Standing there looking at the broken light as the wind screeched down the alleyway he caught the word 'Stay ' somewhere deep down in his subconscious. Stay what he thought 'Stay here' from the Policeman 'Stay awake' from the Ambulance man 'Stay still' from the Nurse? He just couldn't place it and deciding not to spend any more time on it he headed off down the alleyway and across the road to the playing fields that separated the two Estates. With the wind behind him he was almost across the fields when a hand fell onto his bruised shoulder and sensing a large presence next to him he turned round with trepidation as the wind blew into his face only to burst into a huge grin as Sid game him a hug, ignoring the fact his upper body was still bruised and painful. "Nearly didn't recognise you with the flat cap Dave" he shouted over the noise of the wind "Your mum said you were getting out today but didn't expect to see you in this crappy weather. What's with the flat cap, got a job training ferrets!" And laughing at his own humour didn't give Dave a chance to respond before realising where he was headed and saying in his best mimicry" "Are we off to call on the young lady of the house yonder perchance young man?" at which falling into similar character Dave replied "Indeed Sir, I have intentions with the young lady, so move aside and let me on my way" Grinning and bending over to allow Dave to pass Sid added "Let me not delay you further Sir, and safe journey to you" before shouting back in his normal voice "See you to-morrow at the Malt Shovel" into the wind and set off into the wind and home. Having arrived at the end of Sandra's street Dave regained his thoughts which had been interrupted by meeting Sid, and pushed by the wind found himself outside the Front door of Number 9, Church Street trying to decide if this was a good idea when the door opened and he was sure it was.

Sandra had seen Dave come down the street as she was watching nothing interesting on the TV and her attention has been grabbed by the only person she had seen on the street for the last half an hour and certainly the only one who was wearing 'her' flat cap. "Coming in stranger" she said holding the door open wide, and as they passed in the doorway she gave him a kiss on the cheek which he turned into a full blown kiss as he went to pass her in the doorway. "Who is it?" came the cry from the Lounge as the door closed behind them and they took the opportunity to have another longer kiss, before her mother left the Lounge to see who it was as she hadn't been answered. "It's Dave, mum" she finally replied having decided she wouldn't wait any longer for an answer. "Well, bring him in here he must be freezing being out in that wind" and with that, the kisses would have to wait as Dave took off his winter coat and flat cap and followed Sandra into the Lounge. "Hello Mrs Robertson, belated Merry Christmas" at which the expected "Call me Diane please, and Merry Christmas to you, although that really wasn't the case for you was it. Sandra was all over the place. How people can do the things they do beggars belief. Come and sit down" she finished pointing to the sofa where Sandra was already heading. "I'll make a Pot of Tea and you can fill us in with what you have been up to" before realising her error and without correcting herself headed for the kitchen. "You didn't need to come out on your first day home, but I'm glad you did" Sandra said once her mother had gone and holding his hand she kissed him passionately knowing her mother would give them a few minutes, and with perfect timing Diane returned from the kitchen with a full tray of goods that suggested that that was the last interlude they were going to get for some time.

Once the tea and cakes had served their purpose and the story told of Dave and Sid going for a drink and splitting up at the end of the Estate then waking up in the Infirmary and missing Christmas and then getting out today, there wasn't really much more he could say to fill the silence when Diane put them out of their unease saying "Your Dad and Tony will be home for tea in an hour and I haven't even started it yet so I'll leave you two alone, look after him Sandra" she added leaving with the tray and with a grin that they both saw.

As he put his arm around Sandra she moved closer expecting a full blown kiss now her mother was gone, but instead Dave just put a finger on her lips and quietly, staying inches from her face quietly said"I don't remember anything much about the attack, but I do remember thinking a lot about you and me over the last couple of weeks, and well, spending that time in the Infirmary pondering things. Just hear me out before you say anything okay" Taking her hands and holding them in his, while looking into her slightly wary blue eyes, he continued "Sandra, you know I like things to be organised and I kind of have a career path in mind that if it works out will see me as a Senior Council Surveyor in my mid to late thirties, depending in how I do in exams of course. I know you've said you want to move jobs and maybe move into Planning or Estates, which, with your qualifications from school you should be able to do really well. What I am trying to say I want us to make that journey together, and although I know we have only been seeing each other a few weeks since the Council Christmas Party,

I think we are great together, I can't really remember what I did before you came into my life, I miss you every day I don't see you, and if you feel the same as me, I would, if you wanted to, that is if you feel the same, plan to get engaged on your 19th birthday, July 16th next year!"

After finishing talking and awaiting Sandra's response to opening his heart to her, Dave continued looking at Sandra and her blue eyes that were no longer wary, more quizzical. Still holding her hands in his, in what felt like his whole future bound up in their entwined fingers, the silence between them was back dropped by the sound of the wind outside, like dreams, wild and dangerous but beautiful as nature can be, as it blew off the moors and across the Estate.

"How long have I got to think about it Dave?" broke the silence as Sandra finally, almost whispering said as they were so close together still holding hands and still locked eye to eye.

Just as he was considering a reply to the question he hadn't prepared for, but before he had a chance to, Sandra added "Yes"

◆ ◆ ◆

Chapter 7

As the Christmas holidays played havoc with everyone's schedules with extra days booked off and skeleton staff at the Council it was on the 29th December that Sandra returned to work. Aware that most of the Administration Support Department had booked extra days, there was only herself, and Jo in today and her boss Mrs Anderson. Seeing that there was little work as the majority of staff were off, and therefore not generating the workload for the Administration Support Department she waited until she had done an hour and making her way to the Managers Office knocked on the open door and asked "Can I have a word please Mrs Anderson" at which the "Sure come in, it's very quiet in here today and will be all week I think" before adding "What can I do for you Sandra"

"Well it's like this Mrs Anderson, I got good grades at school but there was nothing at the time I left school, so I took this temporary role, which to be fair has been great, but I had rather set my heart on a role in Planning or maybe the Estates Department, and well I heard that there would be a position in the Planning Department in the New Year coming up and wondered if I could apply for it, and would you give me a reference." "Sandra" replied Mrs Anderson "I know the role you are interested in will be coming up as it was signed off at the last HR meeting before Christmas. I would have no hesitation giving you a reference, you're wasted here, just look at Jo all loved up and daydreaming over some boy down there." Waving her hand in the general direction of the desk Jo was sat at."You'll have tough competition as it is a career role, but yes do apply for it, and I'll try to put in a good word for you along the way. Now seeing as it's so quiet in here, tell me did you have a good Christmas? I heard Christmas Eve was a bit lively in Town from the gossips" Caught on the back foot Sandra replied "Just a few drinks with the girls around Town, mainly following Sharon around as always, you know what she's like, a one woman party" she said trying not to turn scarlet and having given all the information she wanted to give, she said she had better get back to work and before Mrs Anderson had a chance for further interrogation she was heading back to her desk, Plan A started. Now there was just the application, interview and hopefully fingers crossed a new job for the New Year.

Dave was still off work until the New Year and with time on his hands he walked into Town each day to meet Sandra for lunch, and look around the sales when he was early, which is when he bumped into Eric Normanton from the Property Department in WH Smiths looking at the magazine section on cars. "Didn't have you down for a car buff" he said standing behind Eric as he flicked through a 'Jaguar Classic' magazine "Neither does Mrs Normanton" and turning to check it was who he thought it was said"Dave, my boy, you gave us all a shock when you didn't come to work on Christmas Eve and we heard what had happened, truly shocking, how are you now, on the mend? Hell of a way to avoid Christmas" he sarcastically added before quantifying it with."Only joking", at which, knowing his sense of humour Dave responded" I wouldn't recommend it to be fair" "Touché" came the swift reply as he patted Dave on the back and having finished dreaming of Jaguars of old he put the magazine under his arm and as he headed for the tills said "See you in the New Year, try not to miss it like Christmas!" and he was gone into the throng giggling to himself no doubt. '"Not a chance" said Dave to no-one as he set off towards the exit and round the corner to where Sandra would just be leaving the Council Offices.

As Dave turned the corner he could see Sandra waiting outside the Council Offices and breaking into a hesitant run, reached her in seconds and entwining her in his arms kissed her like it had been weeks since they had seen each other, knowing that it was only yesterday when they had agreed to a life together. "So, still happy to see me" Sandra said into Dave's ear as they held each other at which he replied "You haven't changed you mind after sleeping on it?" hoping she wasn't going to crush all his hopes. "Don't be silly Dave, I said Yes and I mean Yes!" and hand in hand they walked towards the Carousel cafe oblivious to the rest of the world passing by, lost in the bubble they now lived in.

Ordering two teas at the counter they spotted a table by the window and sat down facing each other, taking a drink both using their right hands, with their left already taken with each other's hand Sandra smiled and said "When do you think we should tell everyone?" at which Dave took another sip of tea, and taking a few seconds grace to think about his response which he had already formatted "I thought perhaps New Years Day!" "You thought!" Sandra responded immediately "You had already made your mind up Mr Organised! But honestly, that is fine with me I can't wait to tell everyone, I nearly told my mum this morning over breakfast as I was in such a good mood. But I didn't" she added squeezing Dave's hand as re-assurance. "I know it's short notice Sandra and I've only just thought of it on the way here this morning, but why don't we get both sets of parents who've never met each other to meet up on New Years Day for a drink at the Malt Shovel and maybe ask a few friends to ostensibly celebrate New Year and an-nounce it to them all?" "Get you using big words, do you even know what ostensibly means?" and seeing that Dave wasn't sure how to take the comment she added "You can use as many big words as you like, it's the little words like" and putting her hand over her mouth, she finished the sentence so Dave couldn't hear ".... that matter!"

With the usual late December weather not relenting and send-ing arctic wind and rain across the region, it was a somewhat dishevelled Sandra who arrived home and hardly had she got through the door that she put Plan B into action. "Mum, are you and dad doing anything on New Year's Day?" she asked taking off her damp jacket and hanging it up in the hall to dry ready for tomorrow. "We haven't got anything planned, or at least your Dad hasn't mentioned anything darling, why?" Returning from the hall Sandra casually said "Dave and I thought it would be a good idea for you to meet his parents and we thought a neutral venue would be good, so we thought the Malt Shovel would do as we could all walk and save having to drive, I just hope this weather is better by then" "What a good idea Sandra" her mother replied without a hesitation, "It would be nice to meet Dave's parents and I know your Dad is off work. I'll ask him when he gets home and let you know but I'm sure it will be fine" turning to check on tea which was nearly done she had a little smile to herself, her little girl was growing up!

Dave arrived home soaked to the skin having walked home in the afternoon after meeting Sandra at lunchtime, leaving her with a kiss on the Council Office building steps. Nothing better to do and the fresh air will do me good he had thought as he set off, which might have been a good idea when the weather had abated a bit, but now it was back to full winter mode and he was walking straight into the wind and rain, but hey he thought, last week I was in the Infirmary and look at me now. Trudging onwards he was feeling damp by now, but as he turned into the Estate the rain intensified and by the time that he reached the alleyway leading to his street, he wished he had put his winter jacket on instead of his denim jacket which was useless against the persistent rain, but he was nearly home and keeping his head down he came out of the alleyway with just a quick thought about his attack. Why, he thought as his Dad had recently said, when asking about the attack, but by the time he arrived home the thought had gone and been replaced by the conversation he and Sandra had had a lunchtime, something he considered had a much higher priority. Seeing his mum in the kitchen rummaging through the freezer for something for tea which was usually at 6pm, some two hours away, he broached the subject with her back to him "Mum, are you and Dad doing anything on New Year's Day?", closing the freezer and turning round with one of her home made cottage pies in her hands she replied "No David, nothing planned, but you might want to wait until your Dad has got home. Cottage pie, carrots and gravy for tea" She finished putting the cottage pie in the oven and started peeling some carrots, then stopped and said "Something important is it David?" and changing the subject he said "Any chance of a cup of tea mum" "Off course dear" putting down the carrot she was peeling and filing up the kettle she turned to Dave and said" I'll join you and you can tell me about your day" and reaching for the tea pot smirked to herself 'you're not getting away that easy' as she picked up two mugs for them and adding "Go into the Front room, I'll bring them in when the kettle has boiled" and returning to finish the carrot she had been peeling she wondered what his question meant hoping it was some good news after the last few days which had ruined Christmas.

Despite Mary's best efforts she was no nearer knowing what David's question was leading to as his "It will wait until Dad gets home" was all she got with that look he had that she found hard to read, just like his Dad she thought. The tea was barely half eaten when Mary announced "David has something to ask you Alan" as he put a gravy laden carrot into his mouth. Looking at David, Alan finished chewing and looking directly at his son intimated with a look of 'Well what is it' as he loaded his fork with some eagerly anticipated cottage pie and awaited the question Mary was so eager to hear. "Are you and mum doing anything on New Year's Day Dad? As Sandra and I thought it would be a good idea for you to meet her parents, we thought the Malt Shovel would be a good neutral venue for you to meet them say around four when it shouldn't be too busy" Before Alan had a chance to ponder Mary had the words out of her mouth "Of course we can make it, that would be lovely wouldn't it Alan" and with a look between father and son, the deal was agreed and New Year's Day was a done deal.

◆ ◆ ◆

Chapter 8

Having finished work on the 30th December taking New Year's Eve off as holiday, Sandra had suggested to Dave that they spend the day together and meet up with friends at night to celebrate. So when Dave turned up at 9, Church Street, just after lunchtime, thankful that the weather had appeased. Rattling the door knocker twice he waited for an answer and hearing nothing rapped the door knocker again just as the door started opening and following the advice from the voice from within he entered closing the door behind him. "Take a seat Dave" said Tony "She's still upstairs probably deciding for the umpteenth time what to wear" and sitting down at the kitchen table, he saw that Tony had a mug of tea in his hand and gesturing to the kettle intimating did he want one, but before he could answer he could hear Sandra coming down the stairs and thankful he had delayed his answer, he finally shook his head to say no just as Sandra came into the kitchen which she saw, and thinking the nod was aimed at her looked at him "Don't you like it?" she said looking down at her outfit that had taken her an hour to decide upon. Tight black jeans, white lambswool jumper as it was still winter, a pink Kashmir scarf with a white bobble hat and her red winter coat in her hand. What's not to like she thought, waiting for his answer. "I was" started Dave before Tony cut in "He was saying no to a cup of tea Sis, as he had his tongue sticking out!" and laughing at his own humour Tony took his mug of tea into the Lounge and left them alone in the kitchen waiting for the first one to break the ice. "My tongue wasn't sticking out" Dave tried but quickly said "I take that back, it was sticking out!" at which Sandra immediately said "I should think so after all the effort I have put in!" Closing in on Dave she gave him a light kiss on the lips and stepping back she did a half twirl left and right, and looking right into his eyes said "You approve?" at which he closed the distance between them in an instance and kissed her neatly glossed lips, until he heard a cough and opening his eyes, saw Mrs Robertson behind Sandra. As she entered the kitchen she said with a smirk "Good morning Dave, where are you love birds off to today?" and heading for the kettle felt rather than saw the look Sandra would undoubtedly be giving her, at which the smirk grew bigger until she composed herself, and with the kettle filled and on she turned to address Dave with the smirk no longer evident "Really looking forward to meeting your parents tomorrow Dave, although I would have perhaps chosen somewhere better than the Malt Shovel" the smirk having returned this time she could see Sandra's look "Mum!" but seeing the smirk on her face looked at Dave and said "She's only kidding, it will be lovely to meet them and I'm sure the Malt Shovel will be fine" reaching out for his hand, she continued before her mother had a chance "We're off out for the day so don't make any tea for me mum, oh and we're meeting friends in the Black Horse tonight, so I'll see you when I see you." Putting on her red winter coat awaiting her mum's response she was surprised when she said "You two have a lovely day and enjoy yourselves, not too much mind, you never know what tomorrow will bring?" and with that, Diane finished making her mug of tea and kissing her daughter on the cheek as she passed on the way to join Tony in the Lounge, she left Sandra and Dave looking at each other as if Diane was a Clairvoyant. Putting her finger to her lips Sandra looked at Dave and headed for the door. It was only when they were outside and halfway down the street that Dave broke the silence "What did she mean by that?" at which Sandra quickly replied "I haven't said a word, I swear I haven't, it's not been easy but I haven't!" and now out of sight of her house Dave pulled her tight to him and kissed her with a longing from where he wasn't sure, but when he released her she caught her breath and looking at him "So you do approve!" she said with a smirk her mother would have been proud of. Adjusting his flat cap and putting her hand in his, they set off out for the last day of 1981.

Having walked across Bedlow Moors they came to the old Toll Bridge, Finkle Bridge and stopping to lean over the edge to see the rushing water coming off the moor over the last few days Sandra let go of his hand and delving into her pocket found a 2p coin, looking at Dave she said "Penny a wish they say, well I've got two so our wishes can go together" and taking hold of his right hand with her left she raised her hand to throw the coin, first quickly sneaking a kiss, and launching the coin she cried out "Don't tell me" as the coin sank into the rushing waters and was gone from sight. 'It could be all the way out to sea in time, or it could just stay here and be buried in mud, like many other dreams over the years' Sandra thought to herself' Let it be out to sea where the world meets and dreams can sail on wishes' she hoped, as they turned away from Finkle Bridge hand in hand, ready for anything the world could throw at them as the wind increased and clouds grew darker.

As the weather was definitely taking a turn for the worse they headed for the nearby Bedlow Arms, managing to get there just as the rain started to pebbledash the windows. They eyed a table by the fire as they went to order a drink. "Pint of Lager and a half of Lager and Lime please" Dave said when the barman had finished serving the previous customer, and taking a sip each they turned to go to the table by the fire, but an elderly couple beat them to it and they had to wait for a few minutes by the bar before another table came free, as two couples decided they had had enough and headed for their car braving the weather with the rain now setting in for the afternoon. With the waitress clearing the plates and glasses away with an efficiency that her mother would have been proud of Sandra quietly said, "Thank you" and looking up at their waitress, who she hadn't really noticed while she was taking off her coat and sitting down, she realised she knew her from school

"Carol Marsh is that you?" and standing back up went to give her a hug, but with all the plates and glasses it wasn't going to work out so standing there looking at each other Carol broke the moment saying "I'd better get these to the kitchen, but I have a break, such that it is at four, so if you are still here we can have a catch up, do you two want to see the menu" she added hesitating before Dave said "Yes" and she disappeared through to the kitchen laden with her workload, and a few minutes later returned with the Festive Menu for them."Pie or the Lasagne is good, be back in a bit" she said and left them to make their choices, as the pub now seemed to be filling up with refugees from the winter weather. Seeing Carol heading their way Sandra asked Dave what he wanted and pointing to the Steak Pie on the Menu as he was taking a drink, Sandra ordered a "Lasagne for me please and a Steak Pie for Dave" and as Carol wrote their order to her pad added "Chips with both please" at which Carol looked at Sandra and said "Saw you on Christmas Eve in Town with a bunch of girls, it was mad, a bunch of us from school had arranged to get together, did you have a good time?" and with an affirmative Nod, Sandra picked up her drink taking a sip asked "You" "Oh yes it was crazy, I'll tell you on my break" came the reply and she was gone.

"Small world" said Dave when Carol had gone "Were you good friends at school?" "Not really" she replied "Just part of a group really" and picking up her drink realised she had finished over half of it and Dave had hardly touched his. Swiftly moving off subject she put her arm in Dave's and smuggled up to him and whispered "This is nice" and as they both settled down to wait for their meals they people watched, which Dave had said was one of his favourite pastimes. Guessing what people did for a living, or if they were couples, were they married, or boyfriend/girlfriend or even Lovers. They would never know if the couple by the bar holding hands were married or Lovers, but as they started to leave the woman looked over at Sandra and Dave and smiled at them even though she didn't know them. 'Kindred spirits' Sandra thought just as Carol arrived with their meals and setting them down with cutlery she quickly added "Enjoy" and turned round before they could answer to attend to the next table as a couple waited for someone to clear the remains of the previous occupants.

As the conversation dwindled between them with their attention on the food in front of them, Sandra concentrated on her Lasagne, as Dave attacked his Steak Pie, grateful for some time to think she tried to plan what to say when Carol would join them on her break. Would she let Carol go on about Christmas Eve, or try and get her to focus on the girls from school she was out with, and steer her and the conversation away from what had happened! Would she even know what had happened? Why did she go out she thought to herself, putting a chip dipped in Lasagne into her mouth just as Dave nudged her and as she looked at him losing her chain of thought. "This is really good, how's yours?" and having finished chewing she quickly said "Lovely, good choice to come here, especially as the weather is horrible and it's busy which is a good sign" and realising she really only needed to say Lovely, she turned back to her Lasagne, Dave, already cutting another slice of pie and ready to stab a chip just smiled at her unaware of the turmoil in her head and the impending return of Carol preying on her mind.

"Another drink?" asked Dave as he finished his Steak Pie, clean plate as his mother liked, and seeing Sandra shake her head to confirm she would, her first drink finished unseen ten minutes ago. As Dave went to the bar for their drinks, Sandra put down her knife and fork next to her half finished meal and looking around noticed that the pub was now standing room only as the weather had enticed people with its best endeavours. As she spotted Dave returning from the bar trying to weave his way through the throng with their drinks, she could see just behind him, Carol almost following him towards their table.

"Wow, that was a bit of a crush" he said putting down the drinks just as Carol arrived. Putting her glass of Cider down next to Sandra's Lager and Lime she sat down and taking a sip said"I needed that, only been working here a few weeks since finishing University, just needed to earn some money, it's good fun but wouldn't want to do it for a living, what are you up to?" she asked, looking at Sandra and taking another drink. "I work for the Council in the Administration Support Department, have been since school, there wasn't much around when I left but I didn't want to go to University like you did, as I really had no idea what I wanted to do, but I have just applied to join the Planning Department which should be good" she finished, embellishing the truth somewhat. "Good for you" Carol replied and looking at Dave continued "You two been going out long?" to which Dave responded before Sandra could think of an appropriate reply "No, not long, pulled her at a Christmas party!" grinning at his humour, but getting a look from Sandra that suggested she thought he had lost his sense of humour. "I hope you didn't take advantage of her when she was drunk!" chipped in Carol with a look that suggested she knew what she was talking about, at which Sandra saw her whole world crashing down, and taking a couple of mouthfuls from her glass tried to change the subject using some gossip she had heard "No one at University for you Carol?"and as if a dagger had been thrown from behind, the usually bubbly Carol shook her head and said "There was, but I found out he had been cheating on me so I dumped him and left University at the end of term, I'm not really sure if I am going back at the moment." Reaching out with her hand Sandra she grasped Carol's right hand and looking into her subdued eyes tried to apologise for her question "I'm sorry Carol, I shouldn't have asked" at which Carol squeezed her hand and said "Not your fault, it was his, you weren't to know. Anyway my break is up, maybe see you again before I go back to University.... if I go" and taking her empty glass headed off to the kitchen, picking up a couple of plates from a now empty table on the way.

Sensing that there was some emotion in the air Dave decided to add his input now that Carol had gone. "Shame that, I would hate to be in that situation, she seems a nice girl" Sandra thought for a second about Carol before replying "It is a shame, especially as they went out together at School then went to University together! We used to tease them as Puppy Love" and realising how wicked she had been to Carol with her comment, she got up and pointing to the Toilets said "Won't be a minute" Taking a left turn she found herself at the kitchen door, from where she could see Carol folding some serviettes and knocking quietly eventually she caught her attention and she came over with a bundle of serviettes and a question on her lips. "Forgotten something ......pudding?" at which Sandra gave Carol a hug and Carol responded and they blocked the doorway. 'Excuse me ladies' came a voice from another waiter above the general noise and they separated "I'm sorry I shouldn't have said that" said Sandra, "But you didn't know" Carol quickly replied, at which a repentant Sandra admitted she did know. "Then why? Quickly she answered her own question "Christmas Eve?" "Listen Sandra, what Andy did to me was awful and broke my heart at the time, after all we had been going out for over two years and had all these plans for the future but if it wasn't her, it would have been someone else, he always did have a roving eye. Yes I did see you in the Cross Keys. So what if you snogged someone on Christmas Eve, everyone does. Now let me pick up these serviettes and get back to work and you can get back to ....Dave" suddenly remembering his name. As Sandra turned and went back to their table, Carol watching her make her way through the crowds of drinkers said under her breath "Andy used to look at me that way!"

Returning to the table where Dave was sat, she looked at him and deciding she needed to leave Christmas Eve behind, she sat close to him and holding his hand gave him a kiss that went on for a bit longer than she had intended, and as they parted she heard him say "They're playing your record" as Blue Eyes by Elton John came on the Juke Box. Looking at him, she smiled thinking back to when they had started going out and he had first mentioned it at The Plough when it came on, and she cringed, but after he said it was how he saw her, she had said she would have to choose a record for him but as yet, she hadn't thought of one when it suddenly came to her, as she had caught what Carol had said. As the record finished and an Adam and the Ants record blasted out of the speakers she leaned into him and over the sound of Prince Charming said "I know what your record is" and by the look in his eyes thinking it was the one currently playing added "Not this, you vain idiot, come here" and pulling him closer said "For your eyes only!" and flashed her eyes at him hoping he would get the not so hidden message, he thought about it before responding "So you think I'm James Bond!" at which she said "I would prefer Prince Charming!" and they both laughed at the absurdity of it and feeling that a weight had been lifted, she took a drink and waited until the music died down and said somewhat coyly, without looking at him "You'll work it out in time" smiling at her own innuendo, she finished her drink and standing up turned to pick up his glass to go with hers and headed for the bar, leaving Dave with a grin on his face, having just worked out the riddle.

"Look who I found at the bar!" her voice said over the speakers and looking up Dave could see Sid and Sandra and a girl he didn't know just behind them. Mouthing "What happened to Marion?" he was beaten to the answer by Sandra saying "and this is Jane" as she put their drinks down and sat next to Dave, as Sid and Jane took the other two seats, close but not too close she thought. "Fancy letting your girlfriend buy your drinks, have you no manners?" Sid said after taking a drink and looking at Jane raised his glass to her and said "Here's to next year" at which they all took a drink and Sandra, sitting next to Jane whether by design, or more likely Sid manoeuvring they started to chat and find out who they both knew, and what they had done over Christmas ignoring Dave and Sid, who she could hear were on about football, but she lost their thread when the music increased, and she had to concentrate on Jane and trying to figure out why she and Sid were together. It soon became apparent that she knew nothing about Marion, and not wanting to drop Sid in it they chatted for a while before Sid got up to go to the toilet . Dave took the opportunity and said they were going to the Black Horse next, and would they both join them as they could share a taxi. Jane looked around for Sid returning and with no sign of him took a second before saying "That would be nice, as long as Sid is okay with it" "Okay with what Jane?" came from behind her and looking up she saw Sid towering over her. Sandra jumped in "We're getting a taxi ,and all going to the Black Horse next Sid" she said making sure he understood the inflection in her voice and as Sid put a hand on Jane's shoulder said "Better get one in then while we wait for a taxi, same again you two?" and squeezing Jane's shoulder a little added "Give us a hand Jane" they set off for the bar with Sid patting Jane's tight fitting jeans as they walked, leaving his fingers in the back pocket as they reached the bar and ordered the drinks.   —

By the time the Taxi arrived they had all but finished their drinks, as the horn sounded for the second time they finished off the drinks and checking they had all their jackets and hats and in Dave's case flat cap, which was getting some merciless ribbing from Sid 'Bought a pigeon' being his favourite, they got in the Taxi and headed for "The bright lights of The Black Horse please" as Sid who was sat in the passenger seat, directed the Taxi Driver who had obviously heard it all before." Happy New Year driver" Sid said as he paid the Taxi Driver. A couple stumbled out of the Black Horse as they reached the door, and headed for the now empty Taxi "They'll never see midnight!" said Sid holding the door open for them and closing the door after them, headed for the bar with Dave, as Sandra and Jane took a beeline to the Toilets 'To freshen up'."Right Sid, the girls have gone for a minute what's the story with you and Jane, and what happened to Marion?" said Dave "Two pints of Lager, half of Lager and Lime, half of Lager and Black please barman" and turning to Dave continued "Still playing in the sweet shop Dave, haven't found 'The One' like you but she's a good laugh once you get to know her, usually after a few drinks so should be anytime now, your round" he finished, holding out his hand as the barman returned with their drinks. Handing Dave his change he added "Marion's got a steady boyfriend so presumably she will be with him tonight.....and me tomorrow" as he took his and Jane's drinks off the bar and headed for the snug, pointing with his head to the left at the girls, who were just coming out of the Toilets.

Sitting down in their couples the drinks flowing, tales told of memories that only alcohol can release from the back of the mind and tell, true or not! As Sid had said Jane really was funny when she had lost her shyness. Her tale of the first time of going to Girl Guides as a young girl where she hadn't really understood what Girl Guides was all about, so she got a raspberry cane from the garden and painted it white and took it with her pet Labrador to use as a guide dog to her first Girl Guides meeting, had them in hysterics that took another round of drinks to recover from. Just as they had settled down Joe Dolce came on the Jukebox and set them off again "Shaddup you face" they all joined in on the chorus as did most of the pub by the noise drowning the song. "God I hate that song" said Dave, before realising he had sang most of it. Sid didn't let it go and dived in with "I suppose you think you are Prince Charming!" which had just come on at which Sandra burst out laughing, thinking about their earlier song conversation and with just having taken a drink, a flow of Lager and Lime shot out of her mouth and landed between the couples on the table."Charming" said Sid, and then reacting quickly followed up with arms open wide figuratively embracing Dave and Sandra."I gave you Prince and Princess Charming"that was going to take some beating he thought, raising his glass to his own humour.

They got two rounds in before midnight "Because we are wise" said Dave when challenged by Sandra, as he and Sid returned from the bar which was now 3 deep in customers. Setting the drinks down they stayed stood up and chatting about nothing in particular, Dave asked Sid if he would be in the Malt Shovel tomorrow as he had arranged Sandra and his parents to meet and it would be good if a few friends were there too! "What was it you said when I asked you last time we were in the 'Shovel' let me remind you. Nah you said. when I asked if you were head over heels, well the bump on your head hasn't changed your mind I see!" With a quick comeback Dave replied "Come on Sid just take a look at her what's not to fall in...." Dave was saying into Sid's ear, when a tug on his arm interrupted him shouting, Five, Four, Three, Two, One, Happy New Year! A now pretty fresh Sandra gave him a huge kiss unaware she had cut of his comment. Letting go of Sandra and giving Jane a kiss on the cheek and then turning to Sid who was by now finishing kissing Sandra, he pulled her close to him and offering his free hand to shake said to Sid who had put his arm round Jane's waist "Happy New Year you two" "And to you two" came the joint response and they gathered arms around each other and celebrated as only true friends can do with honesty, secrets and lies.

Finishing off the last of the two rounds they had ordered, just as the Landlord called last orders Dave shook his head to say enough is enough without actually saying it, and Sid while thinking about 'one for the road' decided that his attentions were required elsewhere as Jane was making a play to be his first girlfriend of 1982. Sandra returned from the Toilets and looking at Dave, who was holding an empty glass, took it as a sign that they were done and ready to go. Bending down to give Jane a hug and a kiss she was enveloped by Jane who she thought said "Thunk you" then realising what she meant said "See you again soon, you two" and giving Sid a quick kiss on the cheek as she stood up. "Yeah, see you soon" the response came from Sid, before he resumed trying to devour Jane by the mouth. "Don't think we're wanted here" said Sandra putting on her Jacket and taking Dave's hand and using each other for some support, they headed for the door and their future.

◆ ◆ ◆

Chapter 9

New Year's Day had arrived in Kirkdale with what can only be called a sharp frost, which had cleared the air outside so much that the low lying sun was trying to make a welcome return, but had yet to make any impression on the near zero temperature.

"Perfect New Year's weather" Jim said to Diane as he entered the kitchen and kissing her gently on the cheek finished with "Happy New Year" as he picked up a mug of tea that Diane had just made, being the first one up this morning. "Yes it will be a nice walk to the 'Malt Shovel' this afternoon but I haven't decided what to wear yet, maybe I'll wait until Sandra gets up and ask her advice" and picking up her own cup of tea sat down at the table and pondered what the day would bring. It wasn't like Sandra to keep things from her, and the meeting with Dave's parents was unexpected to say the least. Taken with the Christmas Day story that they swore would never mention again it was even stranger that they were suddenly meeting Dave's parents. Maybe the day would make things clearer she hoped, as the clock chimed 10.00 she decided to have a shower and see what she could find in her wardrobe for this afternoon, already half decided on a classic Royal Blue two piece that she had worn to Jim's works Christmas party. The sound of the shower running brought Sandra out of her dream, which by the time she had fully awaken and tried to piece together last night had gone from her mind, and remembering the Girl Guide story she smiled as she looked in the mirror and hoped her mother wouldn't be too long. Her hair needed washing and she had to look her best for Dave's parents this afternoon and lying back down on the bed, she thought about last night and the walk home with Dave.

Having left the 'Black Horse' they walked home by the road as the canal path which was shorter was unlit and after Dave's attack they agreed it made more sense, besides the way they were walking and holding onto each other arm in arm, they could fall into the canal if not careful. She could remember stopping several times to kiss, and the walk must have been the slowest ever as it was nearly two in the morning when Dave left her at her door with a final passionate kiss before heading off to his house. What was it she thought that he had said, something about cutting him off? Well whatever it was she couldn't remember it, but it would come back to her, maybe, and hearing the bathroom door open she got off the bed and stretching like she had only just got up, she headed out of her bedroom and getting a couple of towels from the airing cupboard, entered the steamed up bathroom to start the New Year all shiny and new, ready for whatever today would bring.

In the Baxter family house it may have been New Years Day but nothing really different had changed. Dave was up at the first smell of coffee from the kitchen and ravenous after the long evening at the 'Black Horse' was grateful for the scrambled eggs on toast that his mother had made them all and sitting down, ready for the usual questions about what time he got in, and who did he meet was surprised that his father spoke first. "Anything we should know before we meet Sandra's parents David?" and grateful that he was chewing his meal which gave him time to work out exactly what his father meant, he finally responded "No Dad, nothing like that" answering the hidden meaning in the question "We just thought it would be nice for you to meet each other, as everyone is free because of the holidays" "We thought did we" his Dad quickly replied at which Mary gave Alan a look that said 'Don't tease the boy' and returning to their breakfast, the conversation reverted to the weather and if they would get wet walking to the 'Malt Shovel'.

The weather stayed 'Set Fair' as a sailor would say, with some wind, but nothing that threatened rain but with the temperature not improving as the Sun lost its battle with the frost and retreated to the West, it was a well wrapped up Robertson family that set out for the 'Malt Shovel' at 3.30pm for the 15 minute walk. Tony had been coaxed from his bed with a bacon butty, and the promise of his Dad buying the beer, with Sandra and Diane hooked up the Robertson nuclear family that was, made their way walking the pavement route, rather than the usual short cut across the playing fields 'Not wearing these shoes' Diane had stated when asked by Tony, and deciding it wasn't worth the argument he had let it go. 'If Dad was buying what's a few minutes' was his mindset. "Don't wander off when we get there will you Tony?" said Jim knowing his son's penchant for pool, and with a not convincing "I won't leave your side" adding a slight jab to his Dad's side and seizing the moment "Not when you're buying!" and without waiting for a reaction added "Nearly there!" Up ahead Sandra and Diane had been quiet apart from the request for confirmation that 'her outfit was suitable for the occasion' as Diane was still not sure she had chosen the right outfit, despite changing her mind three times before returning to the Royal Blue two piece that she was now wearing under her coat, which was doing a good job of keeping out the cold. "Sandra darling" she started and almost immediately wished she hadn't but too late now as she continued "Anything we need to know before we meet Dave's parents?" Sensing the underlying question, but determined not to give her mother an easy time, the cheek of the question, anything indeed! Taking a few seconds which undoubtedly would worry her mother she started" Well Dave is called David by his mum and dad, he's an only child, his dad is called Alan and works in an Accountants, something to do with Audits, his mum is called Mary and she doesn't work since they had David, sorry Dave, oh and they have coffee rather than tea! That what you wanted to know" and knowing full well it wasn't she gave her a nudge and burst out laughing, at which Diane, realising she should never have asked the question had no option but to laugh along with her Daughter having been completely put in her place. 'Yes her Daughter was indeed growing up' she thought as they arrived at the 'Malt Shovel'.

Leading his Dad to the bar as they entered the' Malt Shovel' Tony was determined to make sure he didn't renege on his promise of 'buying the beer' so much so that he didn't see Dave and Alan Baxter already sat at a table in the snug, but turning round to ask what his mum and sister wanted, he spotted Dave and seeing that his mum and sister were already headed over to where they were sat turned his attention to his Dad who was ordering their drinks. "They're already here Dad" he said taking one of the pints and the half of Lager and Lime for Sandra as Jim picked up a pint and a half of Bitter for himself and Diane. "Over here" he said already setting off to the other side of the pub, Jim following slightly behind having taken a sip of his pint so he wouldn't spill it on the walk across the pub. "After you" Jim said as a woman wearing a Scarlet trouser outfit came out of the toilets and splitting between Jim and Tony, they all three headed towards the table where Dave sat next to Sandra with Diane on her left. Tony put his drinks down and turning round to see where his Dad had got to found himself face to face with Dave's mum and realising what had occurred he offered his hand, much to the surprise of Mary Baxter, "You must be Dave's mum. I'm Tony, Sandra's brother" and shaking a slightly caught off guard Mary's hand, the ice was broken as having let go of Mary's hand Tony let out a general "What" to anyone who could hear. Diane got up and introduced herself and Jim to Mary, before she could sit down and taking his chance Alan stood up and standing next to a now recovered Mary, the final introduction was made and they all sat down thankful that the ordeal had passed albeit thanks in part to

Tony, who had since made himself scarce having spotted a friend when at the bar.

After some brief family chat and comments like 'Haven't been in here in ages, the beer's not bad, good job the weather has improved' and the like it was on the second round of drinks that Dave got a nudge from Sandra which was 'their sign' and realising that there was a lull in the conversation, but not before taking a good half of his newly replenished pint he set off on his longest sentence of his life, in more ways than one. "Mr and Mrs Robertson" immediately interrupted by "Call us Jim and Diane, Dave" starting again he went on "Jim and Diane, mum and dad, we wanted you to meet today as Sandra and I have been going out for some time, although some would say not that long, and rather than tell you separately we wanted to tell you together. As you know while I was in hospital I had a long time on my own to think about things and I made a decision that when I got out, if I got out that is, I would see if my hopes and plans would be reciprocated by Sandra, and a few days ago we had a conversation, I should say I had a conversation and she listened, but we thought it only fair let you know how we feel about each other, as at the end of that conversation, and with much thought Sandra said Yes" The silence went on far longer than he had anticipated when they had decided to tell their parents and just as it was getting tense Sandra added the bit that Dave had missed out."Just in case you didn't quite get Dave's meaning, we are going to get Engaged on my 19th Birthday" and promptly burst into tears as Diane put her arm around her and breaking the stilted silence said "What a great start to the New Year, I'm so happy for your both, welcome to the family Dave" and looking at Mary, waited for her mirrored response, which after a nudge from Alan came with almost an icy delivery "You can't take my David!" which was followed by a depth of silence that was almost theatrical when she breaking into a huge grin finished "Only joking!" and taking a good mouthful of her Bitter "Alan,

I think this calls for something more than Bitter, go and see what they have behind the bar". As everyone caught their breath and the dark humour of the situation turned to laughter, Dave looked at his mother as if he had been shot "Oh cheer up David you've got a beautiful girlfriend and soon to be Fiancé, let your mum have a little fun before you fly the nest". 'Little fun' he thought turning to Sandra who was bursting with laughter, having got the joke before him, and taking her lead he burst into a smile that became a kiss, then a hug before being interrupted by Alan returning from the bar with a bottle of the 'best house Champagne' that had been gaining dust for the last year, followed by Jim with an assortment of six glasses. Tony having found a pool partner had disappeared. Opening the 'Champagne' with a satisfying pop a few people turned to see what was going on, and as quickly returned to their conversations, as Alan poured the Champagne into the glasses and taking 'Master of Ceremonies' in his stride held out his glass and said "To David and Sandra" and as they raised their glasses Tony returned, and having no idea what was going on said "I'd rather have a pint Dad!" at which they all, apart from Tony laughed as one, defeating the Jukebox until a partly recovered Jim said "Come on I'll get you a pint you Neanderthal" and he headed for the bar, with the son he knew they would have trouble getting to leave the nest.

The rest of the afternoon merged into the early evening and despite only being introduced this afternoon, Sandra was hopeful that the initial signs were good that their parents were going to get along. Alan had offered to get a four ball game of golf together with Jim and some of his friends and they could play golf when the weather got better, whenever that may be. Diane and Mary were already starting to plan the Engagement party for Sandra's 19th Birthday in July, when the weather would be nicer, and discussing whether the Bedlow Golf Club or the Cricket Club would be best as a venue. Watching from the side Sandra and Dave had resumed their usual holding hands and talking about 'What if's' interspersed with kisses, that were shorter than he would have liked but he could wait until their parents had had enough and gone home. Just as they parted from a kiss Dave spotted Sid approaching from the bar with a pint and a half, and Marion just behind. "Told you didn't I Marion!" said a cocky Sid seeing the Champagne bottle and glasses "Knew something was up when you said the parents were meeting up" and holding up his pint said "Cheers you Lovebirds" putting a hand round Marion's waist as she took a drink he mouthed 'Sshhh', before turning his attention back to Marion and kissing her a little too hard, he suddenly had a memory and said "If it wasn't for Marion and me at the Council Christmas Party you two would never have happened." Happy with himself turned to give Marion another kiss, then realising he had missed a point added "Course if it all goes wrong don't blame me!" and delighted at his humour finished half of his pint, completely missing the look Marion gave him as he waved at Tony who had lost his game of pool and was now heading their way. "Tony, meet Marion, Marion meet Tony "said Sid and headed off to sate his thirst with another pint, holding out his glass towards Tony to see if he wanted one, but Tony was no longer looking his way. Greeting Marion with a smile and taking a leaf out of Sid's oddball humour Sandra said" So it's all your fault" and leaning in to give her a hug whispered "Thank You" and gave her a kiss on the cheek and seeing that Sid was still at the bar and with Jane fresh in her memory from last night, she took Marion's elbow and steering her gently, pushed her into the direction of Tony. "Marion this is my brother Tony, he's a bit of a lost soul but he's a Robertson so his heart is in the right place" and looking at her brother like he's just won the Pools added "I bet you've got loads in common" not having a clue if they did, but if you don't try!

Organising a Taxi from the phone in the hallway for the parents, Dave was relieved that they were going so he could spend the rest of the evening with Sandra, who was now holding court between Tony and Marion with Sid playing pool oblivious to the ironic twist. "Church Street and then Albion Street please for Mr Baxter" he finished and turning to go back inside he felt the cold as the door behind him opened, and then a hand on his back "Didn't think you would be out and about Dave" came the comment as Daniel Bruce stepped past him, and before he had a chance to reply Daniel had gone through the internal doors into the bar area. Thinking nothing of it Dave followed him into the bar area and seeing Sandra still trying to 'sell' Tony to Marion he took her hand and said "Shall we sit down" and they returned to the table which still had the empty Champagne bottle and glasses on it . Moving them to one side they put their drinks down and holding hands Dave said "Taxi will be 10 minutes and as it is busy you'll have to share" at which Jim volunteered that they be dropped off first as it was nearer, and with a nod of agreement the dreaded parent meeting came to an end with a "We will have to do this again, and soon" from Diane, as a Taxi horn cut into the conversation. Hugs and handshakes finished the gathering, and the two sets of parents headed off in search of the Taxi waiting patiently outside.

Left on their own Sandra gave Dave a hug and whispered into a just kissed wet ear "You did very well" and kissing him properly on the lips sat holding hands until Sid and Marion joined them, Tony having returned to the pool table. "Right you two Lovebirds shall we have a session" and finishing half his pint said "Your round" pointing at Dave. "I got them last night" he was about to say when an elbow from Sandra reminding him it was Jane last night, cut him off and letting the point go, he set off for the bar. "Two pints of Lager and two halves of Lager and Lime please" he said to Ian, their regular barman who had just started his shift "Feeling better I see" he replied filling the first pint and setting up the next."Police got any idea who did it?" "No idea as yet but maybe one day someone will say something, but they're not hopeful" and handing Dave the last of the drinks he added "I'll ask around if anyone has heard anything and let you know" "Cheers Ian, appreciate it" Dave answered and taking care not to spill the drinks he turned straight into Daniel, who had heard the full conversation. "Excuse me" said Dave concentrating on the drinks before realising it was Daniel in his way, without moving Daniel said "Shame you missed Christmas Eve it was a blast in the Cross Keys, ask Sandra if you don't believe me" and moving to one side, he let Dave go past with a look of triumph on his face, as he tried and failed to attract Ian's attention, leaving Dave to wonder what on earth he meant as he headed back to where Sandra, Sid and Marion were sat in discussion about boyfriends and girlfriends from what he could glean as je put down the drinks. "Here we are drinks for everyone, Lager and Lime wasn't it Marion if I remember rightly from the Council Christmas Party" "Yes thanks, I see you didn't lose your memory" and sitting down next to Sandra gave her a hug and seeing he had disrupted their conversation asked what they were talking about. "Well Mr Macho here" said Marion thinks it's fair to have more than one girlfriend at a time, because how do you know it's the right one, until you have tried a few, a bit like cars he says!" and seeing the look on their faces she continued" Oh don't worry you two, I know he has other 'friends that are girls' " and taking a hefty drink looked at Sid, who following her lead took a couple of mouthfuls before attempting to defend himself "Well it works both ways, you wouldn't want to choose a bloke and stick with him all your life, and never know if there was someone better out there that you had missed!" and confident he had defended himself with the ability of a QC, he took another drink and looking at Marion added "Sometimes it's just about having a good time, and we have a good time don't we ?" Reaching out he held her chin in his hand and gave her a kiss that would stand the test of time in any movie, and settling back with arms around each other looked at Sandra and Dave similarly arm in arm and Sid hop-

78

ing he could change the subject soon said "It matters who you love first, but it also matters who you love last, with you two the answers going to be the same, with us who knows, that's what makes love so interesting it's not the same for everyone, but it is if you know what I mean" and taking a drink " Wow, get me, a philosopher!" and burst out into a roaring laugh that set them all off at the absurdity of Sid giving them 'Lessons in Love!'

◆ ◆ ◆

Chapter 10

With only two days before everyone returned to work, Sandra and Dave spent as much of their time together getting to know more about each other, and their respective families, after Dave's shock announcement to Sandra after Christmas after he got out of the Infirmary. As the weather had remained cold but dry, they filled their time walking the nearby Bedlow Hills and moorland above Kirkdale. It had been a manic few days but as they walked, as ever hand in hand, the conversation had lulled for the time being, and Sandra was pondering to herself about the last few weeks and wondering how strange life can be and how quickly her life had changed, and if it could get any better, 18 and in love 'What's not to be happy about' she thought as Dave let go of her hand, and adjusted his flat cap which seemed to be an ongoing requirement and was just a bit annoying. Taking back her hand and giving it a gentle squeeze they carried on walking the footpath route that was signposted to Peddlers Pike. Just as Sandra started falling back into her own internal thoughts and the future to come, the words "Did you see Daniel in the Malt Shovel last night?" shattered her thoughts "No" she automatically said trying to figure out where this had come from, and why he had waited until they were alone on the Moors to ask her. What had Daniel said to Dave she wondered waiting for Dave to continue, hoping that her newly found world wasn't going to come crashing down.

"I have to work with him occasionally at the Council but I don't really like him, he's so full of himself, going on about how he will be running the Department when Eric Normanton retires. He's got such an Ego! I can't believe you went out with him Sandra" and as the wind momentarily picked up and blew directly into their faces having taken a sudden gust, Sandra turned her face away from the wind and giving herself a few seconds as she pulled her hair out of her mouth, blown there by the wind she finally squeezed his hand and said "It was only for a few weeks in summer nothing to talk about really" and pulling him close she kissed him on his cheek, and then before she realised what she was doing, she asked a question that the moment it came out of her mouth, she realised it was a mistake, how big a mistake she wasn't going to know until he had responded. "Did you speak to him?" and as her trepidation increased she looked away from Dave, wishing the wind could blow her stupid question away for good. "Well he spoke to me when I was ordering a Taxi for our parents, just something about didn't expect me to be out and about " "Oh well just being polite" she said thanking the wind for deflecting her worries until Daniel continued "No it was later when I was at the bar that he said something that I put to the back of my mind as we were all having such as good time, especially Sid and Marion" and as Sandra could feel the cold on her face and the wind picking up taking her dreams with it. Dave finally got to the sentence Sandra hoped she would never hear. "He stood right in front of me at the bar and with a smirk rather than a smile, said I had missed a blast at Christmas Eve at the Cross Keys and I should ask you if I didn't believe him!"

Hit like a newborn baby she wanted to cry out, as she could feel her new found happiness destroyed by a drunken night out in Town and Daniel! Taking her time before responding, by adjusting her own hat, she thought one lie doesn't need to lead to another, but I can mitigate that lie by telling a half truth, and hope that it doesn't in time grow into a full blown lie. Pretending that her hat was now fine she finally answered "I told you we all went into Town as the 'Barmy Army' with Peggy and Sharon and some others from the Department. It was fun as they had a Disco and Sharon and Peggy got picked up, but it would have been so much better if you had been there" she added before launching a passionate kiss on a slightly unexpected Dave. Holding him in a hug after their kiss she looked over his shoulder, and saw the expanse of moorland going on for miles and miles barren with no life and empty like her life would be if she lost Dave because of Christmas Eve. Holding back the tears that were almost there, she felt Dave push her slightly away and holding her with his hands on her shoulders she heard the coldly spoken words that broke her like ice underfoot. "So while I was in the Infirmary at death's door, you went out dancing and partied the night away!" As the tears that she had managed to keep under control started to flow down her cheeks, blown in rivulets by the wind, Dave realised he had overstepped the mark and quickly pulling her tightly to him despite her reluctance, he set about trying to undo his last sentence. "Sandra, babe, don't cry. You really are going to have to get used to my chronic sense of humour. Of course you should have gone out, no point in us both staying in, and besides I used the time really well thinking about you and me" Hugging her closer as she eased into him as his words hit home, he kissed her on the forehead and pulling away he started to gently wipe some of her tears away, until she stopped him and getting a tissue from her pocket she wiped her eyes, until she had satisfied herself she looked reasonable. "Sense of humour my foot" she said taking his hand and heading for the Cragg Inn two fields away the conversation was muted until they reached the door, at which Sandra went ahead and holding the door open for Dave said "Shall we? It's your round Mr Sense of Humour" at which he took off and doffed his flat cap in her direction, as he entered the pub and as Sandra headed for the Toilet he made for the bar. Seeing there some spare tables available despite plenty of people eating he ordered a Pint of Lager for himself and Half of Lager and Lime for Sandra, 'their usual drinks', and taking a look at the menu he ordered some food from the barman when he returned with their drinks. Taking a table at the far end of the Bar he waited for Sandra to return from the Toilets, a little disturbed that she had taken his comment so badly.

A reinvigorated Sandra returned from the Toilets, having spent her time wisely washing her face and combing her hair which had taken a battering from the wind. Happy with her appearance she spotted Dave at a far table and heading his way saw that there was a degree of concern on his face, but she kissed him gently as she sat down to let him know they were alright. "I ordered Burger and Chips for us both while you were away" he said and picking up his pint of Lager to his mouth, he was taken aback when Sandra stood up curtly, and with a straight face looked him in the eye "But I'm a Vegetarian" turning away to look out through the window onto the moors where they had come from, she heard Dave put his pint down and stand up next to her, and still looking out at the moors she felt his arms come around her waist as he stood close behind her, and as she felt his breath on her ear, he whispered "Good try, Miss Lasagne and Chips" and as she burst into a strangled laugh he spun her round and looking at her beaming face "I can see I'll have to get used to your sense of humour!" and after a swift kiss they sat down to await their food, Sandra happy that they had come through their first real test and no serious damage had been done, as long as Daniel kept his mouth shut.

Returning to work on the 4th January 1982 after the last two days with Dave, had Sandra on tenterhooks, as she hadn't seen anyone from work apart from Jo since Christmas Eve, what would anyone say she thought to herself as she entered the Council Office building and seeing that there were lots of people already here, providing no one mentioned Christmas Eve she should be fine. Sharon's voice as always was to the fore and Sandra stopped for a second as she heard the dreaded Christmas Eve mentioned, but the story she was telling was how her and Peggy had been picked up by two blokes and had drank them under the table "Didn't we Peggy!" at which a slightly ashamed Peggy answered "I think you drank all of us under the table Sharon... as always" and smiling at Sandra, asked her how her holidays had been. Taking her arm to move Peggy away from the others Sandra asked her what she could remember about Christmas Eve. "Well nothing that anybody needs to know about, if that's what you are asking about. It won't come from my lips but I can't speak for anyone else" she said curving her hand in the general direction of the office, and with a "Thanks appreciate it" Sandra was hoping for an easy start to the day when Sharon joined them, and as she opened her mouth Sandra knew she was in trouble."Get you the dark horse Sandra, Daniel from Estates who would have thought!" Deciding to put a stop to any further gossip Sandra took each of Peggy and Sharon's hands, pausing for breath she let them have chapter and verse."I went out with Daniel in the summer before I came here, but only for a few weeks and Christmas Eve was just too much to drink and he caught me unawares and anyway it was Christmas, so what's in a kiss at Christmas. Can we all move on now and forget it because I'm going out with Dave and he would have a fit if he knew especially as he was in the Infirmary at the time. Speaking of which Dave and I are getting Engaged this year on my 19th Birthday in July, so if you want an invite you'll forget about Christmas Eve, I have!" As they looked at each other and took in the implications of what Sandra had said, they both attempted to give her a hug at the same time and Sharon quietly said "Secret is safe with us... you dark horse!" and giving Sandra a gentle punch to her ribs they all hugged until Mrs Anderson's arrival signalled work was expected, which was a bit of relief to Sandra whose half truth was now heading into a full blown lie.

◆ ◆ ◆

Chapter 11

With normality resumed with the return of work, and Christmas becoming a fading memory the cold of winter closed in over the first week in January 1982 and talk moved to that famous British pass time, talking about the weather and how bad would it get, and would they get snowed in and against this background the first week of work came to an end with Sharon and Peggy arranging to have a quick one after work on Friday, and just as Sandra was about to say she would be coming Mrs Anderson came out of her office and firmly, as was her manner about work related matters, said "Can I have a minute please Sandra?" Heading over to her office she heard Sharon quietly say "You're in trouble!" which a swift look in response from Sandra, made her wish she had kept her mouth shut, but then she wouldn't be Sharon if she kept quiet, and making her way to Mrs Anderson's office Sandra mouthed 'See you there' at Sharon knowing she really meant no harm but couldn't help herself. Closing the door behind her Sandra took the chair offered by Mrs Anderson's open hand, and not quite sure why she had been summoned at the end of the day on the first week back she took a breath and said "You wanted to see me Mrs Anderson?" "Yes Sandra, a couple of things. I like the way you work and would be sad to lose you, but as per our conversation last week the role in Planning you were interested in has been put out to interview, and I have recommended that you be given an interview. I put in a word with the Manager, as I know he was keen to balance up the Planning Department which is 'a bit long in the tooth', his words not mine. Interviews will be confirmed next week, so I'll let you know when I know. I would advise some revision on Planning as it will show your interest. Oh, and if you want to get on, be advised that Planning and Estates is very male orientated and you will have to stand your ground and be careful who you make friends.......or enemies with. Good luck and I'll let you know about interviews next week. Now go and enjoy your weekend." and opening the door to let Sandra out it was only at the last minute, as she was halfway out of the door that she thought to say "Thank you Mrs Anderson, for the opportunity ... and the advice I really appreciate it." Heading out of the Council Office building and heading for the George where the rest of the girls were meeting, she thought to herself, Plan A really could happen.

Ordering her drink at the bar, she felt a hand on her bottom and swiftly looking round to see who had the audacity to pat her bottom, the kiss that landed on her lips as she completed her turn told her who owned the offending hand. "Didn't expect to see you till tonight" she said as Dave left his hand on her bottom, his other hand gripping a pint of Lager. Returning to the barman who was waiting for his money, she apologised with a look as she handed over her money. "I see you've got one" she said pocketing her change and taking a sip from her Lager and Lime. "Yes I'm fine, just having a quick one with the guys I've been on the course today with, then I'll come to yours, seven be alright?" he finished "I've got some news for you tonight", Sandra said adding "but it will keep till then. Got to join the girls in the corner over there as I'm running a bit late" and with a quick kiss she headed off to join her soon to be ex work mates, if she passed the interview.

Fighting his way across the Estate against the freezing wind blowing directly at him carrying light snow that he hoped wouldn't turn into a full blown snow storm, which he would have to deal with on his way home. Sandra answered the door as he was about to knock, as she had seen him walk up the street, the only brave soul out on this freezing night. "Hello boyfriend, or should that be Mr Yeti!" as the snow had given him a covering and his flat cap was a half inch higher than normal. As he shook himself and cleared his flat cap before entering, Sandra took a step back and as he came into the kitchen her mum came into the room and with a casualness that came naturally she said "Get yourselves into the Lounge where its warm, Jim and I are going out to the Pictures although we could have chosen better weather, so you have the house to yourselves as Tony left about 10 minutes ago. There's some beer in the fridge if you want" and taking off his Jacket and putting his flat cap in the pocket, he looked around for somewhere to put them as Diane headed upstairs. Sandra took his jacket off him and hung it up in the hall indicating with her eyes that he should follow as she made her way to the Lounge. Having put the TV on, Sandra sat on the sofa and patting the cushion next to her, Dave immediately did as instructed and joined her, putting his arm around her and pulling her close he kissed her, like it had been a month since they seen each other, until she pulled away and said "Someone has got a cold nose, Mr Yeti" and rubbed it with her fingers until he grasped her fingers and kissing them individually, he pulled her close again at which they settled together on the sofa until they heard Diane come down the stairs and popping her head into the Lounge said "Have a nice time you two, see you when we get back" and with that she and Jim, who was already waiting patiently at the door headed off into the cold of the night.

With the house all to themselves Sandra took the lead and asking Dave if he wanted a beer she headed for the kitchen when he nodded a yes, as he caught something of interest on the TV. Returning with two bottles of Heineken and a couple of glasses she handed him his drink and seeing he was watching the TV like her Dad did, oblivious to anything else in the room, she nudged him as she sat down saying "You could have stayed home if you wanted to watch TV" taking a drink as she waited for his response, she noticed he was smiling at something he was watching, so taking the moral high ground stood up and walking over to the TV turned and faced him as she stood directly infront of the screen. "Anything attracting your attention?" she said posing with her glass of beer in one hand and her other hand resting suggestively on her hip."The beers not bad" he quickly replied with a huge grin on his face and getting up, he walked over to where she was standing and taking the drink out of her hand, he took a sip and then burst out in laughing as she launched a slap across his chest, which he caught with his spare hand and pulling her close, he kissed her firmly and as their tongues met she suddenly remembered her news and pulling away said "Let's sit down I've got some news for you" at which a slightly disappointed Dave took her hand and they sat together beers in hand like an old couple, as Sandra told him about the meeting with Mrs Anderson this afternoon. "That's great news babe" he said returning to where he had been a few seconds ago, and pulled her close to him resuming where they had left off they were locked together, until he decided to breathe and leaving his arm around her they settled back on the sofa at which Sandra said "Dave do you think I have a chance, Mrs Anderson said it would be tough as it is a very male orientated Department" "Babe you'll be fine, Mr Normanton is a bit old fashioned, but he is fair and I know he likes looking at beautiful things" not adding that he meant cars "So you think I'm beautiful do you" Sandra jumped in as soon as he had said it, and realising he had better back it up, he placed his hands on her face and when they were inches apart he said with all the sincerity he could muster "Beautiful isn't a long enough word to describe you babe" and as he kissed her, he was glad he had remembered one of Sid's chat up lines. She knew he had probably heard it somewhere, but it didn't matter, she was his and he was hers.

There was nothing of interest on the TV, but if there had been it wouldn't have mattered, as they spent the evening in each other's arms. As Sandra came back from the kitchen with a second bottle of Heineken this time to share, she settled back into his arms, and after a few minutes they were entwined laid flat on the sofa, as she felt his hand move up her back and move to undo her bra, after a few seconds she felt the clasp give way and her breasts were released from their cage, but still trapped under the material, until she felt his other hand move up the front of her T-shirt and with gentle pushing at the material with his fingers, she felt the bra moving above her breasts as Dave moved his hand to cup her left breast and as she felt him find her nipple, she gave him a sign that everything was okay as she again found his tongue and her hand up the back of his jumper pulled him closer as Dave pulled her T-shirt up from her waist to expose her breasts all the time kissing her intensely. When he pulled away from kissing her and sliding down the sofa a little he placed his lips on her left breast slowly licking her nipple, she for a fleeting second thought of Christmas Eve, but quickly returning to the present she held the back of Dave's head as he found the nipple on her right breast and caressing it with his hand while kissing the nipple on her other breast she held his head rolling her fingers through his hair, her breasts feeling a warmth inside building, as Dave slowly came back up the sofa to kiss her, leaving his hand to play with her nipples and as she responded to his kissing and trading tongues she was lost in the moment when she felt his hand move across her thighs, and lightly rubbed the front of her jeans. When Dave slowly felt for the zip on her jeans, all the while kissing her and caressing her nipples Sandra didn't, despite her first thoughts stop him, and as he found the top of the zip and gently pulled it down, he left his hand at the opening and slowly two or three fingers found their way inside her jeans, as she slightly opened her legs and feeling him reach the front of her knickers he pushed his fingers in through the top of them and sliding his hand inside her knickers, she could feel his hand on her pubic hair and kissing him with increased vigour she let him stroke her pubic area for a few minutes, until she swiftly closed her legs trapping his hand "Dave that's as far as I want you to go tonight" adding "Sorry " as she sat up on the sofa and kissed his slightly puzzled face and quickly pulled up the zip on her jeans. Adjusting her top which was now around her neck, she was about to put her bra back on when Dave said "Don't babe it's alright, about not wanting to go any further, but leave your bra off I don't think I've finished yet" with a look of a boy with one sweet left in the bag. She took off her bra and pulled her T-Shirt down with a smile that said 'Boys and breasts!' as he put his arm around her cupping her left breast through her T-shirt and taking a drink he said "Do your parents go out every Friday" at which the dig in his ribs told him no, but his hand stayed cupping her breast.

Jim gave Dave a lift home as the sleet was coming down when Sandra's mum and dad got home. Kissing her goodnight in the doorway in front of her mother made Dave blush a bit more than he should, as he thought about the evening, but the look of happiness on Sandra's face was apparent and he got into Jim's car with a smile that he hoped Jim wouldn't read. Sandra unseen, waved at them as the car headed down the street in the sleet "Enjoy the picture mum?" Sandra said closing the door and wrapping her arms around herself from the cold. As she went to put the kettle on Diane replied "Yes dear it was The French Lieutenants' Woman, it was very good, but sad, don't think your Dad liked it though" "And you two, have a nice time?" Diane said turning to face Sandra who was now rubbing her hands from the cold "Yes mum watched some TV, had a couple of bottles of beer, thanks for that, and we chatted a lot" and looking at the direction of her mum's eyes suddenly realising she was bra-less she was about to head for the Lounge and retrieve it when Diane said almost laughingly "Yes I can see you chatted a lot!" as the kettle clicked off and she set about making the tea. Ignoring her mother's innuendo Sandra headed for the Lounge and searching for her bra down the back of the sofa, she was wondering where it had gone as she got to the third cushion, when she heard her Mother behind her "Lost something dear?" "Just an earring mum" she replied pretending to continue looking as the heat hit her face and she felt herself turn crimson. "I've left your tea in the kitchen, hope you find it, if not I'll help you look for it in the morning" she finished and Sandra heard her mother laughing, as she made her way up to bed.

The weather finally broke on Saturday morning and Sandra set off for Dave's house on Albion Street. To anyone who saw her it would have been difficult to work out if she had a furious or a comical face. Depending on who answered the door, would determine which face would meet the door opener. Mrs Baxter answered the door with her coat on "Sandra, so glad we didn't miss you, we were just going out for the day, and I so wanted to thank you for introducing us to your parents. We had a really good time and got on so well. I hope you enjoyed it as well. Of course you did. Didn't you? Take your coat off, David will hang it up for you, David" she finally finished as Mr Baxter came into the kitchen."Hello Sandra" he greeted her "Can you tell your Dad, sorry Jim, that I'll be in touch when the weather is better, and we can arrange a game of golf as he seemed quite keen when we met. "Certainly Mr Baxter, he is quite looking forward to it" she said in reply as Dave took her coat and looking at him she was still unsure which face to use, so she smiled like she'd found a pound and lost two 50p's. Taking her out of her thoughts Mrs Baxter said "Say hello to Diane for me will you Sandra and see you soon I hope" Mr Baxter opened the Front door and led his wife outside and opening the door of their car, he waved at Dave and Sandra stood in the doorway like they had lived there forever.

As soon as the car was out of sight the dig that Dave received made him double up for a few seconds "Sandra" he said thinly as he stood upright "What was that for" "Give it back now!" she replied with a furious face and his "What" didn't help matters "You know what!" came a swift response "No I don't give me a hint" and with a smirk coming across his face, he added "Let me think" and putting both hands on her chest, he moved towards her aiming for a kiss that he knew he would be lucky to get. Moving her head to avoid his attempted kiss, she said with her best furious face "So you do know what's missing" and glaring at him so hard that he should have burst into flames she wasn't quite ready for his response "Nothing's missing as far as I can tell, in fact they're just perfect!" he said with a huge grin, as he had left his hands on her breasts, which she had forgotten about as she was so angry. Realising she had lost the battle she looked at him and leant in for a kiss and as he bent to meet her, she quickly brushed his hands away from her breasts and putting a finger between them before they kissed. she said "Good job I've got more than one bra" and taking her finger away they kissed gently, as a kiss mends all arguments when you're in love.

Catching the bus into Town they wandered around various shops with Sandra picking some lipstick from Boots, and Dave a copy of Auto Trader from WH Smiths, as he was hoping to pass his test next month, and was looking to get an 'old jalopy' as he called it if he managed to pass. Walking down by the Bridge Canal Basin, they were looking at the rows of multi coloured barges tied up for the winter, some with small pipe chimneys poking out of their low roofs, blowing their smoke out towards the moors high above. Seeing that a new cafe had opened they headed for the door hand in hand and just as Dave shut the door behind them, they turned and saw Sid and Jane sat in conversation, each holding a mug in their hands as if trying to crush the life out of it. Approaching the counter they were busy reading the hand written menu which seemed to have every variety of everything, and must have taken hours to finish. Deciding to go for something simple Dave said"Two coffees and two sausage rolls please, and sideways to Sandra 'Unless you are still Vegetarian of course!'" which deserved the kick he got. "I'll bring it over, where are you sitting?" came the reply from the woman behind the counter, and turning to point to the table where Sid and Jane were sat, he found himself pointing to their now abandoned table with two empty mugs, and he just had time to swivel round to see the back of Sid as he shut the door. "Over there" said Dave pointing to an empty table, perplexed that Sid hadn't seen him. Sitting down and looking at the door Dave turned to Sandra and said "Odd, very odd" "Do you think they didn't see us" countered Sandra as the woman brought their order. "Sid never misses anything, there must be something up" and taking a bite of his sausage roll, he was trying to think if he could figure out why Sid had obviously avoided them, when Sandra broke his chain of thought." Dave was last night ok.....I mean did you expect....well you know" at which he reached for her hand and looking at her directly facing him he slowly said "Obviously I would like to,, no let me start again. When we ....are ready for that step I want it to be a memory that I can take to the grave with me" and inevitably the tears came for Sandra, and landed on her sausage roll which took some of the romance away, but she wiped them away from her eyes, and having taken a moment to have a drink she said "You are such a softy,.... my softy" she finished, as she attacked her damp sausage role, as she had missed breakfast at home. As they finished their drinks to wash down the flaky pastry that seemed to have spread everywhere, Sandra suggested they walk home as they can pick the path up from the far end of the Bridge Canal Basin out towards the Bedlow Moor, and eventually 3 miles later home.

At the crossroads where the canal went under the railway they sat on a bench 'Dedicated to Brian and Margaret Wilson who spent many happy hours here watching the world go by'. "Isn't that romantic" said Sandra as Dave cleaned off the last of the ravages of the weather on the plaque. "Now who's being soft" he said putting his arm around her, as they became modern day Brian and Margaret for 10 minutes. Having drifted off into a silence that threatened to put them to sleep as they leant into each other, the sound of a train passing overhead broke them out of their moment, and with a quick kiss they set off on the next leg of their journey home. The walk up to Bedlow Moors was always a hike, as it rose from the low lying Canal some fifteen hundred feet, but as the sun tried to break through the cloud to give a little winter's warm, Dave was still thinking about Sid and why he had ignored them at the cafe. As they reached the plateau before the final few hundred feet to the top of Bedlow Moor, they could see on the horizon between them and home the Bedlow Arms, and its welcoming yellow lights trying to beat the sun to creating warmth. Dave just beat Sandra to the question "Fancy a drink?" and with a squeeze of his hand the decision was made. They headed on a cross moor path that wasn't too wet, cutting the distance by a third, just as the sun gave up and went to sleep in the west, they arrived at the door passing the main window that looked out at the moorland, and stopping so suddenly that Sandra almost dragged him the last few feet Dave said "Well this should be interesting" and as Sandra hadn't looked in the window a sudden dread hit her. Letting Sandra go first as she was now infront of Dave, she opened the door with some concern, unsure what or who more importantly, Dave had meant. Peering through the side window into the main room her heart ready to miss a beat, she saw Sid and Jane sat at the table infront of the main window, which Dave must have seen as they approached the pub. Looking back at Dave she mouthed 'Sid and Jane" and with a nod of his head, indicating that this was what he had seen on the way in, he moved past her and led her by the hand to the bar. Ordering 'their drinks' he paid the barman and said "Let's just pretend we didn't see them in the cafe, and see what they say!" and approaching the table Sid looked up as he sensed a presence, and seeing who it was said "Fancy meeting you two lovebirds up here .....again! Come and join us and moving his coat off a chair so Dave could sit down Sid took a drink and looking at Jane "Remember these two lovebirds Jane?" "Course I do" she quickly responded "We had a great night the other week, have you walked here" she added, realising it was obvious they had as they had probably taken the same path as

94

them from the Cafe."Yes we went into Town and then had a meander and ended up here, bit of a hike up from the Bridge Canal Basin though" Dave added to make sure they knew they had been seen, and he wasn't going to let Sid off snubbing them in the cafe.

"Alright Sherlock Holmes" said Sid "We were in the middle of something when you came into the Cafe, and now we're not so shall we move on?" Taking a drink, finishing his pint he headed for the bar with a cursory look at Jane, and a shake of his pint to figuratively sign if she wanted another drink. The positive answer came at a nod of her head, no surprise to Sandra as Jane looked like a woman who needed to drown her problems, and knowing that alcohol caused more trouble than it solved, it was a reticent Sandra who put her hand out to touch Jane and barely had she started her sentence "Anything I can ...." Jane got up and headed for the Toilets with a brief "Excuse me" on her way past Sandra. Looking at each other Dave squeezed Sandra's hand and said "I'll go give Sid a hand with the drinks, won't be long" leaving Sandra nursing her Lager and Lime and wondering what on earth was going on. She knew Sid played the game, but they had a really good night on New Year's Eve, and she thought there may be some future in it for them, but seeing Sid with Marion on New Year's Day had just confused her, how could you be with one person one day and another the next she thought and realising her own hypocrisy, she was saved from her thoughts when Jane arrived back from the Toilets with Dave and Sid nowhere to be seen."Sorry about that Sandra" Jane said sitting down and looking around for Sid. "We just needed some time to sort something out between us, and when you came into the Cafe we were at a bit of a sore point that needed dealing with, we didn't want to blank you, but sometimes it's best dealing with something rather than letting it fester" and having finished what Sandra thought was an apology, but about what, she still had no idea, they both took a drink to fill the silence. Putting down their glasses in synch as Sid and Dave appeared from outside where an intense conversation had taken place, judging by the nearly empty pint glasses they both had. Approaching the table Sid handed Jane her new drink, and without saying anything he set off for the bar for a refill. Holding his glass which was summarily empty Dave smiled at Sandra and pointing to the bar he headed off to follow Sid, intimating he would get her a fresh drink as he shook his glass at her. Returning from the bar with everyone now in possession of a full drink the silence was broken by Sid, who taking a gulp of Lager, began his explanation of what had been going on.

"Look this goes no further, Jane dumped her boyfriend Nigel, her first real boyfriend if you get my drift, before Christmas as she found out he had been playing around as they say, as he took up with this other girl. But seeing Jane out on Christmas Eve he made a beeline for her, and what with it being Christmas and Jane having had a lot to drink they ended up in this situation where he wanted to take her home, and Jane being out of her tree agreed, and they ended up at his flat where, well you can guess what happened, but Jane passed out and when she came to he was asleep but they were both naked on the floor. Jane managed to get a Taxi home but she can't actually remember if they had sex, or not but the fact she was naked suggests that it may have happened. Anyway he has decided he made a mistake and Jane is the love of his life, will she forgive him and he has been bombarding her with calls, and her parents are wondering what is going on. She told her parents it was just a falling out and it was over, but after she ignored his calls he sent her a letter and pleaded with her to take him back"

"God that's awful Jane" said Sandra feeling a kindred spirit with her own Christmas Eve incident.

"Well that's not the end of it unfortunately is it Jane" looking at her as she burst out crying and Sandra moved to give her a hug. "Unfortunately Nigel, the ex boyfriend took some rather intimate pictures of Jane at his flat, when they were going out. As Jane is quite proud of her body, which in my opinion is fully justified, sorry I'll get back to the story. There are these pictures some of which he has already sent to Jane and he has said he will send them to her parents if they don't get back together. Well you can imagine if her parents saw them what the reaction would be. So as you can gather when you saw us in the Cafe the timing wasn't great, sorry Dave" As the silence continued and Dave and Sid took a swift drink Sandra was holding Jane around the shoulders as she cried into her hair and it was only as the drinks went down that the silence was finally broken by a now very angry Jane "Sid get us a Vodka and Coke, ...please" and seeing the look in her eyes he headed for the bar with Dave in tow, and upon returning with the drinks they were more than a bit surprised to see a smiling Jane and Sandra chatting like nothing had ever happened. "Well something cheered you up" he said, handing Jane her the Vodka and Coke, and sitting down the reason for the change became apparent "Sandra here has convinced me that if life kicks you have to kick it back, so here's what's going to happen. Tomorrow being Sunday Nigel will be at home in the morning so we, meaning me and you Sid, go round to his flat and demand the pictures, negatives the whole shooting match and if he won't give us them, which he will, as he's only 5'8" and you're 6'3", well threat isn't the word for it, that's the plan, fight a bully with a bigger bully, sorry Sid you're not really a bully" and squeezing his free hand, she smiled at him as he drained a mouthful of what must have been his 5th pint. Holding up her vodka and coke Jane said "Bring on Sunday, my round!" and finishing her drink she headed for the bar.

The rest of the evening fell into a more normal routine with Sandra and Jane catching up from New Year's Eve, Sid and Dave chatting about football and work, which in Sid's case was not going well as he told Dave. "The work is fine but there's no chance of progress unless Tom retires and he's only 51 so no chance. The place is busy, but stuck in the dark ages as far as modern working methods. Plenty of staff but ancient machines, we could do so much more if they spent some money on modern equipment, it's like they have never heard of a computer!" and finishing his pint said "One for the road" already getting up to go to the bar and seeing that he was getting up Jane held her almost empty glass in the air to let him know she was ready for another, and catching Sandra following suit he was stuck with a full round. Heading to the Toilet Dave gave Sandra a smile, but she was in deep conversation with Jane, and having a full bladder, he set off to relieve the pressure and entering the Toilet was thinking to himself how strange that they had spent a few nights with Sid, one night with Jane, the following with Marion and now Jane again, Sid must have hidden talents he thought as he came out of the Toilets and made for the Bar. Tapping him on the shoulder "Give you a hand Sid" said Dave and careful not to spill, as he took the drinks from Sid, they returned to their table with Sid saying "Hi" to a girl Dave didn't know on the way, which drew a questioning look from Dave which Sid mouthed "What?" Placing the drinks on the table and sitting down the conversation returned to work and who would change their jobs which brought out the fact that Sandra had an interview this week, at which Jane jumped in with "They'd be mad not to choose you, smart, pretty, and I think a little in love" she laughingly finished and gave her a hug which Sandra naturally responded to like long lost friends stuck together. The last orders bell sounded, but the consensus was that they had had enough and leaving just as the time bell rang, they set off to walk home deciding that a taxi was extravagant, the weather was cold but fine and as they made their way down off the moor on the road, a little unsteady but 'life is like that sometimes thought' Dave.

Sunday arrived and an unexpected January sunshine lit up the hills around Kirkdale, as the weather continued to improve after the long freezing December. Agreeing to meet up after Sunday lunch at the respective Baxter and Robertson family homes Dave and Sandra met at 3pm with Sandra in particular worried about what had happened with Jane and her ex boyfriend, as she and Sid were going to 'deal' with him this morning. Hand in hand they made their way to the Malt Shovel where they had arranged to meet at 4pm, with time to spare they took the long way round the reservoir which now had a newly instated public footpath linking it the Bedlow Moor above. Sitting on one of the new benches, watching the regular procession of birds landing and taking off from the still frozen surface, Dave broke the quiet by handing Sandra her errant bra, at which she immediately blushed and snatched from him and put it in her pocket hoping no one had seen. "Dave what if someone had seen, honestly sometimes I do wonder about your sense of humour!" and leaning in to give him a kiss, she stayed resting her head on his shoulder after they had parted, his arm around her as they returned to their own thoughts. "Come on" said Dave offering his hand to Sandra as they stood up "Time to meet the Vigilantes" he added and taking her hand, they set off towards the already setting Sun that had tried it's best, but wisely given up ready for another day.

Taking off his flat cap as they entered the 'Malt Shovel' Dave could see Sid and Jane sat at a table as if they had been there some time, and pointing to where they were he said to Sandra "Go and sit with the Vigilantes" still amused at his sense of humour "I'll get our drinks and be with you in a minute" Heading for the bar, he hoped everything had gone alright this morning, knowing that it could have turned nasty even if Sid was 6'3"! The pub was quiet after Christmas and he was soon back with the drinks, placing them down on the table he knew by the look in Sid's face that things were good. "Well don't keep Sandra waiting she's dying to know what happened!" Dave said after taking a drink at which a look came from Sandra, that yet again his sense of humour was out of kilter. "Jane why don't you tell them, it was after all your call last night!" and handing the 'stage' to Jane, she regaled the story of their morning. "Well Sid picked me up around 10.00 and after he asked if I was sure I wanted to go through with it, which as I said last night, well, I think I said, if life kicks you kick it back! No that was you Sandra, wasn't it, I just picked it up. Anyway we turned up at Nigel's and he opened the door, seeing it was me and then spotting Sid as he stepped forward he kind of turned a funny colour, but before he could move Sid went past him and we were in through the door before he could react. Initially I thought Wow! that was easy, and then I saw this girl coming out of the bedroom wearing just a thong and hair all over the place. Well when she saw us she placed an arm over her tits and shot back into the bedroom, and I think that was when Nigel realised the game was up. He still had the cheek to ask me what I wanted, but when Sid asked him if he had taken any pictures of the girl in the bedroom, he knew why we were there and he just went to a cupboard by the TV picked up a photo wallet handed it to me. Well I checked it contained the photos, as well as the negatives before handing it to Sid, and then I slapped Nigel as hard as I could, which I must say was harder than I thought I could ,as he was caught unawares and ended up resting on the arm of the sofa behind him. I was heading for the door when the girl came back out of the bedroom in Nigel's shirt and asked what was going on. Nigel got up to go to her, but Sid put his hand out to stop him and went to talk to her, and then she disappeared into the bedroom. After that Sid had a few words with Nigel, and then we headed out leaving them to it and good riddance I say!"

"Well done you two, Sandra was a bit worried it might kick off "Dave said knowing his sense of humour had done it again, but no kick or nudge, just a look that said it all from Sandra."Cheers to Jane and Sid" said Sandra holding up her drink, which they all joined and clashed like a winning team. With the relief at the outcome they set down their drinks, just as

Sandra decided she had missed something "What did you say to the girl Sid" and looking at Sandra, and then Jane who he hadn't told as she was just so happy, on the way back from Nigel's, she had put it to the back of her mind. "Well it's like this, Angela is the daughter of Pete, one of the guys at work, so I told her that I worked with her Dad, and if she went home and never came back, I wouldn't tell him that she hadn't stayed over at a friend's house. She got the message.............it's a tough learning curve at 15!" The silence was palpable until Jane and Sandra said in unison "No!" "Afraid so" Sid quickly added"If Pete ever found out, they'd be taking pictures of Nigel in the morgue!"Another silence fell upon them as they all found the right words difficult to find, and sensing silence was better than an ill placed comment, Sid chose the moment and broke the quiet by putting his hand inside his jacket, and pulling out the photo wallet which Jane had given him at Nigel's, but had forgotten about, as she was so glad it was all over, and opening it he took out the first picture and with a smile from ear to ear said "Anyone want to see one of Jane's pictures?"

Stunned at Sid's comment Jane swiftly took the Photo Wallet out of his hands, as he expected she would do, but he still kept hold of the picture in his hand and turning it upside down said looking directly at Jane "Can I keep this one?" Seeing the humour had lifted the awkwardness of the last few minutes Jane countered with "Sure why not" before adding with a hefty measure of sarcasm "Don't you want the real thing? You did this morning!" as she took the picture from him and placing it safely in the Photo Wallet wondered where she could burn it, along with a small part of her heart that she had left at Nigel's.

◆ ◆ ◆

Chapter 12

After a strange Sunday to say the least, it was back to normal on Monday, and as Sandra said hello to everyone on her way to her desk at work, she wondered what they had all done over the last two days and did they have a story to match hers, which she doubted, but she had been asked not to tell anyone so she would never know if they had a more sad, emotional and eventually funny story to share."Hi Peggy" she said passing her desk "Have a good weekend?" "Oh just the usual Sandra, went out with Sharon on Saturday night and, well you can probably guess, had too much to drink and ended up with a couple of lads at Roxy's which was hilarious. The carpet in there is so old and sticky that Sharon fell and landed in the arms of this bloke from the Army, and well you can imagine what happened next. She really knows how to lay it on. 'Why you saved my life' she said 'But can you get your hands off my Tits!' Classic Sharon! Well they bought us both a drink and what with the six or seven we had already had in Town, the inhibitions were down, not that hers are ever that high that is, and we danced like them from Top of the Pops but really more like demented idiots until closing time and wouldn't you know it Sharon asked Mick, the Army bloke, to walk her home and his mate Andy said he was starving so we went for a curry" "Come on Peggy you can't leave it at that" said Sandra not noticing Mrs Anderson enter the room but a look over her shoulder from Peggy told her and that they had run out of time "Tell you at lunch" said Peggy sitting down and moving to her desk Sandra whispered "Can't wait!" and the daily routine of the Administration Support Department began to get into gear as the noise decreased, and piles of paper that had appeared since Friday from all the different parts of the Council were attacked, romantic or otherwise stories would have to wait.

As 12.30 came and chairs were scrapped on the floor as the evacuation, as they liked to call it, started Peggy, Sharon, Jo and Sandra gathered outside the Council Office and headed for the Brazilian Cafe which was run by Martin, one of Peggy's uncles. Ordering four coffees which were quickly poured and taking the frothy coffee cups, they sat in a booth and Peggy continued where she had left off earlier.

"Well you'll have to ask Sharon what happened with her and Mick as she hasn't told me yet, which means she's either feeling guilty or more likely can't remember!" and looking at Sharon who was paying her coffee more attention than the story she continued "Well Andy, who by the way works at Valley Haulage as a mechanic, and has done since leaving school, he did his Apprenticeship there and, "Get on with it" said Sandra "So me and Andy" "Oh it's me and Andy now is it?" said Jo pitching in "Well if you'd let me finish girls" said Peggy before carrying on "Me and Andy went for a curry and got along really well, we were last out of the curry house at 3.30am, and as we live in much the same direction he walked me home" "You can't leave it there Peggy, did you snog him, did he cop a feel, are you going to see him again" said Jo now eager to get the details "Yes, No and Yes Jo" she quickly responded, at which a smiling Sandra reached to squeeze her hand and said "Good for you Peggy about time you had some luck with men" "Men!" exclaimed Jo, they're all the same only after one thing, isn't that right Sharon, let then have their way and they're a...way!" Looking at Sharon for a response which wasn't forthcoming Peggy asked what was wrong "Well if you must know Mick has asked me to visit him at Catterick Army camp, where he is based at the end of the month and I said I would let him know, but I can't make up my mind. We.... well, you know, and we spent all day Sunday together before he went back to camp and it was lovely. He made me breakfast in bed. Well scrambled eggs on toast, we walked on the Canal path and went out for Sunday lunch at the Tower Hotel and walked across the Denton Moor, and had a few drinks at the Copper Pot, before going back to mine and well ….you know" And with that she was finished, and without looking up she returned to concentrate on her now almost empty coffee. "Get you Sharon all loved up!" said Jo, immediately regretting it, as a barrage came from Sharon who had found her inner self. "Jo when I want your opinion I'll ask for it. Has Steve called you yet after Christmas? No. Because you gave him what he wanted and then followed him around like he was god's gift. Well he's not in fact he was in the Copper Pot yesterday, with Linda from Accounts, all over her like a rash he was!" and seeing Jo burst into tears, as she realised she had been waiting for a call from Steve, that would never happen, Sharon touched her hand and trying to mend their friendship said "I'm sorry Jo, but you needed to know. I'm sure there is someone out there for you, after all if Sandra can land a Romeo there's hope for us all" in true Sharon style, she laughed at her own joke as Sandra decided to let her have the moment 'Dave a Romeo, cheek she thought' But as they all took the point they reached out and with all four hands together Sharon proudly announced 'Barmy Army' which they all echoed and laughed at the absurd name they had given themselves.

Returning to work they settled into the afternoon workload with differing moods, but individually glad they had friends that they could talk to about anything, whether they liked it or not. The pile of papers that Sandra was plodding through had become monotonous, as it came from the rent department, so she was pleased when the change in colour in the pile, just after halfway showed they came from the Planning Department. A change is as good as a rest she thought, reading the first file which was some 8 pages. But with little of interest a file dated 1952 attracted her attention, WCarey/McParland/2811952 intrigued her as she spent a little more time on it than she should have, but as time passed she decided she had to get on with her work and she would return to it another time. The instruction on the first page was copy and return pages 3 to 8 to sender with the following letter attached. The next 24 files were of a less interesting nature, and they took most of the afternoon to complete and just as she finished the last one she came to another batch of Rent Department papers as the working day ended, and everyone got ready to leave for home. Finishing tidying up her desk Sandra was thinking about asking Sharon if she had made a decision as yet about Mick, when Mrs Anderson said "Got a moment Sandra?" just as she was about to go past her office. "Sure" she replied and entering the office Mrs Anderson said "Close the door Sandra please" and as the door shut "Take a seat Sandra, Well there's good news and bad news Sandra" she continued and looking at Sandra, who now had a perplexed look on her face she added "The good news is that the interview for the role you applied for at the Planning Department is this Friday afternoon at 14.00. The bad news is that there are six applicants, so you will have to be on your game to convince them to choose you. But you have the rest of the week to get some revision done, so I have written down some pointers that might help" and handing her an A4 sheet which was half full she finished "Good luck for Friday and if you need anything before then please let me know" With that she started to put her coat on, indicating the conversation was done, at which Sandra stood up and quietly said "Thank you Mrs Anderson" as she left the office and headed for home and her future on an A4 piece of paper.

The knock on the door at 24 Albion Street was opened and greeted by Mrs Baxter, who seeing that it was Sandra, ushered her indoors out of the dark "Well hello Sandra, what brings you round here, as if I didn't know" she said, already heading for the Front room calling out "David". As Dave entered the hall he was surprised to see Sandra standing there taking her coat off. "Hello boyfriend" she said and gave him a quick kiss, before Mrs Baxter came back out of the Front room and headed for the kitchen with a smile on her face as she passed her David. "Well this is a nice surprise" he replied having ignored his mum's innuendo ridden smile. "Come into the Front room" he said taking hold of her hand and hoping this actually was a nice surprise, as they sat on the sofa next to each other and he pulled her close for a kiss before his mother returned. Parting after their embrace Sandra explained why she was here on a Monday night, telling Dave about her conversation with Mrs Anderson and the interview on Friday. "I'm a little bit worried that I'm going to mess it up, and not get the job" she quickly said before adding "Dave, according to Mrs Anderson there are six applicants and I've got no experience in Planning, which the others might have, she gave me a list of some pointers that she had written down." Handing the paper to Dave she continued "I saw some Planning files today and they look fairly straightforward, but do you really think I have a chance!" Putting his arm around her and stealing a kiss, he thought for a minute before replying" "No!" he said leaving a pause "Sorry my sense of humour again. No, I don't think you have a chance, I think you will get it! Eric Normanton was setting out the week this morning and mentioned that he had to book Friday for interviews with HR for the Trainee Planning role, and he was saying that he had seen the applications and there were only a couple of applicants that looked good and that only one was a girl, which would be nice to have in the Planning Department ,as it was full of macho blokes, he gave me such a wicked wink that I thought he knew that it was you, but it could just be his sense of humour. Anyway let's have a look at that paper and opening it out he read the pointers advice that Mrs Anderson had given to Sandra. "Have you read this Sandra?" Dave asked having finished reading, to which she admitted she had looked at it but not really taken it in on the bus home. "Well the thing is these are basically the type of interview questions that HR sets out and from memory they haven't changed since I had my interview 2 years ago. I'll write down my answers as I remember them."

"Question One, What attracted you to the role?
Well the answer is working with me! No, really the answer is, I see buildings being changed, knocked down and built and I want to know why, how and for what reason."

"Question Two, Can you work to rigid timescales?
The answer is I already work to tight deadlines and timescales from various departments in the Council maybe add including the Planning Department."

"Question Three, Can you work in a team or on your own to agreed targets.
Same answer nearly as above but you need to add with clear instructions absolutely and can work on schedules."

"Question Four, Where do you see yourself in 5 years?
In bed with Dave would be the best answer. Sorry, I would hope to be finished the Planning HND and looking at doing a further qualification perhaps specialising in one section of the sector."

"Question Five, Good luck Sandra I'm sure you will interview well. I will miss you" Mrs Anderson

"How can you remember something from 2 years ago Dave?"
"Well I had nothing to fill my head with until you came along" he said and pulled her close thinking 'but thinking back to the attack, someone wanted to keep it that way! "No wonder you're doing well at work with answers like that from 2 years ago. I'll try to miss out working with you!" she replied as he leant in to kiss her as the door to the Front room opened. "I've made you both a drink" came the voice of Mrs Baxter as she entered the room and putting two mugs of coffee on the side table she headed for the kitchen with another smirk."Your mum had a wicked smile, don't you think" said Sandra picking up the nearest mug of coffee and handing it to Dave be-

fore reaching out for her own mug and settling back on the sofa there was a moments silence before Dave said "You didn't comment on the answer to Question Four?" "No need to, is there, because it will be a fact!" Sandra said with a huge grin knowing that as they had hot mugs of coffee each he couldn't do anything but smile........and dream!

Dave walked Sandra home at 10pm, satisfied that she was knew what to do and was ready for her interview on Friday "A little revision on Planning issues especially historic or Listed building would be good as Eric Normanton likes people who have an interest in the past, not just the future" he had said as they watched the 9 o'clock news sat in the Front room with his mum and dad, like an extended family for the night. Despite his Dad offering to run Sandra home, he felt like a walk and a little 'us' time and as they set off for Church Street as always hand in hand, he could feel that they were coming up to a hurdle in the plans they had for the future. If Sandra didn't get the job they would both be disappointed, but they might do another round of interviews next year when another place came about. Looking at her as they neared her house he suddenly stopped and putting his arms around her said "I can't wait to celebrate on Friday so why don't we do something different, how about the pictures, unless of course your mum and dad are going then we could just" ...but he never got the words stay in out of his mouth, as Sandra kissed him passionately and as they parted she said "You really believe I will get the job don't you" "Of course I do, I have no doubts about it" crossing his fingers behind his back, he continued "My future is with you, and you are my future" at which she gave him an embrace, mingled in with a long kiss and looking at him as they separated she said" Did you do poetry at school, you big romantic?" and tugging him they made for her house and a final kiss before they would meet again on Saturday. Walking home Dave put his hands in his pockets and crossed his fingers as he walked home hoping his flat cap, and dreams wouldn't be blown away.

A nervous Sandra arrived early at work on Friday, and only Peggy was already sat at her desk and putting her things on her own desk she went to chat to her as seemed a little lost this morning. "Penny for them" said Sandra as she approached her desk."Oh hi, just daydreaming Sandra I got up a bit early this morning, and thought I might as well get to work early than sit around at home" "Dreaming of anything in particular Peggy" Sandra said trying to lead the conversation, but she was cut off as Sharon and Jo arrived together, and as the subject changed to what they were all doing tonight Sandra didn't have a chance to follow up, but thought she might get a chance at lunch when they usually went to the Brazilian Cafe together. "Morning everyone" broke through the general chat as Mrs Anderson arrived and slowly everyone got down to work, and the noise abated until it was almost silent. The morning passed quickly for Sandra as she had the conversation she was going to have with Peggy on her mind, and she was thankful she had something to take her mind off the interview this afternoon. Despite Dave's confidence, she had some doubts about her chances of success but she had done her revision, Dave had given her some good interview question answers, obviously ignoring the bed answer and they were going to meet up tonight to celebrate if she was successful. Pondering what she would do if she didn't get the job, her thoughts were interrupted by Peggy "Now who's daydreaming! Come on Sandra lunchtime" and getting her handbag she joined Peggy as they tried to catch up with Sharon and Jo. "Tell you mine if you tell me yours!" said Peggy as they exited the Council Office and realising she had to go first, Sandra told her about the interview this afternoon and her doubts that she was going to succeed "Is that all, we've known since last week when Sam Brown from the mailroom told us, nothing gets past him! You'll be fine. They'd be mad to choose anyone else. Come on, they're miles in front of us" Peggy finished. Grabbing her hand Sandra said" Just a minute tell me yours before we get to the cafe, unless you want them to know as well?" Looking

Sandra straight in the eye Peggy thought about it and then said" Well Andy has asked me out on Saturday night and he has kind of hinted that if I want to I can stay the night at his. It's too soon Sandra, I like him but if I say no he might dump me, and I do quite like him he's not immature like some of the men, or should I say boys I have been out with, damned if I do and damned if I don't. What do you think?" As they neared the Brazilian Cafe where Sharon and Jo had just gone through the door Sandra said "Peggy, everyone's different, I would tell him it's too soon, and if he cared for you he would wait, and see how he reacts to that. If he does care, even though it's been such a short time, he will wait if he won't then it's his loss and he wasn't the one for you"

Giving her a hug before they got to the door of the cafe which was just opening as a couple left Peggy said "You know there's only one Dave out there Sandra" and headed through the still open door to joining Sharon and Jo who had already ordered."What have you two been dragging your feet about" said Sharon as they took their coffees and sat down. "Nothing concerning you Sharon "Peggy quickly replied and spotting a chance to move the conversation away from herself added "So are you going to Catterick Army camp Sharon?" and the delay told them all that she hadn't made her mind up yet, but putting down her coffee she surprised them by saying "He's coming down on Saturday and going back Sunday so he must be keen!", with a smugness of someone who has been bursting to tell everyone all morning. "So there you lot" Sharon finished leaning back in the booth smiling like a child who has found a present the day after Christmas. As the conversation fell into office gossip and what the rest of them were doing for the weekend Jo quietly said "Steve has been phoning me asking for a second chance, what should I do?" Quickly beating everyone to the answer Sharon said "Tell him he had his chance and blew it, and tell him where to stick his phone!" as they all laughed at Sharon's somewhat crude advice and the rest of the lunch hour swiftly came to an end. As they returned to the Council Offices, Sandra realise she hadn't had time to think about her interview in 30 minutes.

Taking her seat and starting to see what the Mailroom had brought while they were at lunch she was separating the various files into order when Mrs Anderson came over to her desk and quietly said "Pop into my office when you have a minute Sandra" and with a look at Peggy who gave her a thumbs up, she finished her task and set off for the office."Just a quick pointer before your interview Sandra, try and stay calm, if you don't know the answer just say you haven't covered that in your work here at the Council. There's Amanda Wilson from HR and Eric Normanton doing the interview and he's a big softy so you should be fine. Good luck and off you go" she finished holding the door open and forgetting to thank her Sandra headed for the stairs and the interview room like a prisoner hoping for parole, she would either get what she wanted, or stay where she was!

Coming down the stairs after the interview, Sandra was about to reach the bottom step when out of the corner of her eye she saw Daniel coming down the corridor, and quickly turning left she headed for the Toilets. Closing the door she looked at herself in the mirror and upon closer inspection wished she had added a little lipstick, but it was too late now and besides lipstick wouldn't get her the job she thought. Deciding to give herself a few more minutes, she took a cubical and closing the door behind her she put the lid of the toilet down, and sat to contemplate the interview. Eric Normanton as Dave and Mrs Anderson both said was a softy. He had asked her 'Where do you see yourself in 5 years?' and 'What attracted you to the role' just as Dave had said he had asked him 2 years before, which she thought she had answered quite well, but when Amanda Wilson had asked her "What assets make you stand out as a better candidate than others?" she was a bit stuck, but answered that she had got good qualifications at school, had this role come about when she left school in the summer she would have applied then, as she had always been interested in buildings both old and new. Amanda seemed happy with the reply and made a note on her pad and then asked almost as an afterthought "So why didn't you go to University, Sandra?" which came at her out of the blue, and as she sat thinking how to answer the question she couldn't really answer, she eventually said "To be honest I've never really thought about University, I wanted to be more of a learn on the job type of person than all theoretical, and this role seems like a good fit where it is a mix of practical and theory" as her face slowly lost its redness she saw the two interviewers look at each other without giving anything away, and then back to Sandra, "Thank you for your time Sandra, we will be reviewing the candidates and will be in touch to let you know the outcome". She remembered to say "Thank You" before she left and headed for the stairs where she has successfully avoided Daniel, or so she thought when she finally left the toilet.

Standing outside toilets him with his leg bent resting on the wall having obviously waited for her he said "How was the interview Sandra?" which came out of his mouth before she had time to really take in his presence. "Did you kick old Eric in the balls like you did me?" he said with a level of hate in his voice, at which she backed away taking a couple of steps back towards the stairs. "I won't forget what you did you Bitch, I'll get you back for that!" and stepping further backwards, she reached the bottom of the stairs, that she would have run away upstairs like a child a few months ago, but Dave had given her a level of confidence she didn't have when she went out with Daniel. "You got what you deserved Daniel, why I ever went out with you in summer I'll never know, but if you mention that night to anyone, ever, I will say you tried to rape me!" Turning away from Daniel she didn't see the hate in his face, but could feel it is his voice as he loudly said "I'll get you one day just like…" but he didn't finish the sentence, as Amanda Wilson came down the stairs disturbing them, and Sandra quickly headed off towards her office leaving a very annoyed Daniel with a face that could kill.

Flushed with anger Sandra sat down at her desk and immediately, without looking at anyone, started on the files she had arranged before the interview. After some 10 files she looked up to see Peggy looking at her like she had heard there was a death in the family 'You alright' she mouthed and as Sandra responded with 'Fine' which Peggy passed onto Sharon and Jo by a thumbs down signal the office settled into the Friday afternoon routine as the piles of files and papers diminished certain to be replenished by Monday. Sharon was first to stand up, as always and pointing to the Toilets she headed off out of the office closely followed by Jo. Peggy, caring as always, came up to Sandra and putting a hand on her shoulder said" Didn't go well then I take it!" Looking Peggy in the eye it took a second before the meaning hit home her mind still stuck on the confrontation with Daniel "No it was fine, just.... well never mind, time will tell" she finished, realising how true she comment was on both counts.

Peggy and Sandra left the Council Offices arm in arm, discussing what Peggy ought to do about Andy and the decision she faced "It's not going to happen!" said Peggy as they headed for the George for a quick drink before home she continued before Sandra could react "He's a couple of years older than me but I'm 22 and can make my own mind up. So if Mr Andy wants this" and waving her hand down from her face to her waist like a backhand sweep added "he'll have to wait and earn it!" at which they both burst out laughing, as they reached the door of the George which opened towards them just as Peggy went to pull the handle and two slightly inebriated men pushed past them as they left the pub, and as they looked at each other both said "Men!" at precisely the same time and the laughter started again as they approached the bar. "Two halves of Lager and Lime please" said Sandra to the barman who finally served them on what was going to be a busy Friday night. Taking her change Sandra passed one of the drinks to Peggy who was chatting to Jo and Sharon. "Thanks Sandra" said Peggy adding "Would you believe it Jo has decided to meet Steve to tell him to his face that it is over" and with a knowing wink that said 'I don't think it's over' Sharon changed the subject completely " Enough of men ladies, this is our hour, lets ignore men, well for the time being at least! How about a night at the pictures just us girls" and with a nodded agreement the discussion turned to what they should see with 'Arthur' or 'Raiders of the Lost Ark' getting the vote depending on which was still showing next weekend."Arthur for me!" said Peggy at which a quick witted Sharon shot back "Don't you mean Andy, not Arthur!" Seeing the humour in her face Peggy gave her a look that said 'I'll let you get away with that one' before her quick mind retorted "You always come back to men, don't you Sharon!" at which Sharon held her open hand up and they hi-fived each other, and laughing at how smart they both were, they finished their drinks as Peggy headed to the bar for a quick one before home not bothering to look at Sharon, who now had her arm around Jo slowly making their way to the bar, and giving her the benefit of her experience with men in relation to her impending meeting with Steve. All of 5 months was the age difference between them at 21, but in terms of experience of life 5 years. As they were halfway down their second drinks and contemplating making the next bus Mrs Anderson and her boyfriend James entered the pub, and as James headed for the bar Mrs Anderson spotted Sandra, and putting her hand on her shoulder managed to convey over the music, which was now pounding out of the speakers on a Friday night, that she would like a word outside. Leaving Peggy holding her drink she followed Mrs Anderson outside where the music was muffled, but increased as people entered and left the pub. "Sandra, I would have waited until Monday to give you the news, but seeing you just now I thought you would want to know now, rather than wait all weekend!" Sandra was unable to read from the look on her face whether it was good or bad news and Mrs Anderson must have realised from her silence that Sandra thought it was bad news."Oh by the look on your face I didn't put that very well. Eric Normanton rang me just as I was leaving, to ask for a reference for you and after a chat with him he is going to officially offer you the role on Monday, when we are back at work. He did say Amanda was a bit tough on you but that's her job. Well done Sandra I'll be sorry to lose you, but I do think it's the right move for you, now let me get you a drink to celebrate!" Suddenly the emotions of the afternoon hit her and Sandra started to cry at which Mrs Anderson pulled her close, and with a few experienced words calmed her down and once she had wiped her eyes and smiled at Mrs Anderson that she was okay, they headed for the door of the George to give out the good news.

As Sandra followed Mrs Anderson into the pub, a slightly pensive Peggy was keeping an eye on the door for when they would return and seeing Mrs Anderson smile but Sandra with red eyes she couldn't figure out if it was good or bad news, and thankfully Mrs Anderson put them all at ease. "Ladies" she said "Say goodbye to your old work colleague, and hello to Junior Planning Assistant Sandra Robertson" The group hug was almost immediate, the shrieks almost drowned the music as the 'ladies' celebrated Sandra's news. Going home was now forgotten and as Mrs Anderson returned from the bar, shortly followed by James with a full round of drinks between them and with a toast to Sandra, the evening was going to be one to remember.

"I thought when you came back with red eyes that it was bad news" said Peggy as Sandra took a drink "I thought it was but got the wrong end of the stick, so before she could tell me I was already convinced it was bad news and ....well you know me and my emotions" and smiling at Peggy with a look that said 'all is well with the world' they linked arms and joined in with Jo and Sharon quizzing James how he had met Mrs

Anderson which he was trying to avoid answering, but under Sharon's interrogation he had no chance, and was only saved when Mrs Anderson returned from the Toilet and said they had table booked at the Pizza and Wine restaurant, and taking his chance to escape James finished his drink and after saying it was "Nice to meet you al'" he was led by the hand out into the dark night, with a feeling that he would never be allowed in the George again.

By the time 7.00pm came and the first of the night drinkers started arriving as the teatime drinkers left, Sandra was feeling a bit guilty as she was enjoying herself so much. The banter between them had been building as the alcohol released inhibitions, and the half truth's became truth or were corrected whether be it for better, or worse. As they were listening to Sharon describe how she had dumped one of her boyfriends by setting him up with Sandy from Accounts through a friend so he thought he was dumping her. "She makes him sandwiches for lunch, which they sit and eat in the park!" adding "And they still haven't done it!" and with a gently rocking motion Sharon went into full laughter mode that continued until she realised she had finished her drink, and prodding Jo on the arm to get another drink handed her the empty glass. Jo went to the bar dutiful as ever, to replenish their drinks hoping this wasn't going to be a long night, as she had to decide about Steve tomorrow and she was already weakening. The barman was rushed off his feet by now and as she waited for her turn, she felt a hand on her waist and instinctively knew it was Steve as he finally said "And two pints of Lager, Jo" turning to face him she was lost for words and turned back to the barman who she heard say "Next" and not missing her turn quickly said "Half of Cider and a half of Lager and Black please oh, and a pint of Lager as well" seeing the barman start to pull the drinks Steve put his hand on Jo's shoulder and leaning in so she could hear "Two pints Jo I said, one for me and one for Daniel". As the barman returned with the drinks Sharon spotted that

Jo had company of the unwelcome kind, and was on her way to save her friend when she stopped, as Jo paid for the drinks and she heard her forcefully say a comment that Sharon would have been proud of uttering "I can't change the past, but I can change the future and you are not in mine. Have this one on me!" and picking up the Pint of Lager poured it all over Steve's head and picking up their drinks went to join Sharon who was now beaming from the sudden change in Jo's attitude. "Good for you Jo, didn't think I had it in you" she finished, and gave her a hug, careful not to spill their own drinks, all the time looking at Steve, who had now been joined by Daniel who had caught the remains of the drink on his shirt as he stood behind Steve. Just as Steve and Daniel were deciding what to do next, a hand settled on Steve's shoulder and looking up and accepting his fate as the words came from above "I think gentlemen you should come back another night" and leaving his hand on Steve's shoulder, Sid escorted them out of the door without a word from either of them. Dave who was just coming out of the Toilet watched the event start and play out, and realising it was Jo in the middle of it had asked Sid if he would go and sort it out as he couldn't get involved because of work, at which a smiling Sid said he was happy to assist a young damsel, and headed off to do his bit.

After all the action had settled down Sharon and Jo both thanked Sid for his intervention, and realising he was with Dave who quickly introduced Sid, they quickly struck up a conversation when it suddenly hit Jo that where they were stood, Dave couldn't see Sandra and Peggy sat down in the corner so taking her new found confidence another step she said "Excuse me a moment, I'll be right back" hoping Sharon wouldn't set her sights on Sid. Stepping to the side and moving past the wall that hid a quiet corner where Sandra and Peggy were sat chatting, Jo sat opposite them and explained what had happened, up to the point where a tall dark stranger came to her rescue. "You'll never believe it when you see who it is!" she said and taking Sandra's hand pulled her up and was leading her towards the wall when she stopped and quietly said "Christmas Eve never happened!" and before she could work out where this comment had come from she was stood opposite Dave and Sid, who was by now under the attention of Sharon. Lost for words after Jo's comment, seeing Dave when she wasn't expecting to, and after the interview and seeing Daniel was all a bit too much for Sandra as she flung her arms around Dave and buried her face in his neck. "Well I'm pleased to see you to!" said Dave as he kissed Sandra on the ear and finally prising Sandra away from her embrace, they stayed in a hug until he kissed her at which Sharon's "Get a room" comment hit home, and they parted but still held hands. Peggy joined them having followed Sandra and Jo, as they left the table and seeing Dave said" Aren't you going to introduce me to your friend Dave?" at which Dave decided to formally introduce Sid "Ladies I give 'Prince Charming'" at which a now recovered Sandra started laughing at the memory of their conversation about their records and catching the thread Dave got the joke, and as they stood holding hands laughing it was a joint, second perfect comment of "Well he's my, Prince Charming" from Jo and Sharon that set them all off laughing together.

"Hello Boyfriend" "Hello Girlfriend" followed by a kiss was finally their introduction to each other as Sid was at the bar." Didn't expect to see you tonight" Dave added still holding her hand and grasping the pint that Sid held up for him to take." But glad I did" he finished before taking a drink and as Sandra was about to tell him about her day Sharon interrupted "Got to go home, busy day tomorrow if you know what I mean" and Peggy also offered her goodbyes as she had "Things to do tomorrow" and after hugs all round and a rueful look from Sharon at Sid, who was now listening intently to Jo they left to get a Taxi together. With Jo and Sid chatting, Sandra and Dave were finally left alone to talk about their week since they met on Monday, but before Sandra could say a word Sid turned to Sandra and gave her a hug and letting a somewhat surprised Sandra go he said "Got a clever one here Dave, passing her interview" and with a look of slow comprehension Dave pulled her close to him and whispered "I knew you could do it" which Sandra nearly missed , she had so wanted to tell Dave tomorrow when they were supposed to meet, and she was trying to be angry with Jo for telling Sid, and Sid for telling Dave. But if Jo told Dave nothing about Christmas Eve then it was a small price to pay. With the news out it wasn't the time or the place to discuss the afternoon so Sandra said she would tell Dave all about it tomorrow and they fell into that easy routine that good friends can of laughing at bad jokes, filling in gaps in stories and mixing truths with lies but as the evening progressed it seemed that 'Prince Charming' and Jo would be a good match, that is if Marion or Jane would let him go. The couples parted as food began to be the main source of discussion, but Dave and Sandra just wanted some time on their own so leaving Sid and Jo at the Kebab Shop, they got a Taxi to Sandra's house from where Dave could walk home and as Sandra opened the door, a slightly worried Diane was making a cup of tea in the kitchen and as the door shut behind them the comment "You're late Sandra, but at least you have a Prince Charming to bring you home" came out of her mouth at which Dave and Sandra burst into laughter yet again, and with tears rolling down their faces at the ongoing joke Diane, picked up her cup and headed upstairs confused as to why her comment was funny.

After making two mugs of tea for them and going into the Lounge, Sandra sat next to Dave on the sofa and kissing him with a passion that she had refrained from all evening apart from in the Taxi, they settled down with Dave's arm around her shoulders with his hand resting on her breast which she let stay there."It's been a long day Dave, do you mind if we just cuddle" and kissing her on the head "Sure" he replied leaving his hand where it was, and closing his eyes thought to himself 'Prince Charming" and smiled as Sandra fell asleep in his arms for the first time.

◆ ◆ ◆

Chapter 13

A breezy Saturday morning in January greeted Sandra, as she came into the kitchen just after 09.00 just as her mother came back indoors, having put the washing out and the door slammed to from the wind. "Lovely drying weather" she said as Sandra flicked the kettle on "Do you want one mum" Sandra responded putting two slices of bread into the toaster. "Yes please and you'd better make your Dad one as well, as he'll be down in a minute. I take it you'll be out today" she finished putting away the wash basket. "Yes mum, Dave and I are going for a long walk to catch up, yesterday was a bit hectic to say the least!" "Oh so that's why you both fell asleep on the sofa last night" Diane quickly said with a hint of sarcasm. Ignoring her mother as she buttered her toast she waited for the apology that she knew would come, and as she handed her two mugs of tea, Diane quietly said "Just teasing, you looked so cosy I didn't want to disturb you both, but I have your reputation to consider!" at which Sandra pretended to throw her toast at her as she left the kitchen with a huge smile on her face. Sandra finished her toast and taking her tea up to her bedroom to get ready to meet Dave she saw Tony came out of his room, looking like he had only been in bed for a few hours. "A long night was it?" Sandra said in a slightly motherly voice at which Tony grunted and headed for the bathroom, but turning at the door he said "At least I made it to bed, saw you two fast asleep on the sofa , love's young dream" at which he shut the door behind him, giving Sandra no chance to defend herself. So that's what woke us up, Tony coming home Sandra thought and a feeling of contentment was just emerging, when she realised Dave had his hand on her breast the last she could remember and embarrassment replace the contented feeling, but it didn't matter she thought it wasn't like they were doing anything, except sleeping, not like the other night she remembered, and now it was a good job no one could see her red cheeks as she put on her jacket and hat and headed out of the door to meet Dave, the reason for her blushing.

As Sandra came around the corner at the end of her street and saw Dave waiting at the bus stop with his flat cap making him standout, she got the feeling that today would be a day to remember and as she playfully tried to grab his cap, he moved away at which she immediately said a little too loudly "You didn't move away last night when we were asleep!" and realising what she had said she turned away, so he wouldn't see her blushing but it was too late, as he took her hand and pulled her close he quietly said "Our first night asleep together!" and kissed her slowly and passionately, until they both heard the bus coming up the street, and they broke apart with a mirror image grin on their faces as the bus stopped, and they boarded hand in hand.

Getting off the bus they headed for the McDonalds opposite the bus stop and after ordering two coffees, sat in a booth and started to catch up on yesterday and plan the rest of the day together. "I'm so proud of you Sandra for getting the position, I know we didn't really talk about it much last night, so do you want to tell me about it, was it tough?" Sandra put her coffee down and thought for a moment before telling Dave about how the interview was all going well, and Eric Normanton had asked her a couple of questions that Dave had said he would, but then Amanda Wilson had asked her why she hadn't gone to University and that had thrown her a bit, but she had said that when she left school this opportunity wasn't available but when it came up she had immediately applied as she had an interest in buildings past and present. "I wasn't sure I had answered her question but thankfully it must have been what they were looking for because Mrs Anderson told me in the George that I had been successful. She even gave me a good reference to Eric Normanton so the offer should be in the internal mail on Monday. I'm so happy I could kiss you! But I won't ....because you've got a froth moustache!" and laughing as he wiped his mouth with a serviette she let him finish before reaching across and giving him a quick kiss, and sitting back left her hand on the table where he took hold of her fingers and interlocking them said "So he didn't ask Question Four?" and with a beaming smile he stood up as she slowly worked out what he had said, and realising what he meant, she said with a modicum of indignation "He most certainly did not!" and smiling to let him know she was okay with his humour, she hooked her arm in his as they headed onto the street and looking at her slowly he pulled her within kissing range, as they touched lips he squeezed her round the waist as they became one body, and feeling her warmth he held her for a while before releasing her slowly saying "You choose what we do today in celebration of your new job" and realising he was being led by the hand towards 'House of Fraser' he realised he was now secondary to a department store. "I bet you've never been in here have you?" Sandra said as they went through the doors, and the hot air blasted down to welcome them to the store that seemed to go on forever, and had prices to match Dave thought. As he was led, like he was in a maze, around the store he was intrigued as Sandra stopped in the Lingerie section. Seeing the quizzical look on his face she smugly looked at several bra's that she picked up and played with, pressing the cup area and pulling the straps to test the elasticity, all the time looking at Dave for a comment which she knew wouldn't be forthcoming, as he stood playing with his flat cap, looking like he had done something wrong but not quite sure what!

"Hold this please" Sandra said handing him her handbag as she took two bras into the changing rooms without looking back. After a few minutes she returned with a red laced bra and holding it up for Dave to see she said "This will look nice on me don't you think?" and aware that he was being teased he quickly replied" It would look better not on you!" and realising she had taken her little game far enough quietly said "Well we'll have to see about that, won't we!" and turning to go to the checkout till, she hooked her little finger for him to follow and like a lamb to the slaughter, he did.

After a couple of hours wandering around town and saying hello to a few people they knew from work it was as they were passing the Old Cock that they saw Tony and Marion, hand in hand, walk into the pub oblivious to them, and anyone else thought Sandra. "Well, who would have thought?" Dave said without looking at Sandra beating her by a millisecond. Suddenly stopped in their tracks they looked at each other with a decision to make and after a pause Sandra said "Let's get out of this Town" as they passed the door to the Old Cock they could see a couple kissing and looking at each other it dawned on them both, that this was their doing. "What will Sid say when he finds out?" Sandra said as they went past the doorway "I wouldn't worry about Sid if I were you, he's a big boy, in more ways than one" Dave replied and correcting himself unnecessarily "Height I meant, anyway I think Jo might be more than a replacement for Marion, or an addition knowing Sid" and amused at his quick wit, he didn't expect Sandra's response "Dave, It's not fair Sid having three girlfriends on the go at the same time, what if one of them really falls for him. He'll break her heart!" The silence that followed from Sandra gave Dave time to think but didn't give him a solution. They had been through this question at the 'Malt Shovel' and it had been something of a no win situation as far as he remembered, but his thoughts were interrupted by Sandra crushing his hand and asking him at the same time "You wouldn't cheat on me would you Dave?" a question that had a bitter feeling behind it, but that was quickly set to the back of her mind as Dave answered "Never going to happen Sandra it's you and me, full stop" The arms around his neck told him he had hit a nerve, as Sandra kissed his neck she regained her composure and slowly let Dave breathe, as she looked directly at him and said "You are such a romantic Dave Baxter" and taking his hand they headed away from Town, and all its distractions and memories.

"Sandra where shall we go …. sorry, it's your day, you choose" said Dave almost forgetting "Well actually I thought it would be worth trying the Tavern at Ogden if you like. It should only take half an hour to walk from here, or we could get a bus" Sandra quickly responded and added as an afterthought "When you pass your test we can go anywhere!" "Just got to pass it first, though I think the lessons are going well." replied Dave adding "Maybe you should think about learning to drive Sandra, you will need it for your new job at some stage in the future" "I hadn't thought about that" Sandra said before pondering and added " I suppose I will have to visit buildings and sites across the area, doing that on a bus wouldn't work, besides everyone seems to be learning to drive nowadays, okay you're on I'm up for it. I'd really like a Mini!" and looking at Dave she realised she had said the last sentence out loud "A Mini indeed, thinking of going rallying are you?" he exclaimed as they automatically set of walking. "It just came out Dave I'm really not bothered what I get……as long as it's a Mini!" and putting his arm around her he softly said "It's okay to dream Sandra!" at which she gave him a kiss on the cheek, and they slipped into a silence of hopes and dreams.

The Tavern proved to be an inspired choice for a Saturday afternoon with a Carvery, and a normal menu which would explain why the car park looked full and they had to wait for a table at the bar. Ordering their drinks while Sandra looked at the Menu, Dave was relieved that he didn't recognise anyone as he wanted the day alone with Sandra. As their drinks arrived at the bar a table came free and the waiter led them to the back of the restaurant, handing them the menu's he said he would be back in a minute to take their order, and was gone. "Well it's busy, which is a good sign have you decided what you are having yet girlfriend?" said Dave looking at the menu having changed his mind several times already "Yes I'm having Chilli Con Carne!" and putting her menu down as the waiter returned and looked at Dave who was stuck between decisions again. "Chilli Con Carne for the lady and I'll have the Fish and Chips please with Mushy Peas" as the Waiter finished writing their order down and headed off to the kitchen Sandra couldn't resist "Lady, why thank you Sir!" and realising what he had said, he decided to take advantage of the situation "Only a Lady would be good enough for Prince Charming!" at which Sandra gave him a look which a Lady wouldn't use and raising her eyebrows skyward quickly said "My dear Prince I think if you're not careful you will wear out that particular title at least for the time being !" and picking her glass up raised it in a toast, and quietly said, so no one else could hear "But you'll always be my Prince Charming!"

"So what's next in your plan for today?" said Dave having nearly finished his meal. "Well I think we should walk this food off on the way home. We could go by the moorland path and stop at the Bedlow Arms to break up the journey and then we'll see" Sandra replied "Sounds good to me especially the, we'll see bit!" he immediately replied "Trust you to pick up on that!" Sandra responded with a smile as she laid her fork down adding "That was lovely just spicy enough but I'm stuffed now, how was your fish?" "Like Moby Dick very nice but I think it's got me beaten" said Dave putting down his knife and fork and leaning back "Going to have to walk slowly girl-friend" and looking around for the waiter to ask for the bill, he saw Sharon and presumably Mick at the bar who must have just come in as they were looking at menus, and with a bit of a sense of relief they were ushered to a table at the other end of the restaurant. When the waiter brought their bill Dave offered to pay for it but Sandra insisted that they split it as they were both working it was only fair. "Ready girlfriend" said Dave standing up and putting his coat on, "Just nipping to the Ladies, as I am one!" she said picking up her coat and hat. Dave made his way to the exit to await her return hoping she didn't see Sharon and Mick, but he knew by the wait that she obviously had, so he returned to the restaurant just as Sandra was giving Sharon a hug and heard her saying 'See you on Monday, nice to meet you Mick" and turning to see Dave coming over she introduced Dave to Mick and added "Enjoy your meals my Chilli was really good but Dave struggled with his Fish and Chips, like a Moby Dick he said, anyway have to go see you!" and she took Dave by the hand as they headed for the exit "He seems nice Mick I mean, don't you think Dave?" "Bit hard to tell from 30 seconds but you can tell he's in the Army with that haircut!" Not sure how to take that comment Sandra let it go for a minute, as they crossed the road to the moorland path."Well at least he doesn't hide it under a flat cap!" she said teasingly as she snatched it from his head and the wind caught his hair which was now released and blew across his face. "Give it back it was a present from an admirer at Christmas" he cheekily said at which she stopped and slowly came closer to give it back, but as she stood in front of him and quietly said "So I'm just an admirer not a Lady anymore, I'm hurt Mr Baxter!" and turning round with her back now to him she kept the cap in her hand and crossed her arms in front of her. "You're a Lady, always have been, always will be!" Dave said as he put his arms around her and as he held her hands he gently kissed the back of her neck, and she slowly turned round to kiss him properly for the first time today.

The walk to the Bedlow Arms was surprisingly quiet as they both seemed to be holding back a question or two, and as they reached the door Sandra said she had to go to the Toilet leaving Dave at the bar awaiting the barman to finish serving the customer next to him. "Pint of Lager and a half of Lager and Lime please" he said just as Sandra returned and looking around as their drinks were being poured he pointed to the back of the pub which had some free tables and as Sandra nodded and went to take a seat he paid the barman and wondered what if anything was going on. Setting the drinks down on the table Dave looked at Sandra and with no reaction said "Okay Sandra?" "Yes fine just a bit full" and taking a drink they sat for what seemed like ages, and almost at the same time with their comments overlapping each other said jointly "My parents are out tonight!" at which the absurdity of the comment broke the tension and Sandra put a finger to his lips and said "Me first Dave" and taking hold of his hands in hers she began "I think I'm ready to sleep with you , but when we do I want it to be special, it would have to be romantic, you do know how to do romantic don't you!" she finished by placing a pack of condoms from the machine in the Toilets in his hands as if to seal the deal.

"Well that must have taken some thought" he replied trying to get his own thoughts in order. "I won't deny I would like to go further than we have so far, but I'm here for the long run and I'll wait until you are ready. I didn't really put sex into my plans, well I take that back, I did, but not in black and white that is, and I was rather hoping it would just fall into place and when and if ..." A kiss stopped him saying anymore and as Sandra's tongue made connection, caressing his tongue they stayed locked together for a few minutes, and parting slowly with a final kiss on the lips, they had crossed the question that they had both been holding back on asking.

The evening darkened outside but with the conversation back in full flow it was a surprised Dave who returned from the toilet to find Peggy and Andy sitting next to Sandra. "Dave look who I bumped into, Peggy and this is Andy, they're just out for a walk like us, it's small world isn't it!" "Yes isn't it just" said Dave shaking Andy by the hand "Nice to meet you, been here before?" "No usually drink in Town, but when you're out with the girlfriend it's better to go somewhere nice where you can have a chat if you know what I mean?" "Yeah like it here, never any trouble and the beer's not bad either" he added a bit lost for something to say before Peggy sensing the awkwardness said "Are you two celebrating the great news about Sandra's interview? We'll miss you when you leave you know" "Oh Peggy I'm only going to Planning we'll see each other all the time" and giving her a hug the conversation picked up as Dave chatted to Andy about cars and his upcoming test as Sandra quizzed Peggy about Andy. As they came to finish their drinks Dave looked at Sandra and tilting his head in the direction of the door got a positive nod from Sandra, at which she finished her drink and looking at Peggy said " Well we should be off you don't want to spend all night with, what was it now you called us Peggy .. Lovebirds! Cheek of it!" smiling at Peggy's reaction of horror that she had been caught out, they bade their goodbyes and wrapped up for the walk home. "Can't seem to go anywhere without bumping into people we know" Sandra said as they made their way on the moorland path towards the Estate, "Shall we go to yours Sandra, it's nearer so it makes sense, that's if it's okay with you" "Fine by me" she said quickly knowing it wasn't nearer, but she would be happier in her own house.

As they reached Sandra's house and she opened the door Dave said he had to go to the Toilet and headed off up the stairs, which made Sandra's mind up for her. Leaving her coat and hat in the hall, she followed Dave up the stairs and on entering her bedroom opposite the Toilet, she took off her blouse and removed the bra she had been wearing and replaced it with the red laced bra she had bought this morning. With a quick look in the mirror she stood in the open doorway, barefooted and leaning against the door frame as Dave came out of the Toilet to immediately face her "I thought you might like to see it on" she said with a coy grin erupting on her face and the words "Very pretty" left Dave's mouth as he closed the gap between them, and he put his arms around her back to pull her close "You should go shopping more often" he added before kissing her neck and ear as they slowly retreated into her bedroom. As

Sandra spun him around she kicked the door close with an outstretched foot and led him slowly to her bed. "I thought you'd like it" said Sandra as she lay down on her bed still holding his hand, and he gently lay next to her putting his left arm around her shoulder as they slowly relaxed. With his tongue playing tag with hers, he moved his right hand over her breasts and feeling the lace on her new purchase he intensified his kissing until he could feel her nipples pushing through the material and feeling for the hooks with his left hand behind her back he pushed the hooks together, and they swiftly released the bra from its job after only two minutes as he could feel with his right hand that the tension was gone and he moved the bra off her breasts and took a bare nipple in his fingers and gently squeezed at which a slight movement from Sandra and a nibble of his tongue set his mind at ease that all was good. With the bra now superfluous to the activity on the bed, it wasn't long before it had left its owner and found its way onto the floor. Slowly Dave released himself from the intense kissing, and with his right hand having enticed her nipples to stand erect he kissed his way down Sandra's body to her breasts, kissing each nipple gently he heard her give a little moan as his tongue ran in circles around her breasts, with her hand on his head running her fingers through his hair she wasn't surprised when his right hand landed on her leg below her skirt and he moved his hand up and down her leg, each time going a little higher as she parted her legs a little and felt his hand on the front of her knickers. Feeling his hand slowly rub her between her legs, she gasped as he nibbled at one of her nipples, but not enough to stop him as his hand entered the top of her knickers and she could feel his fingers probing lower and lower slowly stroking her pubic hair until suddenly she could feel a finger on her clitoris, and she moaned inwardly as his finger ran backwards and forwards and eventually entered her now stimulated vagina which made her tense her bottom, but Dave didn't seem to notice and leaving her breasts naked and abandoned, he kissed his way backup her body until they were kissing like their life depended on it, all the time with his finger moving in and out of her. With her skirt around her waist and her breasts pointing to the ceiling Sandra parted her legs a little further and felt another finger enter her as Dave's palm of his hand stayed in place on her pubic hair and his fingers were now entering her more swiftly all the time, at which she was now moaning in time with their strokes. As she stiffened and raised her back from the bed and tightened her vagina at the same time squashing Dave's fingers she let out a groan and relaxed as he slowly removed his fingers and moving his hand slowly up her body he caressed her breasts as they stopped kissing and came face to face. Lying on her bed, his hand still on her breast Sandra broke the silence "So you do like it .... the bra obviously!" she said realising she had thought one thing and said another, correcting herself somewhere in the middle. "Oh very much..... an excellent choice" he finished not quite knowing what to say next, but Sandra was way ahead of him "Well if this is how you treat all your presents it a poor do! " she quickly said adding "Dropping it on the floor when you know where it should be , shame on you!" but not to be outdone he quickly responded."Sandra you can buy as many bras as you like, and I'll love them all, but like all presents it what's inside that matters to me!" and with a huge grin and a tweak of her nipple that was under constant attack by his right hand he moved in to kiss her again, as she smiled at his comment and his hand moved lower again.

The headlights shone through the curtains of Sandra's bedroom window as her parents returned home giving Sandra time to redress herself, while Dave looked sadly on. They just made it to the hall where Dave had an arm in his coat as Diane and Jim opened the door. "Hello you two, had a good day?" "Yes it's been very interesting Diane" at which the look from Sandra told him not to push his sense of humour but it was too late. "Been to places I've never been before!" "Oh that's nice isn't it Jim" as she headed for the kitchen to make tea for them both not really listening, smug at his quick wit, the flick on his ear told him otherwise "Don't forget your flat cap" Sandra said putting it on for him and flicking his other ear. "See you tomorrow boyfriend" she said giving him a little kiss on the lips and hoping her mother couldn't see the colour of her face as she opened the door for him. "Can't wait to find out what presents you might have to show me" he said out of earshot of Sandra's mother and knowing he had pushed his luck he nearly missed Sandra's hand as it swiftly knocked off his flat cap and it landed on the ground between them "Hey, that was a present!" he said, knowing he had definitely gone too far, putting distance between them he turned round at the end of the garden path and blew her a kiss which she symbolically caught and held to her heart, her smile telling him all he needed to know.

◆ ◆ ◆

Chapter 14

Sunday lunch was organised at the Baxter and Robertson family abodes, so it wasn't until nearly 3pm when Sandra met Dave and with time overnight to consider what had taken place it was a couple of minutes before a slightly reticent Dave finally said "I really enjoyed yesterday" and without giving him a chance to finish "Oh you did, did you!" Sandra interrupted him. Dave looked lost as to what to say when he saw Sandra burst out laughing "Seriously you should see the look on your face!" as she laughed even harder "Come here you" she managed to say through the laughter pulling him close "I enjoyed yesterday too, I won't break you know! Women have desires too!" and taking hold of his hand they set off to nowhere in particular, on what was now a sharp but fine January afternoon.

"Have you seen Tony to ask him about Marion yet?" said Dave suddenly remembering part of yesterday that seemed a lifetime away. "He made it down for Sunday lunch but didn't say much about where he went although when I asked him if he was in Town, he said yes with a few mates, which we know was a lie. Never heard him come home" and continued "I slept like a baby last night..... even kept my clothes on!" and seeing the look of confusion in his face she finished "Just teasing" and kissed him lightly on the cheek before they wandered in no particular direction, with Sandra now hooked up to Dave's arm.

They were trying to keep warm as the temperature had dropped now the sun had gone, and as they seemed to be heading towards the general direction of the Malt Shovel "Be glad when this cold weather goes" said Dave as they made a beeline for the pub and its large log fire. "Wonder who we'll meet in here?" Dave said holding the door open for Sandra against the increasing wind. Heading to the bar with Sandra following he had already attracted the attention of Ian the regular barman, and ordering their drinks, he looked around and surprised to see no one they knew he intimated a table by the window and they went to sit down with their drinks. "Thanks" said Dave as he held up his Pint of Lager "No problem boyfriend" Sandra replied after taking a sip of her drink. "Think I'll just have Lager in future Dave, they seem to add too much Lime in most pubs, just so you know" she finished, and looked at his bemused face, which was begging to ask a question but he knew he was being led "Alright then I'll go for it, why the sudden change to just Lager?" barely had the words got out of his mouth when the reply came "I've decided to save up for a Mini!" and there it was, a harmless conversation from yesterday and her mind was made up! "You'll have to have lessons and take your test first" he automatically said without thinking "Before you even think about a car, sorry Mini" he added. Not to be put off Sandra took another drink, and with a premeditated smile announced "My parents have said they will buy me a car, sorry Mini, if I pass my test only this lunchtime!" and sitting back with a smugness that says beat that, she smiled at Dave and awaited his response. Aware that he had pushed things a little too far when he left her house last night, he took his time before putting together his answer. "As you know I've got my Driving Test coming up in February well it's on the 11th actually and if, sorry when I pass I was wondering if we could maybe spend Valentine's Day together, away from here to celebrate" and very quietly finished "and stay the night in a Hotel".

"Well that's a month away so you had better get some lessons in before then and pass, hadn't you Mr Confident!" Sandra said and taking a drink, left him hanging as she looked around the pub as if looking for someone before continuing as Dave looked to be holding his breath and unsure how his offer had been taken "I think I have just the present in mind that would go with the occasion!" and with a kiss on the lips, the deal was done with a smile that said more than could be read by anyone but Dave, and a look on Dave's face that said he had got the cream. Which was when Sid and Jane walked in and joining them after getting their drinks, Sid wasted no time in asking a leading question as he put his drink down and looked directly at Dave. "Well someone's has had a great weekend!" but before Dave could answer, Sid carried on "Me of course" putting his arm around Jane and kissing her he continued "Had an excellent couple of days haven't we Jane, she even cooked my dinner today and cracking it was" taking a drink he looked around to see if anyone else had had as good a weekend as him, saving Dave from a question that he didn't want to answer at any cost especially in company.

Trying to find out what happened between Jo and Sid on Friday night would have to wait thought Sandra, as there was no way with Jane here that she could find out without up-setting her, so putting it to the back of her mind and hop-ing for a chance when Jane went to the Toilet, she listened as Sid went over their 'great weekend' together. "Saturday night at the pictures, American Werewolf in London, it was great especially when he transforms into a wolf, really impressive wasn't it Jane?" "Well I seem to remember this morning in the shower someone turning into a monster!" she said looking at Sandra smiling, as she finished "Boys and their toys!" and tak-ing a drink she looked around the pub hoping Sid wouldn't go on about Jenny Agutter and the shower scene in the film, which they re-enacted this morning. "Dave, what have you two been up to this weekend then after Friday in the George" said Sid, without looking at Jane, who was still thinking about the shower this morning. "Went out for a meal at the Tavern on Saturday which was really good and then just a quiet night in" which was delivered with a look that said don't ask which Sid must have read, as he got up to go to the bar and said as he left "Pool" to Dave which Sandra caught, and signalled it was okay and they headed off to the bar together, 'Two boys off to play with their toys!' she thought.

With Jane and Sandra now left alone, it wasn't long before Sandra asked if anything further had happened with Nigel, after her and Sid's visit last week."Dead silence thank goodness" Jane said "and long may it remain, although I do feel sorry for that young girl, I kind of knew what I was getting myself into, she couldn't have known at her age. Part of me hopes her Dad, Pete never finds out, and another part of me wants him to find out" taking a drink indicating she was finished Sandra nodded that she agreed with her and grasping the moment "What made you agree to him taking pictures, if you don't mind me asking that is?" Putting down her drink Jane took Sandra's spare hand and holding it firmly in her hand looked her in the eye and quietly said "There are many types of men out there, Nigel was a player, good looking, money, car and he has a charm about him that makes you think you're a million dollars, as they say. He said he was doing a portfolio for me as I had never had one put together, well the first few were fine, head shots and a little shoulder but after a while it became tit shots, oh with your body, you should be in a magazine he used to say, and then it was full frontal, and well I've slept with him which was great, or so it seemed at the time, so it didn't seem too big a deal and it was of course between us. It was only when he brought a video into the bedroom that I said no and that was when he got quite heavy and threatening and I walked out. The rest you know!" and finishing her drink stood up to go to the bar and pointing at her drink offered to get Sandra a refill "Just a half of Lager please" she remembered just in time as Jane left to go to the bar, leaving Sandra alone with the story of Nigel going through her head.

Sid and Dave returned just as Jane was putting the drinks down and with a light slap of her bottom as she was bent over Sid said "I'll get my own shall I?" at which Jane said teasing him

"I'll have a half if you're going to the bar, that's the least you can do after I scrubbed your back this morning you Monster!" leaving the meaning open and leaving without a word he headed for the bar and Dave sat down having beaten Sid at pool, so he owed him a drink. "Enjoy yourselves Dave?" said Jane as she took a sip "Yep beat him on the black, what have you been chatting about?" "Boys and their toys" they said in Unison, and missing the joke as they both laughed at their own humour, Dave looked longingly for Sid to come back from the bar.

The evening settled into a round of stories intertwined with rounds of drinks, and as it was Sunday no one wanted to stay late, but they were still there at last orders, and unable to stop Sid and Dave automatically heading for another round 'for the road' the conversation between the girls had reached semi drunken gossip and Jane started the story of how her and Sid met up, when she was still seeing Nigel. "He asked me out when I was on a girls night out from work in Town, brazen he was, said I didn't look happy, but he knew a bloke that could make me happy. When I asked him who that may be, he just put his hands up and pointed to himself. The audacity of it was amazing but he has this smile that breaks through occasionally and it just melts you. You know he even said to me, and I still to this day have no idea how he knew. When you dump the loser you're with give me a call he said and he wrote his phone number on a beer mat and put it in my handbag. Then smug as anything he kissed me and said, see you soon. God I thought what an ass but with what happened with Nigel that weekend, I sat at home for a few days and as the weekend came I gave him a call and the following week we went out, and I've been seeing him quite a lot, well all of him obviously to be honest. Talk about chalk and cheese, Nigel and Sid are opposites in so many ways, but they're both boys in a man's body. Hark at me going on and on, what have you two been up to!"

Taking in most of what Jane had said, some of which she was

sure she wouldn't remember as the alcohol took charge, Sandra didn't initially know where to start, but sitting up a little she set off on a long diatribe of the weekend." Well on Friday I had an interview for a role in the Planning Department which was tough, but they have offered me the role, then we had a few drinks in Town and then yesterday we had the day to ourselves and went to the Tavern for lunch, which was really nice then a quiet night in, and today out walking on the moors, until we came here so nothing too exciting really" and finishing she took a drink at which Jane looked at her and said "Excellent news about your new job I hope it goes well for you. If you ever want to talk about men Sandra, just you and me, let me give you my number" picking up a beer mat Jane wrote her number down and just before the 'one for the road' round arrived she quietly finished "It is a big deal ,sex, but it doesn't need to be, but you and Dave, you should be just fine" and taking a glass from Sid glanced up at him before he sat down, with a look that Sandra was sure said to her untrained eye 'I've got your measure' and turning to Sandra raised her glass and said "To Boys and their toys" for the second time tonight, which Sandra automatically mirrored, as Sid and Dave looked on confused like their toys were being taken away.

Monday came and went like a well oiled machine. The workload awaiting Sandra at her desk diminished as the day went by only to be replenished as the day came to the end, from the other Council departments. Mrs Anderson dropped her Job Offer on her desk after lunch and said" You don't have to worry about references, I've already taken care of that, and as you will see the start date is 1st February 1982 which I am fine with, as I said I'll be sorry to lose you, but I wish you well, if you want some more time it would be the 1st March, either way I'll leave it up to you." She couldn't wait to move to the Planning Department and the variety of work that it would bring and the 1st February would be just fine. Picking up her pen to sign, a weird thought entered her mind as she signed and dated the document 25th January 1982, and on a piece of paper next to the form she signed Mrs Sandra Baxter, and pleased with herself she suddenly had a feeling the whole office was watching her, and quickly scrunched up the paper and thought about dropping it into the recycle bin, but slipped it into her pocket with a feeling of contentment.

Tuesday mirrored Monday, with the weather still refusing to appease, the Arctic winds keeping the temperature close to zero for a second week. As Sandra made her way to the bus stop and the journey home she was daydreaming as the bus arrived and as a voice said "Do you want this one Dear?" she snapped out of her thoughts, stepped forward and getting her pass out showed it to the driver and found a seat halfway down the bus and went back to her thoughts. I start a new job next week, Dave has his Driving Test and well there's Valentine's Day coming up, with an agenda that was getting ever nearer especially after Friday night at her house. Lost in her thoughts she just managed to see her stop coming up through the misted up windows and alighting into the cold she pulled her hat down over her ears and made the short walk home, by now hungry and wondering what was for tea before the inevitable night in front of the TV.

Wednesday arrived and the weather finally broke as the Sun made a brave attack on the Arctic currents and the temperature rose above 10 degrees for the first time this month, breaking the cold spell that had enveloped the country. The demeanour of the office matched the change in the weather, as there were a few more smiles and more colourful attire than on the first two days, and as she completed the files from Estates leaving just a few from Maintenance she saw Sam from the Mailroom enter the office with a full trolley containing tomorrow's workload. 'Thank god this is my last week' she thought. Suddenly realising she was being unfair to her friends that she had made while here, and the rest of the staff, she smiled as Sam put down two boxes of files on her desk "Why thank you Sam, that should keep me busy!" "Yes but only till the end of the week then you can start sending your own work down here from Planning, new girl starts on Monday!" and without waiting for a response, he went off to Peggy and then Sharon's desks as his trolley emptied and he was gone. Sorting out her new mountain of work ready for tomorrow, she realised she would be in the Planning Department next week and taking out her diary she checked she had put everything in for February and happy with the content and using it as an excuse that was at best weak, and in reality not an excuse at all, she headed for the door putting her coat on with her hat in her hand, she left the Council Office with a surprising spring in her step.

Deciding to have a quick look in the travel agents on her way to the bus stop, she flicked through a few brochures and took one which had Hotels that she liked the look of for Valentine's Day. Picking up a magazine at WH Smith's she realised her plan was still a little out of synch so she walked three stops on her bus route from Town and waited at the bus stop for the 6pm bus that she knew Dave usually caught. As the bus arrived she was behind an old lady with a shopping bag in each hand and following her onto the bus showing her pass to the driver she looked down the bus for a seat a little perplexed that she couldn't see Dave, then she spotted a flat cap moving behind the old lady, as she sat down a now standing Dave looked up from inspecting his shoes and saw Sandra looking at him an amused smile on her face and closing the distance between them her tapped her elbow with his flat cap and with a confused look said "What are you doing on this bus you usually get the 5.15pm?" "Well I wanted to see you as Sunday was a bit of a long day, and we didn't get much of a chance to chat after Sid and Jane arrived in the Malt Shovel did we?" taking her hand and squeezing gently she suddenly realised her stop was coming up next, and with a quick kiss she was heading towards the exit as she turned and finished "Come round about

8pm, see you then". and as the bus came to a halt she was gone into the night.

Finishing a very filling Sausage Casserole particularly after two portions, Dave went upstairs to get changed, returning a few minutes later he stuck his head round the Front room door "Just going out for a bit won't be late" and the look, and mouthed 'Sandra' from his mother told him she missed nothing, but he was already on his way to the door. It wasn't until he was halfway down the street that he realised he had no idea what Sandra wanted to chat about, and nothing had changed that thought as he arrived at her door.

"Hello boyfriend" said Sandra as she opened the door to a slightly nervous Dave, kissing him as he took his off his coat and put his flat cap in a pocket."Come and say hello to mum and dad" she said leading him into the Lounge. "Hello Mr and Mrs Robertson" he just got out, before it was swamped by "Call us Diane and Jim, Dave we don't stand on ceremonies here, did you make him a drink Sandra?" Looking at Dave, Sandra could see he was a little lost, but she answered "I'll make us a cup of tea mum, stop fussing" and taking his hand led him to the kitchen where she pounced on him when they were alone, and kissed him with an amount of vigour that seemed to confuse him even more. "Tea, or coffee boyfriend" she said letting him go and with a murmured "Tea's fine" she headed for the kettle and Dave sat down at the table. Watching as she made the tea he couldn't figure out what was happening, so as she turned around and put the teas down, he quietly asked "What's going on?" Putting a finger to his lips she took his spare hand and picking up her cup of tea, led him into the hall and at the foot of the stairs loudly said in the direction of the Lounge where the door was open. "We're just going up to my room mum" and not waiting for a reply, she led a now very nervous Dave holding his cup of tea, to her room where his memories were etched for all time, but now doing somersaults in his mind.

Closing the door behind her she went past Dave and sat on her bed and patted the spot next to her where a dutiful Dave sat awaiting his punishment. Taking his face between her hands she slowly pulled him close until his lips met hers and they locked together, until eventually they fell backwards and lay on the bed their tongues playing games until Sandra pulled away and looking at Dave as he lay next to her "I've missed you boyfriend!". Lying with his arm round her staring at the ceiling Dave finally decided to broach the subject that he couldn't work out. "Sandra what is it you want to chat about, if you don't mind me asking?" "Just things really" she started then unable to conceal her excitement "Well not just things but, just listen for a bit. I start my new job on Monday 1st February and you have your Driving Test on the 11th which if, sorry, when, you pass we are going to celebrate, and then there is Valentine's Day, on the 14th obviously and well...." getting off the bed she went to her dressing table and took the brochures she had got from the travel agents out of the top draw, and handed them to Dave with a smile on her face that slowly transferred across to Dave, who realised his misgivings about tonight had been so far off the mark he would have been wearing a Dunce Hat if he had still been at school. ".....well as you can see I thought to celebrate you passing and ....well you know, we could have a romantic night at one of the Hotels in these". Proud that she had managed to get everything out that she had been holding back she looked at Dave who was looking up at her "Well what do you think, boyfriend?" The hands on her bottom as she stayed standing over him gave her a hint, but as he pulled her next to him and ran his hands up her back forcing her to bend to meet his welcoming mouth, told her she didn't need to say anything else as there were better things to do with her lips, as his tongue chased hers, moist and hungry. After they untangled themselves, they lay on the bed side by side looking at a brochure each and Sandra had got to Page 35, when she nudged Dave and handed him the brochure which she had folded over to her chosen page and with a look that said 'deny me if you dare' she lay back with her hands locked together behind her head and waited for the response. "Well ....chosen" he said and rolling over to rest on his left elbow he put the brochure down and kissed her as she closed her eyes, moving his right hand under her jumper, he felt for her bra and as they locked into a kiss he found her right nipple under her bra and gently rubbed until he could feel it stand proud, before moving his hand across to her left breast and nudging her bra over her breast exposed the nipple to his fingers cupping her breast in his hand to cover the nipple he moved his hand to fully push the bra out of the way, as Sandra pushed her tongue further into his mouth catching his tongue with a bite and then relaxing as she felt her breasts exposed to the fresh air and putting her arms around his neck she felt his hand move down to her trousers and lay on top of the zip before sliding it down and entering the opening with his fingers. He placed his fingers on the front of her knickers before sliding over the top of them, as he moved his fingers into the gap between her legs she felt a pressure on her clitoris as he moved his fingers slowly up and down, she sucked hard on his tongue and felt his fingers slip under the material and into her now aroused vagina, which she met with a hand that had disengaged itself, and landed on top of his hand which was still inside her trousers. Seeing him look at her she said quietly "Enough Dave, I don't want to go any further" and taking his hand away he kissed her without saying anything and after redoing all Dave's handiwork they lay in each other's arms both aware that they were closing in on one of life's major moments.

Thursday was a complete wash out in more ways than one. The weather had become mild over the last few days, and with it came the pent up rain which lashed the moorland and ran down into the towns and villages in the area causing flash floods and road disruption. Sandra was grateful that her mum had given her an umbrella as she was heading out the door this morning, but she was still wet not least because the newly created puddle outside the Council Office, had been driven through just as she was on the second step, and although she had missed most of it her ankles were wet though, so the first thing she did was take her shoes off when she got to her desk as no one would see them underneath, and they might be dry by lunchtime. Just before they all started work Sharon came over to a barefooted Sandra and suggested, or was that demanded that they go out on Friday night to celebrate Sandra leaving, even if it was only to another department. Agreeing that it seemed a good idea, they arranged to meet at lunch to discuss the plan of action, which slightly worried Sandra as she started on the two boxes of files that Sam had brought yesterday. Walking to the Carousel which was the nearest Cafe to the Council Offices sheltering two under each umbrella, the four of them had to wait a few minutes as a table just emptied was cleared, but by the time they had ordered and got their coffees the table was free and Sharon taking the lead set off on her plan of action. "A few drinks round Town and then a nightclub followed by a curry how does that sound." The silence went on before Peggy chipped in "Well how about a few drinks then a curry, well she's only going to Planning, not the end of the earth and we'll still see each other" she finished knowing it probably wasn't true, as you lost touch with work colleagues as they moved on. While the two options were being debated Jo decided to pitch in "Why not a few drinks, then a pizza so we won't be out to late and can still have a nice weekend." She said hoping no one would ask, realising she had left herself open with the end of the sentence. Sharon didn't miss it "So Jo, who are we having a nice weekend with?" looking straight at Jo and expecting an answer which to be fair to Jo, she was dying to let out of the bag "Chris from Accounts asked me out this Saturday!" and pleased to have finally got her two day old secret out, she took a sip of coffee that gave her a frothy moustache, at which the others laughed as she put her cup down unaware of her froth covered lip, as she concentrated on telling them about her date tomorrow "What! He's nice and he's got a car" she said which made the others laugh even louder, as her froth moustache moved up and down as she spoke, until Peggy used the back of her hand to wipe an imaginary froth moustache from her own face, and Jo took the hint wiping her lip with a serviette before adding "Well I think he's nice!" at which the three others set off laughing again, and folding her arms she looked out of the window as the rain ran down the large window panes down into the overflowing drains like the tears from the Gods.

Friday finally arrived and as Sandra put her coat on and took her hat from the pocket her mother, sitting at the kitchen table said "Will we see you tonight as it's your last day?" "We are planning to go for something to eat, and a few drinks nothing too heavy because Jo has a date tomorrow so I shouldn't be late, but you never know! Are you and dad going out tonight" she ended. "No darling your dad is working late today so we are going out tomorrow. We thought the Hinchcliffe Arms for a change, but I think your dad has his heart set on a curry at the Kashmir so we'll see. Off you go now or you'll miss your bus, wouldn't do to be late on your last day! With a hug from her mum Sandra put her hat on, and closing the door behind her, headed for the bus stop for her last day at the Administration Support Department.

Arriving in Town Sandra walked from the bus station towards the Council Offices with a little trepidation. After all she thought, this was her last day before she joined the Planning Department. Although the job hadn't been great, she had made some good friends and while she would see them from time to time, it wouldn't be the same as working with them on a day to day basis. It was just that her life was taking a different road to theirs and that is the way things go, she considered as she finally arrived at the steps of the building and looking up, stopped for a second as if to prepare for news that she didn't want to hear. As Sandra entered the office she sensed something was going on, as there was noise before she opened the door, but that had now decreased to almost nil. Looking around she could see everyone had their feet up on their desks with everyone looking directly at her. Not paying attention it wasn't until she got to her own desk that she realised what was going on. "You can leave when you've finished that lot!" rose loudly above the silence, as Sharon the ringleader as always, pointed to Sandra's desk which was under two feet of files covering the whole desk which as she stood there came up to her shoulder. "Anyone got a match?" Sandra said which brought a round of applause, that was curtailed as Mrs Anderson entered the office and the Sandra's last day in the department started in earnest.

The excess load of files found their way back to their rightful desks, and as the morning passed Sandra was determined to leave an empty desk when she finished at the end of the day so she concentrated on reducing the pile in front of her so much, that it was lunchtime before she realised it, and only the scraping of chairs being moved broke her concentration. "Come on Sandra let's go its lunchtime" she heard as Peggy put her hand on her shoulder and stretching she pushed back her chair and went to joining Sharon and Jo already waiting at the door. "Brazilian or Carousel" said Jo as they exited the building adding "Or shall we have a proper drink in the Cross Keys?" said Sharon making a quick left turn towards the Cross Keys, she raised her arm and waving it backwards and forwards, they followed her without a second thought.

After a quick two rounds of drinks it was while Jo was at the bar that the questions started to be asked 'This Chris from Accounts, anyone know anything about him" said Sharon, leading as always. "Not me" said Sandra wondering if it was a good idea to drink at lunchtime."Well, as it happens" Sharon carried on "I heard he had a long term girlfriend that dumped him before Christmas for someone else, and he was heartbroken, even took a few days off!" and as Jo returned from the bar with their drinks Sharon couldn't resist asking and launched into "Well Jo, what about this Chris from Accounts what's he like?" caught unawares, and deciding to stand up to Sharon for a change she answered "I'll let you know on Monday, if he's gone home by then that is!" and putting the drinks down she sat next to Peggy who gave her a look that said 'Good for you girl!' and Chris wasn't mentioned for the rest of the lunchtime.

The afternoon naturally dragged as Friday afternoon's have a habit of doing. Work was completed, new work arrived and the cycle continued until 5pm came and the mood changed from the mundane, to almost joyful, until they saw that the rain had arrived with force and none of them were dressed for the downpour which had arrived. "Never mind" said Peggy looking at the rain beating against the high windows "We'll just stay in the nearby pubs and get wet inside ourselves!" and pleased at her ages old joke, put on her coat and headed for the door with Sharon, Jo and Sandra close behind. As they passed Mrs Anderson's office she was in the process of putting her coat on when Sandra asked her if she wanted to come for a drink with them, but the shake of her head suggested otherwise but the "Good luck in your new job Sandra!" that came almost as an afterthought, suggested to Sandra that she would be forgotten by next Friday.

Friday early evening in Kirkdale was busy as the weather was impacting on people going straight home from work, or having a drink or two while the rain decided if it was staying for an hour more, or all day. It also helped that the Council employees had been paid today, the last Friday of the month, so as Sharon led the way into the Cross Keys for the second time today, she had to push her way through the early starters to get to the bar with Jo in tow, as Sandra and Peggy went to find a table. Finding themselves at the very same table as they had sat at on Christmas Eve they looked at each other and as Sandra shook her head Peggy said "That was a lifetime ago, forget about it and move on, he's out of your life now" and with a smile that said yes, but hid the full story then and since, she was relieved when Sharon came bustling through the crowd with Jo right behind her with their drinks and setting the drinks down with a toast "To Sandra and her new role!" drank a good half of her drink after they clinked glasses. "God I needed that after today, you do right leaving Sandra, can't see me staying another year, they don't appreciate my abilities!" not letting her get away with it Peggy quickly retorted "So what abilities do you possess that you could use apart from drinking, partying and breaking hearts Sharon?" Looking seriously at Sharon, Peggy she just about managed a mouthful of her drink before breaking out into a guttural laugh that grew louder as Sandra and Jo joined in, until finally Sharon also joined in, but not before adding "But I'm very good at those!" and breaking into a smile that was hard to resist she looked at Jo, and like an unwritten command she dutifully stood up ready to go to the bar for another round. "Let me give you a hand" Sandra said joining Jo and they headed off to the bar without looking back as the evening started to pick up, the weather set in for the night and probably the weekend, the early evening drinkers would soon be joined by the regular crowds, the weather outside would be forgotten apart from the short trips between pubs as the alcohol took hold, and more important discussions took place across the Town than the British obsession with the weather.

After three drinks the decision was made to move onto the George, and as they hurried between the two pubs, hands over heads and breaking into a run in a futile attempt to avoid the raindrops they arrived just as Sid and Pete were coming out of the door. Seeing Jo first then Sandra keeping their heads down trying to evade the rain, Sid held the door open and with a slight bow said "After you ladies!" at which Jo recognised the voice, "Why thank you Prince Charming!" she said as they passed each other in the doorway, and quickly handed him her phone number on a piece of paper that she had written today in the hope that they would meet again. Seeing the attempted hidden note passed to Sid as he and Pete left the pub Sandra waited until they were inside and at the bar before asking her as they waited to get served."I saw that Jo, I thought you had a date with Chris tomorrow!" "Yes, but it never hurts to have a backup Sandra" she responded, and handing the barman a £5 note, she handed two drinks to Sandra and picking the other two from the bar led the way through the crowd to where Sharon and Peggy were standing with a smug smile on her face. With no tables free they stood in an alcove and Peggy brought up the question of what everyone was doing over the weekend. "Jo, you've got a date with Chris from Accounts, Sandra you'll be with Dave, I've got a date with Andy at the pictures although God knows what we'll watch. So Sharon you're the only one with no plans, well no plans that we know of that is.... Spill!" Taking a mouthful of her drink Sharon said "Nothing to spill Peggy, quiet weekend, apart from tonight of course then Catterick tomorrow!" "Well you kept that quiet I must say" said Peggy suddenly halting from taking a drink and adding "Are you sure you know what you are doing?" "I'm not 10 Peggy, he's been down twice so I'm going to his just for Saturday night, to see where he lives and if he is different on his own patch as they say!" and taking a hefty drink which emptied her glass, Sharon looked away to end the conversation with a non negotiable "Let's go to the Old Cock they usually have a band on a Friday".

Heading for the Old Cock the conversation had been stymied by Sharon's comments, but as Jo opened the door they could hear a band which was advertised by a flyer on the door but which had been rained upon and made illegible by the rain, trying their best to cover 'Caroline' by 'Status Quo' which changed the mood and the evening was back on keel, as Sandra returned from the bar with their four drinks, helped by Ann and Gill from Sandra's old school, who had come to watch the band, as Gill's boyfriend Steve played Bass guitar in the band.

After making the introductions it was almost impossible to talk as the band cut into one of their own songs that only Gill knew. After four more songs the band took a break, and the conversations restarted with Ann asking Sandra what she was up to while Gill went to see Steve. "Well I start a new job in Planning next week, which I am excited about and that's why we are out tonight to celebrate" said Sandra "What about boy-friends Sandra?" said Ann which was really her original question's meaning "Well as you ask, I've been going out with Dave since before Christmas, and things are going really well. We go out walking a lot as he hasn't passed his Driving Test yet but he will on the 11th February. He works for the Estate Department at the Council he's ambitious and he's met my parents and I've met his!" "Slow down Sandra" Ann quickly interrupted "Sounds like you really like him, do you think he's the one?" "I do hope so Ann" Sandra said admitting it for the first time to anyone.

The band started up again and further discussion was cur-tailed for their second set, and enjoying the band the group of six tried to snatch a few words between songs, but gave up after the third song and as Sandra and Gill headed for the bar a voice pitched through the noise "Hello Sis" and turn-ing away from the bar in the direction of the voice she knew, Sandra saw Tony and his friend Paul who were watching the band. "Small world isn't it" Tony continued as the band ended another song. "Didn't think this lot would be your cup of tea Sis?" "No not really were just here as it's my last day at work, so were celebrating" Sandra managed to get in before the band launched into another song. Pointing to the bar where Gill had now found a place Sandra intimated to Tony that she was going to get a drink, but his attention was already taken by the band, and she joined Gill at the bar convinced that her brother would be single for years to come. While at the bar Gill managed to ask Sandra, if Tony was seeing anyone which came as such a shock, that she spilled some of her drink on herself. "Shaking her head almost in time to the music Sandra mouthed 'No' which as far as she knew was true, but then there was Marion but she didn't know what was going on there, so putting a note in her memory to ask him they headed back to where the others were at the side of the stage, with Gill looking back at Tony but he was oblivious to anything apart from the music.

The band finished with 'All Night Long' by 'Rainbow' which Sandra noticed went down well with everyone, especially her brother, who she figured was now definitely the centre of Gill's attention by the look on her face. Wait until tomorrow when I tease him she thought. As the Jukebox kicked in, the sound had reduced enough that they could discuss what they had been holding back on while the band played. "So are we going for a Pizza or, a Curry" said Sharon who wasn't a great fan of tomato sauce on bread as she called it and awaiting a response "Do you two want to come?" to Ann and Gill. "Thanks but got to catch the last bus" said Ann as Gill nodded in agreement, momentarily averting her eyes from Tony. "Maybe next time" Ann finished. As they both emptied their glasses and putting their coats on turned to leave with a few waves and a "See you soon" from Ann they were gone into the night for their ride home. "Right you lot, one for the road, then Pizza. I don't want to smell like an Onion Bhaji tomorrow when I see Chris!" and with that Jo headed for the bar with Peggy reluctantly following, having already decided that she really didn't need one for the road. Four Vodka and Cokes arrived with a smile from the barman but little change, but Jo didn't seem to notice as she wheeled round handing two of the drinks to Peggy, who seemed relieved that it wasn't another half of Cider. Returning to where Sandra and Sharon were stood chatting Peggy handed her drinks to them and took the spare from Jo. "Here's to Sandra and her new job" she said which Sharon immediately said "I've already said that earlier!" at which Jo decided she wasn't going to be left out "To Sandra's new job!" and to complete the circle Sandra said" To my friends thank you" and as they all raised their glasses in ill timed synchrony "Barmy Army".

The Pizza Restaurant was closing when they got to the door at nearly 11.00pm so it was Curry for the 'Barmy Army' and after taking ages to decided what to order they were just finishing telling the waiter their order of two Chicken Massalas, Lamb Bhuna and a Chicken Dopiaza with two Pilaf rice and six Chapattis, when Tony and Paul walked through the door. "Hello ladies" said a now very obviously drunk Paul, and as he and Tony sat down at a nearby table with Paul waving his hand in the air for service, Sandra had more ammunition with which to embarrass her brother. "Two Chicken Vindaloos with six Chapattis" he said" and some Poppadoms, please" as an afterthought. The food turned up quickly and as the chatter dropped, as they all got stuck into their meals, Sandra looked over and realised that at the other table, Tony and Paul had ceased talking altogether, and were eating like their lives depended on it with occasional drinks of water, before returning to devour their meals. As both tables finished at roughly the same time there was some chat between them about the night, and which pubs they had been in and whether the band was any good. Finally sharing Taxi's became the focal point for discussion and it was agreed that Sharon, Jo and Peggy share one with Tony, Paul and Sandra getting a separate Taxi. When the bill came and they had all chipped in, Sandra asked the waiter if he could get them two Taxis. As the banter about what they each were doing tomorrow went round in circles until the waiter said the Taxi's were outside, it struck Sandra that she had only really thought of Dave once tonight, when she was talking to Gill and that just wouldn't do.

Saturday came blowing in with a strong wind from the West and with it a break from the constant rain that had continuously fallen in the area. The rainfall drained from the moors creating floods in the low lying areas in places where the river

Kirk had broken its banks into the fields alongside the river course, and some local roads were only passable with caution. It was into this wind that Sandra headed out pulling her hat over her ears on the walk to Dave's, with a slight hangover that she hoped her bacon butty and two cups of tea would soon dispel. Tony missed both as he was still in bed, so Sandra didn't have a chance to use her newly discovered information from last night, but it would wait for another time she thought, as a discarded wrapper caught her face and brushing it off she turned into Albion Street, and headed towards Dave's house halfway down the street. Knocking on the door she had to wait for a few minutes and with no answer knocked again at which Mrs Baxter suddenly opened the door which the wind caught and pushed her back a step. "Oh hello Sandra, do come in, I was just vacuuming upstairs have you been knocking long?" and turning to allow Sandra inside she headed for the kettle and picking it up checking it had enough water, she brandished it in Sandra's direction at which Sandra having had two cups of tea already declined "I'm fine Mrs Baxter thank you" "I'll have one please mum" said Dave as he entered the kitchen and moving across to where Sandra was slightly awkwardly stood, kissed her on the cheek and quietly uttered "Hello girlfriend" before pulling out a chair for Sandra which she took and they both sat down at the kitchen table. Looking at Sandra and holding her hand under the table he said "Didn't realise it was that late, I was having a shower so didn't hear you but never mind that, you're here now, if a bit windswept" at which Sandra took off her hat and used her fingers to try to manage her hair that had been hiding from the weather. "Sure you don't want a coffee" said Mrs Baxter handing Dave his mug of coffee but with a shake of her head Sandra saved a few words and "Best get back to it, the house won't clean itself" said Mrs Baxter and taking her own coffee left them alone.

"So, why were you so late getting up late night was it?" said Sandra holding Dave's hand above the table now. "Well you know what Sid's like when he's on one. We didn't leave the Malt Shovel until closing time and the walk home was a bit slow." "How was your night in Town?" Sandra outlined the evening they had had on the pub crawl, and ending up having a curry rather than a pizza and Tony and Paul joining them. Looking out of the kitchen door to see there was no one around she   leaned into Dave and kissed him with a passion that took Dave aback until they separated, and Sandra squeezed his hand and whispered "I've missed you" leaving her cheek next to his for a moment. With no response as Dave picked up his mug Sandra looked him in the eye at which he took the hint. "I've missed you too, especially these!" as he put his hand on her chest with a smile of a child. Removing his hand slowly and keeping it in hers Sandra quietly said "All good things come to those who wait!" and as Dave kissed her Mr Baxter came into the kitchen disturbed by the ongoing cleaning machine that was Mrs Baxter. "Hello Sandra, how are your mum and dad?" and headed across the kitchen towards the kettle. "They're fine thank you Mr Baxter, they send their regards and dad is looking forward to a game of golf when the weather is better" Having filled the kettle he responded "Good to hear , tell Jim we'll get that game of golf as and when" and getting the milk from the fridge turning back to watch the kettle boil. With a sideways look Dave motioned for Sandra to join him in the hall and with a quick aside to his dad Dave said "We're off out dad, see you later, tell mum I won't be back for tea" and with a swift "Okay" from the kitchen Dave put his coat and Flat cap on and once Sandra had put her hat on, took her hand and they left out of the front door into the wind ready to blow the cobwebs from their respective nights out.

Heading down Albion Street hooked up as if it would help to block the wind they got to the end of the street and stopped. Neither willing to make a decision, a brief kiss broke the silence and then Dave said "Fancy a change Sandra?" "What have you got in mind?" she quickly replied trying to work out where his mind was going. "How about we go to Skipton for the day, we can catch the bus on the main road, they have a market on a Saturday and we can have lunch or maybe tea and just have the day to ourselves" Pondering his out of the blue suggestion and wondering where it came from, she thought about her parents going out tonight and her own barely organised plans but sensing he was waiting for an answer she put it to the back of her mind. "Good idea boyfriend let's do it. Will we have a long wait for the bus?" "Thought you might say no, but it will be a nice change and if we hurry, we should be able to catch the 11.30 from Town and be in Skipton by about 12.15" and leaning towards her kissed her forehead, before linking up and heading for the bus stop on the main road at the other side of the estate.

The wind was slowly easing and stood together, arms around each other at the bus stop it was a still pondering Sandra, who said as the bus headed up the main street "I'm still not sure why you chose Skipton, but I guess I'll have to trust you." With no response she boarded the bus in front of Dave and headed upstairs and finding a seat halfway down the bus waited for him to join her, as she looked out of the window perusing the estate as the bus slowly pulled away and she felt Dave sit down and hold her hand. "Better view from up here!" she said squeezing his hand. "You won't be disappointed with Skipton" he replied and looking out of the window, he had managed to confuse Sandra even further.

With a 40 minute journey they had plenty of time to cover what had happened last night, and after Sandra had added some more details to her night out, Dave started to expand on his evening with Sid. "Well we started at the Queens Head but it was dead, so we went to the Fleece which is nearby although it to was pretty quiet, we played a few games of pool and were just thinking of going to the Malt Shovel when a couple of Sid's workmates, Pete and John came in, so a few beers and games of pool later we were just chilling when Pete, who had obviously already had a few beers elsewhere with John, asked Sid if he had seen his daughter Angela on his travels. Sid obviously said no but Pete wouldn't let it go. He knew she was out somewhere with one of her friends, but he didn't trust her after she came home the other Sunday in a bit of a state and he hadn't been able to get out of her what had happened. Anyway after a bit of a silence the night carried on, it wasn't like Angela would come into the Fleece or Queens Head so we thought nothing of it, getting a bit bored with the pool we decided to end up at the Malt Shovel so we left Pete and John at the Fleece and made our way to the Malt Shovel at about 10.00 and got drenched on the way." At which Sandra gave his hand a squash and half listening, half looking out of the window at the expanse of moorland all around them, she let Dave continue his story "Well we got to the Malt Shovel and it was heaving as always on a Friday night, we got a couple of beers and as the pool table was busy we stood just watching, when Sid asked me something that struck me as odd. He asked if I could remember anything about the night I got attacked but as I said to him at the time, all I can remember is the word 'Stay', but when I said it to him I felt that it was more than just 'Stay' more like 'Stay away or maybe Stay awake' than anything else but that was probably nothing. Anyway we were just chatting and it just kind of stuck with me as odd that Sid would ask that question, but he just said that it came to him as we would be walking back the same way as on that night for the first time since the attack. The rest of the night was just a bit of a blur to be fair, but I would have killed for a curry at the end of the night, but probably a good job we didn't as I would stink of curry!" and letting it sink in, the dig in his ribs and "I don't stink of curry I'll have you know" from Sandra told him she was listening but was still struggling with his sense of humour, but she at least now understood it.

Finally they arrived at Skipton, and you could tell it was

market day by the number of people milling around and the weather had even dropped to a wintery bluster, with the rain stuck up high on the hills and moors. Crossing the road from the Bus Station the smell of fish and chips hit Dave almost immediately and he regretted not having a curry last night even more as he said "I'm starving do you fancy some chips or should we wait till later?" and turning to await the answer got some of his humour back "I'm surprised you can smell chips over my curry perfume!" turning away she awaited an apology, which came but in Dave's usual format "Well we can share if you want and then we will both smell of salt and vinegar" and before she could work out the comment, he kissed her quickly on the lips and headed into the Chippy, leaving her on the pavement trying to avoid the stream of people meandering through the town. When Dave returned with a large paper bundle, he took her hand and led them to the canal basin where there were benches to sit, and as they found an empty bench some 50 yards away, he sat down and quickly started to open the wrapper of last weeks newspaper, breaking into the inner paper helped himself to several chips before he realise Sandra was looking at him with an amused smile on her face as she then said. "You really were starving weren't you, serves you right for sleeping in and missing your breakfast!" as she took a chip from the open bag and popped it into her mouth "Not bad, but not as nice as my bacon butty this morning!" as she licked her fingers, and sitting back let Dave finish off the rest of his breakfast which was now his lunch. As he finished and wiped his hands on the wrapper he looked around for a bin to put it in, and spotting one seeing one by the Ice Cream Parlour, he got up and offering his hand to Sandra they made for the bin, with Sandra hoping he wasn't going to have ice cream as a pudding. Dropping the squashed package in the bin he gave Sandra a hug and a kiss which she quickly ended with "Lovely, you taste like a chip!" as he started to respond with "Better than a ....." she cut his comment short with a tug on his hand and he let his retort drop, as they made their way onto the main street which was now a throng of people, with market stalls taking over the usual car parking spaces and some sellers shouting their offerings above the general noise of the day.

Taking their time to mingle with the crowds and avoiding prams and young children who seemed intent on getting lost they were halfway up the left hand side of the street heading towards Skipton Castle when Dave suddenly stopped and pulled Sandra into an alleyway and out of the morass of people. Pulling her close to him he kissed her longingly, until they had to separate as a couple went past them with a cursory 'Excuse us' as they passed."Well what was that for, and why did you stop?" said Sandra as Dave took hold of her hand. "Well I thought you might have missed ....." and without finishing he kissed her again pushing her gently against the alley wall until Sandra pushed him away "I didn't come all the way to Skipton just to get kissed in an alley!" taking her hand he just smiled and they returned to the main street, and the streams of people looking for a bargain to justify the trip out. Ignoring the many food sellers they stopped at a hat stall where Dave offered to buy Sandra a new hat, as long as it was the one that looked like a sheep with ears to match, which not surprisingly she turned down, but not before offering to return the favour and buy Dave a hat in the image of a hound dog with long ears to match, which he similarly refused on the grounds that he was quite happy with his flat cap, which a beautiful lady had bought him.

Crossing the road at the top of the main street by the roundabout they were slowly making their way, mainly in the same flow as the rest of the shoppers and tourists, when they came to a large alleyway where Dave led Sandra by the hand out of the main stream, and into a quiet oasis of calm. Taking it that Dave knew where he was going they went past a sweet shop, and an outdoors clothes shop, before he stopped suddenly in front of a jewellers and looked directly at Sandra "Well I said you wouldn't be disappointed and I really hope you won't be" Before she had a chance to respond he was opening the door and leading her inside, speechless. Wandering from display to display Dave finally settled on the display trays by the counter and asked the woman behind the counter if they could have a look at the Platinum engagement rings tray. As he turned to look at Sandra he said "I was in Skipton last week on a course, and came in here at lunchtime and liked this tray but if you fancy something else just let me know won't you!" the silence told him all he needed to know and when the assistant asked Sandra if she would like to try one on, she pointed to a ring with a single line running around and through the middle, holding out her finger she offered it to the assistant to try on the ring. Holding her hand up against the light coming into the shop from the windows and moving it up and down like her hand was a small bird she gave Dave a look that needed no answer. "If the young lady would allow me I'll check her ring size and see if we have one in stock that matches" and taking Sandra's hand she measured her third finger, left hand as the song goes, and with a smile she said "I won't be a minute" as went into a back room, which gave Sandra just enough time to plant a kiss on Dave's lips before the assistant returned. "I am sorry we don't have that one in your size unfortunately, you could choose another one" at which the look from Sandra told her that wasn't an option and finishing "Or you could come back next week and we can have it resized". Barely had the words been spoken when Sandra beamed a quick reply "We'll be back next week, please" Giving his address and contact details, Dave could feel Sandra at his side with the ring in front of him never out of her sight. Thanking the assistant and leading Sandra by the hand towards the door, Sandra turned at the last minute and said "Thank you, we'll see you next week" and with a smile that could have opened the door on its own, she squeezed Dave's hand as he held the door open. "Well I wasn't expecting that!" she said before pinning him against the wall outside the Jewellers, and putting her hands on his face leant in and kissed him slowly, and then with an urgency before slipping her tongue inside his mouth. They stood locked for a few moments before Dave put his arms around her and moved to whisper in her ear "I said you wouldn't be disappointed" and looking into her face as he straightened up, the tears slowly started to run down her face at which she hugged him, nudging her face into his neck as she tried to recover and failed miserably as the tears of happiness continued.

After a couple of minutes Sandra pulled herself away from Dave and taking a tissue out of her pocket did her best at wiping away the drying tears, and looking into the Jewellers window to see the effect her crying had made on her face she said "We'll have to find somewhere so I can fix my face" and looking at her he replied putting a finger on her nose "Looks gorgeous to me" at which she gently punched him "Don't!" as she almost started crying again. Heading for the pub which they had passed on the way to the Jewellers they struggled to go against the flow of people, but taking an opportunity after a family with a pram had gone by, they entered the Woolly Sheep pub, as Sandra headed for the toilets to 'fix her face', Dave went to the bar and ordering a pint and a half of Lager which he felt they would easily dispose of, he managed to find a table at the far end of the pub and sat to await Sandra's return. Eventually Sandra returned with her coat over her arm, and a smile that said she had a secret that only she knew, but she was desperate to share with everyone. Sitting down next to Dave she gave him a quick kiss, and taking a drink she leaned in for another kiss still without saying a word. Sat together not speaking, it was a few minutes before Dave finally broke the silence and holding Sandra's hand tightly he said "I hope you don't mind waiting another week for your ring, maybe it's for the best" which got a quizzical look from Sandra "Some things are best waiting for!" he finished and she looked at him, gave him a quick kiss and settled back into the world of Sandra and without saying anything thought to herself 'You won't have to wait very long boyfriend'.

Halfway down his pint, Dave looked at Sandra and plucking up a modicum of courage, decided he felt he needed to explain a few things and set off on a bit of a ramble. "Sandra I'm sorry to spring it on you, the ring I mean but I saw it last week, and couldn't wait until your Birthday, I do hope you like it. Let me finish" he quickly added, seeing Sandra about to say something and continuing "It's going to be hard keeping it a secret, but secrets are sometimes worth keeping. Anyway you've got a new job, I've got my Driving Test coming up, and we haven't even broached Valentine's Day with our parents as yet, mine I'm sure will be fine but I don't know how your mum and dad will react. I thought we might tell them tomorrow, and see what the reaction is. Right that's it, I'm done!" and sitting back, he waited for Sandra to respond. Picking up her nearly empty glass she finished it, stood up and headed for the bar without saying a word. Left more than a little perplexed, he finished his drink and trying to figure out what was going on, he watched as she made her way to the bar. Looking around at the various posters and pictures on the walls he was perusing an old 'Welcome to Yorkshire' railway poster when he saw her returning from the bar. Putting the drinks down she sat next to him and held his hand, putting her finger on his lips "Now boyfriend, let me have my say while you have a drink, you might need it. Valentine's Day will be fine I've already had a word with mum and I'm sure she has had a word with dad, but yes I think it would be a good idea to tell them tomorrow, as it is after all only two weeks away. I think as both parents know we are planning on getting engaged on my Birthday, that it will be fine about showing them the ring before, but we can keep it secret from everyone else, but I want to wear it when we go away, so to finish. I don't like the ring........ , I Love it, oh and by the way, in case you didn't already know............................. I Love You!"

"Well I didn't expect that girlfriend, or should that be Fiancé now! Oh and by the way yourself, I think I've always loved you, ever since the first time I saw you at the Council." They tenderly kissed with the rest of the pub blissfully unaware of this precious moment, and upon parting he continued. "I know it's a bit soppy, but you really were the best medicine when I was in Hospital. I haven't told you before but when I was in there you were the only thing I could think of, and that's why I have these plans for us and for the future, I'm so lucky to have you in my life." As the tears started again Sandra leant into Dave and quietly whispered "Oh, not as lucky as I am!" and resting her head on his shoulder she wiped her eyes, and crossing her fingers on one hand hoped no one would ever take this happiness she felt away.

They spent the afternoon walking by the canal and keeping out of the way of people, as they couldn't possibly be as happy as they were. The footpath by the canal eventually brought them to a bridge and leaning over as a barge slowly passed underneath, Dave said "Throw a penny and make a wish" handing her a coin. He watched as she slowly moved her eyes sideways and up and down and created a wish, then tossed the penny into the canal. "All done!" she said and without looking at him as if he could read her mind and find out her wish, she took his hand as they crossed to the other side of the canal for the walk back into Skipton. As they passed the back of the Royal Shepherd the unmistakable smell of food hit them, and without a word they turned off the path and made a beeline for a very late lunch. Sitting with their drinks awaiting their food, the plaque on the wall where they were sat, told the story of the murder of John Southworth in the pub, and the death of Molly Barker and her faithful dog Tag, that haunt the canal towpath to this day."Do you think we'll get a dog?" said Sandra before taking a drink. "Three deaths, and all you ask is if we'll get a dog, it's no wonder I love you so much" and managing a quick kiss, as their food arrived she looked at him as if what she had said was the most natural thing in the world, before picking up her knife and fork and serviette and attacking her Chicken and Mushroom pie. Still shaking his head in disbelief Dave pulled his plate nearer and set about his very full plate of Gammon, Egg and Chips, as a silence nurtured by hunger, mixed in with a day in a lifetime took hold.

With the short days of January, the warmth and ambiance of the pub saw them have another drink after they had finished off their meals. Watching as an old couple entered and took what was obviously their usual place at the bar, and engaged the barman in a conversation about how busy today had been while he pulled their drinks, Sandra and Dave noticed a sheep dog sitting patiently at their feet head looking up at the bar awaiting a predestined treat, which he always got. As the barman finished pulling their drinks, he handed them their change and leaning out over the bar at which the dog reached up and put his front paws on the bar as the barman said "There you go Billy" handing him a bone, which he gratefully took in his jaws and promptly lay down, putting the bone between his front paws started to lick his regular treat, as the old couple chatted about the day. Having seen the episode at the bar Sandra looked at Dave and said"We could get a dog like that!" at which Dave just looked at her, and let it go with a smile and watched as the pub filled up, the market having finished and the traders spent some of their hard earned profits, deserving of a drink and some nourishment after 8 hours standing outside in the changeable weather. Over the next hour they had another drink, and when Sandra offered to get the next drink, Dave had already worked out her ulterior motive as he saw her head for the part of the bar where Billy lay at his owner's feet, having seen off the bone over the last hour. Ordering the drinks she automatically stroked Billy's head, as the barman went to pour the drinks, at which he sat up and licked her fingers as the old woman said "He's a big softy love, he won't hurt you, you'll be fine with him". The drinks were placed on the bar in front of her, and she paid the barman and waiting for the change carried on stroking Billy until the barman offered her the change and she suddenly realised what the old lady had said. Heading back to where Dave was sat she placed the drinks on the table with a smile that Dave couldn't read "What?" he said taking a drink as Sandra sat down next to him "It was something the old lady said, about you being a big softy" and leaving it at that, she sat back as Dave pondered why the old woman would think he was a big softy, but decided to leave it alone and sat back to people watch, as a new group of drinkers entered the pub and headed for the bar.

Realising the evening was moving on as another crowd of drinkers had arrived, Sandra and Dave decided that the day had run its course, and checking the bus timetable, figured they could make the 8.15 to Kirkdale and after one more drink they headed out into the cold and dark night to make their way to the Bus Station and the slow journey home. With nothing to see in the dark they sat downstairs on the bus and settled into each other as the bus set off. After some 10 minutes of silence Sandra was dozing off and to stop herself she said "I've really enjoyed myself today, and you were right I wasn't disappointed, exactly the opposite to be honest. I can't wait until next week when the ring is ready" but with no answer she moved her head off Dave's shoulder to realise he had fallen asleep. Resting her head back on his shoulder she smiled and closed her eyes to join him in his dreams.

Getting off the bus at their stop near the Estate, they were heading for Sandra's home when they walked into the path of Sid and Jane who were on their way to the Malt Shovel and with a little cajoling they joined them, and the night started again. After catching up on what they had each been doing during the day, the couples settled down in the snug and as the effects of the day out in Skipton and the drinks already consumed it was only just over an hour later when Dave and Sandra decided that they had overstayed their welcome, and were ready for home, but they would meet up on Wednesday.

They left Sid and Jane with a ringing endorsement of 'Light weights' ringing in their ears as they headed for the door and the walk home. As they left and crossed the car park holding hands they didn't see Daniel and his mate Steve, until it was too late and they were closing in on each other "Evening Daniel, Steve" said Dave as he realised who it was in the dark, at which Daniel responded "Dave" as he passed by, and as he looked at Sandra he mouthed 'Bitch' without breaking step, and carried on walking across the car park towards the pub without looking back. Taken aback at seeing Daniel and his mouthed comment Sandra was wondering what to say when Dave altered the subject. "Can't wait to get home, it's been a long day. You choose what we do tomorrow and I'll call for you late morning, and I will be at your beck and call, a bit like you were for me today." Sandra thought for a moment about her empty house and the temptation was there, but as they had been drinking all day she just quietly said "Okay boyfriend, that will give me some time to plan a few things although I won't be able to top today!" at which Dave smiled at the success of his plans, as they settled into a slightly wobbly walk home to Sandra's they didn't see Daniel stop at the top step of the Malt Shovel as Steve went in, holding a finger out into the night sky dragged it figuratively across his throat and out into the night as the figures of Sandra and Dave disappearing into the dark.

Sunday turned out to be a bit of a dead loss as the rain returned with increased anger, and with the prospect of getting drenched out walking, Sandra decided it would be a good time to go to the pictures and it was just which film to watch that was the problem and as Dave knocked on the door she still hadn't made her mind up. After turning down a cup of tea from Diane, Dave was taking off his coat and flat cap when Sandra told him she had decided that they should go to the pictures as the weather 'was set in for the day'."Okay that's a good idea what shall we go to see?" he said taking a seat at the kitchen table." "Well there's Reds, Mad Max or ....Endless Love" and walking round behind him she put her arms around his neck and waited. "Mad Max it is then" he said after a few seconds thought, and holding onto her hands pulled her forwards so he could kiss her and after she responded to his kiss they were still hugging when Diane came back into the kitchen. "So what are you two love birds doing today?" at which Sandra rolled her eyes at her mum and said "We're going to the pictures to watch Endless Love, you're welcome to join us" and leaving it hanging awaited her mum's response. "No that's okay we're just having a quiet day in as your dad's been working over this week. You two love birds enjoy yourselves!" and with a grin on her face left them alone in the kitchen. "I thought we were going to see Mad Max?" said a puzzled Dave as Sandra sat opposite him. Taking his hands in hers she with a knowing smile said "We are boyfriend, oh there's so much you have to learn about women. Let me give you some advice. My mum will be looking at the plot of Endless Love the minute we are out of here, and I know she would be happier with that, than Mad Max with its cars and violence" "So we are going to see Mad Max?" said an even more confused Dave. The nod told him yes, but he was no wiser. 'A lot to learn' he thought to himself as he played with her fingers on top of the kitchen table noticing that she was paying particular attention to the third finger left hand and trying on imaginary rings.

Monday came and Sandra started her new role at the Council in the Planning Department. Deciding to look smart casual rather than casual smart, she entered the Planning Office 5 minutes early and was greeted by Mrs Shaw who was obviously expecting her. "Come with me Sandra and I'll show you to your desk. It will all be a bit strange I dare say. Today will be about getting to know where everything is and there is an Induction organised for 10.00 for two hours so that should make things easier for you. There's a coat rack on the back of the stationery door which you can use, Mr Normanton doesn't like us to hang coats on the back of chairs. Likes to have a tidy office he does. The filing cabinets along the walls are set up numerically rather than by alphabet but you will get used to it as you settle in." she continued leading Sandra to one of four desks in the room. "There you go, this one's for you as you can see, all neat and tidy so get yourself settled and I'll make us a cup of tea before we start work, tea okay?" Nodding her head as she tried to take it all in, Sandra sat down at her allocated desk and noticing a few files in the in-tray was reading the second one when Mrs Shaw returned with a mug of tea for them both. "There you go Sandra, a nice cup of tea to start the day, I see your looking at the files, probably won't make much sense to begin with but you'll soon get the hang of it and if you ever need any help please don't be afraid to ask, we all have to start at the beginning" and with that she sat down at her own desk and taking a sip from her tea took the first of a large stack of files and opened it, as Sandra looked at the file in front of her and tried to figure out what it all meant. The rest of the morning passed as various people introduced themselves, and following the Induction it was lunchtime before she knew it, and as she made for the door, she suddenly realise she had no-one to go to lunch with and wondering what she was going to do as she stood on the steps of the Council Offices.

She felt a nudge in her side as Peggy went past her, and with a wave of her hand indicating she should follow her, she soon fell into step with Peggy as she could hear Sharon and Jo chatting behind her as they made their way to the Brazilian cafe. "So how is your first day in Planning?" Peggy said as they reached the door. "Oh it's fine Mrs Shaw seems nice but it's all been a bit hectic so far" and passing Peggy as she held the door open, she made her way to the counter closely followed by Peggy with Sharon and Jo still lagging behind, having only just reached the door. "Four coffees please" said Peggy as she looked around for a table and pointing to the back corner where a couple we just standing up, they awaited the coffees as

Sharon and Jo joined them. Having paid they headed for the now empty table. "You two were hard at it when Peggy and I got here, got something to tell you two?" Sandra said. Looking at each other Sharon and Jo burst out laughing as Peggy said "They've been like this all morning, if it carries on I think I'll have to look for another job as well!" Calming down and taking a drink Sharon was the first, as always, to break the silence. "Well Sandra for your information Catterick Camp is a really nice place to spend a Saturday night, not that I actually saw any of the camp if you get my drift, but I can tell you the ceiling needs a dust!" at which she burst out laughing again unable to take a drink and putting her cup down, as she laughed at her own humour. Trying to change the subject Sandra turned to Jo, and hardly had she got the words "What did you do this weekend Jo?" than Sharon jumped in and through her ongoing laughter said "Chris from Accounts taught her some double entry bookkeeping!" at which an initially furious Jo said "Sharon! ....Well ...oh alright" realising the battle was lost "Chris from accounts took me out on Saturday night to the Pheasant for a meal, and we had a lovely time and when he left on Sunday morning he had a smile on his face! And that's all I'm saying ....but he is cute, and did I say he's got a car!" "Yes" came the answer from the other three at once, and they settled down to their coffees. Desperate to tell them about her trip to Skipton, but even more determined to keep it a secret Sandra quietly said "Dave and I had a quiet weekend we went out on Saturday and then to the pictures on Sunday to see Mad Max which was okay, I think Dave liked it more than me. "We went to see it on Saturday night "said Peggy it was a bit violent for me, but Andy loved the weird cars they had and we had a curry after at the Rhajastan which excellent" "and ....and" came the comment from Sharon "And nothing Sharon we are going out next weekend and then we'll see........if his ceiling needs dusting" and stunned at her own coarseness Peggy let out a laugh that even Sharon had trouble overcoming.

The rest of the afternoon went smoothly as Mrs Shaw showed Sandra how things worked, where workloads were allocated, and the urgent categories which usually were awaiting a legal decision or signature so needed chasing so they could meet legal requirements in line with Council and Government timescales. Mr Normanton came to welcome her in the afternoon and gave her a small pamphlet that outlined what the Planning Department's policies were, and which she should consider the Bible for the Department. "Stick to that Sandra and you'll do just fine" he said before leaving to chase up something that she either misheard or just plainly didn't know. Feeling better after her first day, she left the Council Offices and was headed for the bus station, when she felt a tug on her arm which stopped her, and as she turned round she headed straight into a full blown kiss. Relaxing as she felt Dave's arms around her, she closed her eyes for a second and then as he pulled away, she saw a bouquet of flowers held out towards her. "For your first day girlfriend!" he said with a smile and she leaned in to give him a hug "I can't stop, got to finish something, just popped out to give you these on your first day, so need to get back, but I'll call round on Wednesday and we can go to the Malt Shovel with Sid and Jane, as we agreed on Saturday, if that's okay?" and with a quick kiss they parted with Sandra holding her flowers as she watched Dave return to the building. 'He is such a romantic' she thought, turning to walk to the Bus Station and wishing Wednesday was already here.

Tuesday and Wednesday passed at work as the learning curve that Sandra was now on settled in, and her first course was set for the end of February in Skipton, which did little to speed up time until she got her engagement ring on Saturday. After tea Sandra heard the knock on the door but her mum had beaten her to it, as Dave stood in the kitchen when she got down the stairs. "Hello girlfriend" he said with his hands behind his back and with a quizzical look she couldn't quite figure out what his stance meant "Mrs Robertson, that is Diane, we, Sandra and I wanted to let you know that this Valentine's Day we are planning on going away for the weekend, well actually Saturday night at a Hotel in the Dales and we didn't want to do anything behind you back, so we just wanted you to know and I, sorry, we hope you'll be okay with it!" As he looked at the flowers he had given Sandra on Monday in a vase on the kitchen table he waited for a response, as the time elapsed he started to get concerned that he had completely dropped them in it "Mum!" said Sandra curtly to break the silence at which Diane said "Dave, you take good care of my daughter, she's very precious to us, and obviously I can see she is to you, so yes Dave, Jim and I are okay as you say, with you going away for Valentine's!" and with a huge confined grin on her face she left them in the kitchen as she headed to the Lounge, well aware of the consternation she had caused.

Walking to the Malt Shovel they had got over halfway when Sandra suddenly stopped in her tracks and Dave looked at her unaware of the reason to stop. "Dave, do you think we should do it, you know, before we go away, because well, we could if you want!" "Girlfriend, or should that soon to be Fiancé, I want our first time to be the last first time. It will be special and we will always remember it, and no one can change or take it away, it will be forever our memory!" and holding her close he gently kissed her before saying "Come on now I gagging for a pint, oh and it's your round!" Sid and Jane were already at the Malt Shovel, and judging by the empty glasses on the table in front of them they were already on their second drink. Heading to the bar Sandra ordered their drinks and paying Ian the barman, she awaited the change and as he placed it into her hand with a smile, she turned and joined them at the table by the pool table, where Sid and Jane had earlier taken up residence and where Dave was now getting a cue as Sid stood up. "Come on Sandra lets leave the boys to it and we'll get a seat in the snug" said Jane already picking up her drink. Following her to the snug, Sid and Dave were oblivious to them leaving but they would figure it out.

"So what are you two up to?" said Jane "It was so obvious on Saturday that you had something to tell but, well we had had a load, and you were a bit fresh so come on it's just us two girls spill!" "Well the thing is we've booked to go away for Valentine's Day and well we haven't, you know, done it yet so I'm a bit nervous. I'm sure it will be alright but I've heard you can freeze and it can hurt. I know it's going to be fine but it's not really something you can chat with your mother about is it? Hi mum, what was your first time with dad like, as we are going to have sex!" and realising how strange a comment it was, she laughed and looked at Jane for a reaction. "God no, don't ask your mother it will be with you for all time! Look I've had a few boyfriends, some good, that will do anything to make you happy, and will be grateful for sex, and then the bad ones who treat you like you should be grateful to let them have sex with you. I would put Dave definitively in the good boyfriend category and the best thing I can advise is that you have plenty of foreplay and take your time. Talk to each other Sandra, the sooner you get comfortable with sex the better it will get. Now don't expect an orgasm the first time, as you won't know what it is and yes it can be a tiny bit painful the first time, but it won't be much you might not even notice it, especially if you take it slowly. I take it you're not on the pill yet, but it does make it a lot easier and if you want I'll come to the Doctors with you, but it's all confidential and as you are 18, you can go without your mother and she will never know. Oh and finally, but feel free to ask anything else....... Enjoy it"

The silence didn't last long before Sandra said "Do you think I should wear something sexy?" "Darling you'll end up wearing nothing in the end, but a sexy outfit is a good idea for your first time, unless you are confident with your body in which case go for it! Oh and of course I almost forgot.....don't let him take any pictures!" at which they both burst out laughing which was interrupted by Dave coming over pool cue in hand "Drinks?" he said waiting for an explanation of the laughter which almost drowned his question. "A man of few words your Dave" said Jane adding "I hope his actions are louder than his words!" and bursting into a new round of laughter without answering, Dave left them with whatever was amusing them, not realising it was actually him!

The evening had a light feeling after Jane and Sandra had their chat, when Sid and Dave finally lost a game and came and joined them, the conversation turned to the weekend and doing something a bit different, when Sid came up with an idea that he thought they would all enjoy "How about we go to Leeds for the day, get a late morning train, have a wander, a few drinks and something to eat?" looking at her boyfriend as she now considered Sid to be, Jane quickly whispered to Sandra "We could get something sexy for your weekend at the Corn Exchange, and I might get something for Sid as well!" seeing the smile on her face Sandra quickly said "You're on!" and slowly her plans were coming to fruition. Realising he had been accepted rather quickly, Sid meekly shrugged his shoulders and looked at Dave before saying "Looks like we have a date! Beer anyone?" and headed for the bar, with Dave getting up behind him wondering what had just happened.

Thursday and Friday were just typical early February dull non events, as the weather never got above 10 degrees and rain was always present, in various strengths from off the moors, so it was a very happy Sandra who arrived home on Friday teatime, slightly damp but looking forward to the weekend. Dave was coming round tonight, and then it suddenly struck her that if they were going to Leeds tomorrow, they wouldn't be able to go top Skipton to get her engagement ring. So it was a slightly deflated Sandra who opened the door to see a damp but beaming Dave looking at her. "You're a bit late boyfriend, I expected you half an hour ago" she said as he came through the door. "I had a driving lesson from my dad that went on a bit" he said taking off his coat and flat cap. "I'd forgotten about your Driving Test next week what with all we have been up to recently, how did it go do you think you can pass on Thursday?" she quickly added realising her mind was elsewhere.

"Well we went a bit further than normal, but I have one lesson next week and my dad thinks I should be okay" Dave quickly answered as Diane came downstairs and putting on her coat as she entered the kitchen she saw Dave and after asking how his parents were she put on a hat, before saying they were going to a birthday party for one of Jim's workmates but wouldn't be late so the house was theirs, with a wink that Sandra couldn't miss and which turned her cheeks red. Jim followed down the stairs a few minutes later putting on a winter coat, and wrapped up against the cold and rain they headed outside as the Taxi horn sounded. "Have a good night" said Sandra and closed the door to see a still beaming Dave looking at her. "Okay boyfriend what's got you so happy, apart from seeing me obviously!" she added as he moved to put his arms around her and kissed her softly to begin with and then more urgently, until Sandra pushed him away saying "It was seeing me then" and still unsure why he was in such a happy mood she went to the fridge to get a couple of bottles of beer to take into the Lounge. "Come on then Mr Smiley" she said to Dave as she headed to the comfort of the Lounge. Like a well trained animal he followed her into the Lounge and sat next to her on the sofa still with the smile still on his face. Handing him a bottle of Lager she looked at him and still no wiser said "Come on you'll burst soon if you don't tell me!" Looking at her bemused face he quickly gave her a kiss and taking a mouthful of beer sat facing her. Once he had swallowed his Dutch courage, he held her spare hand in his and suddenly realising he had a logistical problem took the bottle from her other hand, he stood up and placed both bottles on the side table before returning to sit next to her now holding both her hands in his. "Well girlfriend it's like I was saying my dad took me on a driving lesson a bit further than normal, and we ended up in Skipton, and it just so happens I had some business to complete in Skipton so....." but he never finished the sentence as Sandra realised all of a sudden why he had been smiling and wrapping her arms around him pulled him close for a long passionate kiss, which could have gone on for longer, but she suddenly realised that although she now knew the reason he had gone to Skipton, she wanted to see the result of his trip. Pulling away from him slightly she looked at his still smiling face, although it was now a bit too smug as she said "Can I see it ?" "No!" he said and watched as Sandra's face failed to comprehend what he said, but before she had time to say anything, he took the box out of his pocket and opening it said "But you can wear it!" and a split second later it was proudly sitting in situ on Sandra's third finger left hand, held up in the air for adoration as the tears started to roll down Sandra's face, and she buried her face in Dave's neck without a word as none were needed.

Saturday morning came at the Robertson household and Diane was shocked to see Sandra already up and the kettle on when she entered the kitchen at 09.00. "Want some toast mum?" she said as Diane sat at the table a bit perplexed. "Yes darling that would be lovely. You're in a good mood this morning did you and Dave a nice night in last night?" and desperate to tell her mum but somehow managing to keep their secrets she replied "Yes it was lovely we just planned our day out in Leeds with Sid and Jane, and talked about Dave's upcoming Driving Test. He went all the way to Skipton yesterday with his dad" before she realised she was heading into secret territory and changing the subject said "How was the party? I didn't hear you come in" Taking two mugs to the kettle Diane started to make the tea before answering "It was going well until a couple of workmates had a set to over a girl, and your dad had to step in. Kind of ruined the evening but I dare say they will sort it out on Monday at work" returning to finish making the tea, she suddenly remembered the toast and opening the fridge to get the butter she noticed that only two bottles of Lager had been taken. "Not thirsty last night by the looks of it Sandra" Wondering what her mum was alluding to she replied "No mum, as I said we just had a quiet night in, ready for today" and accepting the response Diane took the two mugs of tea and a plate of toast stopping at the bottom of the stairs "Just teasing darling you have a good day, see you when I see you" and with that she headed upstairs leaving Sandra mulling over what her mum was getting at, and deciding it wasn't worth any more thought she finished her cup of tea and set off upstairs to her bedroom to get ready for their trip out to Leeds. Choosing a warm comfortable outfit, she picked up a scarf and a pair of gloves to keep the wind away and happy with her look she left her room just as Tony headed towards the toilet. "Good night Tony?" she said and with no response as the door closed behind him she went downstairs, put her coat, hat, scarf and gloves on and convinced this outfit would keep her warm she set off to meet Dave at the bus stop at 10.05 for the bus into Town, and then the train to Leeds.

"Wow you look gorgeous and very warm girlfriend" said Dave as he moved in to kiss her at the bus stop. "Didn't expect the gloves, I won't be able to feel your warm hands" and as the words left his mouth he took hold of her left hand and feeling a bobble on the third finger he looked at her slightly guilty expression "I knew you wouldn't be able to resist!" at which she put her arms round him and quietly said into his ear "Well you should have seen your face last night, Mr Smiley!" and locked together they were quite in the moment, until the bus came around the corner and after waiting for the queue to board in front of them, they headed upstairs just reaching their seats as the bus lurched on its way around the Estate and into Town. Sid and Jane were waiting at the Train Station when they got there holding hands, at which Dave took his chance "Get you two all loved up holding hands in public!" at which Sid shot him down with a stern look and then realising Dave had misread his humour said "You should see what we do in private!"

thinking it would be an appropriate reply until the dig in his ribs from Jane told him it wasn't. "Really Sid get your mind out of the gutter!" she said, and a silence descended until the station announcement that the 11.14 train to Leeds was arriving at Platform 2 broke the spell and as the train slowly came into view and pulled to a stop, Sid in an effort to make amends opened the train door and ushering Sandra and Jane forward with his waved hand said "Ladies first" with a smile that Jane ignored. As the train set off and they sat on two double seats facing each other, the conversation started again as if the Platform conversation had never happened. "We should definitely try the Merrion Centre, Victoria Arcade and maybe the Corn Exchange" said Jane looking at Sandra with a wink that was reciprocated, but missed by Sid and Dave as they looked out of the dirty windows spattered by rain. "How about a couple of beers at the 'Scarborough Taps', then some shopping, then something to eat and a few beers on the way home?" said Sid without looking away from the window, which got no response as the train went into a tunnel on his first word and was drowned by the increase in noise. As the train exited the tunnel and with no one commenting on his plan Sid let it go, and carried on staring out of the window trying to work out where places he knew were on the line, as the train made its way on the Kirkdale Line through the valleys on its way to the final destination of Leeds.

Leaving Leeds Station they headed up the Headrow, two couples hand in hand and despite Sid's claim that he was parched, Jane kept him moving until they reached the Merrion Centre and as Sandra and Dave headed to the 'Jean Emporium', Sid angled Jane to the Pig and Whistle pub and deciding the principal that 'better the devil you know' applied, Jane let him have his moment of freedom which he would more than pay for later, they entered the pub which was surprisingly busy for 12.40 but it was a Saturday, so finding a table was impossible. Standing at the bar behind Sid as he got served it was only as they got their first mouthful of drinks that Dave and Sandra joined them, Sandra with a 'Jean Emporium' carrier bag containing a new pair of Levi's. Just managing to attract the attention of the increasingly busy barman, Dave ordered their usual and receiving his change he caught the end of a brief conversation Sandra and Jane were having, but made no sense as he didn't see Levi's as a sexy outfit. "This is a strange old pub" said Dave to Sid as they found a gap in the crowd they moved to a quieter part of the pub putting their drinks on a ledge, and the girls took the opportunity to go to the toilet. "Never been here before" said Sid taking a mouthful of his drink "Won't be coming back in a hurry either" he added after finishing his mouthful. "We'll find somewhere better when the girls get back, and then they'll probably want to do some more shopping so we'd best not get too comfortable, or it'll all go to pot!" As the girls returned Sandra held Dave's hand with her left hand and with a look that said they weren't staying, she finished her half of Lager, and allowing him time to finish his pint, she slowly led him to the door and they were out into the daylight before he could speak. "We've come here on a day out together, not a pub crawl Dave" she said as they waited outside for Sid and Jane to join them, and hearing the determination in her voice he quickly kissed her, as Sid and Jane joined them on the pavement. "Get a room will you" said Sid and the dig in his ribs from Jane told him he had erred again, but as he felt he had done nothing wrong he added "What!" as Jane pulled his hand, and they headed for the Victoria Arcade and Sid knew he would have to wait for another drink, it was just how long he was worried about, as the two couples made their way down Merrion Street and onto Briggate which was by now thronged with pedestrians taking advantage of the last of the post Christmas sales and the clement weather, which had eased as the day went by.

"We're going in here" said Jane as she took Sandra's left hand, and they disappeared into 'Chelsea Girl' leaving Sid and Dave standing outside watching pedestrians playing skittles with each other, until their return some 10 minutes later each holding a 'Chelsea Girl' carrier bag, but with no hint as to what they had bought, and none offered. They each hooked up and headed further down Briggate until they came to a 'Tammy Girl" shop at which the girls looked at each other and handing their carrier bags to their respective boyfriends, Sandra with a kiss for Dave, and Jane with a look that said 'Don't say anything'. Some 15 minutes later the girls returned with a colourful 'Tammy Girl' carrier bag each, and in mid conversation as they reached Sid and Dave, Jane said "We could do with a break, so if you want we could go for a drink and maybe something to eat would be nice" and putting her arm through Sid's who had his hands in his pockets, a smile formed on his face "Finally" he said and then pondered where they could go as they joined the slowly moving masses. "Here" he said turning into an alleyway which hid the Ship Inn, whose advertising board he had nearly fallen over, unable to see it until the person in front of him had gone round it. With Jane following his lead as they were hooked up, Dave and Sandra followed them down the alleyway entering a busy but long pub, where Sid spotted a table towards the back, and waving his hand to Jane that she should go in that direction, he returned to try to get the attention of the barman. As the girls headed for the table with their carrier bags Dave waited behind him not quite as desperate for a drink as Sid, but ready for another nonetheless. Taking the girls drinks from Sid, Dave headed for where the girls had managed to set up camp with their purchases. "Thanks boyfriend" said Sandra as Dave put their drinks down "Didn't you fancy one yourself?" she finished as he sat down without a drink, but before Dave could comment, a Pint of Lager arrived in front of him swiftly followed by a second as Sid sat down next to him and lifting the drink to his mouth took a sizeable mouthful before saying "Thirsty work this shopping" and with a smile from Jane, he felt he was back in her good books.

"Well this is better than I thought it would be" said Sid before realising he was on dodgy ground again, and added "The beer I meant!" hoping he had got away with it, but not taking chances he changed the conversation and went on "Why don't we have a couple more here as we have a table, and then we can go down by the Corn Exchange where Cuban Heels is, one of the guys at work said is really good. What do you think?" The silence was interrupted by Jane giving him a kiss on the cheek and said "You never fail to surprise me!" with a smirk on his face, he now knew he was definitely back in her good books, but not really sure why as he had only suggested a drink and something to eat, I'll never understand women he thought, before realising his drink was nearly finished and returning to form said "Dave it's your round, get some crisps while you're there I'm starving! I'll give you a hand" already getting up, as Sandra and Jane looked at each other before bursting out in laughter which Sid missed, already halfway to the bar with Dave following behind with a £10 note already in his hand. "Let me see it then Sandra" said Jane when they were alone. Almost ready to deny its existence, she took off her gloves for the first time today and holding up her left hand offered it up for Jane to see. "Well that explains a lot young lady. I thought you were going to wait to get engaged on your 19th Birthday but maybe things have move on at some pace. It is beautiful you must be very happy" Trying to find the words that expressed her feelings she finally said "I'm so lucky I sometimes have to stop and wonder is it me that this is happening to. It's so hard to keep it a secret I haven't even told my mum yet, but it was close this morning" and explaining how Dave had been to Skipton to get the ring and surprising her with it last night, she almost started to cry but seeing Dave returning from the bar, she just had time to say "I'd like it to stay a secret if that's okay" as Jane leant in to whisper in her ear before Dave got to the table "Your secret if safe, but we'll definitely have to splash out in the lingerie boutique!" and sitting back as Sid arrived with two pints, Dave having gone to the toilet after putting their drinks down, Jane gave Sandra a look that Sid had no chance of reading, even if he wasn't already taking a drink of his new pint.

Leaving the Ship Inn after 'one for the road' they automatically, as couples do when times are good hooked up, they initially squinted at the remaining daylight, as they exited the dark alleyway. The Corn Exchange was merely a short walk along King Edward Street onto Vicar Lane. With the Corn Exchange in view, it took Jane a few minutes to work out a plan to separate the couples as they neared the building. "Sid, you and Dave go and have a drink at Cuban Heels as we'll probably have to wait for a table and we'll see you there in a few minutes. We girls need to visit a certain shop that you wouldn't be comfortable with!" and without any need for further information about girls shops Sid called Dave over and explained the amended plan, and with an immediate consensus of let's leave them to it, Dave gave Sandra a kiss on the cheek and with a joint "See you there!" from Sandra and Jane, the none the wiser Sid and Dave were already 10 yards away, when Jane took Sandra's hand and led them up the stairs and into the Corn Exchange. After 30 minutes and visiting three bespoke lingerie shops it was in the Victoria's Secret boutique that they both found something that they felt happy with, although it had taken several trips to the changing rooms before they each confirmed the other had made a suitable choice. Out went some stocking and suspender sets that Jane felt were wrong for Sandra, as well as a scarlet red Basque, but the white satin two piece outfit she had finally chosen got the thumbs up from Jane, as she stood in the changing room feeling slightly self conscious , but that was soon forgotten as Jane came out of her booth wearing a red baby doll outfit that left little to the imagination, but the smile on her face and her confidence as she twirled around left no doubt in Sandra's mind that this was the one Jane wanted "Sid will love it!" merely sealed the deal, and getting dressed Sandra wondered when she would be ready for an outfit like Jane's and blushed at the thought as she exited the booth and went to pay for her outfit thinking 'I hope Dave loves it!'

Arriving at Cuban Heels, Sandra held the door open and as Jane went inside she saw Sid and Dave sat at a table looking at a menu each. "You took your time, get what you wanted" said Sid as they sat down, before he saw the Victoria's Secret bag in Jane's hand, and his demeanour changed as he finished "Not a problem Dave here, has been filling me in on a few things while you ladies have been..." and losing his thread as Jane sat next to him and slightly opened the bag so he could see her purchase. "Anyway have a look at the menu ladies and I'll get us some more drinks" he finally managed to finish, handing Jane his menu and headed to the bar out of habit. As the waiter took his drinks order at the bar, Sid took a long look at Jane trying to imagine what she looked like in the outfit she had bought herself. "Sir, I'll bring your drinks to the table" said the waiter which brought him back to earth, as he headed back to the table and taking his seat kissed Jane on the cheek "What was that for?" she said looking at him "Well you know" he replied unable to think of anything to add "Oh I know Sid" as she squeezed his leg with her spare hand and left it there, as the waiter arrived with their tray of drinks. "Ready to order ladies and gentlemen?" he said, placing the drinks down and with a nod all round he took out his order pad, once everyone had order he finished with "Gracias" and headed for the kitchen leaving two very happy couples sat chatting about nothing in particular, but looking forward to the future and the unknown promises it brings.

After their meal which was both original, plentiful and would definitely justify a return visit, they set off for the train station full of food and drink linked up as couples, and even Sid had had his fill not helped by finishing off Jane's Banoffee desert. "Top day that!" said Sid to no one in particular as they stood on the platform waiting for the 10.42 train to Kirkdale, which unsurprisingly was running 2 minutes late. As the train pulled in it was already half full so they had to split up into couples, and sit apart and as the train pulled away, Sandra leant into Dave who put his arm round her and snuggled into him, as he looked out at a black dirty window and as they went through the first tunnel he realised she had fallen asleep and slowly moving her hair from her face kissed her forehead as the train rumbled onwards to Kirkdale. Sid and Jane were sat a few seats back and there was no chance of sleep as Sid wanted to find out what was in the Victoria's Secret bag. "You'll have to wait until we get home Sid, it's not like I'm going to wear it on a train!" and giving him a kiss she settled into his shoulder for the rest of the journey, managing to fall asleep just as the train slowed to arrive at Kirkdale station. With a dig in her ribs from Sid, they stood up as the train stuttered to a halt and they passed Sandra and Dave who were getting their carrier bags in order ready to leave, at which Sid looked at Jane and seeing the Victoria's Secret bag missing was heading back to their seats as a hand pulled on his jacket "Lost something Sid?" said Jane with a grin and pulled the Victoria's Secret bag, part out from inside the Tammy Girl bag she had in her left hand. Seeing his dreams in safe hands he caught her up on the platform "Cruel!" and taking her hand they headed for the Taxi rank with Dave and Sandra following a few feet behind, having stopped for a kiss as was their habit. Sharing a Taxi Sandra was dropped off first with a kiss that went on longer than Dave expected, and with an accepted agreement for Dave to come round to Sandra tomorrow the Taxi headed for the other side of the estate, and with little to talk about as Sid was definitely concentrating on something, Dave said "See you" as he shut the Taxi door and headed for his door with a tired but happy demeanour on a very successful day out.

◆ ◆ ◆

Chapter 15

Sat at the kitchen table as the clock struck 11.00 the Robertson family were on the second pot of tea of the day as the last bacon butty was hovered up by a now sobering up Tony "Top breakfast mum" he said as he added brown sauce to the open butty and closing it with his palm took a bite without saying another word. "Glad you appreciate my cooking" Diane said pouring another mug of tea for Jim. "Well what is everyone doing today then?" she added before putting the teapot down waiting for an answer" "Dave's coming round about midday and we'll probably just go for a long walk as we had a long day yesterday in Leeds, what are you two doing mum?" "Well your dad and I are going out for a drive this afternoon and plan on a Sunday lunch somewhere as I don't feel like cooking so we'll be put all afternoon" before she had a chance to add anything else Tony, who had by now finished his second bacon butty took a sip of tea and said "I'm meeting Gill and going to the pictures" hardly had he got the words out than Sandra responded "Gill from School?" "Yeah Gill from school sis, bumped into her and her mate Ann at the Old Cock last night watching a band with Paul. I asked her out, so we're off to see Mad Max this afternoon after a few drinks. Anyway any more tea in the pot mum?" The silence continued until the kettle clicked off and with a clinking of the tea pot lid as a fresh pot was completed and put on the table, Tony realised Sandra had seen Mad Max last week. "Any good sis?" realising Tony was referring to the film she hardly thought about it before responding "I'm sure you will like it I'm not sure whether Gill will though, it's a bit gruesome in parts, not a love story that's for sure!" "Right I'm going for a shave and then your mum and I will be off so remember to lock up when you leave you two" said Jim already out of his seat and heading for the stairs at which Diane started clearing up the table leaving Tony with the pot of tea contemplating something but not willing to add to his earlier announcement. As Diane finished tidying up and went upstairs to join Jim, Sandra offered a still silent Tony some advice "You could always go to see Endless Love instead, it's got Brooke Shields in it" "Nah sis, Mad Max for me, if she's scared she can always look away!". Finishing his mug of tea without another word he left Sandra in the kitchen clearing up as there was a knock on the door and the silhouette of a Flat cap through the top glass of the door meant no introductions were needed. As Dave entered and closed the door behind him, he turned round into Sandra holding out her arms and taking the opportunity kissed her with a growing urgency that was abruptly curtailed by Diane as she came down the stairs followed by Jim a few steps behind."Hello Dave, did you have a nice time in Leeds yesterday?" she said as they quickly parted. "It was a Top Day thanks Mrs Rob.... Diane" he automatically replied taking Sid's comment from last night and added "We all really enjoyed ourselves thanks". "Good I'm glad it was worth it, Jim and I are going out for the day and Tony is off out on a date would you believe it, so the house is yours. Anyway Dave, if I don't see you before good luck with the Driving Test this week" putting on her coat and hat she waited for Jim to find the car keys and as they headed for the door Jim turned at the last moment and said "Dave, just take it easy on the test, sticking to the speed limits is important, easy way to fail that, but I'm sure you'll be fine good luck!" and they were out of the door before he could respond. Returning to the arms that Sandra held out again they were deep into tongue tag when Tony came bounding down the stairs hair combed and throwing on a coat rather than his usual leather jacket, he headed for the door, stopping at the last moment to check he had a key and feeling its impression in his jean pocket he opened the door shouted "See you later" and was gone, leaving Sandra and Dave alone with an empty house.

As they parted and it sank in that they were alone Sandra took Dave's hand and led him upstairs to her bedroom and despite the house being empty she closed the door. Leading Dave to sit on her bed and releasing his hand she went to her wardrobe opening the door to find her purchases from yesterday. As a slightly bemused Dave sat on the bed she took out the Tammy Girl bag although she was tempted to take the Victoria's Secret bag instead, but that could wait until next weekend. "I thought you might like to see what your girlfriend bought in Leeds" she said opening the bag and taking out the contents "I thought this might be nice to wear next weekend for dinner at the Hotel" as she held up a floor length red one piece dress with spaghetti straps in front of her, before he could say anything she hung it on the wardrobe door and took off her sweatshirt exposing her bare breasts, aware of the silence she turned slightly and took off her tracksuit bottoms and standing for a second with just her Lace Thong knickers on, she faced him with a smile on her face and a look of awe on his, before she turned to the wardrobe and taking the dress rolled it up in her hands before she put it over her head and let it fall onto her shoulders. Pulling the dress down so it hung properly she looked at Dave before twisting to the right and left as she felt the material on her legs. "Well you haven't said anything, don't you like it......boyfriend!" "I don't think we'll be going to Dinner if you wear that ... girlfriend!" and getting up from the bed he slowly closed on her until his lips met hers and the answer she expected and wanted went unspoken.

As they found their way slowly step by step back to her bed, Dave gently eased one strap off her left shoulder exposing her breast before using his other hand to nudge the strap off her right shoulder and as the dress dropped to her waist they lay slowly down onto the bed still entwined in a lingering kiss that was under no threat of stopping. Feeling her exposure Sandra thought about where this might be going for a second and then leaned into him, as he found her nipples with his fingers and her arousal increased. Feeling his lips start to pull away she put her arms around his neck as he moved his head lower down her body and started to kiss her breasts and nipples with his tongue making circles on her nipples each one feeling more alert as he moved across her chest with Sandra's hands on his head guiding him, as the intensity increased and she shivered slightly as he pinched her nipples and a sensation she hadn't felt before went through her. Moving back to kiss her open mouth Dave left his hand on her breast, while putting his other arm around her shoulders before slowly lowering his hand down her breasts, across her stomach, and under the waistband of the dress. Feeling no denial he moved his hand into the top of her knickers as his fingertips found and slowly stroked her clitoris, as she moved her right foot up the bed to rest sideways onto her other leg opening up the gap between her legs as his fingers entered her vagina and she felt his hard penis against her thigh. Feeling the movement of his fingers inside her as he entered her, slowly at first and then more urgently as he rhythmically pushed his finger in and out of her now moist vagina, she moved her right hand from behind his head moving it down his body until she found his bulging penis under his jeans. With the palm of her hand she started rubbing his trapped penis until slowly she moved her hand and she found the top of his zip and pulled it down. She moved her fingers inside his jeans and into his Y fronts, slowly putting her fingers around the shaft, she released his erect penis from his jeans until it was standing exposed and rigid in her fingers for the first time. Slowly working up and down his penis with her hand she felt her knickers being pushed down onto her legs as Dave exposed her further by pulling up the dress from the bottom so it was gathered around her waist with her breasts and her dark bush now naked to the sky as it looked in through the window.

The door slam stopped them in their tracks. Almost naked and with her hand around Dave's erect penis they could hear someone downstairs at which Sandra quickly got off the bed leaving a bemused Dave propped up on one arm and his penis protruding erect out of his jeans. As Sandra took off her dishevelled dress, which did Dave no favours, she quickly pulled up her knickers, found a bra, put on a pair of jeans and a top from the wardrobe she had left open in her haste. Dave wrestled his penis into his jeans and standing up he zipped them up before moving next to a now fully clothed Sandra, planting a butterfly kiss on her lips he said "Well that girlfriend, was fun, but shall we wait until next week when there will be no interruptions and you can show me what you bought from Victoria's Secret" as he saw the bag at the bottom of the open wardrobe. The slap on his shoulder told him all he needed to know as they headed downstairs to find the unexpected visitor that was thankfully Tony not her mum and dad, and Gill sitting in the Lounge suddenly caught in the act as Tony removed his hand from under Gill's jumper. "Oh hi sis, didn't expect to find you in!" "I can see that "Sandra quickly replied as a red faced Gill smoothed her jumper but before there was any more embarrassment she added "We're going out for the afternoon so the house is yours, oh one thing, don't forget to lock the door, you wouldn't want to be disturbed!" heading for the door as her own face started to turn red Sandra took Dave's hand and they found their coats and hats. Putting them on as they went down the garden path they reached the gate and heard a firm key lock the door behind them as they both burst into laughter.

"Well boyfriend that was a close call!" Sandra said as they headed out of the Estate onto the Bedlow Moor footpath "Good job it wasn't your mum and dad!" Dave replied before wiping his forehead with the back of his left hand as he squeezed Sandra's hand in his right and found she had put on her engagement ring. "I just like wearing it, no one will know what's in my hand when I have my gloves on" she said as he played with her finger and suddenly realising what she had said had a double meaning, she hoped he had missed it, but the fit to burst smile told her he hadn't, and with a speed that surprised herself proudly stated "Wrong hand anyway!" before realising she had done it again as Dave let go of her hand and bent over double trying not to cry, while she slapped him on the arm nearest her before she curtly finished "Boys and their toys!" at which she walked off leaving Dave to calm down until her last comment cemented in his head and he was off again.

Catching up with her after she had gone some 50 feet ahead, Dave took her left hand in his and put his arm around her shoulders. "Girlfriend you really are one in a million, beautiful, sexy, funny ……. and mine!" at which she smiled and waited for the kiss that landed on her lips just as she expected as they headed out onto the moors both silently pondering after a close call that could easily have been a lasting lifetime memory of an afternoon fumble in her bedroom. Dave spoke first as they could see the Bedlow Arms on the horizon "Sandra……..do you regret not …. well, you know … not doing it?" With a moment's hesitation she replied "Maybe a bit, as we were rather well …………. but in all honesty, next week on our own, in our own time, in our own bed ……….with no interruptions ………will be so much better, and like you said the other day it will be our forever memory for life!"

Some 20 minutes later they arrived at the Bedlow Arms and as Sandra went to the toilet, Dave went to the bar which was quite busy, as was usual on a Sunday afternoon, so when Sandra returned Dave was just getting served at the bar. Looking around for a table, she spotted a small table for two by the window which would do nicely, putting a hand on Dave's shoulder she indicated with her hand and headed for the table with Dave nodding that he would follow with their drinks. Arriving with their drinks and taking off his coat to put on top of Sandra's on a spare buffet, Dave pulled out the page he had ripped from the Travel Agents brochure with the Hotel they were going to stay at on Valentine's Day. "We should be there for lunchtime if the train timetable is anything to go by so we could have maybe have lunch, or go for a walk and wait for dinner. What do you think?" he finished handing the page to her "Oh I think a walk would be best, York has these wonderful city walls you can walk on and then there is the Minster and the Shambles, I'm not sure we'll have time to squeeze any-thing else in ....except of course!" and finishing without fin-ishing, she took a drink as her cheeks turned red for the second time today.

As the light faded and the warmth of the wood fire by bar filled the room, Sandra realised they hadn't really worked out the coming week with all that it encompassed so as they fin-ished their drink she got up and picking up the empty glasses she headed for the bar with a smile and a mouthed 'I'll get these'. Seeing a space at the end of the bar away from the fire she waited her turn to be served and when the barman took her order "A pint and a half of Lager please!", a voice behind her said "I'll get those and a pint and a half of bitter please" as her father moved to take her place at the bar. "Thanks dad, didn't expect to see you here, where's mum?" "Gone to the La-dies, she'll be back in a minute". The barman returned with the drinks and looking around Jim said "Can we join you, or do you youngsters need your space?" "Of course you can join us, but we will need to move to a new table but there's one over there she said, pointing towards the bay window as Diane joined them. "Hello darling didn't expect to bump into you!" "We come here when we want a decent walk and the weather isn't too bad" Sandra said taking their drinks and making for the larger table with a nod towards Dave as they went past the table he was still sat at on his own. Picking up their coats he headed after Sandra as Diane made it to the table first. "Well this is a nice surprise, I must say" Diane said and taking a sip of her drink she looked around at the rest of the pub, resting her hand on Jim's arm just as he was about to take a drink added

"We used to come courting here didn't we Jim" at which he took a drink and nodding said "Yes this used to be our hide-away, none of our friends would ever come here, too posh they used to say, still is a bit, but yes this place brings back memories" and taking another drink settled down to reminisce for a few minutes, as Sandra listened as her mum explained about their day out and deciding to have a drink on the way home at one of their old haunts.

"So what have you two been up to today since we left" Diane said as the conversation stalled "Nothing much mum just a cup of tea and a bit of a chat nothing much at all really" Sandra said avoiding any mention of Tony and his unscheduled return. "So nothing much apart from getting engaged that is!" Diane quickly replied having noticed the ring on Sandra's hand that was no longer gloved. Sandra looked at Dave and with no support forthcoming she let the silence continue until Diane gave her a hug "Couldn't be happier for you both, I wish Jim was as romantic as Dave, let's have a look" taking her hand without waiting "It's lovely no wonder you couldn't wait to wear it. Do Mary and Alan know?" "No mum, and you weren't supposed to know either" Sandra quickly stated looking at Dave for support where there was none."Jim, Sandra and Dave have got engaged isn't that great news!" The smile almost got away with it but Jim knew he would have to do better "Shall I get us all a drink to celebrate, come on Dave give us a hand" and retreating to the bar Sandra and Diane were left with half a drink each as their men propped up the bar. "Honestly Sandra Congratulations and if you don't want we won't tell anyone until your 19th Birthday but I doubt you will be able to keep it secret yourself. You know at least Dave tried to make an honest woman of you. Jim and I went away for the weekend when we were courting and buying me a ring was the last thing on his mind!" "Mum!" a stunned Sandra loudly said, as Dave and Jim returned with another round of drinks "Jim, just telling Sandra about of first weekend away when we were courting, didn't buy me an Engagement ring did you?" Putting down the drinks Jim smiled at Diane and said "No dear I didn't, I bought you a Camisole and that was a waste of money the amount of time you had it on!" and with a wink at Dave he sat down with a smile on his face that Diane couldn't and wouldn't ever remove.

Monday arrived and with it a wind that chased the litter across and down the street, as Sandra crossed over the road to the Council Offices and headed to the Planning Department for her second week in what was now her new career. Waving at Peggy with a hand sign of an imaginary cup which received a thumbs up response, as she made her way to the Administration section, Sandra was already taking her coat and hat off as she went through the door. Seeing Mrs Shaw and greeting her with a confident "Good morning", Sandra hung her coat up and sitting down at her desk started to go through the in tray when she realised she wasn't wearing her Engagement ring, momentarily she thought about checking her coat, before remembering she had taken it off this morning before her shower. There was still a small imprint where it had been all weekend when she was brought back to reality as Mrs Shaw arrived at her desk. "Sandra, there's a lot to get through this week and I know it's only your second week but if you concentrate on sorting out the oldest planning documents this morning into chronological order as per our system checking for any updates, I'll go through them with you this afternoon so you can get a better idea of how we work. If you need any help just ask. I won't bite!" and with that she headed out of the door with a pile of folders. Sandra started to work her way through her in tray and by lunchtime with a couple of breaks for advice, she felt she had done a good job on the 94 folders now stacked up on her desk, ready for the afternoon.

Stood waiting for Peggy on the Council steps Sandra couldn't resist playing with her empty finger so she didn't hear Peggy come up behind her until she was hooked up with her as her hand stayed in her pocket hiding a secret that she was dying to release "A penny for them, or should I just ask how Dave is!" Peggy said as they set off for the Brazilian cafe "He's got his Driving Test on Thursday so fingers crossed, I do hope he passes" "He'll be fine, when he sets his mind on something he doesn't give up until he succeeds. Don't you remember all the good mornings and hellos when he came into our office, he was always looking at you, but you usually had your head down, we all knew except you!" said Peggy and realising Sandra really had no idea she shook her head and smiling at Sandra opened the cafe door to let her go first. Seeing Sharon and Jo already sat with their drinks, Sandra ordered for her and Peggy and when the coffees arrived they joined them at their table, just as Jo finished complaining about Mrs Anderson and with hardly a break, she carried on to tell her story of her weekend."Well, let me tell you about my weekend. Chris picked me up on Saturday teatime and dropped me off on Sunday teatime" and taking a drink she looked around the cafe waiting for a reaction and when none came she continued "So you don't want to hear about my weekend then?" leaving the question in mid air "Jo, just tell us before you burst, will you" said Sharon shaking her head. "We went to the football, it was freezing and no, I don't know who won. Chris seemed to enjoy it but I didn't know he could swear so much! Anyway then we went into Town for a Pizza and had a couple of drinks before we went back to his for the evening." "And" said Sharon "And he has a log fire so we got all cosy" "and get on with it" said Sharon getting bored "and his carpet needs cleaning is all I'm going to say" as she finished with a recollection of their fireside lovemaking which she definitely wasn't going to share. "So you had sex in front of the fire is that what you are saying" Sharon quickly said, taking Jo's memories of the evening down a peg or two. Seeing the disappointment rising in Jo's face, Peggy decided to raise the mood and give them chapter and verse of her weekend with Andy "Right you lot, no interrupting or I won't finish" she started her short story "Andy picked me up on Friday night and we went to a party for one of his friends at the Royal Oak which was excellent, the DJ really knew his stuff and there were a few of my old schoolmates there so got all the gossip, anyway we had a bit too much to drink and well I ended up staying at his on Friday night, nothing happened before you ask Sharon, we just slept in the same bed. In the morning he brought me a cup of tea and toast and we just talked for a while before he went to have a shower. I don't think he was expecting me to join him but for some reason, which I'm still not sure where it came from, I crept into the bathroom and slowly got into the shower without him knowing as he was washing his hair and couldn't see me. So when I put my arms around him he just kind of groaned and turned to face me, and then I could tell that he was happy to see me as his dick hit my stomach. That's as far as I am going the rest you can imagine." A brief silence followed before not surprisingly Sharon said "Good for you Peggy, can't beat a bit of clean sex! The rest of the day is going to be dull after that, not sure I'll be able to concentrate without thinking of you and Andy soaping each other up" "I knew you couldn't resist Sharon!, anyway it's time to get back to work before you think of any more clean jokes in your dirty mind" and pleased at her response Peggy led them out into the wind and back to work as she smiled at the memory of the look on Andy's face in the shower. Happy doesn't do it justice she thought.

Monday afternoon quickly went as Sandra and Mrs Shaw ploughed through the stack of files Sandra had worked on in the morning, as the day neared an end she felt that she could probably manage this part of the job on her own next time, and as she put on her coat Mrs Shaw walked her out of the office with a "Well done this afternoon Sandra, I know it's a lot to take in but once you get the basics sorted I think you'll do just fine. Your course at the end of the month will help, but I just wanted you to know you're doing well, see you tomorrow" and without looking back she headed off to the car park at the back of the building, leaving Sandra standing at the top of the steps putting her hat on ready for the walk to the bus station, when a hand knocked her hat off and turning round to see who it was the kiss on her lips gave her the answer. "Hello girlfriend" Dave said once he had pulled away from the kiss and bending down he retrieved her hat and placing it on her head he patted it down with a little smile "There that's better" he said just as Sandra took it off and checking it was now the right way round pulled it onto her head before taking his hand and heading towards the bus station she realised he must have finished early and with a slight questionable look on her face she said "What are you doing finishing early on a Monday?" "Got a driving lesson and Mr Normanton said I could go early, if I made it up tomorrow so here I am" he replied as they neared their stop. The bus pulled in as they joined the end of the queue, sitting upstairs as downstairs was full, Dave said as the bus set off." This time next week there'll be no more buses for us, I'll be able to give you a lift home" and squeezing Sandra's hand continued " My Dad told me this morning that there's a guy at work that's getting a company car and so he's selling his. It's an old Fiesta but it will do for a start. He said if he can get it for a decent price, he'll sort the money out" Bringing him back to earth Sandra quietly said "That's presuming you pass your test" but not to be put off Dave rapidly answered without thinking "If I put my mind to something I usually succeed" and as he kissed her cheek she wondered where she had heard that recently.

Thursday came, and with it a sense of anxiety for Sandra as she hadn't seen Dave since their unscheduled Monday meeting. He was confident of passing his Driving Test this morning, but she was still nervous, as this was a part of Dave's plans and he hated not to succeed. They had spoken on the phone last night and she thought he sounded confident, but they had mainly talked around the weekend coming up, arranging train times and things to see in York, and there was always that unspoken thought about the first night they would spend together, another step in the plans that were now theirs, not just Dave's. The sound of Sam Brown from the mailroom arriving with a new batch of work brought her back to her work as Mrs Shaw followed him through the door. "Sandra can you give Sam a hand with these please?" she said without stopping as she headed to her desk. Sam looked put out, as if he couldn't manage his workload, but handing Sandra an armful of folders he smiled and said "Settling in okay Sandra?" taking the folders in both hands she relied "Early days yet Sam, but working out fine so far, Mrs Shaw is helping me settle in and it's more interesting than just doing Administration." Quickly with a sense of angst he said "Wouldn't know, all I get to do is do this four times a day around the building, maybe I'll apply for your old job!" "Oh I'm sorry I didn't mean it like that" she quickly countered. "It's okay Sandra I know you didn't, anyway I'd probably get eaten alive by the likes of Sharon and Jo, so maybe I'll stay where I am" he replied with a smile "No Sam, you go for it and Sharon and Jo are really nice, I'll put in good word if you want!" she said with a raise of her eyebrows "You could do worse!" she finished and tapping him on the arm she headed back to her desk trying to imagine Sam and Sharon together, but she shook her head as she sat down. Now Jo and Sam might work she considered, opening the first folder and all thoughts of the Driving Test which was currently happening were gone from her mind. Lunchtime came suddenly, as Sandra was engrossed with her new set of folders, when a tap on the door made her look up and she saw Peggy waving her hand to encourage her to finish. Putting down a particularly fat folder, she headed for the door and a desire for a coffee, and maybe a piece of cake suddenly hit her as they left the building, all thoughts of Dave's Driving Test buried by her hunger.

The afternoon disappeared for Sandra faster than the pile of folders she was working on, and when Sam arrived with the end of the day mailroom run, she realised despite her best efforts there were still around a dozen folders that she had yet to finish, with a half plan in mind she offered to stay a little late to finish them off to which Mrs Shaw said "That's fine Sandra", delighted that her new employee was settling in as she herself headed for the door putting on her coat leaving Sandra alone in the office. Finally finishing the last folder ,as the clock moved towards half past five Sandra picked up her coat from behind the stationery door and headed out of the office suddenly realising her plan may not be one of her best, if things hadn't gone well for Dave and his Driving Test this morning. Arriving at the bus station she saw Dave waiting at their stop, despite seeing her he had a somewhat bemused look on his face which Sandra took as negative, but which she actually couldn't read. "Hello girlfriend" he said planting a kiss on her lips which still didn't ease her sense of uncertainty. "Been waiting here for half an hour, I thought maybe you had got an early bus so was going to get on this one" Still unsure how to read his demeanour she replied " I stayed behind to finish some work thinking we could get the bus together" and realising her plan had gone wrong added "Sorry". The bus arrived on time and as they were at the front of the queue, due to Dave being early, they boarded the bus but it wasn't until they were sat upstairs that Sandra plucked up courage to ask the question, to which she still had no idea what the answer would be as Dave was giving nothing away. "Good day boyfriend?" she started "Yeah fine, plenty to do" How about you girlfriend, you must have been busy staying late" he countered. "Dave! Will you just tell me how the Driving Test went don't keep me hanging on!" she said firmly squeezing his hand. As he turned his head and whispered in her ear "No more buses for us!" firmly squeezing her hand, he sat back as a huge grin spread across his face. "You are so hard to read sometimes, I was worried you had failed" before adding "I should have known better, if you are going to do something you usually succeed. Well done boyfriend, I'll have to think of a present for you for passing" and leaning into his shoulder she heard him say quietly "I can wait until Saturday!" as his grin became an almost permanent feature as he looked directly ahead lost in thought.

Friday opened with a dull but dry day as Sandra caught the bus to work, just catching Sharon at the door of the Council Offices and agreeing to meet at lunchtime, which was almost an unwritten agreement nowadays they said "See you" at the same time as they made their way to their different offices. Sam from the mailroom had been and gone before Sandra had arrived, as evident by the pile of folders as well as some files that now sat on her desk. "Morning Sandra did you finish those folders last night" said Mrs Shaw as she took off her coat and hanging it up made her way towards Sandra's desk. "Yes Mrs Shaw only took half an hour, but it meant I have a clean start today" she responded. "Excellent, well looks like you have enough to keep you busy today, but let me know when you get to the Estates files, and I'll show you how we deal with them as you haven't done them before" and with that she left the office and Sandra settled down to make inroads into the folders some of which were definitely seeing the light of day for the first time on some years. Lunchtime soon came around and meeting Peggy, Jo and Sharon on the Council Office steps, the quartet set off for the Carousel cafe and a catch up before the weekend.

"So what are you lovebirds doing this weekend?" Sharon said and taking a frothy sip of her coffee awaited the response from Sandra when Jo said "Well Chris is taking me out for a meal for Valentine's and he has promised me a surprise!" "Jo, I was asking Sandra not you although the way you are going on I might have to call you and Chris lovebirds, and Sandra and Dave just the old couple!" and sitting back Sharon waited for a response "Well I don't mind being an old couple" Sandra replied at which Sharon pretended to put her fingers down her throat and said "Yuk" before smiling at Sandra and addressing Jo "Well you lovebirds have a nice time, I hope Chris's surprise doesn't involve handcuffs!" at which she burst out in laughter as Jo's face turned bright red and failing to find an answer to Sharon she took a sip of her coffee as Sandra tried to steer the questioning away from her. "So Peggy are you and Andy doing anything this weekend?" but Sharon was having none of it as she said "So what are the old couple doing this weekend Sandra?" and despite feeling a bit trapped she gave Sharon a little ammunition but not enough to kill her."We thought we might go to York on Saturday and have a day out. There is plenty to do and it's not far on the train" she finished. "Oh God you two really are the old couple. Peggy, tell me you and Andy are going to have some good clean fun this weekend!" and with a wink alluding to last weekend's shower story Sharon paused hoping for something to lighten up the lunchtime. "Well we were planning on getting to know each other a bit more, so the plan is to meet some of his friends on Saturday for lunch and then we'll see what happens with the rest of the day and the weekend but I am staying at his so I've bought him a soap on a rope just in case!" Peggy finished with a smile on her face and realising Sharon was avoiding telling her own story she quickly challenged her "Well I'm having good clean fun as you say Sharon, but what about you? You've been very quiet about your plans". Not one to be put off Sharon finished her coffee, and with a smirk that hinted at much more she quietly said "Mick is coming down from Catterick tonight, he said he would be in full uniform so he said he wants me in uniform too. So I've got my old school girls uniform out so he can teach me a few lessons" at which she burst out in laughter which they all joined in together before she added "It only fits where it touches so I hope I don't get disciplined too much!" at which they all roared with laughter such that the rest of the cafe customers looked at their table, which made it even worse and once the laughter has subsided a little Peggy said "Come on you lot back to work, or I'll have to discipline you all!" at which the laughter started again and was still in full flow as they left the cafe and made their way to the Council Offices. Parting upon entering the offices the "Have a great weekend" resounded across the foyer as they left to go to their respective offices, with Sandra in particular grateful for being let off easy over lunch, but intrinsically wondering who could possibly have a weekend that would better hers.

Friday night had been arranged as a quiet night as the weekend was going to be so important for both of them. Dave headed for Sandra's house on Church Street and it was almost 8pm when he arrived, and within a few minutes as Sandra was ready and just had a coat to put on they were out and off to the Malt Shovel, hand in hand, happy and relieved that the week was behind them with a positive outcome and the future ahead lay wide open for them. Arriving at the Malt Shovel they went to the bar together and with each holding their respective drinks they found a table in the snug and finally after a drink Dave turned to Sandra and with a quick peck on the lips said "I hope you're looking forward to tomorrow as much as I am! That is the whole going away bit, and York and everything I mean as well as ......" finding Dave's comments amusing she let him carry on as he continued "Wonder if they have boiled eggs for breakfast?" at which she took his hand and as a little smile came over her face, she took a drink before looking at him, with an uncomfortable look on his face. "Boyfriend I think you should stop thinking about tomorrow. It will be a weekend to remember forever and I'm looking forward to our first night together. I've even bought a present for you, well actually for us but then you know that after Sunday afternoon, don't you " and as the embarrassment flooded his face she put her drink down and leant into his shoulder and whispered into his ear "I do hope you've still got those condoms I bought in the Bedlow Arms" and with a smile that told him everything was going to be alright he downed half of his glass and put his arm round her as they sat each with their own thoughts about the impending weekend, and its implications for them and their future.

They were brought out of their moment as Sid and Jane arrived and joined them, before after one drink, Dave and Sid made for the pool table leaving Jane and Sandra to catch up since their day in Leeds. "So you ready for your big weekend then" Jane said after they were alone."I think so, just think we'll take it easy and see what happens. I haven't got any preconceptions but I do know it's not like in the movies but we almost did it last weekend" "Wow, do tell" Jane quickly said putting down her drink and with the comment already half out Sandra carried on "Well my mum and dad were out, and Tony was meeting Gill from my old school so we had the house to ourselves all afternoon, so I wanted to show Dave my dress from Tammy Girl and well it wasn't really on for very long, but just as we were getting to the ...... well you know, and Tony came back, thinking it might be mum and dad .... well needless to say we stopped, but you know if felt so right, so I think this weekend will be absolutely fine. "Sandra you'll be absolutely fine you can see Dave is head over heels, and he would never hurt you in fact I wish Sid was a bit more of a softy like Dave but hey he is what he is, and he's mine" at which Jane picked up her drink and raising it towards Sandra who automatically had picked hers up said "To us girls!" and proceeded to finish her drink and without saying a word stood up and headed for the bar. Sat on her own Sandra looked around the pub which was filling up as usual for a Friday night and decided that if anyone else in the pub was happier than her then good luck to them!

Chapter 16

Saturday started with a rain shower but by the time that Dave had made his way to Sandra's house the weather was beginning to abate, as he stood proud with a small weekend bag in his hand he checked himself in the Lounge side window and happy with his look, he adjusted his Flat cap before knocking at which the door was opened almost as he removed his hand. "Come in Dave don't stand out there, do you want a drink?" said Diane "No thank you Mrs ....Diane I had one before I left thanks" "I've told Sandra that I'll run you to the train station, and she should be down in a minute so take a seat while you wait, oh and congratulations on passing your Driving Test" and almost as he sat at the kitchen table he could hear the sound of feet coming down the stairs and Sandra appeared at the kitchen door with a smile on her face that immediately set a still slightly nervous Dave at ease. "Hello boyfriend, I'll just get my coat and hat and mum's going to run us to the train station" and as she turned away to get her coat and hat Diane said "Why do you two call each other boyfriend and girlfriend still, we called her Sandra when she was born and I'm sure your parents were happy calling you Dave, just wondering, that's all!" "To be honest Mrs ... Diane it kind of started as a bit of a joke but it's stuck and we are happy with it. It's kind of quirky and different and well it works for us" as Sandra returned dressed to go, carrying a bag that looked too big for one night, but which he wasn't going to question. "Right if you're both ready, best get going" said Diane picking up the car keys from the kitchen table and heading off out of the door. As Dave and Sandra sat in the back of the car Diane set off and looking in the mirror commented "Look at you two sat there like royalty, going away for the weekend and chauffer driven!" as they looked at each other they sat holding hands but were still uneasy about having a kiss, even if it was behind Diane's back. Stopping outside the train station Dave was first out of the car and taking Sandra's bag as she slid across the back seat to where Dave was stood waiting, Diane wound the window down as Dave shut the back door. "See you Sunday enjoy yourselves and don't ...." which was cut off by Sandra's sharp "Mum" and taking her punishment Diane waved her hand and putting the car into gear set off for home leaving them stood outside the train station locked in a kiss that had been waiting for the last 20 minutes and with a bag each they set off for Platform One holding hands for the 10.04 train to York and a weekend of the past, present and future in more ways than one.

As the train pulled away from Platform One, Dave turned to face Sandra "Happy girlfriend?" "Very boyfriend!" and she hooked up to him as he contentedly looked out at the passing countryside on the start to their plans and lives together. It was as they pulled into Leeds station before Dave spoke again "Do you want to do anything special while we are in York..... sorry that came out all wrong, what I meant was" and as his face reddened Sandra cut in "I thought we could drop our bags at the Hotel then go around the City walls and see the Minster and if we can find the Shambles maybe find somewhere to have something to eat or maybe a pub by the river, what do you say?" a calmed down Dave looked at her and struggling to find an appropriate answer whispered "Bossy girlfriend" and kissed her gently before she had a chance to react. The journey continued with the train now pretty full as the day trippers from Leeds headed for York, Sandra and Dave settled into a quiet peace as the train sped them onwards, as they each quietly considered the day and night ahead of them both.

The train ground to a halt at York Station and slowly the passengers made their way onto Platform Nine with Sandra and Dave stuck behind a family with three children, who weren't helping with the smooth exit from the train, but as the father picked up the youngest and the rest of the family followed him off the train, Dave took Sandra's hand as they made it onto the platform with their bags in their other hands and joined the queue to pass the Ticket Inspector. The sign 'Welcome to York' stood proud above them as they handed over their tickets, turning left out of the station they took the short walk to the Royal Station Hotel, their home for their weekend. Taking the steps up to the main entrance Dave looked at Sandra, and seeing her slightly nervous look he squeezed her hand and feeling the engagement ring he smiled at her, before saying quietly "I've booked us in under Mr and Mrs Baxter, just to give you a chance to try the name out!" without giving her a chance to reply he led her through the main door and headed for the Reception desk, with a slightly amused and bemused Sandra almost in step as they arrived at the desk. Greeted by a smiling blonde Receptionist "Good morning Sir, welcome to the Royal Station Hotel, how may I be of help?" "Mr and Mrs Baxter checking in!" Dave confidently replied, at which Sandra turned bright red and looking anywhere but at the Receptionist, put her bag down and her hand over her mouth to stop the giggles that were starting. "Certainly Sir, if I can ask you to register here" she said putting a Registration Form in front of Dave together with a pen, and turned to pick out a key from the pigeon holes behind her. "Thank you Sir" she said as she took the completed form and filed it in the pigeon hole where the key had been. "You're in Room 317 which is on the 3rd Floor overlooking the Castle walls, the lifts are on the left by the dining room. I hope you and Mrs Baxter have a lovely stay and I see you have booked to dine with us this evening. Dinner is served between 7.30pm and 9.30pm, would you like to book a time now, alternatively you could turn up and have a drink while we find a table for you if you're not sure of your plans for the day." and awaiting a reply she handed him the room key, which gave him time to think as he replied "We'll just turn up if that's okay, as we will be out for most of the day thank you" and taking the key he picked up his bag and went towards the lifts where Sandra had moved to stifle her giggles, out of the sight of the Receptionist." "Come on Mrs Baxter!" Dave said pressing the 3rd Floor button on the lift panel, and took hold of her hand as the lift doors opened, once inside as Dave leaned in for a kiss Sandra said "I could get used to Mrs Baxter, boyfriend!" giving into his lips as they touched hers, they were still kissing when the lift stopped sharply and they parted as the doors opened, following the number signs they headed for Room 317 with the key already out of Dave's pocket. Opening the door and leaving it open for Sandra to go first, he kept hold of her hand stopping her entering and as she looked at him wondering why he was holding her back she figured it out before he had a chance to ask "Yes I 'm sure it's what I want!" she said, letting go of his hand, she went to the window putting her bag down on the bed on the way. As she heard the door shut and moments later his arms around her waist, as she looked over the City walls and York beyond in all its splendour, as the sun tried to make an appearance, she felt him kiss her neck and she turned to respond with her arms around his neck as he found her tongue, and they slowly made their way to the bed behind them.

As Dave started to loosen her coat buttons Sandra put a hand on his and whispered "Mr Baxter there will be plenty of time for that later. Can we go out like we said and see the city, this will be here to see later" waving her hand up and down her body "Sure Mrs Baxter whatever you say!" at which Sandra burst into a full blown bout of giggles which only went away when Dave looking at the bed raised his arm out towards the left then the right side at which Sandra smiled and with a mischievous grin replacing her giggles said "I rather hoped I would be underneath!" and the giggles returned as Dave suddenly became the one not to know where to look. Taking his bag and putting a shirt and trousers in the wardrobe, he went into the bathroom where he placed his travel toiletries bag from Christmas, which he had thought he would never use, on the side as he heard Sandra close the wardrobe door and join him with a pink flowery cosmetics bag in her hand which soon sat next to his and with a kiss Dave decided they had better get out of the hotel now or they never would. "Come on girlfriend let's go and see what York has to offer" with a sad look that appeared on her face Sandra quickly said "So what happened to Mrs Baxter, I was quite getting used to that!" "Well girlfriend, some things are worth waiting for!" and taking her chin in his hand he kissed her as she closed her eyes and envisaged being Mrs Baxter.

They left the room key at reception and exiting left they headed out of the Royal Station Hotel to explore York. Crossing the road to find an entrance to the City walls, they joined several groups of other likeminded people who took advantage of the views of both the internal and external buildings and houses from their lofty walkway as they made their way along the City walls towards York Minster, stopping regularly to catch a kiss and wonder how many others had made the same trip though the ages. Coming off the City walls near the Minster, they joined a healthy mass of people headed in the same direction until they were out in the open and the Mister stood large and proud directly in front of them as they stopped hand in hand and tried to take in the sheer size of the building "I want to work on buildings like this one day" Dave said as Sandra held her hand over her head, to shield from the low lying sun shadowing part of the building "Beautiful isn't it " Sandra responded without averting her eyes, only to be aware of the silence next to her, as she turned to face him the words "Yes she's beautiful" hit her as he put his arms around her as she got the double meaning, half a second before his lips hit hers.

Taking a right turn they headed for the Shambles area, taking their time as it was very busy as always, they found La Piazza pizza restaurant, and deciding to get out of the crowds entered an already busy establishment and were seated by a waitress who said they were lucky to get a table at this time of day, which judging by the queue of people waiting to be seated was an underestimation. Ordering two cokes the waitress left them with a menu each and a promise to be back with their drinks to take their order in a few minutes, and true to her word she appeared in less than 5 minutes with their drinks, just as they put their menus down and she took their order of, a House Special and a Pepperoni Pizza before disappearing back into the kitchen with their order, before quickly appearing in the entrance to take the next customers to a newly vacated table."Gosh she's a real whirlwind isn't she "Sandra said before taking a drink, "Sure is" Dave agreed putting down his drink "I hope the wait isn't too long I'm starving and this place is so busy." Changing the subject he continued" York has so many old buildings imagine working in their Council, it must be quite something, anything from Viking, Roman to Victorian buildings all over the place. The newly unearthed Coppergate Jorvik area, plus of course there is the Minster which is a lifetime project." "Get you, back into work mode, while we are supposed to be on a romantic weekend away, but I get your interest with all these old buildings, but we have loads in Kirkdale, they're just not as well known" Sandra responded deciding to match his interest. He took her hand and looking directly at her said "Didn't see you bring a Victoria's Secret bag with you" as a grin grew across his face "Why Mr Baxter I don't know what you mean, that particular present was for my boyfriend, and he will have to wait until later to find out if he can have his present!" she confidently said squeezing his hand, feeling a little bit of embarrassment at her implication, and she took a drink to cool her cheeks as Dave excitedly said "That's a present that I'm looking forward to playing with!" at which Sandra just managed to get out "Boys and their Toys!" as their waitress returned with a pizza in each hand and a large peppermill under her arm. After finishing their lunch with some small talk about work they made their way around the rest of the Shambles, getting a couple of ice creams they headed back onto the City walls to complete the circuit, and the long route back to the hotel, stopping at the King's Arms by the River Ouse for a drink. Sitting outside despite it being February, they watched the various birds swooping down to pick up any bits of food dropped by a casual tourist. "We should come here again in summer" Sandra said and looking down at her left hand added "after we get engaged that is!" "Now that's a good idea girlfriend, but will I get a present!" he said expecting a dig in the ribs but Sandra's response shut him up completely "I'm your present for ever, so yes you will get a present, you lucky man" and with that they set off for the Royal Station Hotel across the bridge silent in speech, but not in thought.

The Receptionist welcomed them as they entered the Royal Station Hotel and headed towards the lifts with a "Good afternoon Mr and Mrs Baxter, I hope you enjoyed your day out in York" and handed Dave the room key without asking the number "Thank you yes it was lovely" Dave replied without breaking his stride, as Sandra tightened her grip on his hand and looked away sure that the Receptionist knew she wasn't really Mrs Baxter, as a bit of guilt hit her. The doors to the lift opened and as they entered and turned around, the second the doors closed Dave put his arms around her waist and slowly placing his hands on her bottom he pulled her into him, as he kissed her with a building passion that was interrupted by the lift reaching their floor. "Come on Mrs Baxter" he said taking the room key out of his pocket and opening the door, he let Sandra in first before closing the door behind them leaving them alone as the clock on the wall struck 4.00.

Having taken off her coat Sandra sat on the edge of the bed and took off her shoes before moving up the bed to rest her head on the pillows putting her hands behind her head. Watching Dave who was standing by the window looking at the view she quietly got off the bed and barefooted went and stood behind him putting her arms around his chest. "Stay there for a few minutes and I'll be right back" and stretching up slightly she kissed the back of his neck before disappearing into the bathroom leaving Dave with a view in front of him and a completely different picture in his mind. Taking off his jacket and shoes he put them in the wardrobe to kill a little time, and lay on the bed trying not to stare at the bathroom door, but still feeling slightly awkward he went back to the window to find something to occupy his mind, other than the picture that was now firmly in place. The door to the bathroom opened and Sandra stood wearing her Victoria's Secret white satin two piece outfit and looking directly at Dave she said "Does Mr Baxter like his present?" and with a look that left little to the imagination, but that said Yes in so many ways, Dave stood rooted to the spot as Sandra slowly moved towards him until she was leaning into him and he finally reacted "Mr Baxter very much likes his present!" and slowly he kissed her lips as his hands slid over the satin top and down to her partly exposed bottom as her tongue flicked his and they were locked in a moment until Sandra opened her eyes and realised that even though they were on the 3rd floor they were stood in the main window which looked onto the City walls and which looked onto them. Taking one of his hands off her bottom she led them away from the window towards the bed. Letting go of his hand she lay down on the bed on her side, with her head resting on her hand, Dave looked at her without a word being said. Taking off his t shirt with a yank over his head he undid his belt and took off his jeans, all the while looking at Sandra who was trying not to laugh as he struggled with one of his socks, but as he came towards the bed she could see by the bulge in his Y Fronts that the outfit she had chosen for his present had had the effect she had wanted.

Laying down beside her he put his arm under hers that had been holding her head and pulled her tight so he could kiss her with a desire that was building between them. As she slowly rolled onto her back she could feel Dave's hands working up and over her breasts and she could feel him slowly unwrapping his present as her breasts became exposed to the diming sunlight coming though the window. Feeling him pull away from her mouth she could feel his wet kisses going over her nipples as his hand slowly went into her panties and over her bush. Holding his head with her hands as he kissed her breasts, she felt his finger find her clitoris as he gently moved his finger up and down until he moved his hand further down and she could feel his finger inside her damp vagina as his tongue slowly curved its way over her nipples. Taking her hands from his head she put one arm around his back as he lay aside her, and with the other hand she felt down to her panties and slowly slid them down her legs as far as she could, until she could see Dave's hand covering her bush with his finger still inside her. Moving her hand across to his groin she felt for, and found his bugling penis under his Y Fronts, slowly putting her hand inside she took hold of his erect penis and slowly started to massage it, until finally she released it as Dave moved his body slightly to make it easier. She moved her hand up and down the shaft until she could feel a trickle of fluid on her fingers and she quietly said moving her hand from his back and put her hand on his head, which was buried in her chest "Dave you need to use a condom".

Slowly he pulled his finger from her vagina sliding it over her clitoris, on the way to her breasts kissing her intensely, as his lips moved up her body before he rolled over to get a condom from the bathroom. Returning naked from the bathroom he lay beside Sandra who had taken his present off and lay naked on the double bed, her head rested on her hand looking in the direction of the bathroom "Are you sure that will go on that!" she said at which he smiled and ripping the pack open sat on the edge of the bed and proceeded to put on his first condom, rolling it gently along his erect penis. Rolling over so that they were face to face, he kissed her tenderly as he put one leg over and between hers. As Sandra parted her legs and Dave moved to lay between them, he took hold of his covered penis and slowly rubbed it between Sandra's legs until he felt her vagina with the head of his penis, and gently he rubbed it up and down until he could feel it easing inside her, and after a few gentle pushes he felt his erect penis inside her, as she made a little sigh and tensed a little but her arms were around his back pulling him into her, as he began to move his body back and forth until he was rhythmically using his hips, as Sandra pulled him ever tighter and he put his hands under her shoulders as he pulled himself further into her, feeling his tension rising he came inside her and their breathing slowly retreated as he stayed inside her kissing her gently until his erection dissipated and he rolled off her to lay by her side. Putting his arm around her, he pulled her next to him and she lay her head on his chest, his hand on her bottom, her breasts squashed against his side and closing her eyes as he kissed the top of her head, they both quietly fell asleep naked to a darkening world outside, but safe in their sated cocoon of passion.

A shiver woke Dave from his spent passion sleep and slowly trying to not wake Sandra he moved to get off the bed when the words "Leaving now you've had your wicked way with me!" came from dark as Sandra slowly pulled the sheets up to her neck covering herself up and as Dave put on the sidelight he leaned back towards her and kissing her tenderly on the lips said "Was it ....okay?" as she put her arms around his neck and pulled him closer she quietly said "It was just as I hoped it would be!" and kissing him slowly she suddenly released him and pulling the sheets off them she said as she headed for the bathroom "I hope you don't think you're going to use that again!" pointing to the used condom hanging from his flaccid penis, as she closed the door with a hearty laugh she left Dave with a completely embarrassed look on his face, that hadn't quite gone when she returned a few minutes later having taken a quick shower, still naked but with a grin on her face as she sauntered past him and went to close the curtains, taking a second to show York her nakedness before her innocence overcame her and she closed the world out. Turning around she saw that Dave had gone to the bathroom and she returned to lie on the bed positioning herself so that her hand held her head in a classic Marilyn Monroe pose. As he opened the bathroom door still towelling himself dry from his shower, his hair still wet, the sight of Sandra lying naked on the bed stopped him in the doorframe with the light behind him "Not bad boyfriend" Sandra said staring at the rising bulge under the towel nor quite covering his naked body, before a smile came across her face as she added "You'd better calm that down until after dinner, I'm famished!" and she burst out in laughter as Dave looked down at his newly erect penis and not knowing whether to comment or hide it behind his hands he chose the former "You shouldn't be so beautiful as my little friend has a mind of his own!" and realising his Freudian comment, he sat on the edge of the bed without looking at her and put on his Y Fronts, before heading to the wardrobe from where he took a shirt and turning back to the bed where Sandra lay without moving he said "I'm starving as well, but unless you get dressed we are going to miss dinner" and without moving an inch she smiled at him before replying "I don't think your little friend is interested in dinner!" and she burst out laughing as Dave looked down at his Y Fronts as his erect penis refused to relent as he turned away from her and adjusted himself before returning to see Sandra still laughing with gusto on the bed "There that's better!" he said looking at her as she slowly edged toward the side of the bed and came towards him as he stood still at the wardrobe. Brushing past him with her breasts catching his elbow, she went to get her dress that was hung up "Sorry about that" she said reaching for her dress and slipping it over her head having decide to go braless she went past him brushing his elbow with her now covered breasts quietly saying "You might want to put some trousers on boyfriend, before your little friend escapes!" at which she burst out laughing again before heading into the bathroom where Dave could still hear her laughing. As he pulled his trousers off the hanger from the wardrobe and moving to the edge of the bed, he only just managed to get his trousers on before Sandra returned, no longer laughing but with a smile on her face and her hair tied up, accentuating her breasts as she came out of the bathroom with her arms raised."Will I do?" she said and came close to him to give him a gentle kiss as he put his hands on her bottom "For me absolutely, but you might find it a bit draughty at dinner" and realising she hadn't put any knickers on, she kissed him gratefully before retrieving some knickers from the wardrobe and she slipped them on one leg at a time, under her dress before adjusting her dress with a slight twirl "Better?" she smiled at him and with a nod he looked at her as he finished tying his shoes laces. Standing up and taking her hand as she balanced to put on her high healed dress shoes he made stuck out his elbow with his arm on his waist and when she was finished she responded by hooking up as they made their way out of the room, a memory created for all time behind them as they closed the door and headed downstairs for dinner.

Seated in an alcove towards the back of the room the waiter recited the day's specials as he handed them each a Menu which failed to register with either Sandra or Dave, as they uncoupled their hands across the table both in their own little worlds, when the waiter, having seen it all before over the years, slightly louder than usual said "Would Sir like to see the Wine List?" at which Dave realised he was being spoken to said "Yes please" and nodded at the same time as the waiter produced the Wine List from behind his back. Choosing a Chardonnay as his mum drank it sometimes he waited until the Waiter had left before putting down his Menu reaching for her hand and saying quietly so no one nearby could hear "Girlfriend, I just want to say thank you for my present it was..... sorry, you were, are the best present I've ever had" and turning bright red as his mind returned to the afternoon of passion

Sandra cut in quickly seeing the Waiter returning with their wine "I'm glad you had me too!" leaving Dave speechless, as the Waiter poured out a glass for him to taste. He just about managed "Thank you" after the wine hit his stomach when Sandra said "You're welcome" and Dave was grateful that the Waiter had left them alone, as he once again blushed as Sandra took her glass of wine and slowly looking around the room she finally looked at Dave and said brazenly "Wonder if anyone else spent the afternoon in bed!" at which Dave decided enough was enough and put his menu in front of his face, so she couldn't see how red he now was. "I think I'll have Chicken Kiev came the voice from behind her menu and relaxing a little he put down his menu to see Sandra smiling at him as he reached for her hand. "Good choice girlfriend, think I'll have the Sirloin Steak with all the trimmings" and squeezing her hand he lifted it off the table and gently kissed her engagement ring saying "We could get engaged earlier if you like and then you can wear it all the time!" "Honestly boyfriend I am happy with our little secret, well apart from my mum and dad who know that is, and anyway we have a plan, and I'd hate to disrupt it as it's going so well wouldn't you say!" "Oh yes, it's going much better than I hoped!" he said just as the Waiter returned and having taken their order as he headed for the kitchen Sandra leant into Dave and said "I think so too boyfriend......, but god I'm starving!" at which she leaned even further until she could give him as kiss before sitting back and picking up her glass she said "To plans, to the future" as they clashed glasses Dave added "To us" and as they both sat back with glasses in hand, the time passed with barely a word before the Waiter returned with their Dinner and with an unfeeling "Bon Appétit" he was gone. "Starving " said Dave picking up his knife and fork expecting an answer, but Sandra was already cutting into her Chicken Kiev at which he followed suit stabbing two chips and popping them into his mouth as they both sated their hunger and it wasn't until he had eaten two mouthfuls of steak that he said as he looked up "Beautiful" the

"Thank you!" from Sandra caught him unawares "I meant...." he stumbled "I know what you meant boyfriend, but a girl will take a compliment anytime!" she added returning to cut her Chicken Kiev, with a smile that didn't leave her face even when she was ready to put a forkful in her mouth. Looking at him she placed the Chicken in her mouth and watched as Dave cut a chunk from his Steak, pierced a mushroom and placed them in his mouth wondering what he had done to be so lucky sat across from this beautiful girlfriend. Finishing the main course the ever attentive Waiter brought them a Dessert Menu and after a short discussion they agreed they would have Profiteroles and Black Forest Gateau which they could share at which the Waiter said "Good choice Sir!" for the tenth time tonight, meaning it even less each time before heading off to the back of the room where the desserts were kept in cabinets. Returning in rapid time the Waiter placed the plates in front of them in no order and seeing an arm raised nearby he was gone before they had a chance to say 'Thank you'. Taking a forkful of profiterole from the plate in front of him, Dave offered it to Sandra at which she opened her mouth and took the offering before closing her lips and tasting the sweet chocolate covered choux pastry and cream hit her palate, she uttered "Mmmm" as Dave helped himself to some Black Forest Gateaux and mimicking Sandra with a mouth full he managed to get out "Yummmm" as Sandra swapped plates and cutting another piece of profiterole she said "You don't mind do you, that cake looks so filling and well this is beautiful" "Not at all, and it certainly is!" he quickly replied, as she put a forkful in her mouth, she let her answer wait until he had placed another piece of Black Forest Gateaux in his mouth "You're not just saying that because you had your wicked way with me, are you!" getting his innuendo. Struggling to finish the Black Forest Gateaux and speak at the same time he almost made it before Sandra beat him to it "Don't choke to death Dave, I want to wake up with you in the morning, that is after we have spent our first night together of course! At which Dave having finished chewing turned as red as the cherry he had just eaten before taking a sip of wine and gaining his composure replied "What makes you think you're going to get any sleep!" then it was Sandra's turn to get embarrassed as she watched him empty his plate and wipe his mouth with a serviette as she had just finished doing a few seconds before. Taking a moment Sandra took his hand across the table and leaning towards him said "Well Mr Baxter I'm full, so would you like to take Mrs Baxter upstairs and we can see if practice makes perfect!" Standing up he moved round to pull Sandra's chair away as she got up from the table, leaving a tip on the table he put his arm around her waist and they headed for the lift and their first night together, feeling as all lovers do, that nothing could get in the way of their happiness.

The morning tried to peek through the curtains of Room 317 as the early morning light flooded the front of the Royal Station Hotel but it wasn't until nearly 09.00 that Sandra woke up to find Dave had woken and was already in the shower as the noise from the bathroom hit her senses. Propping herself up on the pillows she decided to leave the curtains for now and pulling the sheets up to cover her breasts she heard the shower stop and a few seconds later a towelled Dave came out of the bathroom and seeing she was awake he came over to the bed to give her a kiss "You smell nice!" she responded after his kiss "Good morning Mrs Baxter I must say you look lovely this morning" he said laying next to her on the bed with the towel around his waist. "Why thank you Mr Baxter "she replied kissing him quickly and getting out of bed she pulled the towel from his waist and headed for the bathroom leaving him naked with a growing smile and penis as she headed naked for a shower. Lying back, he put his arms behind his head resting his head on the pillow and thought back to last night, their first night together and closing his eyes he was dozing as Sandra returned from the bathroom, wrapped in a towel with another on her head which upon seeing Dave lying in the bed naked with his thoughts transferred to his penis which was now erect, she threw the towel from her head over his groin. "Come on boyfriend, your little friend will have to wait, I want some breakfast!" Heading to the wardrobe she put on her knickers, bra and a pair of jeans before turning back to see a grinning Dave doing a matador bull fight tease with his penis behind the towel prodding the towel in motion."Boys and their toys" Sandra said with an inflection that Dave couldn't miss, and pulling a jumper over her head she set about drying her hair with her towel, as Dave finally accepted that breakfast was the only thing on the agenda, and started getting dressed, suddenly realising he too was hungry as he pulled on his jeans and a T shirt and sat on the bed waiting for Sandra to dry her hair in the bathroom. "Ready" Sandra said as she left the bathroom and going over to the bed where Dave was still sat, she took hold of his chin and arching it upwards she kissed him tenderly on the lips before taking his hand and led him to the door stopping before she opened it, and looking at him she squeezed his hand and said "Mr Baxter, I'd just like to say Mrs Baxter has had a lovely weekend thank you" and opening the door she led Dave by the hand to the lift still awaiting a response. As the doors opened and they stepped inside he finally managed to put into words what his heart was telling him "Mrs Baxter should know that Mr Baxter has very much enjoyed himself not only this weekend but every day since the Council Christmas party and very much looks forward to having many more breakfasts together" adding quietly "Must remember to get some more condoms" and grinning he leant in for a kiss that he just managed to complete, as the lift reached the ground floor and the doors opened Sandra squeezed his hand and they headed for their first breakfast together and the impending end of their weekend away.

Packing their bags after breakfast Sandra finished first and went to look out of the window for a final time before they left and it wasn't long after that she felt Dave's arms around her waist and she nuzzled backwards into him and twisted her head for him to kiss which he needed no invitation to do. As he pulled her round to face him she gave in to his hungry tongue and they passionately embraced until a far off clock chime 10.00 which broke their attention and they parted slowly, holding hands until the last moment as their fingers gradually let go of each other and they picked up their bags taking a last look around the room before heading for the door, their week-end and their passion soon to be a memory as the door closed behind them, keeping its secrets for ever.

After a walk down by the River Ouse the weather started to deteriorate and finding a riverside cafe they took refuge from the February squall ordering two coffees and taking a seat by the window with their bags at their feet. "I'll never forget York" said Sandra before taking a sip of coffee "Me neither" Dave quickly answered with a smile that had a double meaning before he realised he needed to clarify his comment "Our first weekend away was very special girlfriend, and it will always be in my thoughts" and unable to resist he added "and the sex as well!" seeing the grin erupting on his face Sandra punched his arms but smiled at her own recollection of their first night together before saying "Well I have some news for you on that account boyfriend!". Sandra took full advantage of the silence that followed her comment and taking another sip of coffee she watched Dave's face grow more confused and quizzical by the second. Deciding she had pushed her luck far enough she took hold of his hand and quietly as the cafe was filling up she said "Jane and I were speaking when we went to Leeds, and well I've decided to go on the Pill so we won't have to ... well interrupt .... you know what ....and your little friend won't have to wear a condom." The smile on Dave's face replacing his worried look was what Sandra expected but deciding to tease him a little further she added before he could say anything in response."There is a downside Dave" at which the worried look returned as she continued "It takes two weeks after I start taking the Pill before it is safe to have .....sex, so your little friend will have to put up with it for a couple of weeks as my appointment at the Doctors isn't until Wednesday" "Well girlfriend, you really know how to make a boyfriend happy!" and pulling her hand so she moved closer he reached to give her a kiss before deciding to add "I've waited all my life for you to come along so a few weeks is nothing...... although I might need some more practice in the next two weeks, and my little friend as you call it, will have to put up with it!" and bursting out laughing at his own humour he could see Sandra looking aghast at his comment before she too joined in laughing, as the weather slowly eased and finishing their coffees, they picked up their bags and headed back the way they had come towards the Railway Station and the journey home back to normality, memories made and saved forever.

The train journey with little to discuss seemed to take for ages but finally they arrived in Kirkdale Railway Station after a delay at Leeds Railway Station, and letting the other passengers disembark before them and head off on the next part of their journeys, they stood on the Platform as the train slowly engaged gear and headed onwards to its next destination. Putting his bag down he pulled her close and his arms wrapped around her as they were left alone which suited their moment until Dave whispered "I think we should go back" and quietly he heard her say "There's no going back now you're stuck with me ....forever!" and a smiling face reached up to him and a kiss landed on his lips that sealed their future, on a now deserted train platform.

Monday morning came with a whimper as Sandra headed into work, all thoughts of the weekend now put in a private part of her mind that during the night had surfaced, as she reached out and Dave wasn't next to her, but as she fell back to sleep she swore she could feel his hand on her breast. Taking the steps up to the Council Offices she was running a little early, and so was alone in the Planning Department, when Sam from the mailroom arrived pushing the day's workload on his trolley. "Morning Sandra, have a good weekend?" he said as he approached her desk and after Sandra had responded with "Yes thank you, we went to York for the weekend, and you?" Sam replied "Quiet one with a few mates but went to see Town on Saturday who actually won, so not too bad really" Placing a bundle of files on her desk, he replicated the action at the other desk before heading out of the door with a backward "See you" and was gone leaving Sandra to ponder how different people's lives were depending on who they were with. Sam Brown was a nice boy but at 20 he was still single, with no girlfriend she had heard about, and probably would always be single unless he changed things in his life. Funny how things turn out she thought, it was only a few months ago she had met Dave and look at them now. Lost in her thoughts she didn't see Mrs Shaw arrive, but felt her presence at her side, and looking up saw that she had a batch of folders under her arm. "Sandra, hope you had a good weekend but we have a load of work to catch up on, most of it you will be fine with but this afternoon there are a couple of interesting files on the Manchester Road Power Station site, so when you get to them, come and see me and I'll help you through them" Depositing her folders on top of Sandra's already numerous in tray she turned and headed for her office leaving Sandra to wonder how she was ever going to get the pile down by this afternoon. No more daydreaming then she decided to herself and set about the first folder which was headed 'Daly Road Sewage Works-Amendments', charming start to the day she thought as she opened the folder and she could swear she could almost smell the sewage on the paper as she set about dealing with the folder.

Dave was last into the Estates Department Offices seeing Daniel Bruce and John Marshall, already at their desks heads down. "Nice of you to join us" said Mr Normanton just as the clock hit 08.30 at which Dave saw Daniel and Peter look up, and seeing the time realised it was another one of Mr Normanton's not so funny critical asides, and returned to their work without a comment. Dave settled at his desk and started on the files left over from Friday before starting on the newly arrived folders. Wonder what today will bring he thought to himself trying to put the memory of the weekend behind him and failing miserably as he brought up the image of his matador impression on Sunday morning and with a smirk on his face he settled down to clear his backlog and his mind.

The morning disappeared faster than their respective bundles of files, but when 12.30 came Dave headed for the door without looking back, putting his jacket on and his Flat cap, which he had almost forgotten this morning as he was running a little late, due to a dream that his mother's yell of "Dave you'll be late if you don't get up now!" had disturbed involving Sandra, who was now stood at the top of the Council Office steps waiting for him, but fully clothed, unlike his dream. Putting his arms around her as she had her back to him he quietly said "I had a dream about you last night" "Funnily enough so did I" she replied with a smile as he took her hand and they headed down the stairs. "You were...." he said at the bottom of the stairs "I don't want to know what I was, ...or wasn't wearing, it's enough that you were dreaming of me boyfriend!" she interrupted as they headed across the Town Square towards the George which was usually quiet on a Monday lunchtime. Ordering two cokes they took a seat in the alcove where he put his arm around her as they sat watching the nearly empty pub slowly serve a few regulars at the bar before Dave remembered they weren't here people watching and had some plans to make as was his want. "So girlfriend, did I say I missed you last night?" "No you didn't, but I suppose a dream counts" she answered before taking a drink and turning slightly to face him she continued "What we talked about on the train on the way back from York, did you have a think about it?" Putting down his drink he quickly responded "Absolutely, as we dis-

220

cussed, we are too young to have children at the moment, and you going on the Pill makes complete sense as we don't want any... well accidents. So yes that bit is fine, and we both have careers now, which in 5 years will mean we will have a chance to rethink things when you will be 24, and I'll be 26, so yes that just leaves the Engagement, and as much as I know you want to wear your ring and tell everyone, it wasn't in my original plan!" "Okay boyfriend I'm happy with that, but I do want children sometime, but I'm happy to wait. We'll just have to have recreational sex in the meantime!" she replied watching as he choked on his coke at her last comment. Not letting him get a word in she continued "There are a couple of things I've thought about that I think should go in your... or should I say our plan. Namely I want to learn to drive and I think ....no, I know, I want to go on holiday this summer with you, somewhere abroad, we could do it after my birthday and finally I think.." and taking a drink, she finished "We should get a place and move in together when we get back from our holiday abroad!" and sitting back with an amused look on her face she waited for Dave to respond "Wow, I've created a Monster!" he said before heading to the bar without waiting for a response. Returning with two halves of Lager he placed one in front of her and sitting down he held up his glass "Can't make decisions like that with coke, so if that's what you want then I agree... OUR Plan is officially given the go ahead!" and as he clashed his glass with hers, the deal was sealed and they settled back in their seats with the next 5 years arranged, only time would tell if it came to fruition, or life would get in the way. As they made their way out of the George and back to work, the barman took their empty glasses throwing one in the bin as a crack had appeared unseen by either of them on Sandra's glass.

Chapter 17 – Five months later

"We've got Five Years" said David Bowie and what a Five Years it was going to be. Sandra and Dave got engaged officially on her 19ᵗʰ Birthday the 16ᵗʰ July 1982, with a party at the Malt Shovel, which had become very much their local drinking hole and a meeting place for their friends. Jane and Sid had announced that they were going to live together but that was as far as Sid would commit "Too young to be tied down he said" out of earshot of Jane. Sandra's workmates all turned up Sharon with Mick, Jo with Chris, and Peggy with Alan which taking their recent boyfriend history must be some kind of record Sandra thought, welcoming them all with a hug and not forgetting to show off her engagement ring each time. Tony her brother, brought Gill who had become a regular visitor to the Baxter house over the last few months. The party carried on until the 1.00 am closing time as Ian the barman shouted "Time please ladies and gentlemen!" and slowly the various couples finished their drinks and headed for the door to await their Taxi's. "It's been a great party "said a slightly drunk Sandra holding onto Peggy outside as Andy had gone to the toilet."It certainly was a night to remember and don't forget my wedding invitation will you!" she replied "Oh we're not getting married yet it's not in our plan but you will be the first to know if the plan changes!" Not sure what plan Sandra was on about Peggy felt Andy take her hand and intrigued she asked Sandra what she meant by the plan. "Well, we are going on holiday in a month, and when we get back we are going to look for somewhere to live together. Then we are going to concentrate on our careers before thinking about children in Five Years!" "Wow" said Andy listening whilst watching for the next Taxi to arrive "That's a plan and a half, what have you got planned for me Peggy?" he added. "Well if you can stay awake for five minutes you'll find out!" at which Sandra and Peggy burst out laughing as a Taxi pulled up and Peggy and Andy got in, soon disappearing down the road to Town as another set of headlights headed towards the Malt Shovel. A very drunk Sharon and Jo were helped into the next Taxi by their boyfriends with a "See you Monday!" shouted retort coming from the open window as the Taxi set off propelling Jo across Sharon's lap in the back seat. Hand in hand Dave and Sandra for no apparent reason waved after them, although they had already disappeared into the dark. "Come on girlfriend time for home" Dave said leading her towards the newly arrived Taxi "You're not going to take advantage of me are you Mr Baxter?" she said stopping before getting into the open Taxi door. "Not tonight Mrs Baxter I'm afraid!" he regretfully said getting into the Taxi alongside her, "Shame" Sandra quietly and mischievously said, leaning into him and was half asleep before the lights of the Malt Shovel had disappeared in the background.

Sid and Jane were among the last to leave and Ian the barman said to Sid, as Jane went to the toilet as they waited for the last Taxi. "Sid, you know when Dave got attacked at Christmas and no one has been found" "Yes what about it?" an intrigued Sid quickly responded keeping an eye out for their Taxi. "Well I've asked around as you were drinking in here that night, and I don't like it when my customers get attacked, whatever the reason, and the only people who left here after you were Daniel Bruce and his mate Steve Parker. Anyway Pete who was working that night reckons that they spent the night watching you two, and left straight after you." "Daniel Bruce, Steve Parker, no way I'd eat them for breakfast!" said Sid failing to see the logic in Ian's statement. "Just saying" said Ian "But weren't Daniel and Sandra a couple in summer?" and as Jane came out of the Toilet and the conversation was curtailed a seed of concern entered Sid's subconscious as he led Jane to the Taxi now waiting outside."That was a really good party" said Jane as Sid sat next to her and closed the Taxi door behind him "They're such a lovely couple, and to think they only met at Christmas, you were there weren't you, you little match maker!" and leaning into him she squeezed his hand, unaware that a reminder of the circumstances of the Council Christmas Party had just been recollected.

"Sid" Dave had said at the time "I really fancy this girl called Sandra Robertson at the Council, I hear she's split up with her boyfriend, so the plan of action for tonight is to get to know her and ask her out. She's really pretty, long black hair, blue eyes so help me out and I'll buy the beers!" as the Taxi made its way to their flat it all came together in Sid's mind, the problem was what to do with the information that was racing around his head as Jane watched the street lights go past leaning into his shoulder unaware of the turmoil in Sid's mind.

The silver Ford Fiesta pulled up at Church Street and hardly had Dave got out of the car than Sandra was already closing her house door and walking up the path to greet him. "Why good afternoon boyfriend, did you sleep in dreaming of me?" Sandra said before planting a kiss on his responsive lips. Parting he caught his breath and replied "It's only five past twelve, but yes I did dream of you ...as did my little friend!" he ended with a smirk as he opened the passenger door for her. Sitting down and searching for the seat belt, she put her hand out to stop him closing the door and said "Boys and their toys!" at which he closed the door, and making his way around the car he got into the driver's seat, but before he put on his seat belt he leant across to Sandra and placing his left arm around her shoulders pulled her nearer to him, kissing her somewhat passionately for the time of day he cupped her left breast in his right hand, as she found his tongue seek out hers and relaxing she responded to his kisses until she felt that parked outside her house wasn't the best place to make out and pulling away with a smile on her face said "So I accept you were dreaming of me but we can't make out here!" realising the truth of her comment he sat back into his seat and put on his seat belt, before putting the key in the ignition. Turning the engine on, he looked at her and said "Where to girlfriend?" "Let's just do a drive round and see what's for sale" she said settling back into her seat adding "I hope I get as nice a car when I pass my Driving Test, do any of your Dad's work mates by any chance have a Mini?" Smiling at the thought of his Dad's colleagues having a Mini, he concentrated on driving and headed towards the South of Kirkdale, and the area known locally as Hilltop, as it looked down on the Town but after 20 minutes of driving as they were heading down Greenwood Street, Sandra suddenly turned to Dave averting her eyes from number 52 and she said "Let's try up towards Bedlow Moor, I know the prices are higher but there may be something in our range" and turning right at the end of the road neither of them had seen Daniel Bruce standing with foam dripping from his sponge washing his car on the drive watching them disappear round the corner as he gripped the sponge until he threw it angrily down on the ground by his feet where it lay, seeping suds into the gravel as his anger rose.

After trying the Bedlow Moor area where they found a couple of possibilities, they moved onto the North side of Town called Northfield, and after driving around the area they had a total of six houses that they would look at in the Estate Agents come lunchtime on Monday. Finding themselves on the 'wrong' side of Town they decided to take a chance on the Sportsman for Sunday lunch and pulling into the car park which was almost full they took off their seat belts but didn't get out of the car. "Didn't give Hilltop much of a chance did we?" said Dave looking at Sandra who had her answer ready and waiting "The schools aren't very good there, and when we have children I want them to go to a good school" and holding his hand she smiled at him awaiting his response. "Well girlfriend, if we stick to the Plan, sorry ....our Plan, children are at least four years away and then they won't go to school until they are 5, so 9 years away, hang on a minute ... them .... you said .... how many children are we planning to have?" he said turning to face her in his seat with a concerned look on his face. "Depends on how well your little friend performs!" and opening the door without giving him a chance to reply she got out of the car and stood waiting for him to join her with a huge smile on her face. Dave closed his door and locked the car and standing next to Sandra said as he pulled her close leaving his hand on her bottom "Had no complaints so far!" "No" she said turning away and taking his hand that was on her bottom before adding "He's doing just fine thank you boyfriend, now come on I'm starving, they do a Sunday Roast Carvery here according to the sign so you can stuff your face" and as they entered the Sportsman he realised she had managed not to answer his question.

Having 'stuffed his face' Dave waited for Sandra to return from the Toilet before heading back to the car. Taking his hand as she joined him at the doorway where he was waiting she quietly said "I think we should go for a walk around the Northfield Reservoir path, which is over there" pointing to a Footpath sign "Maybe we can get an ice cream if there is an ice cream van" and without waiting for an answer she set off through a narrow hole in the wall by the signpost, leaving Dave stood on the edge of the car park, wondering if he was ever going to get an answer to his question. Catching up with Sandra he put his arm around her waist, and they walked together in step on the rough track around the edges of the reservoir, until seeing another couple, a few yards ahead, get off a bench, they made their way to replace them. Sitting down, with Dave's right arm now around Sandra's shoulders, his hand hovering over her right breast as they lay back a little on the bench. "I suppose you want an answer to your question boyfriend?" said Sandra taking his right hand in hers but leaving it over her breast. "Well we do have a plan, but we, or rather I, never, well you know" he replied deciding to leave the question open "Well boyfriend…. I thought we would just leave it to nature, but I would like to have a girl and a boy, so two children, but ….and I know it's not in Our Plan can we just let things happen rather than plan, and see what happens?" and letting his hand rest on her breast she waited for his reply which came in the form of a kiss on her cheek, no more words were spoken as they both took onboard the addition to their plan, as the sun shone down on them reflecting off the rippled water until a cloud covered the sun and standing up, Dave took her hand and they headed for the ice cream van at the far end of the reservoir, which was calling with its children's melodies.

Walking back to the car park at the Sportsman with their half eaten ice creams, a question occurred to Sandra from nowhere, that she had meant to ask some months previously and as they had seemed to have run out of conversation she asked "Boyfriend, I've been meaning to ask for months, do you by any chance have a relative called Windsor Carey?" "Yes, why do you ask?" he said before returning to his now melting ice cream. "Well your mum said something yesterday at the party that reminded me about Windsor Carey, your mum said I would be lucky to be Mrs Baxter….that is, …..if we get married, as her mother married Windsor Carey which she had told me before, and she got a lot of nicknames at school like 'Hairy Mary Carey' and 'Scary Mary Carey' so as your mum said our children will be Baxters, which will be a lot better than her name" and as a drop of ice cream ran down her hand, she finished and concentrated on her ice cream "Well as we have decided to have well …..two children we can call them Albert and Victoria and that should be fine" waiting for a response he finished his ice cream just in time to hear a loud "Over my dead body Albert and Victoria!" from behind him, as Sandra fought to finish her ice cream before it ran down her hand, but failed and put it into a bin, before taking out a tissue and wiping her hand "Albert and Victoria!" Sandra reiterated before looking up to see Dave howling with laughter as his humour failed yet again, but he didn't mind. "You, boyfriend, are very naughty distracting me, while my ice cream melted" she said sternly before hooking up with him and after a few seconds said "Alistair and Caroline will do just fine" with no response from Dave they made their way to the Sportsman car park and it wasn't until he had fastened his seatbelt that Dave thought to ask. "Girlfriend, going back a bit, why Windsor Carey, what was it that you remembered?" "Something to do with work but it was ages ago and to be honest I can't really remember. Maybe it will come back to me" As Dave turned the car around, left the car park and headed for Sandra's house the sun rested on the moorland before slowly disappearing as they reached Sandra's house as the engagement weekend came to a close, an opportunity taken, and one still to see the light of day.

Monday duly arrived and as had become the routine, Dave picked Sandra up in the morning and she made her own way home unless he was finishing early, which wasn't very often as the workload seemed to be growing, and site visits could be anywhere in the area. This Monday was like any other apart from Sandra now proudly wearing her Engagement ring for all to see and it was evident as they walked hand in hand, up the Council Offices steps and onto their respective offices with a quick kiss before parting, that word had got around as Mrs Shaw came over and congratulated Sandra before looking at her ring. "He's a lucky boy that Dave Baxter!" and turning to head off to her own desk, she stopped halfway to say "Busy day today Sandra, so no daydreaming" and with a smile continued towards her own stacked desk, leaving Sandra to wonder how she knew about the engagement, as if she daydreamed! Sam had already done his rounds, and her own desk was piled high with folders that she hoped wouldn't include the Daly Road Sewage Works, which from memory she expected back on her desk at some stage. There was something else but she couldn't put her finger on it so she settled down to deal with the first folder, which was about a new Primary School at Bedlow Moor, which had been earmarked to replace two smaller schools in the area. Taking her time and reading through the various documents enclosed, she finally finished scrutinising it and placed it in the out tray with notes to various departments, for comments on access, road safety, soundproofing and bats among many other points. Strange world she thought schools and bats, as she opened the second folder suddenly realising it was the Daly Road Sewage Works, where an additional amendment had been added for the Engineering Department to look at the access road and its suitability for Tanker access. The rest of the morning seemed to pass without incident, and at lunchtime the 'Barmy Army' had arranged to meet for a catch up as Saturday night was a bit manic. As they sat down in the Brazilian cafe, it was obvious something was wrong as Jo hardly said a word as Sharon manipulated the conversation as usual, until even she realised something was wrong and being Sharon and sat opposite Jo, she said with no room for manoeuvre "Come on Jo spill, you've been quiet all morning, has the wonderful Chris dumped you!" "Sharon!" Peggy quickly said before looking at Jo and more subtly said "What's wrong Jo?" and finally Jo looked up from her half cold coffee and said "I think I'm pregnant!" after which a silence hung for a few seconds, before Sharon as only Sharon could said "Well I didn't see that coming.....neither did you!" and bursting out with laughter at her own joke, which was ignored by the others, she finally calmed down and added "Coming, get it.... well she obviously did!" pointing at Jo, at which even Jo started to laugh until all four were laughing together until Peggy reached out for Jo's hand, swiftly followed by Sandra and finally Sharon, who reached out on top of the stack of hands on the table and softly said "We're all here for you!" before wiping a tear from Jo's face, and a small smile appeared as she released her hand from under the stack and taking a sip of cold coffee said "He doesn't know yet, I only missed my period yesterday but it hasn't come today and I'm as regular as clock-work" "Give it a few more days and we'll keep our fingers crossed" said Peggy before suddenly adding "Unless you want a baby of course!" "Good God, No!" Jo said immediately and finished her coffee, suddenly bolstered by making a decision, and standing up with conviction said "Come on you lot, work to do it'll be fine you'll see" crossing her fingers behind her back.

Returning to the Council Offices they had a group hug on the top step before going to their offices, seeing Sam had brought even more work while she was away at lunch there was no time for sentiment as Sandra set about the folders she had left from the morning and it was nearly 3pm when she started on the next block of folders which she knew she wouldn't get through before the end of the day. Deciding to have a word with Mrs Shaw she approached her desk a little uneasy and ex-plaining her concern that the work was getting on top of her she was pleased to hear Mrs Shaw say "I wondered when you would get around to asking for help Sandra, you're doing just fine the workload in June, July and August is always heavier as the new financial year started in April and funds are released, which means that projects that were refused get appealed, and new projects are agreed which are at the start of the system. This year we have quite a lot of new schools on the rota but it will settle down, and I'm happy with your work, so just stay with it and it will ease up in time. Your review will be due at the end of the month but there's nothing but positives, and no complaints so you should sail through, now off you go, back to it" she finished and a smiling Sandra headed back to her desk and taking a folder titled 'Northfield Primary School Refurbishment' she set about her work reinvigorated, and de-termined that she would finish the pile before Sam returned at the end of the day. She failed as Sam placed 20 files in her in tray at 4.50, saying "Enjoy" as he went around the rest of the desks placing similar volumes of folders on each desk, which each received a sarcastic thank you, before he headed back to the mailroom, leaving an apparent never ending workload on each desk. Defeated by the stack of folders in front of her, and not really looking forward to the bus ride home as Dave was out on site, she made her way down the corridor to the exit to find Daniel stood at the top of the steps with his back to her blocking her way. Slowing her pace she was unsure what he was waiting for, until she suddenly realised it was her, as she had to pass him to get to the Bus Station. Looking down and hoping to pass him without him noticing, she immediately knew that wasn't going to happen, as he turned to face her at the top of the steps.

"Well if it isn't the engagement girl" said Daniel face full of hate and a rising anger in his voice "News travels fast around here, you must have finally let him screw you for the price of a ring! You really missed your chance with me, but one day I'll get my own back....Bitch" turning away and heading down the steps without looking back, Daniel headed towards the Council car park as the tears flowed down Sandra's face as she stood alone arms hanging limp by her side, on the pedestal of the Council Office's steps, for all the world to see her pain!

The journey home passed in a blur as Sandra struggled with Daniel's outburst, and what she should do about it. She couldn't tell Dave as he would be so angry he might do something stupid, and all their plans would be ruined if he confronted and attacked Daniel, as she was sure he would. He could lose his job and probably Daniel as well, but while Daniel losing his job would serve him right it wouldn't be fair if Dave lost his as well. If she told Personnel at the Council there would be an enquiry, but it was her word against his and even if he told his version of the truth it would still come down to who they believed. Whichever way she thought about it, he had been very clever as there were no witnesses to either of their clashes at work. Getting off the bus she slowly made her way home and with the tears now replace by anger, she decided to keep it quiet and bury it with her lie about Christmas Eve. Even if Daniel said something he had no witnesses and she could call him a liar and a jealous ex boyfriend. Daniel could go to hell she thought, he wasn't going to break up her and Dave's future and closing the front door behind her she called out "I'm home mum what's for tea?" burying a lie that only stays a lie, until it finds and meets the truth!

The week stumbled along and as the weather improved towards the weekend, Sandra was ironically grateful that she had seen Dave only on Wednesday night, as she put her altercation with Daniel to the back of her mind, and as a sign that things were getting better Jo announced at lunch on Thursday that she had got her period and they should celebrate with a couple of drinks after work on Friday "I'm up for that!" said Sharon "But only if you go to the Doctors and get on the Pill, this week has been awful wondering if you were, or weren't pregnant" and putting down her coffee she was shocked to hear Jo quickly respond "What I do with my body is my business I'll have you know!" before adding "Who's coming with me?" and without giving anyone a chance Sharon quickly took Jo's hand and said "We'll get it set up today, for next week. We don't want any more little Accountants in the world do we?" The "Hey you can't say that, Dave's dad is an Accountant!" that came from Sandra, before she had a chance to think, was swiftly responded to by Peggy "But Dave's not an Accountant!" at which Sandra ruefully said "Ah didn't think that through did I?" "Well no you didn't" said Sharon adding "So when are you and Dave going to start making little babies?" "Well not for the next four years as it wouldn't fit into our plan if Alistair, or Caroline came along before then!" and realising she had spoken without engaging her brain, she got exactly what she expected. "Alistair and Caroline well that sounds just lovely" Sharon said holding her coffee cup little finger extended "I think that's really sweet!" said Peggy trying to deflect some of Sharon's sarcasm. "You have a plan! With children's names already chosen WOW! Sharon how soon can I go on the pill?" and between the laughter of Sharon and Jo, and the look of understanding from Peggy, Sandra just sat there glad the week was nearly over and she could put it behind her, hopefully for good.

Friday at work passed without incident, and as the day ground to a finish it was a good humoured Sam who arrived at 4.45 and placing 5 folders on Sandra's desk smiled at her and said "I think the rush is over, for now anyway" and headed off to Mrs Shaw's desk, with what looked like two fat folders and seeing that he only had a few folders for the other desks, she eased back in her seat and decided this weekend was about to start, and damn the week about to be gone. Picking up the folders Sam had left it came as no surprise to see the Daly Road Sewage Works folder at the top. 'Well that can wait for next week' she thought to herself, and as she finished the folder in front of her she placed it in the out tray, her work done for the week as her mind wandered to tomorrow night when her mum and dad were going to a Conference in Manchester for the day, and more importantly were staying at a hotel for the night, and she and Dave would have the house to themselves, and it was about time her white satin two piece saw the light of day, and night.

Seeing Peggy at the door ,Sandra went to get her jacket from behind the stationery door, and hooking up with her at the door they headed off to the George, where they had arranged to meet Jo and Sharon and a couple of other girls from the office. "Good week?" Peggy said as they descended the Council steps "Had its moments!" said Sandra eager to get off the steps where she had cried her heart out on Monday. Crossing the road to the George, they failed to see a furious looking Daniel watching from the top of the steps wishing them dead from his lofty position "One day bitch" he said quietly to himself, as Sandra and Peggy went down the alley to the George unaware of the threat behind them ,as they entered the pub to find Jo and Sharon already halfway down their first drinks. "Come on you slow coaches it's your round!" said Sharon finishing her drink as Jo gave her a look and said "Watch out Sharon's on a mission" picking up her drink from Peggy as she returned from the bar, Sandra smiled at Sharon's ability to put things behind her in search of a good time.

As they headed for the Old Cock coupled up, Sharon and Jo, Peggy and Sandra, leaving Sue and Mandy from Administration Support in the George, they were almost at the door when Sharon stopped and putting her arms round Peggy and Sandra said "It's been a shit week, Mick has gone off to Germany for three months, so any good looking blokes out tonight are mine OK!" and with that Sharon left the trio standing outside, taking in the shock news as she opened the door and with a "I'll get them in" almost lost as the door closed behind her the three said almost in unison "Oh God!" and headed for the door knowing that 'A few quiet drinks' would be anything but! The pub was filling up with an eclectic mix of office and manual workers, and the bar was doing a healthy trade already even though it was only 6pm. They spotted Sharon at the bar with a couple of admirers already in tow, and it was left to Peggy to give her a hand with the drinks and the admirers! Returning to the back of the pub with their drinks, and a disappointed Sharon, Jo broke the silence with what can only be described as a bolt from the blue. "I've decided to give Chris the elbow!" at which Sharon, now on a man hunt said "Plenty more fish Jo" taking a drink, she hooked up with Jo as she looked around the pub and added "But not in here!" at which she burst out laughing at her own humour, which was contagious as Jo joined her in a joke that was cruel, but honest.

The quiet few drinks became an impromptu pub crawl as the evening wore on. The Old Cock was followed by The Shears, and then it was onto The Line where Sharon and Jo finally became the point of attraction for a couple of well dressed drinkers who insisted on buying them drinks, which gave

Peggy and Sandra the chance to make a break for freedom and home. With a quick hug all round, Sandra and Peggy took their opportunity and as Peggy headed for the Taxi rank as she lived in the opposite direction, Sandra used the phone box to call Dave who had said he was staying in as he had some course work to finish for Monday, and he would give her a lift home rather than get a Taxi if she called.

"Just a few quiet drinks girlfriend!" he said as he tried to help her with her seatbelt which was met with no comment, but a pair of arms round his neck and a passionate kiss as he leant into her. Returning her passion with his own he eventually pulled away from her and at the second time he managed to secure her seatbelt, as she sat back with a smile on her face before finally saying "Mrs Shaw says you are a lucky boy Dave Baxter" "Oh she does, does she!" Dave responded wondering just where this comment came from "Just saying boyfriend!" Sandra added without looking at him with a smile fixed on her face, as Dave took the opportunity to drive away from the Town centre and head for Church Street, with a story to tell but it could wait for another day, as the silence from the passenger seat told him without looking that his girlfriend had dozed off, with the warmth and motion of the car not to forget the effect of the alcohol after a quiet few drinks!

"Good morning boyfriend!" said Sandra opening the door for Dave as the clock struck 11.00 on Saturday morning "Would you like a cup of tea, mum's just made a pot?" she added before putting her arms around his neck and adding "Thanks for bringing me home last night...Prince Charming!" and planted a kiss on his lips just as Diane came into the kitchen. "You could at least wait until we have gone you two!" she said heading to the fridge for some milk, which drew a scowl from Sandra but not enough to stop her kissing Dave for a second time as if to prove a point. "Cup of tea, Dave?" Diane said ignoring Sandra's scowl with ease "Yes please Diane" Dave responded slapping Sandra on the bottom and taking a seat at the kitchen table.

"I'll just finish getting ready ... only be a few minutes" said Sandra heading out of the kitchen and going upstairs to her bedroom. "How's work Dave everything going okay" Diane said waiting for Jim to come downstairs so they could head off to Manchester. "Yes, everything's going well, I've got a couple of courses to finish, but can't complain" he finished taking a drink of tea. "Excellent, you've got the house to yourselves tonight as Tony is away with work so make yourself at home, there's plenty in the fridge and a pizza in the freezer if you want it......about time too we'll be late" she finished as Jim made an appearance at the kitchen door. "It's only an hour away and it'll be quiet on the roads on a Saturday, so we've got plenty of time" Jim responded picking up a spare cup of tea and taking a drink, as Diane went to get their bags from the bottom of the stairs. A look between Dave and Jim needed no words, as Jim finished his cup of tea Sandra came downstairs, and with a hug between mother and daughter Jim picked up their bag and with a "Don't burn the house down you two" headed out of the front door without looking back as Diane and Sandra waved at each other, like they were going on a holiday rather than a night away.

"So boyfriend what shall we do today?" Sandra said as her parent's car disappeared round the corner. "Well I thought we might do some more house hunting, but maybe look at a map before we set off, and we could have lunch or tea out and then...." "And then what boyfriend?" she butted in pouting her lips "And then I thought we could watch Match of the Day!" at which the pout disappeared until she realised his awful sense of humour was on the go, and thinking two can play that game she said "Excellent look forward to it, are Kirkdale on tonight?" and realising she had made a faux pas, but with no idea of what it was, she picked up her cup of tea as Dave tried not to choke on his "Girlfriend you are priceless, you really are!" "Oh that's nice, so are Kirkdale on tonight?" and unable to control himself, he spat his tea out into the sink, before turning to see Sandra laughing at him "Good job my mum and dad have gone, that's disgusting boyfriend!" regaining his composure he pulled her close to him, and placing both hands on her bottom he leant into whisper into her ear "If we aren't in bed before Match of the Day, I'm going home!" at which he slapped her bottom with his right hand leaving his left on her bottom and pulling her even closer into him, he kissed her slowly and then more passionately before he put his hands inside her bottom jean pockets, as he searched for her tongue which she twisted around his, gently leaning into him before putting her arms around his neck as their passion rose in the empty house. Taking her arms from around his neck she prised his hands from her pockets, and keeping hold of his right hand led him into the Lounge, sitting down next to the sideboard she pulled her dad's A-Z from the bottom draw and giving a now disappointed Dave the book, she patted the seat next to him for him to sit down as he flicked through the pages. "So where shall we go to eat and then we can make a plan where to go on the way there!" he said looking at the index "You and your plans!" Sandra said with a smile on her face as he quickly responded with a similar smile "Well this one is working out quite well wouldn't you say girlfriend?" without a moment's hesitation she replied "Oh yes boyfriend, this plan is definitely working out!"

Having finally decided to head to the Bedlow Moor and Northfield area and having picked up a few brochures from the Estate Agent in Town on Monday, they could afterwards go onto the Hobbit Inn for a late lunch or early tea. Dave held the car door open for Sandra as she headed up the garden path after locking the front door of the house. "Why thank you Sir!" she said as she felt for her seat belt and feeling the click as it found the lock, she looked at Dave who was smiling at her "What?" she said looking around for something wrong "Nothing girlfriend, just still can't believe you're mine!" and without replying, but with a smirk on her face, she sat back as Dave set off towards Bedlow Moor, and the start of a day that they both knew would not end with Match of the Day.

Having decided that Hilltop wasn't for them, despite looking at several houses in the Estate Agent brochures, which were either too expensive or too small, they arrived at Bedlow Moor where they knew their hopes would be difficult to match as prices were always at the top of the market, as it was commuter belt for the cities of Leeds and Huddersfield as well as further away Manchester. So it was no surprise when the first few houses they saw were out of their bracket even if they would accept a lower offer. Rose Cottage on the edge of the Moor looked quite promising, but it was only one bedroom and that wouldn't suit their plan! The next two houses were ex council houses so plenty of space and gardens, but were definitely out of their budget. So it was a disappointed Sandra and Dave who headed to Northfield, their search enthusiasm already waning. The road into Northfield was wide and with some navigation up and down the streets of the main road they found themselves outside Number 15 Windy Hill Street which looked of interest. An all day open day was taking place according to the Estate Agent in Town on Monday, as the owners were relocating so they needed a sale, and open days had worked before, the Estate Agent had said, adding that it saved him having to keep turning up to meet potential buyers on different days and times. Allowing a couple with a little boy exit the front door as they arrived, they slowly made their way around the property without a word between them. Heading upstairs they looked out of the front bedroom window onto the road outside, before moving to the smaller back bedrooms and finally the bathroom which had seen better days. Standing looking out over the garden from the back bedroom Sandra felt Dave's arms around her waist, closing her eyes for a moment she could see a little Alistair and Caroline with a swing in the garden. "Well?" he said squeezing her waist "Yes" she replied and headed off down the stairs and stood by the car. "Yes what, girlfriend?" he asked "Yes I can see us living here, it needs some work doing, like a new bathroom and some TLC, but it's in our budget and they're going to refurbish Northfield School next year, so that's a plus and there's plenty of room for our little family so, Yes boyfriend!" Opening his car door, he turned to take another look at the slightly tired house, he closed his eyes for a second and breathing in and slowly letting his breath out he opened his eyes and got into the car."Well I have to say girlfriend, I agree shall we add it to Our plan?" and the arms around his neck needed no words as Sandra kissed him before quickly stopping. "Let's leave the car here, and take a walk around the area to see what it's really like. We haven't really got anything else to do today have we?" adding with a blushing smile "apart from missing Match of the Day that is!" as Dave locked the car and taking her hand they set off to walk round the area where they would build their life together.

The walk around Northfield took them nearly an hour and returning to the car they took another look at the house leaning against the car as they stood, each trying to envisage what it would look like with the alterations they had discussed on their walk around the area. "Let's have another look inside!" said Sandra letting go of Dave's hand and heading towards the still open front door. Catching up with her, as she entered the house to a "Hello again!" from the Estate Agent, Dave followed Sandra through the kitchen and into the back garden, turning to face the back of the house she took Dave's hand and for a second he wondered what she was thinking, but when she finally decided to let him in on her thoughts, he knew she was right "We could get a kitchen extension which would make the house work better for us, there's enough room and I know this person in Planning who could deal with it!" looking at her and then looking back at the house Dave tried to imagine an extension, and she was right there was enough land, and it would make sense to add an extension, as the current kitchen is from when the house was built. Turning back to look at a thoughtful Sandra, he waited until she turned to look at him before saying "Girlfriend there's one minor problem that perhaps you haven't thought of!" with a pensive look she tried to think what he was on about before giving up and saying "What boyfriend!" waited for his answer as she turned back to look at the house "Well girlfriend, there's the little matter of the fact that we don't own the house!" "Oh we will!" came the swift reply as she took his hand and led him back into the house, seeing the Estate Agent having a cigarette in the front garden they went through the house and joined him as he finished and put out his cigarette under his shoe on the gravel path.

"Simon isn't it?" said Sandra as they stood on the path next to him, before Dave even had a chance to say a word "Yes, how can I help you" he replied adding "I see you came back for a second viewing, so I take it you are interested in the property?" looking at Dave for a second Sandra realised they should have spoken in the back garden, but she had made a decision and she was determined to get some answers before they left the house. "Yes Simon, we are interested in the property, but it needs a lot of work doing, like a new kitchen and bathroom as well as the roof needing some attention, so my question is what will it take to secure the house, before we take it any further?" Taking a copy of the brochure from his briefcase he looked at Sandra, almost ignoring Dave and after a quick look at the picture of the house with the price next to it he said "If this house was in Hilltop it would be up for £29,995 the price of £25,995 is a fair price" "But Northfield, isn't Hilltop!" Sandra cut in and added before he had a chance to add anything else "We would like to offer £22,000 to take into account the amount of work that needs doing. I understand the owners are relocating, and as the housing market is stagnant, I think it is a fair offer, oh and we have nothing to sell so we can move on this quickly. If you could put the offer to your clients and get back to me Simon, I would appreciate it thank you!" and writing her phone number on the brochure she had taken from him, she handed it back to a now somewhat speechless Simon.

Taking Dave's hand, they headed for the car, without looking at each other, or looking back. Unlocking and opening the car door Dave got in, still trying to figure out what had just happened. "Well that was fun boyfriend!" said Sandra as she sat back in her seat and reached for the seat belt. "Fun!" said Dave finally finding his voice "You've just offered to buy a house for £22,000 without asking me!" Pulling on his seatbelt, he started the engine as Sandra suddenly realised she hadn't given him a chance to say anything, as they drove away from Windy Hill Street in silence, and headed for the Hobbit Inn, some 5 miles away. On reaching the Hobbit Inn and pulling into the car park. Sandra broke the silence as she undid her seatbelt "Dave, I'm sorry, I got carried away and I know we should have discussed it. and maybe put in an offer, or not, on Monday. I am sorry" she repeated looking at him as he released his seat belt. "Seriously girlfriend, I think I've created a monster!" at which a hurt look came over Sandra's face, at which he put his finger up to her lips to stop her saying anything "A beautiful monster. who I want to spend the rest of my life with in Windy Hill Street, even if we will be poor!" the hurt look was replaced very quickly by a smile that he would remember forever, before her arms wrapped around his neck. and they kissed with an intensity to cement an agreement that needed no contract.

After being shown to a table at the Hobbit Inn, the waiter left them perusing the menu while he went to get their drinks. Looking out of the window Dave saw the clouds slowly pass by as the sun chased them out of the sky with its heat, and as the rich blue sky looked down on the hills he looked at Sandra who was still studying the menu and playing a game with himself, he decided she would choose Lasagne and Chips, and while he waited for her decision, he reflected on the last few hours as a huge addition to his, and what was now their plan had occurred. £22,000 on a house, just like that, I hope I've passed my exams he thought for the first time in weeks with the results due at the end of the month, the pay rise if he passed would come in handy, especially if their offer got accepted. "Penny for them!" broke his thoughts as Sandra put down the menu and caught his attention. "Sorry I was just daydreaming, have you decided what you're going to have" he replied. "Lasagne and chips for me" she said as a smile came over Dave's face "What?" she said aware that must be a reason behind the smile "Oh it's nothing, think I'll have the Beef Pie and Mash" and with a smile Sandra said" I knew you would order that!" and realising he had been beaten at his own game, he let her win without letting on he had also guessed her meal. As the drinks arrived and they gave their meal orders to the waiter, Dave picked up his Pint of Lager and raising it into the air he held it out to Sandra who raised her own glass to his as Dave said "To 15 Windy Hill Street, may it be ours!" and with a clash of glasses Sandra smiled as she quietly said "And our children's!" and taking a couple of gulps Dave put the drink down and took Sandra's hand "Monster!" he said and squeezed her hand as they waited for their meals, completely oblivious to everyone else in their own little world.

Taking advantage of the location of the Hobbit Inn and with plenty of light left in the day even though it was now nearly 7.30pm they left the car in the car park, and followed the Kirkdale Way signposts leading off the car park, after some 30 minutes they were at the top of a ledge that looked across to Northfield and as they stood arms around each other as the summer sun warmed them Sandra leaned into Dave and said "I know it was all a bit rushed, but I just feel that the house will be perfect, well eventually that is, and I promise I'll never spend £22,000 ever again without asking you!" "Monster, you'd better not!" he said as he kissed her gently adding "If the offer gets accepted you know we'll have to cancel plans for a holiday this summer!" with a few seconds thought Sandra quietly replied "There'll be other holidays but not another Windy Hill!" and joined together physically and mentally in agreement, they looked out across at Northfield before they made their way in a circular route back to the Hobbit Inn, and the drive home which naturally had to be by way of Windy Hill Street.

Pulling into Church Street, Dave parked next to Sandra's house and turned the engine off. Not moving, Dave sat for a moment as Sandra released her seatbelt but seeing he hadn't moved she looked at him "Something wrong boyfriend?" she said sitting back in her seat "No nothing, it's just been a bit of a strange day that's all, definitely one to remember" seeing his mind was still obviously on the house Sandra thought she had the solution to his dilemma. "Come on, the day isn't over yet, unless of course you want to watch Match of the Day on your own that is!" and with that she was out of the car and heading down the path to the front door, as Dave's libido overruled his mind and he got out of the car and picking up some clothes he had brought, he lock it and as he twirled the keys on his finger and headed off after her, all thoughts of Windy Hill now pushed to the back of his thoughts as he closed the front door behind him. With no sign of Sandra he heard a noise upstairs followed by her calling out "Make yourself at home and can you close the curtains while you're at it!" Heading into the Lounge he turned the side lamp on and drew the curtains before heading to the kitchen, and getting a bottle of Lager from the fridge he was about to turn round, when he thought he had better get two bottles and opening the fridge again he picked up another bottle of Lager and felt rather than saw a figure go into the Lounge. With a bottle of Lager in each hand he headed towards the Lounge and said as he neared the doorway "I got us both a bottle of..." and never finished the sentence as he saw Sandra stood with a hand on the fireplace wearing just the satin two piece outfit she had worn on their first night together in York. As a silence came over them both, Sandra slowly walked over to where Dave had remained static and taking the two bottles of Lager from his hands, she put them down on the sideboard, before returning to where he still stood. "I thought you might remember this little number, boyfriend" at which a simple nod was all Dave could manage as she put her arms around his neck pressing her breasts against his chest, and as she raised herself onto her toes she felt both his hands on her bottom as she quietly said in his ear "So you do remember!" at which he moved his right hand to cup her breast as he found her tongue with his, and they entwined as he slowly caressed her body, as they forgot all about the rest of the day just gone. They slowly ended up next to the sofa and taking his hands off her body he pulled off his T Shirt, momentarily stopping kissing her as he pulled it over his head and looking at her face as she smiled at him, he put his fingers at the bottom of the slip covering her breasts and pulled it over her head, leaving her naked above the waist as they resumed kissing as her bare breasts warmed his exposed chest. Standing next to the sofa he slipped his fingers over and then under her panties and slowly prised them down her legs until his fingers could reach no more, but a shake of her hips lowered them to her feet as she stood in front of him naked. Feeling an arm move from his neck he soon felt a tug on his belt as Sandra released the buckle, and popping his top jean button, she lowered his zip until she could feel his hard bulge against her, as Dave put a hand on the top of his jeans and pushed them down his legs she could feel his erect penis against her stomach. As she put her hand inside his Y Fronts Dave put a hand into the side of his Y Fronts and pushed them down leaving Sandra holding a very erect penis in her hand as his tongue urgently found hers again. Gently Sandra gripped his shaft and working her hand up and down she could feel his fingers enter her vagina and somewhat awkwardly they ended up on the floor in front of the fire. As Dave fingered her clitoris lying on his side, he felt Sandra move her leg and finding himself on his back he looked into her eyes as she moved to sit astride him, her hand still holding his penis. Sitting astride him with her knees on the ground, she gently lowered herself onto his erect penis using her hand to guide it into her now very moist vagina, and with a thrust he was inside her as he found her breasts with his hands. Moving slowly up and down, as she felt his penis inside her, she concentrated on keeping him inside her and moving more quickly she rocked back and forth until she could hear his quickening grunts, which she knew meant he wasn't far from coming and quickening her motion even more, she could feel his hands squeeze her breasts harder pinching her nipples, before he pushed up with his thighs and he came inside her as she clenched her own thigh muscles and held him in position until he slowly relaxed and pulling her shoulders down with his hands she leant down to kiss him and stayed lying on top of him nuzzled into his neck, as his penis slowly slipped out of her and their nakedness warming them as they gently held each other.

The slap on her bottom woke Sandra from her dreams of swings, and suddenly shy, as she realised she was naked she rested her head on her hand, with her elbow resting on Dave's chest. "What time's Match of the Day on?" she said looking in the direction of the TV in the corner, at which the second slightly harder slap on her bare bottom told her she had pushed it a little bit. Standing up she looked down on a naked Dave and grabbing her satin outfit put her panties on, all the while looking at him as he was looking up at her. "I think your little friend has died, boyfriend!" and giggling she headed for the bathroom, returning to the Lounge a few minutes later with a dressing gown on she found Dave with just his jeans on drinking from one of the bottles of Lager they had abandoned. "Match of the Day is on in 20 minutes girlfriend" and taking a swig from the bottle he sat back on the sofa and crossed his legs. "Then you've just got time to finish that bottle before we have to be in bed, presuming that your friend isn't dead that is!" Picking up and taking a swig from the other bottle, she sat next to him on the sofa letting the dressing gown fall open revealing her breasts, as he put an arm round her making sure his right hand could reach inside her dressing gown to settle on her breast. "He'll be just fine, as you will find out girlfriend!" and once they had finished their bottles of Lager, Dave stood up and holding out his hand he took hers in his, and said "Come on Monster, lets see if my little friend is dead, or just sleeping!" and they headed off to Sandra's bedroom to miss Match of the Day.

Sunday morning crept through the curtains of Sandra's bedroom and woke her up as the sun crept higher in the sky. Rubbing her eyes she looked at a still sleeping Dave and carefully crept out of bed and headed naked for a shower leaving him lying on her bed, the duvet just about covering his naked bottom. Closing the bathroom door she turned on the shower, and when it was hot enough she stepped into the shower. As the heat of the shower hit her, she thought about last night and making love in the Lounge, and again when they went to bed, she was turning into a Monster she thought as she set about washing her hair. The hands that suddenly covered her soapy breasts made her jump, but with her eyes closed and her hair full of shampoo she leant back into Dave as he caressed her breasts, before his right hand moved down between her legs as his left hand roamed over her breasts. Feeling his erect penis on her bottom, she turned to face him and with shampoo running down her face, she squinted at Dave as he put his hands on her bottom and gently lifted her up as she put her legs around his waist, with a little movement she could feel his hand between her legs guiding his penis inside her as she felt her back against the cold shower tiles which she soon forgot, as Dave with his hands on her bottom moved with ever increasing motion until he finally leant heavily into her, crushing her against the tiled shower wall as he came. Catching her breathe she kissed him tenderly on the lips as her legs locked behind him, her arms around his neck and seeing his smile which needed no answer, he pulled out of her finally at which she gasped a little before her feet slid down his back and touched the floor. Dave reluctantly stepped out of the shower leaving Sandra to finish washing her hair, finding a towel, he dried himself before heading back to her bedroom and got dressed putting on clean clothes that he had brought with him. Once dressed he headed downstairs and putting the kettle on, he took two slices of bread from the bread bin and popped them into the toaster and getting the milk from the fridge he decided to make a pot of tea and adding a couple of tea bags into the pot he had just finished pouring the now boiled water into the pot, when Sandra came into the kitchen. "Well get you boyfriend, all domesticated, surprised you had any energy left!" as the toaster popped up, he turned to take the toast out and spreading some butter on the slices, he cut them each into two and put them on a plate in the middle of the kitchen table, placing the teapot and cups next to the plate he sat down and smiled, as Sandra took a bite of toast. "Morning girlfriend!" he said taking a piece of toast and sitting back in his seat he added "I could wake up to that every morning!" and with a smile he took another bite of toast as he thought of the shower sex they had just had. "Now who's the Monster!" Sandra said before picking up another piece of toast and with a wink she poured them both a cup of tea and adding milk she took a sip before she finally added "Imagine what we could do if we lived in Windy Hill!" taking a drink of tea Dave took his time before responding "Not in that bathroom we won't!" and as Sandra laughed, he took her hand and they sat in silence reflecting on the last day, as they finished their tea.

As Dave put the teapot and plate on the sink drainer he heard from behind him "Come on boyfriend" as Sandra headed upstairs. Following obediently he was disappointed to see as he entered the room, that Sandra was stripping the sheets from her bed and with the evident disappointed look on his face Sandra bundled up the sheets and held them out for Dave to hold."Don't look so sad, if you had stayed up and watched Match of the Day I wouldn't have to change the sheets! But I'm glad you didn't, stay up that is, well, you did actually..... and we had already.....well you know!" as her face turned red, he smiled and headed off downstairs to find the washer as Sandra put clean sheets on the bed where she would sleep alone tonight.

Deciding to go for a walk they headed for Bedlow Moor and after an hour of walking and talking about nothing in particular Sandra finally broached the subject of 15 Windy Hill Street. "Boyfriend do you think we, sorry I should say I, did the right thing putting an offer on Windy Hill yesterday?" hearing the doubt in her voice for the first time he squeezed her hand and carrying on walking thought about it for a few moments before responding. "Well it was certainly a shock, but they have to accept it first, before we need to start thinking about it, but yes I do think it was the right thing to do. If last night told us anything it was that we need to be in our own place. I do like to be clean!" he finished as a hand slapped his chest, before Sandra smiled at her memory of the shower this morning. Taking the long way around Bedlow Moor they arrived at the Bedlow Arms at 1pm and the enticing smell of Sunday lunch proved too much, and they followed a family of four inside and waiting for a table they looked at each other as the family were led to a table by a waiter, and without a word, but with a knowing look between them their plan was sealed as a waiter approached them and led them to a two cover table by the window, looking out towards Northfield where their dreams lay basking under the summer sun.

After a very filling Sunday Roast Beef lunch together with a couple of drinks, Sandra and Dave were grateful for the chance to walk off some of the food and drink, so they ambled back to Church Street in no particular hurry, and seeing that Jim and Diane had returned from Manchester as they spotted the Ford Escort parked next to Dave's Fiesta the weekend was effectively over for them. Stopping at the end of the street they looked at each other and with a gentle kiss they set off down the street, towards where the sheets from Sandra's bed danced in the light breeze. Opening the door Sandra called out "We're home" at which Diane said "So are we!" and entering the kitchen where Jim and Diane sat nursing a cup of tea from a newly brewed pot the words "Did you....?" echoed across the kitchen as Sandra and Diane both spoke at the same time, and Diane opened her hand to indicate her daughter should go first "Did you have a nice time in Manchester?" taking a sip of tea Diane quickly said "Yes darling it was lovely, although your Dad did have a few too many last night which is why we are a bit late getting home!" Jim scowled and deciding silence would be the best response he took a drink of his tea, but managed to mutter "Kettle and black" before concentrating once again on his tea. "What did you two get up to? Although by the sheets on the line I can guess!" and her knowing smile was replied to curtly by Sandra "Mum!" taking a few seconds to regain her composure she finally said "Well if you must know we, that is I, bought a house!" as the sentence soaked in Jim managed to beat Diane to the question "You did what?" Looking at Dave for support his smile said 'You started this and she was on her own "Well there was this open day at a house in Northfield, and well you know we have been looking, so we went on Saturday afternoon and although it needs a lot of work we both love it and well, I made an offer there and then!" as Jim and Diane both looked at Dave for his input he smiled and said "Your daughter is a Monster!" and shaking his head indicating he was done, Sandra went on "We don't know if the offer will be accepted until tomorrow, but they wanted £25,995 and I offered £22,000, as the people selling it are relocating so need to sell but I, sorry we, are hopeful and we had a walk around the area and it's really ice, there's a school for the children which is going to be refurbished next year as I've seen the plans at work and.... Dave!" seeing that she had run out of steam Dave stepped into the conversation "Jim, Diane, as you

249

know we have this plan going on, starting with the engagement and Sandra getting a new job, and although a house wasn't actually in the plan it does make sense, and well it might seem a bit rash, but if we get it at £22,000, with a new bathroom and a kitchen extension it will be a bargain" a silence settled as Dave finished only to punctuated by Diane grasping part of his statement "Children! You're not...." "No Mum I'm not, but we do intend to have children in the future, just not now, it's part of our plan so yes all things considered you will get to be Grandma Diane!" and with a hug that told her that her mum was happy for them, Diane looked over Sandra's shoulder and wiped a tear from her eye, and looking at Jim she said "You'll be Granddad Jim, oh God I suddenly feel old!" and with the news spent, Diane suggested they move into the Lounge and the afternoon slipped by discussing house prices and costs of renovation, and who they could use as a solicitor, all of which would be wasted time if their offer wasn't accepted tomorrow. But tomorrow was such a long way off.

Monday came and the sun heralded in a day that could make or break all their plans, as Dave arrived at Church Street to pick up Sandra for a lift to work. "Good morning boyfriend" Sandra said getting into the car and with a quick kiss she put on her seatbelt as Dave looked at her "Nervous girlfriend?" the silence answered his question, as he set off and it wasn't until they were near the Council car park that she finally answered his question "What if they don't accept our offer, and I gave them my home phone number, and I won't be home until after 5.30 so I might miss the call?" with a smile Dave took hold of her hand, after they had parked. "Girlfriend calm down, why don't we meet up at lunchtime say 12.30 and go round to the Estate Agents, and see what they have to say and ....." he never finished the sentence as Sandra put her arms around him, and kissed him a bit too passionately for the time of the morning. Breaking away she returned for a butterfly kiss before saying "Sounds like a plan!" and getting out of the car she waited for him to lock the car and join her as they made their way up the Council Office steps "See you at 12.30 don't be late!" Sandra said with a kiss on the cheek, before she headed down the corridor to the Planning Department leaving Dave at the entrance with his fingers crossed behind his back, before he turned and took the steps to the Estates Department.

The morning dragged for Sandra as she counted down the minutes, and it was with a relief when Mrs Shaw arrived at her desk. "Sandra the workload has settled down as you will have noticed, so we should book some training in for you, so I just wanted to know if you had any plans for summer. You haven't booked any holidays yet, but before I look at dates I wanted to make sure you haven't booked something over the weekend." "No Mrs Shaw, we didn't book anything over the weekend and in fact we've decided not to go on holiday this year, so any time would be okay for me" with a smile that gave nothing away, Mrs Shaw looked at Sandra and said "Okay I'll let you know what dates are available, and we can get something booked this afternoon" as she left, Sandra watched her return to her own desk, as the clock above her desk moved past 11.00. Taking her time to finish the folder she was working on, she placed it in the out tray and looked at the thick folder that was next and seeing the title Manchester Road Power Station, she realised this was going to take all afternoon so seeing that the next one was Daly Road Sewage Works –Amendment, she replaced the thick folder to deal with in the afternoon, picking up the smaller Daly Road folder she managed to finish it, just as the clock moved past 12.30, swiftly getting up she headed for the stairs where Dave would be waiting, their plans for the future sitting waiting at the Estate Agents 800 yards away.

With no sign of Dave, Sandra started to get even more anxious, until she saw him sitting at the bottom of the stairs, as she joined him, he stood up and taking her hand he pulled her to him and after a light kiss he pulled away and said "Come on Monster, I have a good feeling about this!" and unable to agree with him as her stomach churned, she fell into step as they neared the Estate Agents. Opening the door to let Sandra through first, Dave watched her hesitate for a second before she approached the desk where Simon was sitting. Looking up he opened his hand and said "Take a seat Mr and Mrs Robertson, I'll just get the folder" as Sandra looked at Dave wondering why he had called them Mr and Mrs Robertson, it hit her as he returned with the folder and her number on the top of the brochure inside the folder "Sandra Robertson" and just as she was about to correct him she heard him say "I spoke to the Vendors this morning, and while they were hoping for a better offer they will accept your offer of £22,000 subject to you having nothing to sell. So if you can let me have the name of your Solicitor, we can get the wheels in motion Mrs Robertson. Congratulations!" and as a speechless Sandra looked at Dave, and back at Simon, she heard Dave say "We will be using Mr Sanderson at McParlands here in Kirkdale, but actually it's Mr Baxter and Miss Robertson if you could correct your records please." Picking up his pen Simon, added the solicitor as Mr Sanderson in the allotted space and corrected the name at the top of the file to Baxter/Robertson. "There just remains the address you want the correspondence to go to" and as Dave gave his home address a speechless Sandra sat looking at their future sat on the desk. "Thank you Simon, and I look forward to hearing from you in due course" she heard Dave say, before he stood up and shook Simon's hand, at which she felt a hand on her elbow as Dave helped her up, as Simon finished "Miss Robertson" holding out his hand which she shook automatically and she felt Dave take her free hand, and using his other hand he opened the door and they were out into the bright sunshine. "Not quite the Monster now are we?" Dave said once they were outside. Finally finding her voice she said "I'm going to be a pussy cat from now on!" "Oh no, I quite like the Monster, especially in the shower!" at which the smile followed by a prolonged kiss, still standing outside the Estate Agents told him she did too.

"Well girlfriend shall we get a sandwich for lunch, it's probably all we can afford!" Dave said as a slap landed on his arm and Sandra hooked up, and they made for the precinct and its many sandwich shops. "Dave, you are okay with this aren't you I know I was a bit rash on Saturday, but it is what we want isn't it?" "Sandra, it definitely is what we want, and although you were a bit rash to say the least, on Saturday it is absolutely what I, that is, we want. Now look at us using our formal names that should tell you something! Now let's see what sandwich we can afford!" entering Carters Bakery they joined the queue before appearing with two sausage rolls and two cans of coke. "This must be the best lunch I've ever had" said Sandra as they sat on a bench by the Library as a piece of pastry made an escape from her sausage roll, and landed by her feet ,where a pigeon who as always had lain in wait anticipating his own lunch would be found around here. "I think yesterday's was better! Especially as I was so clean!" said Dave expecting a slap at the least and surprised when a kiss landed on his cheek, and a hand took hold of his and placing it over her shoulder left it dangling to rest on top of her breast for all the world to see, as the sun shone down over Kirkdale.

The afternoon went better than the morning but Sandra's attention wasn't really on her work as she slowly came to turns with what they had done in buying 15, Windy Hill. 'Must be mad" she said quietly to herself even though the office was empty. Returning to the Manchester Road Power Station folder that she had shelved this morning, she sighed upon opening it at the sheer volume of files, papers and notes in the folder. Her mood didn't get any better when she saw on the index that Daniel Bruce had been the last person to sign out the folder, and he had added notes about an enquiry from Anderson Developments Ltd pertaining to the potential use of the land once the Power Station had been closed, which was due in 2002.

'A meeting between Michael Anderson (Director of Anderson Developments Ltd) and Daniel Bruce (Kirkdale Council Estates Department) had taken place at which Mr Anderson had advised that upon the closure of the Manchester Road Power Station, that Anderson Developments Ltd would be interested in developing the site for industrial usage and potentially some leisure facilities subject to planning permission. Anderson Developments Ltd would like to work with Kirkdale Council to develop the land for the benefit of the people of Kirkdale. The note was signed by Daniel in his usual illegible scrawl dated Friday 3rd September 1982.'

Copying and adding for information purposes, no further action required, she sent a copy to Eric Normanton and Legal Services for their files and leafing through the various other documents in the folder Sandra slowly worked her way through the whole folder for the first time. She noted there was a reference from January 28th 1952 from McParlands Solicitors asking to be informed should the land ever be put up for sale with a reference of WCarey/McParland/2811952. The pages of references contained documents and notes from after the war when the land was originally purchased by Manchester Road Power Station Ltd from the Ramsbottom family in 1952, for the sum of £17,500 on a 50 year commercial lease. There were lots of other documents with modifications to the original plans in 1952, as well as additional land purchased for access in 1954 and a mini folder with buildings and their planning certificates, as the Power Plant expanded in 1960. There was a Government paper outlining the 1956 Clean Air Act and a paper modifying the Clean Air Act in 1968. After 1970 there was little additional paperwork from planning until 1980, when a feasibility study was undertaken to review the site and potential change of use, as the coal industry reduced capacity after the discovery of Oil and Gas in the North Sea in the 1970's The study was undertaken by Kirkdale Council Estates Department under Mr Eric Normanton. The results of the study were that the land would be best used for industrial use, and potentially for social housing which the council were currently short of stock, and expected to remain so as the local population was increasing at a rate of 2.1% per year over the last 5 years from 1975 to 1980. The land was expected to achieve a premium, as it was effectively the last large parcel of predominantly flat land in the region. McGuigan Commercial 'Property Valuers' had put a value on the land of c£20million, subject to how many houses were built the current number of social houses on the study being 420. There were notes from McGuigan Commercial 'Property Valuers' stating that should Kirkdale Council decide to move ahead with a redevelopment of the site it would be beneficial to have a mixed development, with the addition of private housing as well as social housing, which could see a figure in excess of c£20million perhaps rising to c£30million by the time the site lease was due to be sold in 2002.

Placing all the files back in the folder Sandra, sat back and happy that she had pieced together the history of the site in her head, she looked at the site plan at of the front of the folder and seeing that Northfield was on the edge of the plan, she tried to envisage what the impact of the development might mean to Northfield, but as it was 10 years away she decided it was a waste of her time and realising it now 5pm she put it to the back of her mind as she had more important things to consider like 15 Windy Hill Street. Placing the folder in the out tray just as Sam added some folders to her in tray she smiled and said "That one can wait until tomorrow Sam" as he made to pick it up "Too late Sandra, already seen it, once seen never forgotten!" he said placing the folder on his trolley and heading towards the door, as Sandra got her jacket from behind the door. Seeing Dave waiting for her at the top of the steps for the second time today, she put her arm through his and for a second stood watching as the offices emptied and people made their way home. "Happy boyfriend?" she said as she looked at him "Oh yes, can't wait to tell my parents I'm leaving home, my mum will be devastated!" he replied somewhat sarcastically, and suddenly Sandra realised she hadn't thought about anybody but herself over the last few days. "Your mum will think I'm a Monster ,taking her little boy away" with a smile on his face he kissed her gently on the lips and said "At least she'll know I'm clean!" at which a slap on the arm told him he had pushed it a little, but as they descended the Council Office steps she said quietly "So do I!" and they headed off to the car park, both smiling at a memory no one would ever know about.

Somewhat surprised at seeing Sandra with Dave coming down the garden path, Mary opened the door and with a intrigued smile said "What a nice surprise we haven't seen you for ages, how are you Sandra?" quickly looking at Dave, she returned her smile and said "Fine thank you Mrs Baxter, we've been a bit busy recently" and stepping into the hallway, she took off her jacket and Dave took it from her and hung it up with his in the cupboard through habit, even though they didn't expect to be long. "Go and sit in the Front room, I'll put the kettle on, coffee alright?" and without waiting for a reply, she was already headed for the kitchen. Returning a few minutes later with a tray of coffees and a plate of biscuits Mary said "I've made enough for us all, as your dad will be home in a minute and tea is a casserole, so it won't harm if it's left in the oven!" handing Sandra a cup of coffee just as the Front door opened, she almost spilled it into Sandra's lap as she turned to say "In here Alan!" as he closed the door and followed her instructions, entering the Front Room to find Sandra sat next to Dave. "Well this is a nice surprise, we haven't seen much of you lately Sandra, is David looking after you?" Slightly blushing Sandra quickly replied, nervously holding her untouched cup of coffee "He's been very busy recently both at work, and.....and well we've got some news for you haven't we boyfriend!" looking at Dave for some support, she took a drink from her coffee hoping he would understand that she wanted him, to tell his parents their news. Giving it just enough time to give both Sandra and in particular Mary some concern, he finally, having taken a drink of coffee explained about their news which although of much interest, was obviously not what Mary had in mind for an announcement.

"Mum, Dad, we viewed a house at Windy Hill, Northfield over the weekend and Sandra put an offer in on the day, and we went to see the Estate Agent today and Sandra's offer was accepted so we are buying a house, and moving in together!" Picking up his coffee he awaited a response that came in the form of a dig in the ribs from Sandra, before Alan spoke up "Sandra put in an offer?" and taking a drink he awaited a reply which came as a result of another dig in the ribs from Sandra. Dave replied "Well it was an open day at the house and we looked around, twice actually and although the roof needs looking at and it needs a new bathroom, well Sandra fell in love with the potential the house has, so she told Simon, the Estate Agent that we would only offer £22,000 when the asking price was £25,995 but we both love it so, it doesn't really matter who made the offer!" at which a squeeze of his hand told him he had said the right thing. "Good for you Sandra" said Alan and taking his chance he added "Mary here won't even take driving lessons, will you dear!" and seeing that she had been backed into a corner Mary said, retaliating "Well if we had a smaller car I would learn!" and seeing an opportunity Sandra said "We could learn together, I've always wanted a mini!" seeing his plan to get Mary driving now had potential Alan looked at his son and said "You've got a Monster there David!" at which they looked at each other and taking a few second to finish their coffee, the look told of a not long ago memory. Bringing the conversation back to the house, Alan asked out loud to both of them "So how are you going to raise the deposit you two?" Looking at Dave for confidence Sandra was surprised to hear "I know I have some money left from

Granddad Windsor, so that should be enough as they will want a 5% deposit on £22,000 so that's!" but he was cut short "£1,100 plus solicitors fees so you need about £1,500" said Alan the Accountant, back in work mode. "There will easily be enough, although you did use some to buy your car, but the Trust Fund does have Compound Interest so when the annual statement comes through you will be able to see what you have, although until you are 25 I will still have to authorise any withdrawals as you know. So yes you will have the deposit, but you might want to take a bit more out maybe to round it up to £2,000 if you have work to do on the house" and sitting back his work done, Alan finished his coffee and wondered when he was going to get his tea, which was now aromatically seeping through the house. "Well done you two, I thought it might be something else but that's for the future!" Mary said, alluding to her hopes of being a Grandmother before adding "Congratulations to you both, we might take a run out this weekend to have a look for ourselves. Now I'd better get tea served, are you staying Sandra?" "Thanks for the offer Mrs Baxter, but mum will be wondering where I am, maybe another time?" and standing up Sandra gave Mary a hug, before Dave took her hand as he joined her and following Alan through the house as he headed for the kitchen and his delayed tea, Dave said with his hand on the door handle "Leave mine in the oven mum, I won't be long" and opening the door to an "Okay" from behind the kitchen door they headed for Dave's car and the short journey to her home. As they pulled away from Albion Street, Sandra said "I didn't know you had a Trust Fund!" and taking a quick look at her before concentrating on the road, he chanced a comment that she would either realise was his odd humour or a downright slight "Well I didn't know if you were a gold digger!" and expecting a slap at the least he was surprised and amused when she finally replied "Monsters not a Gold digger!" and folding her arms as they neared her home, she wondered who Granddad Windsor was, who had left Dave a Trust Fund, but as they pulled up outside her house

Dave and he took off his seatbelt he leaned over to give her a kiss, and her thoughts went elsewhere.

Chapter 18 – Christmas 1982

"Our first Christmas together!" said a naked Sandra, opening the curtains of 15 Windy Hill Street on Christmas Day. "I can't believe we have our own home!" she added turning to face the bed where Dave lay propped up on the pillows "Come back to bed, and I'll give you your Christmas present!" he said with a wink, and slowly returning to their bed, she looked at him and pulling the duvet cover off him, she said with a grin "Is that all I get for Christmas!" as he reached for her hand and pulled her towards him she kissed him slowly at first, and then with more intensity as she felt his hands on her bottom and before long in a twirl of bodies, she found herself underneath him as he rested on his hands on the pillows, before he slowly moved his body down to kiss her as she felt him slip between her opening legs and his penis came to rest on her vagina, as she closed her legs trapping his penis between her legs leaving him unable to move. Whispering in his ear, she quietly said as she opened her legs releasing his penis "I'd like my present now ....please" and with a smile her mouth locked onto his and searching for his tongue, she felt for and found his erect penis guiding it into her vagina she could feel his shaft in her hand as it entered her as she let go and with an adjustment of her hips, she wrapped her legs around his back, as he increased his thrusting, until her bottom was just off the bed, as he continued to thrust, until with an arched back she felt his warmth as he came, with a hug of her arms around his neck they slowly relaxed, before he rolled off her leaving an arm under her neck. "Happy Christmas girlfriend" he said lying back catching his breath "Happy Christmas boyfriend thank you very much for my present!" she replied leaning to face him and placing a leg over his, as they lay wrapped together, without saying a word they lay as the cold winter's rain started to ruin every child's dream of a white Christmas, until she suddenly realised he had fallen asleep. Getting up she covered Dave with the duvet at which he turned over encompassing himself in its warmth before leaving the bedroom heading to the bathroom to get a shower.

As the heat from the shower worked its magic, she finished washing her hair and she was drying herself when Dave opened the door, and seeing Sandra wrap a towel around herself before doing an impression of a turban with another towel on her hair, Dave looked at her and said in a sad voice "I woke up alone" and with a smile Sandra drew SAD ! on the steamed up mirror, standing to one side to let him see he nodded up and down, before she turned and changed the S to a M making MAD ! Looking back at him he smiled, and went past her and adding J and C, and amending the exclamation mark into an I, the mirror now said MADJIC , at which they both smiled, and with a short hug which included a quick grope of her bottom beneath the towel, before he pulled it off her, and as the turbaned, naked Sandra headed off to the bedroom, slowly with a smile on her face, before she abruptly shut the bedroom door, leaving Dave to have a shower having already had one present before he got out of bed, as Christmas Day 1982 started in earnest.

After a quiet breakfast of tea and toast Sandra put the dishes on the drainer and looking out of the kitchen window as the weather looked to be getting better, she turned round to see Dave staring at her. "What?" and with a smile he said "Oh it's nothing I was just thinking maybe next year we can get the kitchen extension done. I got my raise and with the increment increase next year we should be able to afford, and could add it to the mortgage, as it would increase the value of the house" sitting back down at the somewhat cramped kitchen table Sandra first took his right hand and then reaching out she took his left hand, without breaking her look into his eyes she said "I love this house, as you may have gathered, but a kitchen would finish it off and then we could move on to the next stage of Our Plan" seeing the determination in her eyes he asked the question he already thought he knew the answer to "So girlfriend that would be what?" and squeezing his hand she said holding his gaze "Why children of course, you do seem quite keen on the practising, so what do you say?" and with a smile that was followed by a laugh he replied "I thought for a minute you wanted to get married!" slightly taken aback that Dave hadn't realised what she was going to say, she changed tack and thinking as she spoke said "Oh I do want to get married at some stage, but I'm waiting for a Prince Charming to ask me! But if Prince Charming doesn't ask, I can't make him!" and taking her right hand away she looked away for the first time in minutes. "Well kitchen, children and marriage let me see, I don't think Granddad Windsor left enough for all three so how about we do them in reverse order?" said Dave playing devil's advocate, thinking about it for a second Sandra opened her mouth and having said "I so wanted a new kitchen!" realised it came out all wrong "That is, can't we have all three I mean, Kitchen, Marriage and then Children, oh I don't know what I'm saying, you decide!" and waiting for his response she took hold of both his hands again. "Okay we'll go for the kitchen next year when the weather gets better, I'll check with dad about Granddad Windsor's Trust Fund as there are various stipulations in the Trust Fund, then we'll get married the year after when I've asked you that is, and presuming you accept, so maybe 1986, unless of course we have a happy little accident that is, and children after that, if we don't! What do you say?"

"I'd say I love you Dave Baxter, and always will, you will ask me though won't you!" seeing the question in her blue eyes, Dave leant in to kiss her tenderly on the lips and sitting down he said, still holding both her hands "I have always loved you Sandra Robertson from the first time I saw you and when the time is right, I will definitely ask you to marry me, and I look forward to spending the rest of my life with you" and as they kissed again Sandra pulled away and asked "Who on earth was Granddad Windsor?"

"I'll tell you when we have a bit more time as it does go on a bit, but without him there would be no car, no house, so wherever you are Granddad Windsor thank you!" as he raised a hand to the skies "Oh yes thank you Granddad Windsor who- ever you were, thank you!" said Sandra getting out some car- rier bags to put the presents for the day into, still no wiser about Granddad Windsor, but now more interested as Dave returned from the Living Room with presents for his parents, and a bag full of presents that were for Sandra's family. So with a bag of presents for each family sat on the kitchen table and suddenly realising they had time to kill Dave put the kettle on and decided now was a good a time as any, to let Sandra know about their benefactor Granddad Windsor.

Dave took Sandra's hand and led her to the Living Room and sitting down on the sofa and said"It is quite a story and it needs telling in full as he is no longer with us, and history is full of stories from the first world war that are left in Libraries and Archives, so as we have a bit of time, here's the story of Granddad Windsor as told to me by my Dad"

'Windsor Carey was born in 1898 to Ellis and Nellie Carey, one of seven children, three girls and four boys. Two of the girls and one of the boys died in infancy and although not poor, the family wasn't well off and the four living children all started work as soon as a suitable job came up, which was around the aged of 10 in 1906, but with the death of William Carey who was the eldest when he was 11 at the local Sowerby Mill. Nellie Carey managed after many arguments with Ellis Carey, to make sure that the remaining children would stay at school as long as they could afford it, and true to her word Windsor, Robert and Maude all went to the local Bolton Brow School, where they would stay until they were 14. As he had been at school and could read, write and do arithmetic, Windsor Carey worked in the Sowerby Mill Office, rather on the mill floor where his brother had been killed which while not a great job with little prospects, it was safer than on the mill floor, and it did pay more. After the outbreak of war in 1914 Windsor volunteered to join the Duke of Wellington Regiment at the age of 16, and joined thousands of like minded Volunteers completely unaware of the horrors that awaited them, and even completed trench training at the local Copley Woods where he used to play as a child just a few years before. During the war Windsor was injured twice, the last time in 1917, as he helped to repel a German counter attack, after which he was the highest ranking able officer at Lance Corporal when the battle had been won. During the battle Windsor went into the field as the front line moved several times back and forth, and under repeated machine gun fire and constant bombardment he saved several other ranks, including Major George Ramsbottom whose family owned the mill where he started his working life in the office back in 1912. Major Ramsbottom was seriously injured, but despite losing a foot and an ear he was brought back to the field hospital by Windsor, and eventually made it back to Kirkdale where he continued his recovery. Windsor got the George Cross for his bravery, but Dad says he should have got a Victoria Cross. It was only Major Ramsbottom that put pressure on and made it happen for saving his and many others lives, and he sought out Windsor when he returned after the war ended and offered him a job back at the mill as Office Manager and he stayed there until 1952, when the mill was demolished and the land sold for the Manchester Road Power Station. With the land sold Windsor decided to move away only to have to come back in December 1952 at the death of Major Ramsbottom. He left a daughter by his wife Mary who died in 1934 during childbirth, also called Mary, who is my mother. She was looked after by Windsor and various aunts, until she married my dad in May 1952, and maybe because he was happy that Mary was safe he went off to spend the rest of his life as a lorry driver across the UK. There were rumours that Major Ramsbottom left him some money in his will for saving his life in the war, but it's never come out although that does make sense as he may have left me some money, but it could just as easily been an insurance policy. He died in a road accident in 1956 so maybe that's where the money comes from. I've never seen the full document as dad has authority until I am 25, so quite looking forward to that, in a weird morbid grateful way that is"

"Wow a real life hero in the family, and he leaves his money to you how strange is that, why didn't he leave it to your mum?" said Sandra asking a question Dave had often thought about "Not really sure, I presume it was first born male, as was the usual way of doing things then, don't really know but boy am I grateful!" he said genuinely grateful as he heard "Me too" from Sandra adding "Thank you Windsor Carey, for our house, oh and Dave's car and maybe, maybe a kitchen!" "Enough" said Dave curtly "He was a person, not a bank!" and seeing the realisation he had gone a little too far Dave added "But I'm sure if he had ever met you, he would let you have the kitchen. Now come on we're running late after your history lesson" Picking up the bags of presents from the kitchen they headed for Dave's car as a Winter Sun shone down, and they set off for Church Street and the Robertson family Christmas Day now expanded to include the Baxter family, and a table of 7 for Christmas Dinner for the first time, all thoughts of Windsor disappearing as they left Windy Hill.

Chapter 19 - 1984 – Two years later

The two years since they had purchased 15 Windy Hill, North-field, had been good to Dave and Sandra. The kitchen extension was completed in the summer of 1983, and despite it taking some time to do all the redecorating following the works, the house was now as they had both envisaged it on the open day back in 1982, when Sandra rather spontaneously bought it. Dave had continued with his studies, and if all went well he would be a fully qualified Surveyor at the age of 25. Despite all Dave's hard work, Daniel Bruce had been fast tracked to the position of Assistant Chief Surveyor at the age of 24, and it was no secret he had his eye on Eric Normanton's job when he was due to retire in 1992. Sandra had done well in the Planning Department and was now the Assistant to Mrs Shaw who was now not just her boss, but also a friend as a result of going on several courses together, where they got to know each other. Sandra had passed her driving test in summer 1983 but as yet hadn't managed to get a beloved Mini, as Dave had a new car which was actually Jim Robertson's old Escort, as Jim now had a company car. Mrs Baxter finally passed her driving test in March 1984 and was the proud owner of Dave's old Fiesta. Sid and Jane were still living together despite several dalliances by Sid over the last two years. Tony and Gill were living together at her mum's as she had lost her husband a few years ago, and had the space. Peggy was engaged to Andy but they were in no hurry to get married. Jo finally met the man of her dreams and went to live in Manchester with her fiancé James who worked for a bank. Sharon was still looking for Mr Right, but while she was looking she had found several Mr Wrongs.

The summer wasn't bad with some decent sunny spells in

June and July, but apart from the Olympics in Los Angeles, life moved at a pretty sedate speed for the people of Kirkdale. The ongoing Miners Strike rumbled on all year with the Manchester Road Power Station having to get their supplies brought in with police protection, as the striking Miners tried to barricade the site. But after several attempts the Miners focussed more on sites in South Yorkshire and Nottinghamshire. With the house finished Dave and Sandra took to a regular pattern of visiting parents and walking at weekends to fill their time. On the weekend of the 14th of July, Dave and Sandra revisited York for her birthday, unluckily choosing the weekend after the fire at York Minster on the 9th July. Despite a great weekend they came back from their weekend away thinking that the fire was an omen as Sandra was sure she would be pregnant by now, but still nature hadn't worked its magic.

Dave and Sandra booked a holiday for the end of September to celebrate Dave's 25th Birthday on the 27th September, despite looking at Spain from recommendations from their work colleagues, they decided at the last minute to choose Portugal and the resort of Portimao on the Algarve, where they could "Just have time for themselves" as Dave said on many an occasion. Booking a flight on the 22nd September from Manchester they would be back on the morning of the 29th September. Before they went on holiday, there was the little matter of a 25th Birthday party, and despite Dave's protestations, Sandra organised a party at their old favourite the Malt Shovel where a delighted Ian, who was now Manager said he "Would put on a spread" and the date was set for the day of their return from Portugal.

The sunburned couple were picked up at 7.40am by Dave's parents in Alan's brand new August 1st registered, Jaguar XJ from Manchester Airport, and on the way home with Alan explaining all about his new car, which he got as a result of being made a partner in the Dysert and Co Accountancy practice at the end of the financial year in April 1984. Cruising along the

M62 Alan relaxed as the traffic was light on a Saturday morning. "So was Porti-meow any good?" he said looking quickly at Dave, before concentrating on the motorway "Seriously, Dad, it's Portimao" Failing to ignore his dad's little joke, "And it was absolutely beautiful. We went for long walks on the beach, you should see the cliffs they're really spectacular, and the weather was stunning in the 80's every day. We even did some swimming in the ocean although it was a lot colder than it looked, but yes we had a great time" Keeping his eyes on the road Alan said "I can see you caught a tan and Sandra looks well but you'd probably best get some rest before the party tonight, or you'll miss your birthday. Your mum is so looking forward to it as are Jim and Diane, we went for a meal with them last week when you were away to plan things" Looking at his dad, as a smile appeared on his face, he couldn't figure out whether he was being set up or not and rather than ask, he sat in silence as the noise of Sandra and Mary chatting broke through the sound of the motorway rumble. "You haven't done anything silly I hope!" he finally said unable to resist "Don't worry nothing embarrassing, but I think it will be a party to remember!" at which Dave knew it wasn't worth trying to figure out what his dad had arranged and leaving the conversation there, he watched as the Jaguar ate up the miles, taking the turn off for home he missed the rest of the journey, as he dozed off just before they left the motorway at the first signs for Kirkdale, and home.

"We're home, house" Dave said to no one, as he opened the door and picked up the small avalanche of mail before placing their cases inside the door. He waved off the shiny new Jaguar as his parents headed home themselves. "Cup of tea?" he said as Sandra closed the door behind him "No, it's only 8.40 in the morning so I think I'll have a few hours sleep before the birthday celebrations start" she replied, putting the suitcases at the bottom of the stairs. He got caught between his first cup of tea for a week and the potential of morning sex "Good idea" he said and as the answer he didn't want to hear came from the top of the stairs "You had your present on Thursday, Birthday Boy!" and with one option blocked he went into the kitchen to make himself a mug of tea, picking up the mail which he had placed on the sideboard when they came in, he waited until the kettle had boiled and adding some almost out of date milk, he held a beautiful smelling mug of tea after a week away, as he sat at the kitchen table and started ploughing through the letters, mailshots and shopping offers in front of him. The usual bills were put to one side and cursing Jim for the mail shots that his company produced by the thousand, he left the important looking letter to the last. Picking up the official looking letter, which carried the printed name McParland and Co. on the top of the envelope, he got a knife from the drawer and after sliding it into the open part of the seam and running it along th edge to open it, he put the knife down and took out the contents.

28th September 1984

Dear Mr Baxter,

We would be grateful if you could make an appointment with Mr Ramsdale, our Director of Wills at your earliest convenience to arrange for a full reading of the Will of Mr Windsor Carey who was the instigator of the Trust Fund that you are a beneficiary, of under the supervision of Mr A. Baxter of 24 Albion Street, Kirkdale. As of your 25th Birthday on the 27th September 1984 you are now of legal age to inspect, and administer the Trust Fund and any other relevant legal documents.

I look forward to your response

Mrs G. Sands (PA to Mr Ramsdale)

Reading the document again, he stood up still holding his mug of tea, and put a note on the Calendar hung behind him on the kitchen wall for Monday 1st Oct 'Call McParlands' and crossing his birthday off, he briefly thought of the present Sandra had given him for his birthday on Thursday in Portugal, and with the thought still in his mind, he spilt some of his tea down his leg, reaching for a tea towel he wiped his jeans until he gave up and with his jeans still wet, sat back at the table where the letter sat staring at him.

Sitting looking at the letter and with thoughts going round in his head he had almost forgotten the party at the Malt Shovel tonight. "I'll ask my dad tonight" he said to himself and eager to tell Sandra, he went upstairs to find her fast asleep, and deciding on reflection she had made a wise choice, he took off his still damp jeans and top and getting into bed he put his arm over Sandra and with no response and feeling her warmth he cuddled up next to her, as the tiredness of getting a flight at 4.00am caught up with him, he momentarily thought what on earth could relevant legal documents mean, before sleep quickly found him without an answer.

The sound of the shower running woke Dave, and turning over to see Sandra was missing he sat up in bed, putting an extra pillow behind his head he waited for her to return. "Morning sleepyhead!" he said with a smile as his eyes rolled over her naked body except for a towel on her head "Morning my backside, it's half past twelve and you've got a party to go to. "We've got time for a little party here!" he said pulling back the duvet, and suddenly he realised he still had his Y Fronts and socks on as he heard Sandra say "I'll give it a miss if you don't mind!" as she turned to get some underwear, he honestly couldn't blame her as he stripped naked and headed for the shower.

A mug of tea and some toast were on the table as he entered the kitchen. "Where did you get the bread?" he said "Freezer dummy!" came the swift reply, and deciding to keep his mouth shut while he finished the toast to save any more embarrassing put downs, he suddenly remembered the letter from earlier this morning, and going to the sideboard he pulled out the letter and handed it to Sandra as he finished his tea. "Well that makes interesting reading, the mystery of your Trust Fund will finally be revealed, what does relevant legal documents mean?" she said and putting his arms around her he replied "Not the foggiest babe, suppose they'll tell me when I see them" and kissing her neck he said "We've still got time to...." "No we haven't we need to do some shopping as we have nothing in as we've been away, I need to get some new makeup and I saw a dress before we went, that I thought would be nice for tonight so we need to get a move on, oh and one more thing, if you come to bed like this morning, Mr Y Fronts, there'll be no more present s....ever!" and kissing him lightly on the lips, she went to get her coat from the rack and he knew his birthday was over, until tonight that is, and whatever his dad had lined up!

The Malt Shovel was full when Dave and Sandra arrived in their Taxi, and pushing his way to the bar to slaps on the back, he saw Sid in front of him, placing a hand on his shoulder he shouted "Pint and a half of Lager Sid and get one for yourself!" with a cursory look back to see who it was, he smiled and turned his attention back to getting a drink at the bar. Turning to hand Dave his drinks after getting served, Sid nodded to indicate to Dave where to go, and following the unspoken instruction he set off towards the far end of the pub, trying not to spill his and Sandra's drinks, with Sid mimicking him a few steps behind. Upon reaching the table where Sandra and Jane were already sat chatting, with Dave and Sandra's parents sat at the next table, Dave handed Sandra her drink before looking at his dad who seemed to be in deep conversation with Jim Robertson, seeing Sid give Jane her drink he turned to Sid and over the noise said "Great turnout I must have more friends than I thought!" and taking a drink he looked around and although he recognised most of the people there were quite a few that he was sure he didn't know. Seeing the look on Dave's face Sid answered his question before he had a chance to ask it."Your dad arranged it all, bit of a dark horse your dad!" and even more confused, he looked around again and saw that the pool table was missing and over the heads of the now rammed pub he could see a band had set up their equipment, but unable to see the name on the drum kit he looked at Sid again before asking "Any idea who they are?" a shake of the head answered his question, without answering it. As Sandra and Jane caught up with what had happened since they last saw each other a month ago, before the Portugal trip, Sid and Dave got halfway down their drinks before they found common ground. "I see you got a promotion Birthday Boy!" and with a mouthful of lager Dave took his time before replying "Yes about time, but Daniel Bruce who is on the fast track scheme, got the Assistant Chief Surveyor role, which he is no way ready for!" taking a second to answer Sid, decided now was not the time to tell Dave of Ian the Manager's information about the attack on Dave, only adding "You watch out for Daniel Bruce, he's determined to get to the top, and he won't stop at anything to get there!" looking at Sid and wondering why Sid was so against Daniel, he didn't have a chance to ask further as Tony joined them, with Gill sitting down with Sandra and Jane. "Got to say it Dave, your old man has really pushed the boat out!" and about to ask who he was on about he heard rather than saw the band now behind him strike the opening chords of "Let's Dance" by David Bowie started up, and the attention of everyone in the room concentrated on the cover band, leaving Dave to ponder what Sid meant as Sandra joined him and despite there not being much room, soon half the audience were dancing along, as the music pounded out the thoughts in his head.

The evening was a huge success and when the cover band finished with "Jump" by Van Halen the who pub joined in so much so, that Ian the Manager said later that he feared he would have a load of broken glasses to deal with, such was the enthusiasm of the crowd. Leaving the temporary stage of the pool room the band gave way to a DJ, who, taking his lead from the band started with "I want to break free" by Queen and although a good number of people sat down there were a steady stream of dancers who had got into the atmosphere as the night continued without a break until closing time at 1.00 am suddenly approached. A slightly inebriated Sandra was attempting to dance to "Girls Just Want to Have Fun" by Cindi Lauper surrounded by Peggy, Sharon, Gill and Jane as they tried to out sing the sound system and did, as the record ended but they didn't, being a few seconds behind, and the resulting howls of laughter as the DJ finished before them made them all laugh, and hugging in a group they slowly made it back to their boyfriends, as the pub slowly emptied Dave and Alan were sat having a chat about nothing in particular when Dave suddenly remember to tell his dad about the letter from McParland and Co. and despite hoping he could add some insight as to what it would entail, Alan said he had no idea what the Trust Fund meeting would be about, other than giving him authority to use the Fund as he saw fit, now he was 25. "To be honest it was a bit of a burden as everything went through the solicitors, and they were quite thin on giving any further information other than it will all be addressed when you are 25, so your guess is as good as mine." A bit taken aback as he expected his dad to know more he replied "So how much is in the Trust Fund dad?" finishing the remains of his pint Alan looked at Dave and said with a look that said the answer before he spoke "I really don't and have never known, if you needed money like the car and the kitchen I asked McParland and Co. if there was sufficient, and to date they have always said yes there was enough. I guess it will be interesting to say the least!"

Sandra and Jane were ready to leave and as Sid and Dave came back from the toilet they headed outside to the line of Taxis waiting to take the many guests home on what everyone agreed had been brilliant night, which was already tomorrow, Dave asked Sid "What did you mean about Daniel Bruce?" before they reached the Taxi. "Not tonight Dave, I'll tell you another time, don't want to spoil a great night with something that could be nothing !" and opening the door of the Taxi he got into the front seat of the Taxi, wondering if there would ever be a good time to tell Dave.

Getting up late after the Birthday Party at the Malt Shovel a still tired Dave managed to get enough energy to make two mugs of tea and taking them back to bed, he saw that Sandra had gone for a shower while he was downstairs. Getting back into bed he plumped up the cushions and taking a few sips of the hot tea he awaited the return of Sandra from the shower while wondering what they should do today, as it was work again tomorrow after their week away. Having decided a walk and a Sunday Roast should definitely be on the list he forgot all about the list as Sandra walked into the bedroom naked apart from a towel around her head, and with defined lines where her bikini had been highlighting Dave's areas of interest, she saw the look on his face and although she smiled knowing his interest, she turned her back on him as she opened the wardrobe to choose an outfit. "I thought we could go for a walk and maybe have a Sunday Roast, what do you think?" she said turning towards him holding a pair of jeans in her hand. "Well I thought that we could....!" he started before he was cut off as Sandra anticipated his thoughts "I know what you thought, but it'll take more than a mug of tea!" and leaving the comment hanging she turned back to the wardrobe and picked a white blouse to go with her jeans, once dressed she sat at the dressing table and with the towel still on her head, she chose some light make up for the day as she had a tan that she wanted everyone to know about. Finishing her makeup and brushing her hair she looked in the mirror at Dave still in bed, drinking his tea and smiling at him she said "Are you getting up?" and with a smile that she knew meant trouble he replied "Already up, just haven't got out of bed!" and as the towel landed on him thrown by a head shaking Sandra she said as she left the bedroom "Boys and their toys!" and heading downstairs she left a disappointed Dave with a damp towel, and ardour.

Once Dave had had his shower and got dressed, he joined Sandra in the kitchen where she stood as always looking out of the window towards the moors on the horizon. "Hearing him enter the room she said without turning "I fancy a long walk today after yesterday, what do you say to going round the Northfield Reservoir and then Sunday Roast at the Sportsman, what do you think?" pausing to consider if he had a better option he joined her at the sink, resting his head on her shoulder as he put his arms around her he said "I think that's an excellent plan, wasn't quite what I had in mind when I woke up this morning!" at which Sandra cut in "I know what you had in mind, maybe we can go to bed early tonight as it's work tomorrow!" and with a quick kiss on his cheek as his head rested on her shoulder, she looked out over the garden, and secretly wondered if they would ever need a set of swings.

The walk over Bedlow Moor from Northfield was part of circuit that they had figured out in the two years they had lived there, and as they reached the top of the Moor to look down on Northfield Reservoir they had completed two thirds of the circuit and making for The Sportsman for lunch, they hadn't really spoken very much apart from Dave telling Sandra about his dad's comments on the Trust Fund and agreeing the party last night was a big hit. "So how much do you think is in the Trust Fund?" said Sandra as they negotiated a wooden style that was on their path to The Sportsman. Helping her down he took her hand again, and walking slowly he said without a clear idea in his mind "As dad said I have no idea either, it could be a few thousand as obviously I have had money for the car and the kitchen, but dad did say they were very secretive about it, and just said there was enough when he asked, all a bit strange if you ask me, but I'll have to wait until tomorrow to call McParland and Co. and arrange to see them. So if I can, it will be Wednesday as I have no meetings on that day and they are in Town so I could do it at lunchtime so I don't have to take time off work. No letting it go Sandra said as they crossed The Sportsman car park "Have a guess and I'll have a guess and if I'm nearer, can I have a Mini?" Laughing at the audacity of the comment and the reference to the Mini which was becoming a regular occurrence, Dave said "£5,000 is my guess so that would leave about £2,500, after what I have taken out so what's your guess?" Stood outside the door of The Sportsman Sandra was determined to get this dealt with before they went inside, and ignoring Dave's subtraction for money already taken she said "£10,000 and I'd like a red Mini!" letting go of his hand, she opened the door and held it open for a slightly bemused Dave, and without a word he went through the door muttering "Red Mini indeed" as the smell of the food hit his nostrils, all though of Red Mini's disappeared as a waiter went past them holding two large plates of Roast Beef with Yorkshire Puddings and Roast Potatoes, with another waiter following with a large bowl of vegetables and a gravy jug. Looking at each other they headed for the bar without a word, and ordering a pint and a half of Lager and two Roast Beef dinners they found a table by the window before they spoke again. "Here's to us" said Dave raising his pint, as Sandra lifted her own glass and touched his she decided to start the conversation of the Trust Fund up again before their lunch arrived. "Dave, is it all right if it is £10,000, to ask for a Red Mini? It seems a bit mercenary, but with you going to meetings and various sites it would be easier if I had my own car!" and with a slightly pleading look she let the question hang, awaiting his answer. Taking a drink he deliberately let her wait until he had put his drink down before he took her hand and said "Let's wait until Wednesday and then we'll see but the deal is £5,000 against £10,000, so if you are nearer, yes you can have a Mini!" and with a kiss that sealed the deal, suddenly broken as the Waiter brought their lunches it was some 5 minutes, and half a Yorkshire Pudding eaten later, that Dave added "After all this food, and a long walk, I think I might need to go to bed early tonight, ready for work tomorrow!" Finishing cutting a roast potato and placing it on her fork she paused and said "I know what you're ready for, and it isn't work!" and popping the roast potato in her mouth she looked at him and raised her eyebrows, which he acknowledge by putting a piece of Roast Beef into his mouth and tried to smile at the same time, which only made his smile awkward, but she knew what it meant as she cut a chunk of Roast Beef from her plate, adding a carrot to her fork she dangled it in the air, as she considered whether red was really a good colour for a mini convinced in her own mind, that she was going to be getting one.

Monday came and with it Portugal and Dave's birthday became a memory, as the routine of their separate jobs kicked into gear. It was after 11.00 by the time Dave had a chance to call McParland and Co. and taking out the letter from his pocket, he called Mrs Sands number to arrange a meeting. A very efficient Mrs Sands was delighted to hear from him, and giving nothing away she set up a meeting with Mr Ramsdale for Dave on Wednesday 3rd October at 12.30 at their offices and with a "Look forward to meeting you" from Mrs Sands, she put the phone down with Dave no wiser. He had asked if she could advise him of some facts, but she had said that only Mr Ramsdale could give out that information at the meeting.

Sandra had coffee with Sharon and Peggy and with comments of "You look gorgeous with that sun tan" from Peggy and "Did you do it on the beach" from Sharon, Sandra soon felt comfortable back at work and when Mrs Shaw approached her on her return from lunch she was delighted to know she had passed her last exam, and would now go onto year 3 of the course to become a Planning Manager "Well done Sandra, you've worked hard, and if you keep that up you should have no problems and I must say Portugal agrees with you " slightly embarrassed Sandra didn't know at first how to answer but eventually she replied "Thanks Mrs Shaw I thought I had done well in the exam, and you can be sure I'll put the effort into the next year. You would like Portugal the people are so friendly and the weather is brilliant even in September, but don't get the Sardines if you ever do go!" and after relating the story of the Sardines on holiday, they eventually returned to their work and the small mountains of folders that required their attention, as always topped up every end of day by Sam, who had whistled as he saw Sandra for the first time since her holiday, this morning "Bet you've got some interesting tan lines!" he had said this morning which received a joking "Dave thinks so!" and a smile from Sandra, at which Sam mumbled a comment ,as he left the office which sounded like "I bet he does!" The first day back at work finished and waiting for Dave at the Escort in the Council Car Park Sandra bent down and looked in the wing mirror, moving her hair behind her right ear she corrected a bit of eye makeup that was hardly there, with her face covering the whole mirror she felt rather than saw the hand on her bottom and turning round expecting to see Dave she was shocked as Daniel Bruce stood there sarcastically smiling at her "Have a nice holiday, Bitch?" he said and walking away to his car she found herself unable to speak as she stood next to the Escort. As Daniel Bruce drove his Audi out of the Council Car Park, Daniel approached Sandra unseen as she was watching Daniel's car, putting a hand on her bottom without saying anything he was as surprised as she, as she turned and slapped him for no apparent reason. "Well that's some welcome!" and suddenly aware of what she had done she tried to cover up her mistake "Well you could have been anyone touching my bottom!" and leaving a dumbfounded Dave standing as he unlocked the car, she opened the car door and sat in the passenger seat hoping she had time to think her way out of this before Dave got in the car. "Shall we start again?" said Dave, as he got into the car and put on his seatbelt. "How was your first day back at work?" he said, starting the car and heading out of the Council Car Park and out towards Northfield. As they went through the second set of traffic lights Sandra having finally regained her composure said "Bit tiring, but I passed my Planning Exams and can go onto the 3rd year!" adding more lightheartedly "So that's good news isn't it?" before waiting for Dave's response. Stopping at yet another set of traffic lights Dave was trying to concentrate on driving, while at the same time trying to work out what had just happened in the Council Car Park. Deciding it was not worth thinking about he finally said "Well that is good news to come back to!" and leaving it at that they completed the rest of the journey home in silence, neither wishing to revisit a strange incident, so out of character.

Over a tea of Pepperoni Pizza and Chips, Dave decided it was time to tell Sandra about his day and with a mug of tea in his hand and the last chip on his fork he started to outline his own first day back at Kirkdale Council. "I spoke to Mrs Sands at McParland and Co today and have arranged to see Mr Ramsdale on Wednesday at 12.30, so I thought we could have tea out and I can tell you what they tell me about the Trust Fund what do you think?" with a moment's hesitation she replied, finally shaking the memory of Daniel's hand on her bottom "That would be nice, do you want to invite your parents, or do you want to tell them at the weekend?" without hesitation as he'd already made up his mind during the day, he said "I'll tell them at the weekend, a few more days after 25 years won't make any difference!" and finishing his last chip he looked at Sandra as she chewed a piece of Pizza and seeing he was looking at her she said questioningly "What?" and looking directly at her he said slowly "I was... I was just thinking about the Pizza in Portugal on the first night and how we........" and for the second time today a slap arrived, but this time on the arm with a smile, and a reply that it wasn't just his memory, the kiss on the cheek as she picked up his plate to go with hers and put them in the sink, and with that the tension was gone.

Wednesday 3rd October 1984 finally arrived and as they walked into the Council Offices Sandra said as they parted at the top of the steps "I won't be disappointed if there's not enough money and I don't get a Mini!" and with a smile on his face at the obvious little white lie, he replied as the gap between then increased "It's a Red Mini!" and with a smile on his face he went into the Estates Department Office, as Sandra headed for Planning. With the smile still on his face he went to his desk just as Daniel Bruce came out of Eric Normanton's Office with a look of thunder on his, which while not unheard of certainly was unusual for this time of the morning. Looking around for a hint as to what had gone on the rest of the office were head down at their work, which meant no one would be telling, at least not until lunchtime which was unfortunate as he had a meeting with McParland and Co. arranged. With little chatter in the morning as Daniel's aura pervaded the office, it was a grateful Dave who left the office at 11.00 for a site meeting in Hilltop, and then back into Kirkdale for the Trust Fund meeting.

Arriving back at the Council Office Car Park at 12.15 Dave locked the Escort and although he was running slightly late it was only a 5 minute walk across Town so he decided to miss a sandwich or pasty for lunch, and arrive a bit early for his meeting.

Entering the offices of McParland and Co., Dave went to Reception and announced himself to the young Receptionist who had a badge on with the name Laura. "David Baxter to see Mr Ramsdale" and as Laura replied "I'll let him know you are here Mr Baxter, please take a seat!" and indicating with her hand the seat behind him, he duly sat down to await the result of 25 years of history. Looking around the smart decor, he was wondering how many people throughout the years had sat here for whatever reason when Laura approached him and said "If you'd like to follow me Mr Baxter" and leading the way down a hallway, she opened the door with the nameplate Mr Ramsdale, and holding it open until he was inside, she announced his entry Mr Baxter, Mr Ramsdale and without a further word she closed the door behind him.

Standing up, Mr Ramsdale offered his hand which Dave still standing, shook, and taking the lead from Mr Ramsdale as his bold sweep of the hand and comment. "Please do sit down Mr Baxter", he sat down as Mr Ramsdale took a folder from the top of a pile, taking out some documents he put the contents down on the desk between them. "Well Mr Baxter, this is a document outlining your Trust Fund which was set up by Mr Windsor Carey in 1954. Your father Mr Alan Baxter has been the acting on your behalf until you came of age on the 27th September 1984, at the age of 25, so this will be the first time you will have seen these documents. In principle the documents are pretty standard, although there a couple of legal documents that are attached to your Trust Fund, but they are sealed until May 2002 or until certain events pre-empt that date, which unfortunately I am legally bound not to disclose until that time, whichever may come first. As a look of confusion came across Dave's face Mr Ramsdale tried to offer some further information. "Mr Baxter, the Trust Fund was set up in your favour, as a result of Mr Windsor Carey being the benefactor himself of a will, and although the Trust Fund is now open to inspection, as it has served its purpose and legally has served its time, the rest of the legal connections are still subject to various limitations, so cannot be released at this time. However I can say that when the Trust Fund was set up by your Grandfather, Mr Windsor Carey, he did so taking no reward for himself, which means that as of today, your Trust Fund, which accrued compound interest throughout its 30 year lifetime, currently stands at £105,391.10, minus of course two funding requests of £2450.00 authorised by your father, Mr Alan Baxter leaving at today's date the sum of £102,941.10 in the account. The account has now fulfilled its intended purposes, and as such needs closing, so the funds can be transferred by BACS, or I can arrange for a cheque to be raised in your favour. Which would you prefer Mr Baxter?" and with the silence from the other side of the desk Mr Ramsdale stood up and said "I'll give you a few minutes on your own to look at the documents, I'll see if we can't get some tea and when I return if you have any questions I'd be happy to answer them" Leaving the room in which Dave sat trying to get his head round the numbers and legal jargon Mr Ramsdale returned before Dave had had a chance to really think about any questions. "Now Mr Baxter, tea will be with here in a minute, have you had a chance to think about what I have told you today?" and as the tea tray including a plate of biscuits carried by Laura, arrived, it was a still dumbstruck Dave who sat nodding when asked if he wanted milk in his tea. The heat of the tea as he took a drink, brought him out of his sense of disbelief, as he heard Mr Ramsdale say "Perhaps you'd like to arrange a meeting next week when you have had a chance to think about things?" and deciding this was the second best thing he had heard all day Dave said quietly "Yes that would be a good idea!" and taking a sip of his tea, together with a bite of a biscuit Mr Ramsdale sat back and let Dave have a few moments before he said "Same time next week Mr Baxter?" and with a forced "Yes that would be good!" Dave finished his tea and leaving his biscuit in case it choked him he stood up, and offering his hand, said as Mr Ramsdale shook it "Thank you very much, you've been very helpful. See you next week Mr Ramsdale!" with that he headed towards the door and some much needed fresh air leaving Mr Ramsdale to finish his tea and biscuits and think behind his closed door of how the fortunes of some, are unknowingly changed by the fortunes of others.

As the fresh air struck him on leaving the offices of McParland and Co. Dave suddenly realised he was running late and with his watch showing 13.20, he went straight back to work without bothering with lunch. As he walked towards the Estate Office he bumped into Sam from the Mailroom on his rounds. "Hear about this morning's bollocking Dave?" he said with a smile on his face "No I missed it what happened?" Dave replied, all thoughts of his Trust Fund now forgotten. "Well Daniel the Bruce, as I like to call him, apparently had a meeting with Michael Anderson from Anderson Developments Ltd, and put all the info on file about them being interested in Manchester Road Power Station when it shuts in what 20 years, but he didn't tell Eric Normanton, so when he found out because someone left a folder on his desk by accident, Eric went ballistic and Daniel the Bruce retaliated by saying Eric wouldn't be around when 2002 came, at which Eric lost it and gave him a right telling off and said he was going to be suspended for a week after he had spoken to personnel. Anyway he's off for the rest of the week so we have peace, until he comes back of course!" "Wow, wished I'd been here to see that! "Dave said, in all honesty, the row of the year and he'd missed it, serves Daniel right always was too sure of himself. "Thanks for the info, bet it's all round the Council by now!" he finished "I think you may well be right, but if it isn't, it soon will be!" said Sam as he went on his rounds smiling to himself, as his accidental folder plan had worked out better than he hoped.

"Hey boyfriend" came the words from behind him as Dave stood at the top of the Council Office steps "You haven't called me that for ages.....girlfriend" he replied as Sandra gave him a quick kiss on the lips "Well maybe I've got so used to you I've forgotten what to call you, anyway did you hear about Daniel Bruce?" she eagerly asked "Oh yes!" Dave replied with a smile continuing "Sam the Man filled me in, and from the sound of it Eric would have filled Daniel in from what he said" "Serves him right after what......." Sandra blurted out without stopping to think and suddenly cutting short her sentence "After what .....girlfriend?" a slightly confused Dave asked wondering where she was going with the un-ended sentence "After what he said to Eric, he deserves all he gets, is what I meant to say, but I was going to say something stronger!" and hoping that Dave would accept her explanation, and she wouldn't have to explain about her behaviour on Monday night after Daniel's verbal and physical attack on her in the Council car Park. "Well knowing Daniel he'll plead ignorance and try to blame someone else, anyway where shall we go for tea ... girlfriend?" and knowing she had added another little white lie, to the others all involving Daniel Bruce, she paused ready to tell him everything, but decided that a lie buried should stay buried, and changing the subject she took his hand and as Dave said "Why don't we go to The Tavern, it's been ages since we were there, and I can tell you all about my meeting" "And if it's good news we can go past the Mini Garage on the way home!" she replied. As they walked to the Escort Dave was trying to think of a way that he could explain about the Trust Fund without blurting it out before they got to The Tavern, but as the traffic was very busy tonight he had to concentrate on his driving, so it was a slightly nervous Sandra who said as the car came to a halt in The Tavern car park, and Dave switched off the engine. "It's not good news is it, you've been quiet all the way here, I don't really mind if I don't get a Mini but maybe we should save up for one next year!" and seeing the look of disappointment in her eyes Dave almost crumbled and told her but at the last minute his strange sense of humour kicked in "Yes we could do that, but let's get inside and get a drink and something to eat, and I'll tell you all about the meeting" and holding her hand they walked into The Tavern without another word and asking for a table and a pint and a half of Lager they were shown to a table in the restaurant by one of the windows which looked out onto the car park, where a Red Mini was parked three places away from where Dave's Escort sat, unseen he hoped by Sandra when they arrived.

Looking at the menus with seemingly little to say, the drinks arrived and Dave picked it up and said "To us!" Not quite sure what to make of the gesture, Sandra picked up her drink and touching glasses said "To us" with little enthusiasm. "I think I'll have the steak!" said Dave adding "What about you?" and wondering why he was having a steak, as he never had steak, Sandra took a look at him, but his face was hidden behind the menu "I'll have Scampi and Chips please!" and putting down the menu, she waited for Dave to put his down, which he did after a few more seconds which he needed to keep his emotions under control. Almost immediately before she had a chance to ask about the meeting, the waiter arrived to take their order, and as Dave finished telling him their choices, he looked out of the window as the waiter left with their order "Quite an array of cars out there" he said to a confused Sandra who was struggling to figure out what was going on. "There's even a Red Mini over there" he added pointing to the car Sandra had actually noted when they parked, but ignored as she was convinced the Trust Fund news wasn't going to be good. Looking at the Red Mini she had only seen from the back, she saw there was something in the top of the window screen that she couldn't make out as the restaurant windows had steamed up a little. Standing up and wiping the window with a serviette, she could she thought, see some words and when Dave said "Why don't you go and see?" Sandra suddenly caught onto Dave's strange sense of humour. As she went out of the door and into the car park she could see, as she approached the Red Mini the words 'Sandra and Dave' in letters at the top of the window screen. As she turned round she threw her arms around Dave, and suddenly aware again of his strange sense of humour she said stepping back "This isn't one of your jokes is it?" and as he smiled at her, he shook his head sideways at which she gave him a passionate kiss and a hug which finished when the waiter called from the door" Excuse me Sir, Madam, your meal is served" and with her arm around Dave a beaming Sandra, and a slightly smug Dave went back to their table to start their meals with Sandra lost for words.

"How's the Scampi" said Dave after a few bites of his steak "Well it's very nice, almost a nice as the Red Mini out there!" she said waving her knife in the direction of the car park "You and your sense of humour! I thought the news from the meeting must have been bad as you didn't say anything. I should have realised your idea of humour is strange, so what happened, and more importantly how did you manage to get the car so quickly?" taking another bite of steak and a piece of onion ring Dave was smiling by the time he finished it, as he saw Sandra getting frustrated. "Okay, I'll put you in the picture. First the car, I rang them after my meeting and said if they could get the car to The Tavern this afternoon with Sandra and Dave in the window screen, I would buy it off them. The Sandra and Dave will have to go obviously!" at which Sandra put on a sad face and looking at her he said "Seriously!" at which she shook her head and smiled, as she popped a piece of Scampi in her mouth and waited for the rest of the story. Explaining that he had arranged another meeting with Mr Ramsdale for next week he outlined the story of the Trust Fund and leaving the question Sandra was desperate to hear he said "As you now have a Red Mini, you might have guessed you were nearer the figure than I was, so what do you think the Trust Fund was worth... girlfriend?" spearing a couple of chips with her fork, she put them in her mouth and chewing slowly playing for time she eventually said somewhat hopefully £15,000?". Playing her at her own game Dave finished a bite of steak before answering "Well... girlfriend it was set up with £17,500 so you were quite close with your second guess. But let me ask you this, what do you think the Trust Fund is worth today?" and picking up the last bit of his steak and a piece of tomato, he bit them off his fork and awaited her reply. As Sandra tried to figure out what she could guess, she finished off the last piece of Scampi and placing her knife and fork on her plate she tried to multiply £17,500 times 25 years, times 2 and came up with a hopeful "£30,000!" and having given her figure, she was hoping Dave would answer immediately but the waiter returned and picking up their plates asked if they wanted to see the Sweet Menu at which Dave quickly said with a smirk "Yes please" much to the annoyance of Sandra. As he returned with the Sweet Menu Dave took barely a second to order "I'll have Apple Crumble and Custard please" and looking at Sandra he wasn't surprised to hear her say "Nothing for me, thank you" and as the waiter left she finally had had enough "So...... boyfriend, am I near with my guess?" seeing her getting a little perturbed by his delaying tactics, he took hold of her left hand and said "Sandra you need to treble it and add 10!" and sitting back while she worked it out, she had just figured it out when the waiter returned with Dave's Apple Crumble and Custard, halting her just as she was about to tell him her answer. "Thank you" Dave said to the waiter, picking up his spoon and cutting into the steaming bowl before him, but before he could place it in his mouth a hand came across the table to stop it halfway to his mouth. Looking at her with a huge smile on his face he said quietly "Yes £100,000!" and seeing her drop her hand from his spoon, he placed the delicious sweet into his mouth, as Sandra sat with hers open.

Finishing her half of Lager, Sandra attracted the waiter's attention and ordered a refill for both of them. Looking at Dave as he worked his way through his dish of Apple Crumble and Custard, she waited until he had finished and as he put his spoon down she leapt in "Seriously!" she said leaning towards him with her elbows on the table. The smile and nod of the head told her it was true, and she sat back in her chair, to let the facts soak in. "How?" she said eventually already halfway down her Lager. Dave took a drink and explained "Although the £17,500 was a lot of money in itself at the time in 1952, with compound interest rather than straight line interest it came to £105,000, less the car and kitchen of course, so there was £102,941.10 left when I became 25, so Sandra Robertson what do you think of that!" The silence continued until they had finished their drinks, and having paid the bill, they went out to the car park and standing looking at the Red Mini, she put her arms around him and reached for a kiss that she knew would be there. The journey home in Dave's Escort was done in silence until they pulled up outside 15 Windy Hill "Did we have to leave Scarlet in the car park?" and working out she meant the Red Mini, he took her hand as he locked the car. "It was a rush job, so we need to go in on Saturday to do all the paperwork and get it taxed etc, sorry!" "Oh, it's alright, it just seems a shame, that she has to stay there on her own until Saturday!" smiling at the comment he opened the door and after Sandra had gone into the kitchen, he locked the door and joined her as she made a cup of tea. "Scarlet will be back at the garage tomorrow, until Saturday when we pick her up!" and realising he too was talking about the car as a person, he shook his head at the absurdity of it, his thoughts broken as Sandra finished making the tea and with a mischievous look in her eye said "Come on Mr Moneybags, if you want to see my tan lines, let's see if that steak has given you some energy!" and with that she was already heading for the bedroom with a huge smile on her face, which was replicated by Dave, follow-ing her quickly, trying not to spill his tea, up the stairs.

The journey into work on Thursday was unlike any other they had taken. Sandra had asked him a few questions over tea and toast for breakfast, and while he was doing his best to answer all her queries he just didn't have the answers to some of her questions. The legal connections were a particular problem because he honestly had no idea what they meant, now or in the future and as he thought about it he decided that until he had had his second meeting with Mr Ramsdale, they would only tell close family and ask them to keep it a secret until then. Sitting in the Escort in the Council Car Park Dave finally said turning off the engine "I want to keep this a secret until the weekend, and then we can tell your and my parents, but until I have had the next meeting with Mr Ramsdale I don't want this getting out. So can you keep quiet about Scarlet until then, you can keep a secret can't you?" Oh I can keep a secret thought Sandra before replying "Yes I can keep a secret, but can we tell our parents about Scarlet?" and seeing he wasn't going to win this battle, he nodded and she kissed him gently, before they left the car and went about their daily tasks, burdened by a secret that would take years to unravel.

Saturday came and with it the first hint of winter on its way, with a squall that went on most of the day, after tea and toast for breakfast Dave and Sandra went to the garage to release Scarlet as Sandra called the Red Mini. The paperwork and handover took an hour ,and by the time they got to Church Street the house was empty and a slightly disappointed Sandra got into Dave's Escort leaving Scarlet parked outside the Robertson house to which they would return later after visiting Dave's parents."Hello, you two!" Mary Baxter said as she opened the door against the weather. "Take your coats off and go into the Front room your dad is in there, I'll get the kettle on!" and without another word, she was headed for the kitchen leaving Dave and Sandra in the hallway taking their coats off before Dave went first into the Front room and with a "Morning dad" he sat on the sofa as Sandra hung up their coats in the hallway before joining him on the sofa. Putting down his morning paper Alan looked at them and seeing they were holding hands as always, he knew this wasn't bad news, but waiting for Mary to turn up with a tray of coffee which he knew she would, he asked "Did you enjoy your birthday party son?" and without hesitation Dave answered "I told you on the night dad, it was fabulous the band were great, the DJ was great it was a top night, thanks to you!" and as if on cue Mary arrived with four coffees and a plate of biscuits which she handed to each of them, eager to hear why they were here, already knowing about Dave's meeting on Wednesday.

"Well mum, dad we're here to tell you about last Wednesday's meeting at McParland and Co. which was about the Trust Fund. Well it's a bit complicated but the end result is that there was ... no ... have a guess how much there is, both of you!" and as Alan looked at Mary he quickly did some mental arithmetic and said £40,000, at which Mary looked shocked and said "I know you are an Accountant but £40,000 honestly Alan, £30,000 is my guess David, now tell us who is nearer!" with a smile breaking out on both their faces Sandra and Dave looked at each other and leaving Dave to deal with his parents Sandra sat back and took a sip of coffee."Well actually mum, dad is nearer, but way off!" looking disappointed Alan quickly added "Ah I forgot about the car and the kitchen so take of £2,400 that would be £37,600!" Laughing, Dave found it difficult to get the figures out, but after a quick drink of coffee, he put his cup down and said "The fund started off at £17,500 in 1952 and as of Wednesday it stood at £102,941.10 exactly, including taking into account the car and kitchen" The silence was interrupted by a very rare "Bloody Hell!" from Mary, as Alan sat nursing his coffee trying to do the maths "How?" ....he started before answering his own question..."Ah ...Compound Interest!" and the silence invaded the room again.

"That's not all of the story either, I am seeing Mr Ramsdale again on Wednesday to talk about the Fund, and well there are some legal connections that apparently have a timeline on them to 2002 or before, but the information about them is sealed, so I am going to ask him about them, but he did intimate that he couldn't tell me. But say it goes to 2002, then whatever it is will be when I am 42, which seems a strange age, but the fund was actually setup in 1952, so 2002 would be 50 years which makes more sense, but I have no idea what it can be about! Got any ideas?" Getting up Mary headed out of the Front room and came back before the conversation had got going again. Seeing the look on Mary's face and the letter in her hand Alan sat back in his chair, knowing full well what the contents were as she said "David, Sandra, I never really knew my Dad as he worked so hard, and as you know I was brought up by various Aunts or women who I called Aunts. Anyway I never wanted for anything and when I married Alan he gave me this letter to be opened in the events of his death, which I thought would be many years from then but as you know was only two years later. Let me read what he wrote as it does have an impact on you.

"*Mary, it will be in sad circumstances that you read this letter. Although I wasn't always there when you were growing up, I tried my best to make sure the people who looked after you were good people, and I feel confident that they were as you have grown up a confident and beautiful young woman. Alan will look after you until you are both old and grey, of that I am sure. Before he asked for your hand, we had several meetings and he convinced me that his Love for you was pure and true, I have known many people over the years and rarely have I been wrong.*

In the fullness of time there will be a story released that relates to my time in the First World War. Please understand I was just doing my duty like many others who didn't make it back from France. I was lucky and due to the actions of one particular person whose name I can't at this time release, I have been in a position to make your first born the beneficiary of a Trust Fund that will mature when they reach 25. The details are sealed until then, but if you need to use the Trust Fund before maturity please contact McParland and Co, on Kirkdale where the Trust Fund is lodged.

I loved your Mother Mary, so very much, and we had so little time together, we had such plans for the future, but when she was pregnant she made me promise to never forget her, like she knew the future, and I never did, never a day went by when I didn't think of her in all the time between then and now, when I hope I will see her again.

As the tears started Mary handed the letter to Alan, and heading into the kitchen for refuge Sandra close to tears herself, joined her in the kitchen leaving Alan and Dave in silence in the Front Room. The sound of the kettle going on and the clink of crockery broke the silence and a few minutes later a laden tray was brought into the Front Room by Mary with Sandra holding some side plates following closely behind."Always gets me, that letter" Mary said managing to hold back the tears and placing the tray on the coffee table she added "Its 30 years this year since he died and I can't hardly remember him it seems so unfair!" and picking up a coffee she sat down once again silent.

Alan broke the silence as he picked up a piece of fruit cake and placed it on a side plate "So David what do you intend to do with such a large sum of money!" and taking a chance to lighten the mood he quickly said "Well actually, I bought Sandra a little present called Scarlet, actually it's a Red Mini and it's not new or anything but it was worth every penny of..... . what it cost" deciding now wasn't a good time to talk about money. The rest I think will depend on what Mr Ramsdale says on Wednesday, but I might think about paying the mortgage off, as interest rates seems to be going up" Finishing his fruit cake Alan offered "Not a bad idea, you might want to put a sum away for a few years, that will earn a better rate and ..." "Get yourself a nice new car David!" cut Alan off as Mary joined the conversation adding "You're both young, enjoy your good luck you never know when it may change, just look at my Dad he only had four years with my mum. Life can be cruel, you two enjoy yourselves. Now, where's Scarlet Sandra, is she pretty?" and seeing Mary change the mood, Sandra told her all about Scarlet and her two big extra headlights at the front and promised to bring her round tomorrow, as the conversation moved away from the pain and hurt of yesteryear.

"That was more emotional than I expected "said Dave as he pulled away in the Escort from his parents house "That letter was so sad, I have to say when I went in the kitchen with your mother I had a little cry too!" Sandra replied as they headed back towards her own parents house, where she knew Scarlet was waiting for her. As they pulled up behind Scarlet the Jim's company Cavalier was parked on the drive and patting Scarlet on the roof with her spare hand as she passed, Sandra squeezed Dave's hand and said "Thank you for my present! Immediately realising she had left herself wide open "Don't thank me, thank the steak!" and pushing him into the Cavalier as she let go of his hand and went down the garden path opening the Front door, leaving Dave grinning as he followed her into the house. "Hello darling, did you manage to get parked, someone's left an old Mini at the top of the drive!" returning from hanging up her coat Sandra quickly replied "Don't insult Scarlet mum, she's very sensitive!" and after about 10 seconds the penny dropped for Diane "Scarlet! Is that your Mini Sandra?" Proudly she said "She certainly is mum, and if you don't apologise she'll never forgive you!" looking at her completely serious daughter, she had no choice but to say going to the window "I'm sorry Scarlet, but my daughter didn't tell me she had lost her marbles" and laughing she put the kettle on for no other reason than, that was what you do when people visit. "Is dad in the Lounge?" the nodded head told her yes, and as Sandra and Dave headed out of the kitchen Diane said "Go into the Lounge dear, I'll bring the tea in when it's ready" "Hello you two!" said Jim putting down his paper and with a feeling of Deja Vu, Sandra and Dave sat down on the sofa holding hands as always. "So what brings you two round here apart from Scarlet of course, I heard the conversation with your mother, ignore her my new Cavalier is called Lancelot" and with a smile was rewarded with a smile from Sandra, and confusion from Dave, as Diane appeared with a tray of cups and a Teapot together with a plate of biscuits "Won't need lunch at this rate!" Dave said quietly to Sandra, which as ever was met with a small slap on the arm.

"Well Jim, Diane, you wouldn't know but my Grandfather Windsor Carey set up a Trust Fund for me back in 1952, and now I am 25 it has come to maturity so I, that is we, wanted to let you know the outcome" After revisiting the story he had already told his own parents it was a slightly tongue weary Dave who finished and took a sip of tea, and a Kit-Kat from the plate. "Wow! Alan told us the story at the weekend at your Birthday Party, but I don't think even he thought there was that much in the Fund, you must be a bit shocked yourselves!" said Jim finally "More than shocked, absolutely dumbstruck I was, in the Solicitors Office!" replied Dave adding "I've got another meeting next week when I hope to get some information, but it's mind blowing to have that amount of money" and unable to resist Diane said "Less the cost of Scarlet of course!" and giggling at her own sense of humour she didn't even look at Sandra, knowing a scowl would be waiting for her. "Well good for you, suppose a new car and some foreign holidays and a new house are in order!" Diane continued as she was in full flow "Well actually mother we are thinking of paying off the mortgage, and the rest can go in a bank!" said Sandra falling into her mother's trap "I know darling, Dave will be sensible apart from your little present of course!" at which both Sandra and Dave turned bright red and trying to hide behind his Kit-Kat Dave managed to drink his cup of tea leaving Sandra pretending to choke, as a way out of the still recent memory in Portugal.

Heading home in the dark Sandra drove Scarlet with her extra Front Headlights on, and made it home before Dave's Escort despite blinding a few oncoming cars before she found the switch to turn them down. Pulling up behind her, he turned off the engine and watching as Sandra walked down the path and opened the Front door, he sat for a moment and wondered why he had been so lucky and quietly as he got out of the car, said to the sky "Wherever you are Windsor Carey, I hope you found Mary, thank you from both of us" and walking through the door he saw Sandra putting the kettle on and having had enough tea and coffee already, he put his arms around her and whispered in her ear. Forget the tea babe, lets go and have a pint at the The Murg, to Windsor and Mary, and get a curry from the Paradise, what do you say?" turning round to face him she kissed him quickly adding "What a lovely idea, you really are an old romantic you know!" and returning her kiss he added "Less of the old" and he slapped her bottom bringing back for a second, a memory she had consigned to join a lie.

♦ ♦ ♦

Chapter 20

Wednesday soon came around, and with the atmosphere at work at an all time low as Daniel Bruce returned to work, and his obvious anger at being suspended pervaded the office, so Dave was glad when lunchtime came and he headed off to see Mr Ramsdale at McParland and Co. Laura welcomed him like she had known him all his life, and leading him into Mr Ramsdale's Office, she asked if he wanted a cup of tea, or coffee, but determined to get his lunch, he politely said "I'm fine thank you Laura" wondering why he had used her name. "Mr Baxter, do come in" said Mr Ramsdale from behind his desk and taking the seat opposite he sat down as Mr Ramsdale asked him "Have you decided what you want to do with the Trust Fund Mr Baxter?" and with his prepared answer Dave quickly replied "If you can BACS Transfer it to this account" handing him a deposit slip "I would be grateful, but there are a few questions I would like to ask if you don't mind?" picking up the deposit slip, and adding it to the file Mr Ramsdale replied "I thought there may be, but as I told you last week there is little that I can add, but please ask away and I'll do my best" realising he was probably going over old ground, he tried to remember the questions he wanted to ask, but after the third question had been answered by Mr Ramsdale with the same answer "I'm afraid that information is privileged, but it will come out on time!" he was wondering what to ask next when it occurred to him that he was going at this from the wrong angle "Can I ask Mr Ramsdale, presumably the account was set up from another account, do you have that information and is it available?" after a few seconds while he looked though the file he answered "Mr Baxter the account was set up by your Grandfather Windsor Carey, but I have no evidence as to where he got the money, and I know it is frustrating for you, but if you were to do some research around 1950 to 1956, when he died there may be some joy for you. I understand you work in the Council Estates Department so you are in a good place to start if I may say so, I'm sorry I can't answer your questions but the Trust Fund stood for 30 years, and that's where I would start, alternatively I look forward to seeing you in 2002, or rather I should say one of my colleagues, as I will have retired or worse by then. If that's all I'll arrange for the transfer of your funds this afternoon and they should be in your account in 3 working days. It's been a pleasure Mr Baxter and if you ever need our services we would be delighted to assist!" realising his time was up Dave shook Mr Ramsdale's extended hand and with a slight bow left the office where all his answers had lain, with none of them answered.

Patting Scarlet on the roof as he got home, had become a habit. Dave put his key in the lock and putting his jacket on the hook he found Sandra in the Lounge watching TV. "Hello you had a good day?" she said with a smile. Sitting down next to her on the sofa he wearily replied "Not really Daniel is still making the office like a fridge with his demeanour, I spent 30 minutes with Mr Ramsdale, and he said he couldn't answer any of my questions as to where Windsor got the money for the Trust Fund, but advised me to do some research as I work in the Estates Department. Like I haven't got enough to do!" still smiling Sandra turning the TV down quietly said "So you've no news then?" sighing Dave replied "Nope I've got no news!" taking his hand, Sandra while slowly moving his hand over her stomach and placing it on top of her other hand said "Well I've got some news............ I missed my period and I thought it may be with all the travel, but well, it's only early days, but I think I'm pregnant Dave!"

"When did?" he managed to get out "Portugal obviously" Sandra replied amazed at his inability to take it in "What about the pill I thought it was fail proof?" smiling at his lack of knowledge she replied "Nothing is completely fail proof didn't you do biology at school, besides I had a dodgy tummy before we went so I took some pills to counter it, so that may have been something to do with it, anyway aren't you happy?" rubbing his hand over her stomach he leaned in to kiss her and finally finding the words said "No not happy.... ecstatic is the word I would use. If I thought I was lucky before this tops it all although of course the money will help when little.......Victoria or Albert comes along!" allowing him his moment of humour, she looked at him with a face that said no and said "Caroline or Alistair as we agreed, but I think it's a girl!" "How on earth....." he started but didn't finish as he put his arm around her, and they sat watching the silent TV screen, having just made their own little bit of history.

Sounding the horn as Sandra parked Scarlet outside Albion Street, brought Mary out to have a look at Sandra's pride and joy. As Alan joined Dave while Sandra and Mary looked around the car, Dave asked him what they were doing for the day "Well nothing planned but I dare say your mum will want to go out somewhere as the weather is okay, and now we're in October there may not be many more decent days before winter sets in, why have you got something in mind?" trying not to blurt out their news Dave, almost nonchalantly replied "Well we thought it would be nice to get together as a family and celebrate my, that is our good fortune so I thought the Bedlow Arms would be good and Jim and Diane will be there as well as Tony and Gill, my treat of course. What do you say?" Looking on as Mary sat in the driver's seat Alan shook his head knowing that Dave's old Fiesta would need replacing soon but he hadn't got a Mini in mind for Mary but it was obvious that she would now. "What time do you want us there son!" and figuring out what his dad was looking at Dave said "3pm will be perfect dad" as the Mini headed off with Mary waving her arm out of the passenger window, leaving them stood wondering where they were going, and more importantly for how long.

The Red Mini, now known by everyone as Scarlet, was parked in the Bedlow Arms car park at 2.50 as Sandra was desperate by now to tell everyone, and had nearly told Mary earlier on the impromptu drive. Sitting in the car park she suddenly felt nervous, looking at Dave she pondered and said "Is it too early to tell everyone? We could put it off for a bit if you like" opening the door and stepping onto the car park he put his hands on Scarlet's roof, and waited as Sandra joined him after locking the car. Stood with Scarlet between them Dave smiled and said" So the projectile vomiting this morning was a result of cereal poisoning then!" Taking her hand they went towards the Bedlow Arms entrance, just as Alan's Jaguar turned up, soon followed by Jim's Cavalier with Tony and Gill in the back seat."No going back now, girlfriend!" Dave said as he opened the door and as she went past him, Sandra kissed him on the cheek saying under her breath "I love you Dave Baxter!" and only just catching the words as the inside noise hit him, he smiled and heading towards the table with a Reserved for Mr Baxter note, he pulled out a chair for her to sit down and leaning down as he pushed the chair in, he said "Not as much as I love you, mummy!" as the rest of the invitees joined them Dave waited until they had all ordered before standing up and holding up his drink he said with a degree of sobriety "A toast to Granddad Windsor Carey" and as they all raised their glasses he stayed standing, with a now desperate Sandra staring at him he raised his glass again, and with a huge smile on his face said "And a toast to my beautiful girlfriend Sandra, who brought a little present back from Portugal!" and sitting down he waited for all of 5 seconds before both mothers looked at each other and standing up in unison they went to give Sandra a hug and a kiss. "You'll need that money now David" Alan said almost immediately, and Dave replied "I couldn't be happier dad, even if didn't have the money, although you're probably right!" he added ever the pragmatist.

The afternoon seemed to go on forever, as after their meal

they stayed for a few drinks. When Sid and Jane turned up out of the blue just as they finished their meal, they managed to squeeze them onto the table and it was after 7.00pm when the party finally broke up with all the cars driven home by respective wives and girlfriends, with their husbands and boyfriends taking full advantage of the situation. As Dave got out of Scarlet in the dark and stumbled towards their house Sandra locked the car and followed him down the garden path at 15, Windy Hill she arrived at the Front door with the key in her hand. "I do love you Sandra Robertson you know!" smiling as she opened the door he was leaning against, he just about kept his balance as the door opened behind him. Heading into the kitchen, he sat down and as Sandra put the kettle on she joined him at the table "I hope you're not going to make a habit of getting drunk Dave Baxter!" she said taking his hand "Oh, I won't, I'm just so happy, although you have ruined my plans!" looking confused, and a little shocked she asked "What do you mean?" and gulping air Dave said "We were supposed to get engaged, and we did. Then get a house, which you did. Then get married, which we haven't. Then have children, which we are having. So Sandra Robertson what do you say to that!" as the kettle finished boiling and clicked off she took his hand and said "I think you need to go to bed Mr Baxter!" Standing up she led him towards the stairs to the mutterings of "You'll be gentle with me won't you!" until he fell on the bed and leaving him there Sandra went downstairs to make a mug of tea and watch some TV on her own while she still could.

Christmas 1984 came and went in Kirkdale, and with each month Sandra became more convinced that she was going to have a girl. With the money from the Trust Fund, Dave paid off the mortgage on 15 Windy Hill and life settled down to await the arrival of their first born. The Miners Strike continued until the 3rd of March 1985 almost a year after it had started, and with supplies no longer under threat Manchester Road Power Station was given a new lifeblood, where once it had been under review in the summer of 1982 as the impact of North Sea Gas and the Clean Air Act made the 30 year old site bordering on unprofitable. Sandra left work at the Council in May of 1985 and with all the best wishes from her colleagues at work, she was looking forward to some time to herself before her due date of July 25th 1985. The third small bedroom they had decided would be a good nursery, which was her project for when she was off, despite Dave offering to do the decorating and as summer arrived with a blast in June, Sandra turned the previously neglected room into a little girl's haven without a thought that her baby would be anything other than a girl.

◆ ◆ ◆

Chapter 21

On the night of the 27th July 1985 Sandra went into Kirkdale Infirmary at just after 10pm and after 9 hours Caroline Mary Baxter, was born weighing 6lbs 7oz to an overjoyed Sandra and Dave. Two days later they took her home to 15, Windy Hill, and a pink and yellow nursery designed and painted by Sandra, with a little help from an anxious Dave. Settling into a routine the rest of the year was a blur in the words of a very proud Dave, who had passed another exam and was well on his way to his goal of being a Surveyor, and eventually Senior Council Surveyor. Sandra returned to work and despite her concern about leaving Caroline with Mary while she was at work, once the arrangement had settled down, it worked like clockwork. With no doubt as to who her mother was, with her dark hair and blue eyes, Caroline blossomed as she grew from a baby to a child. Going to nursery broke Mary's heart as she had got so used to having her, but she did have the daily pleasure of picking her up from Nursery, until she decided to get a job when Caroline left Nursery and went to a now refurbished Northfield School in September 1990 at the age of 5.

The first two years at Northfield School had brought out more of Caroline's personality and with a smile that he knew would one day break hearts when she grew up, Dave took responsibility for dropping her off each day and Sandra would pick her up from her mum's at the end of the day, as Mary had taken a job after years of not being interested, probably brought on by being so busy when she had Caroline. The plan worked perfectly, and with a substantial balance of money still in the bank from his Trust Fund, the world looked pretty good as they planned a summer holiday in Portugal with each hoping for completely different things, but both knowing what each other was hoping for. Looking forward to the slightly out of synch Labour Day holiday, they were both hoping for a relaxing long weekend, but with Caroline that was never going to be likely. Arriving home from Church Street in Sandra's aging Scarlet, Caroline had a picture she had painted at Grandma Diane's of the seaside, with a family of three, some very lopsided sandcastles and an elephant in the sea blowing water out of his trunk. "Well what have we here baby, is it a circus?" said Sandra as they went into the kitchen, waiting for the indignation from her daughter, at her inability to work out what her picture was about, she got the admonishment she was expecting "No mummy, it's an Elephant on his holidays, and he's giving everyone a shower!" and taking the picture from her mother, she looked at it before raising her arm in the shape of an elephant's trunk and making a water noise with her lips she pretended to shower her mum. Laughing as she made some sandwiches for her daughter's tea, together with some orange juice she had just put them on the table when Dave arrived home. "Daddy!" came the shout and tea was forgotten for a moment as she grabbed her picture, not giving him time to put his briefcase down, she said "Daddy look at my picture, mummy thought it was a circus, what do you think?" and placing his briefcase at his feet he took her picture and looking for help from Sandra which wasn't forthcoming, from the shake of the head, he looked again before saying "Well baby it's an Elephant at the seaside giving everyone a shower!" and as Sandra shook her head again at the uncanny way Dave and Caroline's minds worked in tune, she heard "See mummy!" as Caroline put the picture down and returned to her sandwiches happy that someone could see the world as she could. With the weather for the weekend looking quite good it wasn't long before Dave said "Why don't we go to the seaside tomorrow, as it's a long weekend?" and getting the response he expected from Caroline, he looked at Sandra for support but unsure how she was going to react he played his trump card "Dad's going to lend us the Jaguar as I don't think the Escort has got much life in it! It's been a tough week at work as well so we deserve a break" and knowing that Dave had had a few problems at work, especially with Daniel Bruce the deal was agreed with a smile and a nod, unseen by a smiling Caroline still admiring her picture.

Saturday 2nd May 1992

After breakfast most of which Sandra left, unseen by Dave, they put some warm clothes in the car and headed for Albion Street and Grandma and Granddad Baxter's house to pick up his now 7 year old Jaguar. "Take care of her won't you?" said Alan as he handed Dave the keys to the Jaguar, and with a shake of the head as he still didn't understand why people treated cars as people, he opened the car and putting Caroline's car seat from the Escort onto the back seat, he finished securing it and let Caroline escape from Mary's hug as she clambered into the car. "I'll bring you back some rock dad, or would you like a Kiss-Me-Quick Hat?" "Some rock would be lovely David" said Mary before Alan could choose. "Okay then we'll see you tomorrow, take care of the Escort won't you!" and with an air slap that missed Dave by two feet Alan said "Enjoy yourself especially you, young lady!" pointing to Caroline, as she sat like a Princess in the back of the Jaguar."Love you, see you soon!" said Sandra through the open window as Dave turned the ignition, and with waves all round the Jaguar headed out of Albion Street, destination seaside.

The journey was uneventful apart from the demands from the little Princess Caroline for a different song a she had heard 'Incy Wincy Spider',' Grand Old Duke of York', 'Twinkle Twinkle Little Star' and 'This Old Man' already. As they drove into Blackpool singing 'Ten In a Bed' with Dave leading the singing, the sight of Blackpool Tower faded the song. Realising they had arrived Caroline had a huge grin on her face as she saw the waves and she shouted "Seaside!" as they drove along the front parking close to the North Pier they got their warm clothes, "Just in case" Sandra had said, and holding a hand each, they swung Caroline until they got onto the beach and letting her go they joined hands and watched their beautiful daughter chase seagulls and pick up shells for the next half an hour, until she tired of not catching any seagulls, but with a handful of shells, she came to where they were sat watching her on the sea wall, handing them all her shiny shells she held her arms up and as Sandra picked her up, she sat on her knee as Dave looked at the sand encrusted shells and slowly let them drop back to where they belonged.

"Do you want something to eat baby, Daddy and I were going to get some chips" said Sandra as Caroline's hair tried to blind her, with the wind coming directly at her off the sea. Looking about her Caroline spotted the Ice Cream stall, but before she could say anything Sandra beat her to it. "If you have some chips you can have some Ice Cream later baby, but you can't have Ice Cream for lunch!" and realising the deal was non-negotiable she nodded her head, disappointed, but smart enough to know it was now just a matter of time before she got Ice Cream. Sandra handed Caroline to Dave and said she would get the chips and returning with two trays she answered the question in Dave's eyes before he could ask it "I just got two portions, so we can share as she'd never eat a full portion!" happy with her decision Dave was soon ploughing through his portion as Sandra and Caroline struggled with theirs stabbing the chips with wooden forks. "Big portions!" said Sandra as she and Caroline finished leaving nearly a half portion "You're not kidding be better if they gave you less and reduced the price, good job we didn't get three portions!" and putting the remains in a nearby bin he stretched his arms out wide and said "Now who's ready for the funfair!" at which Caroline jumped up and down, as did Sandra's stomach. Heading for the funfair with Caroline between them, they looked at the height restrictions and finding a couple of rides which

Caroline would be allowed on they joined the queue and as the squeals of delight echoed along the pier they treated their bundle of joy to three rides, before they headed to the slot machines where Caroline spent 50p to win 6 penny coins, but she was so happy it would have been wrong to tell her she was on a losing streak. With a handful of old coins in her hand the inevitable happened and they had to pass an Ice Cream stall at the end of the pier, and having had her chips Caroline wanted the other half of the deal. "Mummy you promised!" and realising she had been boxed in Sandra said "Give me your money and we'll see what you can have!" and as Caroline opened her hand the coins fell into Sandra's hand, quickly put underneath to catch them. "Well let's see, well you did really well baby, so you can afford anything!" at which Caroline jumped up and down before pointing at a swirly ice cream cone, with red sauce dripping down it in the picture. "Can I have a cone with sauce please" before turning and saying "Do you want anything?" a shake of the head and rub of the stomach saved him saying anything, and as she turned back the Ice Cream was already waiting for her. Taking it from the stand with one hand and paying with the other, she handed it to a very excited Caroline taking her spare hand once she had paid, and they went for a walk down towards Blackpool Tower while Caroline concentrated on her now dribbling Ice Cream. Sandra lent into Dave a little and said "Why did your dad lend you the car?" aware the question would come he replied "Well the Escort is getting on and dad's been putting off getting a new car for a couple of years so he's decided he would like something a bit smaller, so he said why don't I try it, as we have a family, and if I like it we can come to an agreement!" Smiling at his answer she took her time before answering "Smart man, your dad!" as they continued walking with Caroline trying to lick her Ice Cream before it melted down her hand, just like her mother some years ago. The trip up Blackpool Tower did nothing for Sandra's queasy stomach, but Caroline and Dave loved it, especially when Caroline realised you could see all the way to the ground. The wind blowing her hair around and the seagulls circling, made Caroline run around in circles and despite a few looks, it wasn't until Dave finally got hold of her that Sandra felt better. "Come on you two, let's get down to ground level and we can see about getting Granddad some rock!" said Sandra as they headed for the lift and another unpleasant journey for her.

Arriving on the street Sandra took Caroline's hand as Dave took her other hand he said. "Let's take her on a Donkey ride, then we can head for home if that's okay with you?" and as Sandra nodded he looked at Caroline and talking to no one in particular said "Who's for a Donkey ride?" barely had the words got out of his mouth, than his arm was being pulled downwards "Me daddy, Me daddy!" and walking towards the beach they saw the small queue for the Donkey ride, and once they were on the beach they let her go, and she quite independently joined the queue. When they reached the Donkey ride Caroline was second in the queue and paying the ticket price despite a look from Dave that said it wasn't worth it, Sandra helped her on when her turn came around and holding onto the reins Caroline set off on her Donkey that she had named spot as he was dappled. Standing watching as a strange looking man, wearing a Kiss-Me-Quick hat took their daughter along the beach Sandra said "We should have another one of those!" and as the Donkey set off back towards them Dave answered "I don't think we can make another one of those!" pointing at the returning Caroline "But always willing to try!" and with a smile on his face he gave her a kiss on the cheek and put his hand in the back pocket of her jeans, where he left it until it was time to get Caroline down from the donkey. "Enjoy that baby?" Dave said as he lifted her down onto the sand "Oh yes daddy spot was lovely, can we get a Donkey!" and with a shake of his head, a slightly disappointed Caroline took his hand as they headed back to the Jaguar. They stopped at a 'Rock Emporium', after choosing several flavours of rock for

Granddad Baxter, and a lolly for Caroline, they walked fresh faced, and smiling to the car park where they had left the Jaguar and the journey home.

Joining the M55 the smoothness of the car soon had Caroline asleep, and as Sandra took the lolly from her hand and put it back in its wrapper she turned slightly in her seat to face Dave as he concentrated on driving. "If we did manage to make another one of those" she said intimating with her hand to the now fast asleep Caroline "Would we move house, or just manage?" she added. Keeping his eye on the traffic Dave thought for a few seconds before replying "I hadn't really thought about it to be honest, suppose if it happens we'll have to make a decision, but the house is big enough for now, but I suppose we should think about it, why brought this up?" "Well this is a lovely car and suits your job, but you've got money in the bank and could get any car you wanted and if you're not getting a new car the money could go to a new house, if …. and when, we have another child that is" taking his left hand off the steering wheel, he reached for her hand and momentarily holding it he replied "That's our money in the bank , well actually it's Windsor Carey's but that's splitting hairs. If and when we need it, a new house might be a good idea, as we could probably make a bit on Windy Hill after 8 years, and I'm not that precious about cars as they lose so much money, but I must admit that I am tempted by this beauty!" Taking the turn off for the M6, the Jaguar cruised along as Sandra slowly fell asleep like her daughter, until the junction for Kirkdale came up, with the motion of the roundabout Sandra woke up and realising where they were she said "Sorry, I fell asleep" and turning to see Caroline still asleep she added "Can you put her to bed and I'll sort tea out" and with a "Yeah no problem" reply Dave pulled up outside 15 Windy Hill and switching the engine off, he set about not waking up Caroline, as he took her from her car seat. Sandra went ahead and leaving the door open, she went into the kitchen to see what there was for tea.

Picking up Caroline he managed to rest her head on his shoulder, she stirred a little as he lifted her but stayed asleep. Heading upstairs he could hear Sandra putting the kettle on as he gently put her down on her bed. Undressing her gently and managing to put on her pyjamas without waking her fully, he tucked her in and headed somewhat relieved downstairs into the kitchen. "All sorted?" Sandra asked even though she knew it was. "Sleeping like a Donkey!" Dave answered wondering where that had come from. "You and your sense of humour!" she said handing him a mug of tea adding "Tea will be 20 minutes so why don't we go into the Lounge until it's ready?" and without responding Dave headed to the Lounge as the smell of Pizza and Chips slowly hit his senses.

Sunday 3rd May 1992

"I'm going to see what there is about Windsor Carey at work when I have a moment next week" said Sandra out of the blue, holding a mug of tea, as she looked out of the kitchen extension onto the garden where Caroline was playing, and as Dave looked at her back, sat at the kitchen table finishing his toast he wondered where this comment had come from. "I never did get around to doing that research, that Mr Ramsdale suggested in what 1984, I guess it just got put to one side maybe now would be a good time to start?" Turning around Sandra looked at him and in added "It's the least we can do, after all we are sat in his kitchen!" and seeing the logic Dave thought about the logistics of finding out about his Granddad but while he was pondering Sandra carried on "I can start in the Manchester Road Power Station folder first as it has been across my desk before, so shouldn't be too difficult to get a starting point, you said he worked at Ramsbottoms before and after the war, and presumably they owned the land so I could try there. What do you think?" putting the last bite of toast in his mouth he finished chewing and replied "I'll ask dad tomorrow if he knows anything else and let you know okay?" and interrupted as Caroline came downstairs still in her pyjamas he said "Hello sleepyhead, do you want some toast?" and with a shake of her head she went to where Sandra was still looking out of the window and taking her hand Sandra said "Shall we have some Rice Crispies, or Sugar Puffs?" with a quick pointed response in favour of Sugar Puffs, Sandra pulled out a chair opposite Dave, putting the box of Sugar Puffs on the table she went to get a spoon, bowl and glass before opening the fridge to get some milk and orange juice. Returning to sit at the table next to Dave, she poured her daughter a glass of orange juice and let her daughter fill the bowl too full of Sugar Puffs, adding the milk which spilled a little Caroline picked up her spoon and set about her mini mountain of cereal. Sandra looked at Dave and with a smile of pride between them they watched as a newly awakened Caroline slowly finished the bowl and half the orange juice before slipping off her seat and saying as she walked out of the kitchen "Going to get dressed!" the proud parents shared a moment before Dave broke the silence "We should have another one of those!" and as Sandra gave him a kiss on the cheek she said mischievously "The practising is fun!" the reply when it came got the slap it deserved "I remember when we used to practise when your parents were away in the Lounge and the shower and...." as he was curtailed, not just by the slap on his arm but also by the sight of Caroline standing unseen in double quick time at the kitchen door in a summer flowery dress with a huge smile on her face but no shoes on her feet. "Come with mummy and we'll get your hair done and get your shoes, then we can go off to see Grandma and Granddad Robertson" and taking her hand Sandra led her back to her bedroom, to put some clips and a bow in her hair, returning to the kitchen she stood next to Dave and said "Daddy, can we go now?" and with a look that had only one answer, he stood up and taking his daughter's hand headed for the Front door only stopping to get them each a coat from the rack by the door. Following behind them Sandra took a coat from the rack and locked the door behind her. Hoping the funny taste in her mouth and the missed period, were a sign that another part of their plan was coming good and Caroline would have a brother soon, she stroked her stomach unseen by Dave as she put on her coat and made her way down the path towards the car, as he helped Caroline into the now old Escort, the Jaguar returned reluctantly to its owner for the time being.

Arriving at Church Street, Dave got out of the car first and opening the door found Caroline had undone her seat belt, and taking her hand he helped her step onto the pavement. As he turned to close the door she was gone when he turned back, seeing her halfway down the garden path he looked at Sandra who had closed her door and was walking round to him "I hope they're up!" he just managed to say before the Front door opened and Grandma Diane held her arms out to await the hug she knew she was going to get, and picking Caroline up she waved at Dave and Sandra to come inside and holding hands they followed the instruction, and the smell of bacon as they neared the door. "Good morning mum, I see you're spoiling dad again!" alluding to the half eaten bacon butty sat on a plate in front of her father "Nonsense he works hard, he deserves a treat" and looking at Dave she added "There's enough left for you Dave, if you want one!" and having only had a slice of toast , knowing he would get a bacon butty, he sat down opposite Jim and hardly had he poured a cup of tea from the pot on the table, than a cut in half bacon butty appeared in front of him from a smiling Diane who offered "There you go Dave , us girls are going into the Lounge" and without a look back the three generations of women left the kitchen by age, leaving Dave and Jim to devour their butties and discuss yesterdays football over the remains of the pot of tea.

"How's Tony getting on?" Dave asked after finishing his bacon butty, "It's been a couple of years since he moved to ....Sunderland isn't it?" he enquired "Oh, he seems to be doing fine he got promoted after Christmas to an Assistant Manager role, so the extra money will come on handy as Gill is expecting at the end of the year." Thinking back to the time Tony brought Gill back to the house and interrupted Sandra and him upstairs, he smiled at the thought, looking subconsciously at the ceiling and looking back at Jim he said "So are you planning to go on holiday this year Jim?" Getting up Jim picked up a brochure from the sideboard and handing it to Dave said "Portugal in September, the page is folded so you should be able to find it, Praia da Rocha, it's near Portimao, where you and Sandra went, before Caroline came along. It looks good and it's only a 3 hour flight, listen to me rambling on, you've already been there. Anything we should know food, drink etc?" Looking at the pictures of the resort brought back memories of their time in Portimao, and Sandra's look of horror, as a plate full of Sardines appeared in front of her, head, eyes and tail still on."They're looking at me!"she said swapping her plate with his steak and looking grateful, he remembered she added "I'll make it up to you!" and without doubt she had, as Caroline was conceived on that holiday 7 years ago. "The sardines might not be to your liking, but everything else is fine, plenty of choice and loads of fish dishes but if you get stuck go for the Peri Peri Chicken, it's a bit spicy but gorgeous. You'll love it, so much better than we hoped, and we went in September if I can remember" and trying to quickly count 9 months back from Caroline was born he said "Yes that's right the weather was 80c every day!" hoping Jim hadn't guessed how he had worked it out. "Good to hear, it was recommended by someone at the golf club, and he also mentioned the sardines! So we will give them a miss, but Diane is looking forward to it and to be fair with the way work is, if I don't take this holiday I'll miss out" "Still busy then Jim?" Dave asked already knowing the answer "Yes we took on a new line in mailshots, and to be honest it's more than we can handle, but with overtime it works and we'll have to get some new machinery to cope long term, it's a shame Tony left as he would been promoted by now, but when he left it wasn't so busy, and well you go where the heart takes you, so good luck to him!" and getting up Jim put the used crockery on the drainer before saying "Well we'd better see what plan the women have hatched!" and headed for the Lounge leaving Dave to follow in his own good time.

The plan involved a short trip to the local Shibden Park where there was a boating lake, miniature railway and of course Ice Cream. Getting into the Cavalier, Jim said, as Diane adjusted the seat belt "Do you think Tony would come back to Kirkdale? I think I could get him a similar job at work and we could do with an experienced extra set of hands. What do you think? I know you speak to him and Gill more than I do, and I doubt you tell me everything!" with a sideways look at him she replied "Jim Robertson, are you insinuating I keep secrets? After all these years!" and deciding to wait for the next sentence, Jim started the car and as they pulled away from Church Street to join the main road to Kirkdale, Diane finally released the secret she had been keeping. "Well not that it's a secret, which it isn't, but Gill isn't happy in Sunderland, and she would jump at a chance to come back to Kirkdale, but Tony is fine at work, so if you do have a job in mind for him, you will have to speak to him yourself to convince him to move, although with a baby on the way and the way he adores Gill he might not take much persuading, they're only renting so go on and ask him. Tony is off work this week to do some DIT at home before the baby comes. I'd like to see more of them and it would be lovely to have both our children, and their children, round at the Robertson's!" and with a smile at the thought of a new baby to go with the gorgeous Caroline, she almost missed Jim's quietly spoke "No secrets my foot!" as he pulled into Shibden Park closely followed by the Escort containing Sandra, Dave and a very excited Caroline.

The afternoon sun kept the light wind at bay, as Jim and Diane took Caroline out on a boat on the boating lake, skippered and rowed by Granddad Robertson, as Dave and Sandra walked hand in hand as always, along the path running round the edge of the lake watching their precious daughter as she ran her fingers in the water. The screams from Caroline as she got splashed, were mirrored by several other children as their parents and grandparents took advantage of the sunny conditions and played on the water. Slightly disappointed at having to get out of the boat as she had been having so much fun, a nevertheless still smiling Caroline, was helped onto the pier by Jim as their time came to an end as Diane, taking hold of her hand led her off the pier to meet Sandra and Dave, with Jim following behind as he struggled to get out of the boat. It was apparent from the look on her face that the lure of the Ice Cream stall, and the miniature railway had her spoilt for choice, and taking his daughter's hand from Diane, Dave chose for her and headed towards the miniature railway as Caroline skipped alongside him, the Ice Cream temporarily at the back of her mind, but by no means forgotten!

After two laps of the train circuit with Caroline sat in front of Dave with his arms around her the miniature train ground to a halt at the Platform, as Dave lifted her off the little train he put her down and she ran to where Jim, Diane and Sandra were waiting. Taking her mother's hand she stood looking at the pictures of the ice lollies and ice creams, on the poster by the side of the Ice Cream stall. "What do you want baby?" said Dave as he joined them and the answer that came back was unexpected to say the least "I'm not a baby, I'm six and I'd like a 99, please!" pointing to the poster with her finger on the flake, she looked up at Dave who in turn, looked at the others and they shared a look among the themselves that said it all, but needed no saying. Wandering around the park with their respective ice creams and lollies, the conversation was curtailed until Jim said quietly "I'll ring Tony tonight and sound him out about the job, and if he is up for it I'll have a word with the MD tomorrow and see if we can set up a meeting this week, he can stay with us for a couple of days" and the silent smile from Diane, as she struggled to stop the ice cream running down the cone and onto her hand, told him he was doing the right thing, even if he didn't know it wasn't his decision at all and he had just been manipulated by a very smart Diane.

Taking their time walking around the park it was nearly 4pm when they reached their cars parked next to each other in the car park, and not willing to let the day end Jim said "Why don't we go to the Bedlow Arms for something to eat my treat, tomorrow's Labour Day Holiday and with all the overtime I'm doing, why not enjoy some of it!" and without pausing for breath he finished "Good, no objections" and getting into the driver's seat he waited for Diane to join him. "I do like it when you surprise me Jim!" she said closing the door and with a wink Jim added "Later dear when the children have gone home!" and securing her seatbelt Diane looked across at him and smiled before responding "Promises, Promises!" and settling into her seat they made the journey to the Bedlow Arms, without so much as a single word between them.

"Mummy!" the voice came from the back of the Escort, and without waiting for a reply the rest of the sentence came out "Can I have fingers and chips?" and turning to see a smiling, as always Caroline, she said "Of course baby, do you want peas as well?" a sudden silence occurred as Caroline thought about the question and answered "No mummy, I'm not a baby, peas are for babies, can I have beans?" and a laughing Sandra said as she turned back to face the front "Beans it is....bab.... darling!" and catching Dave's smile she burst out laughing as the voice from the back seat finished with "and Ice Cream mummy!". They were still laughing as they pulled up next to Diane and Jim in the car park of the Bedlow Arms. As Dave helped, although she didn't actually need any help, Caroline out of the back seat, Sandra retold the story of the conversation in the car, as Mother and Grandmother walked towards the main door with Caroline swinging between them, they looked at each other and smiling together, they lifted Caroline onto the top step, before opening the door and letting her in first, as Jim and Dave caught up with them at the door.

"Table for 5 please" Jim said to the waiter and picking up some menus he led them towards the back of the room where a table for 6 stood empty "Perfect" said Jim as Diane and Sandra sat down with Caroline between them. Dave returned from the bar with a tray of drinks, and putting the tray down on the table, he handed the drinks around before sitting down next to Jim. "Well I think Sunday Roast is called for, what do you say Dave" said Jim and with a nod of the head Dave agreed. "Lasagne and chips for me please" said Sandra "and me too please" added Diane before turning to Caroline "Now young lady have you decided what you want?" despite knowing from the story of the car conversation what she wanted "I would like fingers and chips and beans please, and Ice Cream!" and as the adults laughed, Caroline sat on her hands and looked around the room as if she had eaten there all her life!

"Thanks for a lovely day out!" Diane said as she hugged Sandra while Dave put a very sleepy Caroline into her car seat. "I don't think I'll ever forget the smile on Caroline's face when her Ice Cream Sundae turned up, talk about happiness!" looking at her daughter now asleep in her seat as Dave closed the door gently, Sandra said "I know mum, she really is growing up fast, peas are for babies indeed!" and smiling at the memory she gave her mum an extra hug, before going over to her dad and repeating the hugs, she whispered in his ear "Thanks for the dinner Dad!" and before she could add anything he said "Thank you for Caroline, Sandra, she really is going to break some hearts when she is older! Bye for now!" and with a final short hug, Sandra let her dad go saying "Love you, see you soon" as she always did.

Monday 4ᵗʰ May 1992

The forgotten holiday of Labour Day started slowly at 15 Windy Hill and it wasn't until after 8.30 that Caroline popped her head around the bedroom door and seeing her mum was missing Caroline went downstairs where she found Sandra sitting in the kitchen with a mug of tea. "Hello.....bab.......darling did I wake you up?" "No mummy, I needed to go to the toilet and you weren't in bed when I looked just daddy" Do you want anything darling?" and looking at the toast in front of Sandra she said "Can I have some toast and jam please?" standing up Sandra picked a couple of slices from the breadbin and dropping them in the toaster, she got the Strawberry Jam and some butter from the cupboard. When the toaster popped, she buttered and covered the toast with Strawberry Jam before cutting each slice into diagonal and placing them on a plate put them down in front of her proudly sitting down daughter "Can I have some orange juice mummy?" Just managing not to sit down Sandra headed for the fridge, and taking the carton of orange juice in one hand she reached for a glass with the other on her way back to the table, before putting them both down in front of her now red lipped daughter. Sitting down as "Thank you, mummy" came from the red lipped Caroline. "You're welcome bab....darling" she managed to change at the last second slowly getting used to her very old 6 year old, and her new preferred choice of address. Sitting there watching as Caroline slowly finished off the toast between drinks of orange juice she hoped her intuition was correct about being pregnant, but she wouldn't know for a few days yet for sure so didn't want to say anything to Dave just yet. This weekend she would tell him when she was sure and had taken a test.

The Labour Day was anything but, as the day rolled slowly away with a walk round Northfield and a stop at the cafe on the high street for a drink and obligatory cake which Caroline devoured in record time, although it took a bit of cleaning up afterwards as the chocolate éclair had managed to get its own back with a chocolate smear all the way up to her right ear. "How did you manage to get it that far up darling?" said Sandra trying to clean her face with a tissue that made little effect. Smiling like she had an extra wide brown smile, Caroline thought it was funny and tickly at the same time, and realising she was wasting her time Sandra looked at Dave for help, which was met with a smile that said he also thought it was funny. As he took a bite of his doughnut which produced a stream of red jam down his chin as it was upside down Caroline giggled even harder and realising what he had done Dave joined his daughter in laughing, while trying to stop the jam running off his chin and down his white T Shirt. As she sat looking at the two most precious people in her life, she was now sure that next year there would be a fourth person sat with them, and their plan would be complete.

Tuesday 5<u>th</u> May 1992

As normality returned to the Baxter house once the morning rush had been dealt with it was a refreshed Dave who entered the Council Offices and headed for Eric Normanton's Office after checking his mail. Knocking on the open door he was disappointed to see Daniel Bruce already sat in front of Eric, his presence hidden by the open door. "Sorry if you're busy....." he just got out before Eric cut him off "No come on Dave just going through a few things with Daniel. What can I do for you?" Hoping he would be able to talk to Eric alone he almost changed his mind, but decided to go ahead with his question. "Well we, that is Sandra and I, would like to do some research on the Manchester Road Power Station site, in our own time of course and I just wanted to ask your permission first" "Anything in particular you're looking for as I know a lot about the site and did a feasibility study in 1980. Can't see it having much more of a lifetime as it's about 40 years old from memory and what with the Clean Air Act it's just a matter of time before the old coal fired Power Stations get closed down, sorry that's probably enough from me. I have no problem with you doing research Dave, in your own time of course but if you want some help don't hesitate to ask. See Daniel that's how you keep the Boss on your side! Now, where were we?" realising his time was up Dave returned to his desk and started organising his diary for the shortened week and with his head down he didn't see Daniel leave the office and head for an outside telephone box with information that he was desperate to share with Michael Anderson of Anderson developments Ltd, that was hot off the press after 10 years of waiting.

Sandra was working on a complex planning case that took up most of her morning and when she finally sat back, happy that she had covered all aspects she noticed that it was nearly 12.30pm, and not feeling like a lunch she was going to just have a cup of tea but was surprised to see Dave enter the office with two sandwiches and cokes. "What are you doing here?" she said trying to decide which of chicken salad or tuna and cucumber, she wanted as he put the sandwiches on her desk. "I thought I would treat my beautiful girlfriend, one day to be future wife, to lunch!" and proud of his statement he put the cokes down next to the sandwiches. Trying to figure out his angle she took advantage of his statement and replied "So just when in the future, are you going to ask me to be your wife, boyfriend?" Realising he had raised the issue that had been put back after Caroline was born, he stumbled out "All good things come to those who wait!" almost cringing as he said it. As he waited for a stinging rebuke he opened a can of Coke and taking a drink to play for time the words "I'll wait then boyfriend, but your plan had better get back on track!" Picking up the Chicken Salad sandwich as she couldn't face the Tuna sandwich, she opened the remaining can of coke and as Dave sat on the corner of her desk he suddenly remembered why he was here "Almost forgot, I've spoken to Eric and he says it's alright for us to do some research, in our own time of course, into Manchester Road Power Station, I didn't tell him what it was about as Daniel was there, but at least we can make a start on finding out where the Trust Fund came from!" and taking a bite of the Tuna sandwich he looked on enviously, as Sandra ate the sandwich he had chosen for himself.

Out on site in the afternoon Dave finally went back to his old school Kirkdale High after 14 years, and seeing little had changed it was no surprise that the Board of Governors wanted a survey doing on the site as it had exhausted its life, and the addition of a couple of Portakabins hardly replaced the crumbling east wing. Taking his time to do a thorough job under the keen eye of Mr Adams, the Headmaster who had been in situ for 5 years, it became obvious that at best the entire east wing would have to be replaced, and at worst the whole school could do with re-siting and a new school built. Signing out after shaking Mr Adams hand, he walked out to the car park in the shadow of the East wing to where his trusty Escort sat next to a new Cavalier, and getting into his now 11 year old slightly tired looking Escort he looked across at the parking space with 'Headmaster' on a plaque on the wall, and seeing a Mercedes 190 parked under the plaque he made up his mind that it was time for a change, he would speak to his dad tonight to see what he wanted for the Jaguar.

Sandra didn't have a chance to start on any research in the afternoon as the workload on a short week needed all her attention. With a stretch she picked up the last file she felt she could deal with before the end of the day, and seeing it was from Northfield School her interest was immediately heightened and reading through the application for an extension to house a Nursery, she felt a wave of emotion and seeing that the land was currently unused where the old boiler room and bike shed were located she checked with the legal department as to ownership, satisfied that all was in order she stamped it as 'Recommend for Permission" before placing it in her out tray. Putting a note on her desk for tomorrow 'Research MRPS lunchtime' she saw Sam approaching which was a sign that the day was nearly over and leaning back she said as he picked up the day's workload "All yours Sam!" and never one to miss an opportunity for a joke, he quick as a knife said "Okay but don't tell Dave!" and without waiting for a reply he loaded the folders onto his trolley and was gone as Sandra sat with a smile on her face "Cheeky devil!" she said picking up the phone as he left the office. "I'd like to make an appointment with Doctor

Peters please" she said as her call was answered by the Receptionist at the Clinic "5pm on Friday 8th May would be just fine, thank you" she said putting down the phone and writing it in her desk diary. Standing up and heading to get her coat already wondering what Caroline had been up to for the fourth time today, she waved at Mrs Shaw as she left the office for what would be the last time.

Wednesday 6th May 1992

Sandra asked Sam if he could, with his photographic memory, help her find some papers that she was sure were in the Manchester Road Power Station Folder the last time she had seen it but seemed to be missing now. "Maybe if we cross reference them they will have been misfiled" she said, at which a look of horror came across Sam's face "We don't misfile in the Archive section!" and heading to the door he stood waiting for her as Sandra realised he was sensitive about his newly promoted role to Assistant Head of Archive, she stopped at Mrs Shaw's desk saying "Sam and I are going to try to find some files that seem to have gone missing shouldn't be too long" and noting it was already 3.20pm she realised she had better get a move on if she was to find the files and get back to her desk and complete her work, before picking up Caroline from her mum's at 5.30pm as she always did on a Wednesday, she hurriedly caught up with Sam and followed him down the stairs to the Council Archive Chambers.

"Come on then Sandra let's get stuck in, what are we looking for in particular?" said Sam as he logged into the computer system on the Front desk of the Archive Chambers. Suddenly realising the size of the task ahead of them as she looked down the rows and rows of files that seemed to go on forever "Well" she said collecting her thoughts "The file I am most interested in is the Manchester Road Power Station folder, and if we can start from that and work from there we should be able to find what I am looking for. Seeing Sam put a fingertip on the computer screen with his left hand and write the location of the folder down on a slip of paper, he set off down an alley of wooden bookcases that seemed to make him smaller as he went further into the Archive, but it was only minutes later that he came back with a confused look on his face "It's not there, which is strange as the computer says it is, let me ring Sally Small, my boss and see if she has taken it to a client although I doubt it, she is a stickler for systems and procedures so would have signed it out, anyway I'll check, just give me a minute" picking up the phone, he dialled a number and following a quick conversation he put the phone down and looking at Sandra said "Nope it's not with her so it's here somewhere, let's cross reference and see if we can find it, not that it will be misfiled of course, but just in case!" With a look of concern on his face he took the piece of paper and he had written on, and looked at Sandra, who was also feeling something wasn't right as Sam started scrawling details on the paper "Manchester Road Power Station lets see, well there will be a 1952 or was it 1954 purchase so that will be in the Legal files, then there's that feasibility study by Eric Normanton around 1980 that will be in the Estates files, and then there's the Clean Air Act around, well actually I don't know, as it was before my time, but it will be in the Legal section. The various building works should also be in Estates. There should be something that gives a clue as to where the file is from one of those, and there was that company that was interested in the land" "Anderson Developments Ltd" said Sandra before Sam had a chance to think, wondering for a second why she has remembered it so easily, before realising it was because Daniel had taken the meeting. "You could get a job in Archive with that memory Sandra!" said Sam putting the pen down "That should be in Legal as well so that should give us plenty to go on today, and if it still isn't found I'll have escalate it, but if you do the Estates section as you know that better, which is way down there on the left, I'll do the Legal section which is five rows further over and as I'm more used to it I'll come and find you, sound like a plan Sandra?" and realising the number of times she had heard that expression, she smiled at him before replying "That's a plan Sam!" and with a high five out of nowhere she slapped his hand, before picking up the paper Sam had written on, and heading down the alleyway of bookcases she felt a feeling of slight claustrophobia, as she neared the end of the alley and turned left into the section with Estates printed in bold on the first bookcase.

Looking through the Legal section Sam soon found the first folder from 1952 about the sale of the land and looking through it found that there was a reference to buying more land in 1954 for access to the site, but found no references to anything else that cast any light on the Manchester Road Power Station folder which it should have being such a large and important site. Having located the file on the Clean Air Act and its revision he realised there was nothing to cross reference either file with anything else, which seemed a bit strange but he grew more concerned when looking for the Anderson Developments Ltd file as it was missing altogether ,between Andersen Printers Ltd and Anderson Freight Holdings. Checking that the folder wasn't in a folder either side of where it should be he stood still for a moment "That's odd" he said to himself quietly, before returning to the sale folder where he noticed the index section, which has to be signed by anyone taking out the folder only went up to 1980, and the reference to the feasibility study conducted by Eric Normanton, placing the folder back in its place where it had come from, he headed to the Estates section where he would find Sandra who he hoped had had more luck.

As he approached the end of the alleyway of files before turning left he heard raised voices, which was so unusual he quickened his step, as running was frowned upon. Turning the corner into the Estate section he saw Daniel Bruce shouting at Sandra as she sat on the ground nursing her face, with files strewn on the floor at her feet, and shocked at the scene in front of him he stopped in his tracks and said "What's going on?" at which Sandra looked up at Sam, and Daniel moved towards him. Daniel quickly said "Nothing Sam just a friendly discussion between colleagues, we're fine you can go about your duties!" and with a look from Sandra that said anything but, she said "Sam, I found the feasibility study, and it says the site could be worth between £20 and £30 million and I was just looking through it, when Daniel appeared with the folder we were looking for and several others, he was trying to say he was getting them for Eric Normanton, but I didn't believe him and asked him what he was doing with the folder, then he started having a go at me and then he slapped me!" Sam took a couple of steps nearer, and looking Daniel in the eye from a foot away he said angrily "I think Daniel, you should leave now" and standing to one side to let him past he looked down at a still sitting Sandra, and didn't see Daniel taking hold of the fire extinguisher on the wall that hit him on the temple knocking him unconscious before he even hit the ground, and as Daniel pulled the pin it exploded in a blanket of foam which covered Sam as it went off. Daniel threw the fire extinguisher away towards the far wall, its purpose fulfilled. "Daniel!" screamed Sandra trying to get to where Sam had fallen but as she did so Daniel kicked her in the stomach and she rolled over bent in pain, gasping for air and instinctively rolled in a ball just as he kicked her again, she felt him kneel over her, and grabbing her hair he forced her to look at him. "You and me, Sandra, we should have been something special, we could have been the King and Queen of the Ball, instead you ended up with steady Dave and now you're finally going to pay after all these years. Remember I said I would get you one day Bitch, well that day is today!" and taking the piece of paper she had dropped he saw the contents and put it in his pocket, before kicking her again as she lay in a ball he stood looking at the scene in front of him and quietly he said to a prostrate Sandra "I think we'll have a little fire, that will get rid of any evidence and I will be a hero when I get out of here, if I play it right. You,

Bitch, will be an unfortunate casualty, as will poor Sam here". Daniel went around to the next set of bookcases and putting his back into the metal bookcase case, he managed to rock it slowly at first until he leant heavily into it and the bookcase toppled and landed on Sandra as she lay in a ball, crushed and screaming by the weight of the books, folders and the bookcase itself, as Daniel with a smile on his face repeated his action on the metal bookcase on the other side of where she lay, trapping her underneath the collapsed metal bookcases and their contents. As the screaming stopped and silence pervaded the Archive Chambers, Daniel casually lit a cigarette and slowly and deliberately walked to the Legal section on the far side of the Archive Chambers and checking even though he knew it wasn't there, but safely at home, he looked for the Anderson Developments Ltd folder and doubly confident that his off the cuff actions were going to work in his favour, he took the files next to the empty space, and ripping up the papers put them into a waste bin, adding the paper he had taken from Sandra, and taking a last drag of his cigarette, he dropped it into the now full waste bin which after a few seconds caught alight. Placing it next to a full bookcase he pulled several files out so they would catch fire more easily and the flames soon searched for more material and within a few minutes, as Daniel looked on, the whole length of the legal section, which was full of old dry documents was soon on fire.

Walking slowly to where Sandra and Sam lay, Daniel lit another cigarette and taking a drag he looked down at the broken body of Sandra and the unconscious body of Sam under two bookcases that had spewed their contents. Standing considering his next move, he put his lighter and cigarettes in Sam's pocket and went to the far corner of the Estates section where a table was set up for the use of the staff, sitting down with his back to the outside wall facing the result of his actions, he finished his cigarette and flicked it still lit, towards Sandra saying "Bitch!" as it flew in the air, landing some ten feet away from him on the edge of the debris from the book-case and slowly a flicker of flame began its journey. Looking at his watch which showed 3.55 he closed his eyes and settled down with his future in jeopardy, but not already decided like Sam and Sandra. As the flames from the Legal section moved across from bookcase to bookcase heading in the direction of the small, but now established fire some ten feet away from where Daniel was sitting, seemingly in a trance, as he rocked backwards and forwards he could feel the heat of the fire get-ting closer. As the noise in the background broke Daniel out of his trance as a bookcase collapsed, he could see the result of his work was now getting out of control, and seeing his moment had come, he went to make a run for the door and freedom, only to be halted as he left the dubious safety of the corner of the Estates section, as a concertina effect cut off his escape route as the bookcases lost their strength to the now raging fire and knocked each other down directly into his path and freedom. "Bastard, Bastard, Bastard!" he shouted, banging his head against the wall between each utterance, to the avar-icious fire as it continued to eat up the mass of paper. Slowly heading back to his refuge, his escape cut off, to what he knew would now be his grave with blood trickling down his face from his head butting the wall. he pushed the table onto its side and pulled it towards the outside wall creating his own makeshift coffin. Curling up into a ball he heard the sound of Fire Engines in between the loud cracks as the fire devoured the Archive Chambers snapping old wood as it went, looking at his watch which showed 4.32 he closed his eyes and awaited his fate as the fire and smoke engulfed the Archive Chambers.

Wednesday Evening – May 6<u>th</u> 1992

Diane Robertson was wondering where Sandra had got to, as she tried to keep Caroline's attention as children's TV was about to end. It was unlike Sandra to be late picking her daughter up, but maybe the traffic was heavy tonight she thought as the clock silently touched 6pm. Handing her granddaughter a book and some crayons to colour, Diane turned the TV Channel to the news and choosing ITV as the local news was on first, she missed the beginning of the news having gone to get Caroline a drink. As Penny Sams the News Reporter stood in front of the Kirkdale Council Offices with a glowing background of flames and smoke, and Fire Engines and Police cars with lights adding to the illumination of the night sky, Diane had a sudden feeling of impending pain as the News Reporter explained that a fire had broken out in the Archives section of the Council Offices and that at this stage there were unconfirmed reports that 3 people were missing. Turning to interview the Chief of Police, the glow from the flames seemed to increase in the background as he read out a statement.

"A fire broke out in the Archive section of the Council Offices at around 4.00pm at which time Council employees were ordered to leave the building, as per their established Fire Evacuation Plan, and following the completion of a head-count it has been established that three people are currently missing. At this stage we are still looking for the missing employees, but the situation is developing as we fight the fire and we will update you as soon as we have further information. Thank you" and with that he was gone leaving the Penny Sams to add "As you can see behind me" as the camera panned over the Council Offices which were masked in smoke and flames, rising into the dark night sky "the building is well on fire and I have it on good authority that with the seat of the fire in the Archive Chambers, and the combustible nature of the paper files it will mean it will be difficult to put the fire out, and the building may actually collapse. This is Penny Sams, ITV News reporting from Kirkdale" she finished as the Front door closed and Diane rushed to find her Sandra standing in the hall.

As her mind took in that Jim was stood in the hall, not Sandra, Diane burst into tears and putting her arms around him, she felt unable to say anything as the tears ran down her face, as the feeling of impending pain heightened, until finally Jim pushed her away a little. "What's wrong love?" he said aware that whatever it was wasn't going to be good, trying to wipe her tears away from her face with his fingers as she tried to compose herself. "It was just on the news that there's been a fire at the Council Offices and three people are missing and ....Sandra's late and she's never late to pick up Caroline and ...." the tears started again, as Jim thought what to say without sounding stupid as Diane was obviously very upset. The best he could manage was "The traffic was terrible to-night, presumably because of the fire, so maybe she got caught in the traffic and is just running late!" and looking at her face he didn't believe a word he had just said, as Caroline came into the hallway, and with a smile of innocence that children have, that can break any heart, she held up a picture of a Princess with dark black hair, blue eyes and a crown, tugging at Diane's elbow she held up the picture and said "Mummy!" with a smile that Diane would remember forever, as the door opened and Dave walked into the hall. "Surprise, it's me" said Dave closing the door behind him. Seeing Caroline with a picture of her mummy, he picked her up and said "Mummy's a Princess, isn't she pretty" and kissing her on the head looked at Jim and Diane hugging each other, and aware of something, but with-out a clue what it was, he said to Caroline "What about a pic-ture of Daddy for a change baby?" "Okay Daddy "she quickly said and headed off back into the Lounge still holding the pic-ture of her Mummy. "Thought I'd surprise Sandra and we'd go somewhere for tea" said Dave looking at Jim and Diane, and looking at their faces he awaited the news which he now had a gut feeling, wasn't going to be good.

Diane explained as best she could between the tears that re-fused to relent, what she had seen on the ITV News and as the three of them sat in the kitchen it was Jim who said, as he held Diane's hand for the first time in years. "Until we hear anything we need to act like Sandra's late and Caroline can't get an idea that anything is wrong. It might be traffic, let's not think the worst!" and getting up to put the kettle on, as people do when stuck for something to say a tear ran down his face as he feared the worst.

The Front door opening and shutting startled all three of them, and despite their best efforts it was Caroline who got to the hall first and seeing it wasn't her mummy, she returned to the Lounge to finish her picture of Daddy, leaving Tony stood in the hall looking at Jim, Diane and Dave staring at him, and then making it obvious that he wasn't the one they wanted to see, as they all looked crestfallen and headed back into the kitchen. "Hi son, good interview with the MD?" Jim said, as Tony sensing something was wrong, followed them and without a word Jim pulled out a chair for him, which without a word he took, understanding automatically that it wasn't his turn to speak. Putting a pot of tea and four cups on the table Jim went to the fridge to get the milk and taking a few seconds with his back to the table he finally turned, and after placing the milk bottle on the table, he looked at Tony and having regained a little of his composure he said "There's been a fire at the Council Offices apparently in the Archive section, there are three people missing and Sandra's late picking up Caroline and.........well we haven't heard anything from her and it's not like her and.........." the words failed to come as he looked at Diane, and then Dave, as they both looked at each other as their hands met across the table eventually in a circle as it suddenly dawned on the four adults that today would be a day to remember for all the wrong reasons, as a small voice quietly said "Daddy" next to Dave and holding a picture she had completed that looked nothing like Dave, but had a Flat cap, so he knew it was him, he carefully picked her up said "Thanks darling" and sitting her on his knee with nothing left to say he cuddled her, until there was a knock on the door.

With a sense of foreboding having seen the police car pull up outside their house, Jim held his hand up to the others as the tears started to flow unrelenting down onto Diane's cheeks. Dave kissed the top of Caroline's head and asking her what she had done at school, he never heard her reply as the sight of a uniform headed for the Lounge with Jim directly behind. "Tony can you look after Caroline for a few minutes, maybe best if you take her to your old room, and you can watch one of her VHS's if you don't mind" and with an acceptance that his role for now was set, his interview and move back to Kirkdale very much in the background, he took Caroline's hand and picking up a drink and some crisps headed off to his old room with a copy of Postman Pat, with Caroline lagging behind, aware that this wasn't normal before deciding she couldn't work out what was wrong, but she loved Postman Pat, so she headed off after Tony as he reached the top of the stairs, and the Lounge door closed.

Constable Adams stood by the TV and after Jim and Diane sat on the sofa, her hand squeezing his, Dave took a seat by the window and finally sitting down Constable Adams readied himself before starting to explain the reason for his visit. "As you may know there has been a major fire at the Council Offices in Kirkdale which started at around 4.00 this afternoon and once a roll call had been taken it was revealed that three people were missing. One of those three people is listed as Sandra Baxter" at which Diane buried her face in Jim's chest as Dave tried to hold it together, for the sake of their unknowing daughter upstairs. Resuming, Constable Adams added looking at Dave "We called at your home address in Northfield, Mr Baxter, but with no one at home we came here next, to inform the parents leaving a Constable at your address. At this moment I don't have any further information for you other than that we are still looking for all three people, and we haven't given up hope that we may find them as the Council Offices are vast. The Fire Service is in control of the fire now, so we will know more when the fire has been put out. I'm sorry I can't give you anything more positive but as soon as we know anything I will let you know." and standing up he headed for the door just as Dave opened it for him and finding his voice he quietly asked out of Jim and Diane's hearing "Is there any hope ?" "There's always hope Mr Baxter, I'll be in touch as soon as we know any more" and Dave could feel the underlying sympathy in the Constable's voice as he put on his hat and headed up the garden path.

Going back into the Lounge, Dave stood in the window as the police car pulled away, taking all his hopes with it. He knew in his heart that he would never see her again, with her long dark hair and blue eyes like the picture Caroline had left on the sideboard, but without the love that they had nurtured over the last 10 years since the Council Christmas Party, where he had made his play for her. As the tears rolled down his face he saw his reflection in the window, a broken man, his plans, his love and dreams gone forever, as he put his hands on his head and let the tears fall he slowly felt a hidden anger rise at how cruel and unjust the world can be to the innocent. The anger he felt gave him the strength to make a decision and wiping his face he turned to Jim and Diane and said "I'm going to take Caroline home, it's what she knows and I'll let you know as soon as I know anything" adding "Fingers crossed!" not now believing anything but the worst, and he headed upstairs to Tony's old bedroom where he could hear Postman Pat through the part opened door. "Come on darling let's go home it's been a long day. Thanks Tony" he added as she joined him at the top of the stairs, and getting her coat from behind the door, they headed off out of the Front Door and into Dave's car, as Jim pulled the curtains without waving, as they closed the world to their grief unable to understand why they would never see their daughter again, as the clock moved quietly towards 7pm and the world stopped turning in the Robertson house.

Dave and Caroline arrived home with the house in Northfield the only one in the street with no lights on, and the presence of the police car outside already intriguing the neighbours, some of who had already put the news and the police car together, and as a few curtains twitched as Dave and Caroline passed the policeman who had by now got out of his car. "Nothing further to report as yet Sir" he said before returning to his car and heading back into Town his duty now done. Dave opened the door and only just managed to hold it together as Caroline shouted "Mummy we're home!" into the blackness of the house as Dave turned the lights on and said "Mummy's working late tonight darling, let's get you some supper and off to bed it's after 7pm now!" and somewhat placated by Dave's comment she headed for the kitchen for her milk and biscuits unquestioning as Dave held onto the door that would remain forever closed to Sandra.

Once Caroline had cleaned her teeth with a big smile to show Dave she had done it properly, he tucked her into bed under her duvet with a kiss on the head, as she settled down pulling her duvet cover up to her neck and closed her eyes. Dave stood looking over her wondering how she would deal with the now inevitable news that she would never see her mummy again, and how he was going to tell her and how she would react as she and Sandra were so closely matched in so many ways. "Like mother like daughter" Diane used to say he thought, knowing that she would never be able to use that expression again. Heading downstairs he put the kettle on for no other reason than it being something to do, and letting it boil before it automatically switched off, he left it alone and went into the Front room and pulled the curtains to the outside world, which he knew would soon be banging on his door, as he sat and putting his head in his hands he cried for the first time in his adult lifetime and eventually he ran out of tears and the anger rose in him again. Heading into the kitchen he put the kettle on again and this time he made himself a cup of tea in 'His' mug which was hanging next to 'Her' mug on the Mug Tree by the cupboard. Breathing out he opened the fridge door and seeing the cottage pie that they were going to have for tea he took out the milk and slammed the fridge door for no apparent reason other than he wanted to slam something, but it wouldn't wake Caroline.

Taking the mug of tea into the Front room he sat for a few minutes before he bowed to the inevitable and turned the TV on and catching a meaningless documentary, he found himself caught between wanting to see the latest news and avoiding the report that would cut to the bone. As the clock on Big Ben struck 10pm and the ITV News started, the Kirkdale story was the headline and as the program switched to a now floodlit scene Penny Sams reported "Following the fire at Kirkdale Council Offices this afternoon when three people were announced as missing, I can report that one person has now been found and taken to Kirkdale Hospital but isn't thought to be in a life threatening condition, meanwhile the search was continuing for the other two still missing people. The cause of the fire hasn't been established but the Fire Service will be doing a full review once the fire is completely out. This is Penny Sams, ITV News reporting from Kirkdale"

As the report finished and returned to the studio Dave sat staring at the TV unable to believe what he had just heard "They've found someone!" he said quietly to himself then slowly starting to believe the impossible he said louder "They've found someone!" before adding for a third time as he stood up "They've found someone!" even louder and realising he might wake Caroline up, he sat down again and wondering why no one from the police had been in touch he switched channels in the hope of more information, but he had missed the BBC news, so turning to Channel 4 he watched a couple of reports before the report came on about Kirkdale and the miraculous escape from the fire. "Following a fire earlier today in the Archive section of the Kirkdale Council Offices, three people were originally reported as missing, but after the Fire Service had control of the fire a search and rescue team located one of the missing council employees unconscious, but not in a life threatening condition who has been transferred to Kirkdale Hospital. No further details are available at this time"

The silence that followed the report before the adverts appeared, left Dave with a huge quandary, hope, or give up on hope. Despite a sliver of hope that rose out of nowhere, he knew in his heart that Sandra was gone. Surely they would have been in touch from the hospital if it was Sandra, no phone call or police car, it must mean it must be someone else who was found, and with a plummeting heart he turned out the lights and headed for their bed, alone but for their darling daughter blissfully asleep next door, unaware that her world was going to come crashing down in the morning, like the sandcastles they made a few weeks ago on the seashore, it was all just a matter of time, before the inevitable crushing of the dreams of the innocent.

Thursday 4th May 1992

The police car was back just as Dave was about to get Caroline up and ready for school. Constable Adams knocked just as Dave opened the door "Good......Sir, may I come in" he said realising his day had got off to a bad start, but not as bad as some. Holding the door open Dave suggested by his hand movement towards the kitchen and still standing Constable Adams holding his cap crushed Dave's life, his plans and his dreams. "Following a search of the building last night, all three people that were missing are now accounted for and I am sorry to inform you that your wife's body was found and identified by her staff badge. We will need an official identification at some stage Sir, but not just now. An enquiry is underway but I really am terribly sorry and if we can be of any assistance please ask!" Awaiting a response Constable Adams was shocked to hear Dave reply "Why the hell didn't you tell me last night. The news said someone was found alive, why didn't you tell me last night, have you lot got no feelings?" Taken aback Constable Adams who had been warned about the TV Report quickly said "Sir, I understand that the News item last night may have given you false hope, but the gentleman they found was unconscious and the news leaked out without our permission and I am sorry for any pain it may have caused" "Pain!" said Dave feeling the anger once again rising "Pain!, I'll tell you about pain, what am I going to tell our 6 year old daughter, your mummy is dead, but the News let me think she was alive, but it was only a leak, so actually yes your mummy is dead! Get out you've done your job" and heading for the door Constable Adams put on his cap before heading to his car, aware that he could have done a better job, but knowing that death is a story told with no happy endings.

"Excuse me, just a moment!" Constable Adams heard as he opened his car door and turning he found Dave standing a few feet from him. "I'm sorry I got angry, I know you're just doing your job but where did they find her..........her body. "It will all come out in the inquest Sir, best leave it until then" Constable Adams replied but Dave wanted to know. "Please, just for my peace of mind where did they find her.....please" "Well actually Sir, the three that were missing, were found together if that helps, perhaps shielding from the fire together! Again I am sorry for your loss!" and getting into his car, he took off his hat and placed it on the passenger seat before fixing his seatbelt and heading off down the road, as the getting ready to set off to work neighbours began to appear and speculate once again as Dave shut the door, as some strange thoughts attacked his consciousness, already wondering what he was going to tell Caroline about her Mummy, who would now forever be just a little girl's memory.

As Dave finally steeled himself with another cup of tea he heard Caroline going into the toilet upstairs and heading slowly up the stairs, he sat on her bed and waited for her to appear. "Hello darling, ready for your breakfast?" and holding out his hand she took hold and followed him downstairs, where, confused that her Mummy wasn't making her breakfast, she broke the spell that Dave was living in "Daddy, where's Mummy, is she still asleep?" Taking his time to reply, he got some orange juice and milk from the fridge together with a glass and reaching for the Rice Crispies box, he breathed in, before turning to face her as she helped herself to the orange juice. As her orange smile greeted him, he poured out some cereal and putting some milk in the bowl, he pushed it towards her as she picked up a spoon and she leant into listen to the snap crackle and pop of the bowl. Realising he wasn't ready to break the news he let her finish her breakfast before realising he could no longer put off the inevitable and as she put down her spoon he went round to where she was sat, and moving his seat next to hers, he held her hands and tried to explain to her that she would never see her Mummy again.

"Baby this is really hard to explain, but last night Mummy was in an accident and although she fought really hard to come home to us, she was so poorly that she didn't make it ....and she's gone to sleep forever, and God will look after her until we see her again, when we go to Heaven" and despite trying to hold back the tears they fought their way through his pain and hugging his now also crying daughter they sat at the kitchen table as the world outside, carried on without them.

Picking Caroline up he took her upstairs to her bedroom and laying her on her unmade bed he left her to cry, while he picked out her school clothes and a summer dress from her wardrobe and returning to her bed, he picked her up and hugging her as she slowly seemed to stop crying, he thought about helping her get dressed and whispering said "Darling, before you get dressed shall we go to school, or Grandma's" he said apprehensively, "School Daddy, it's a school day!" came the quick response from Caroline, and surprised at her reaction he got her jacket from behind the door, as she put on her school uniform and helping her on with her jacket, he wondered at the resilience of youth as she headed down the stairs in front of him, picking up the picture she had drawn of her mother last night and folding it so it would fit it into her pocket, she headed for the door. The short walk to the school ended at the school gates as she let go of his hand as her friend Mary arrived and took her hand before Caroline turned back and letting go of Mary's hand she held out her arms as Dave picked her up, and planting a kiss on his lips just as Sandra used to do, she said "Love you, see you soon" and she was gone leaving Dave once again broken as he cried, slowly and quietly, on the walk home, as the words from a six year old struck home again and again, as he recalled the words Caroline had picked up from Sandra which her mother said each morning, "Love you, see you soon" as he went out of the door to work every morning. Tthe tears blurring his vision by the time he got home, at what would now only ever be a beautiful memory.

Seeing the clock on the kitchen wall head for 8.50, he automatically picked up the phone and called work but the number went to Reception, so asking for Mr Normanton he waited for the call to be transferred, and hearing the voice of his boss, he started to explain that he wouldn't be in today and could he have the rest of the week off, but was stopped before he finished his first few words as a weary sounding voice said "Dave, wasn't sure if we would hear from you today but the Department is closed until further notice after the fire, I will be in touch when we are ready to opened again." and having gathered up some strength he added "I'm so sorry about Sandra, we'll all miss her, you look after yourself, and young Caroline and I'll be in touch" and putting down the phone Dave looked in the mirror, and saw a man that wasn't him, but a sad man that looked like him that was fighting to deal with something that wasn't in his and Sandra's plan and shouldn't be in anyone's. Heading for the bathroom, he washed his face and cleaned his teeth for the second time today and looking for and finding his Flat cap which he had forgotten on the school walk, he placed it on his head, and looking in the mirror after putting on his coat, he saw a reflection of a man that was nearly him, but one that he knew would never again be the same. Heading towards his car he felt, rather than saw a few neighbours watch as he unlocked his car, and turning off the radio he headed for Church Street and another test of his humanity and humility.

The moment his car pulled to a halt, Diane opened the Front door and standing in the doorway afraid to head towards the answer to her questions, she knew before Dave had taken a dozen steps that her worst fears were on their way down the garden path. Leaving the door open Diane disappeared as Dave entered the house, and closing the door behind him, he headed in the direction of a crying mother in the Lounge, her face buried in Jim's chest. Sitting down in a chair opposite he barely got a word out before Diane stood, and with tears streaming down her face hugged Dave as he tried, and failed to hold back his own tears as Jim stood up and joined them in a triangle of grief, that means everything to those who have been there and nothing to those who have it yet to come. Pulling away slowly Diane looked at Dave and with a quizzical look said "Where's Caroline?" returning to some semblance of normality Dave said "She wanted to go to school, so we walked there this morning. I told her that her Mummy had been in an accident and God would be looking after her, and after she had cried I asked her and she said 'It's a school day Daddy' so we went. Kids are tough, aren't they!" and breaking into a fresh bout of tears he sat down putting his head in his hands, as Jim hugged Diane until they too sat down and a silence of pain covered the room.

Jim broke the silence "Did the Police say what happened, Dave?" and thinking about all Constable Adams had said, and how best to phrase it he took a breath and revisited his darkest hour. "Well he said the three missing people were all found together in the same area of the building perhaps sheltering together, but only one was still alive and he is in Hospital.

Sandra was identified by her Council badge, but a formal identification would be needed. An enquiry was already underway and an inquest would take place. That's all he said, presumably the Inquest will give more details but ...." and letting the sentence drop, he looked at the carpet unable to look at Sandra's mum and dad without a feeling of guilt that had suddenly arisen from nowhere that he didn't look after their daughter. "Did she suff.." started Diane before thinking better of it, as Jim squeezed her hand to not go any further, and another silence fell over the room as the day moved slowly on.

The sound of the kettle broke the silence as Diane had got up to make tea, as people do when not sure what to do and pouring out three mugs, she set them down on the kitchen table as Dave and Jim joined her unspoken from the Lounge. The taste of the tea cut through Dave's thoughts and it suddenly hit him that his parents didn't know about Sandra, and as he was deciding what to do Diane had the same thought "Dave, do Mary and Alan know about Sandra?" and with a sideways shake of the head from Dave she carried on "Well we'd like to come with you, if that's alright that is!" "I'll ring Alan at work" said Jim adding "It would be best tell them together!" as he headed for the phone in the hall, without waiting for an answer leaving Dave and Diane, sat with nothing to say at the kitchen table nursing their mugs of tea and broken hearts. Jim returned and said he had spoken to Alan and he would be home in half an hour, as he sat down and looked at his watch, he figured out they would have time to get to Albion Street and back, before Caroline would need picking up. Let's get through the afternoon first, he thought playing with his empty mug of tea as the three of them struggled to find a sentence between them, as the kitchen clock ticked onwards.

Reaching Albion Street in their own cars they were just in time to see Alan getting out of his car "What's this about Jim?" he said as he approached the car door "Best we are all together Alan" he replied and taking Diane's hand he followed him through the Front door and into the Front room where Mary was sat in a chair doing some knitting. Looking up as Alan entered the room she said "Forgotten something dear?" immediately realising something was wrong as Jim and Diane followed Alan into the room. Seeing the sight of her son red-eyed, and unable to look at her, she slowly looked at Alan for an answer as Dave found an inner strength and said "Mum, Dad, ...we're here because Sandra was caught in the fire in Kirkdale last night, and well.....they found her body this morning........she's gone!" and sitting down on a chair directly behind him, he lost his strength and cried whatever tears were left as Diane and Mary comforted each other, while Alan and Jim had a short hug with a slap on the back, before Alan asked the question they had all thought about, but never asked over the last few hours. "How?" he said to Jim, realising his son was lost in his grief, and deciding to leave him to come round in his own time, like he had always done as a child. "They don't know Alan, Dave said the policeman told him there was an enquiry already going on, and there obviously will be an Inquest, but I suppose it is still a bit too soon for any answers at this stage" As the enormity of the situation settled into the Baxter household, Mary looked at Diane as she wiped her eyes "What about little Caroline, where is she?, does she know? Oh God this is awful!" as she looked at Jim for an answer Diane still holding her hand said "Dave took her to school this morning, apparently her choice. Yes she knows, but she's too young to really take it in, but she's now our priority above all else, so we need to help Dave as much as possible through this, and after when it all settles down. Come on Mary let's put the kettle on, I'd like something stronger but now isn't the time!" and they headed into the kitchen, leaving the men alone with their thoughts and feelings.

Dave eventually lifted his head and seeing that only Alan and Jim were in the room said "I'm so angry why her! Why not someone else! It's so unfair she had everything to live for and then there's Caroline. She'll grow up never knowing what a beautiful mummy she had. I just don't get it, why her!" and despite over a hundred years of life between them, neither Alan or Jim could think of a single answer that would match his question, as Diane and Mary came into the Front room with a tray of hot drinks, Dave returned to his thoughts until his mother handed him a cup of tea, and realising it was the first time he had had tea in the Front room rather than coffee, the tiny change to their old family routine, brought him out of his thoughts as he took as sip of tea. He looked around the room and with a maturity that didn't altogether surprised his parents he said "There's a lot I need to do tomorrow, after I take Caroline to school tomorrow, presuming that is, she wants to go, can you Mum, or Diane pick her up from school, so I can have the day to talk to the police, the school, her work, her friends and all the things that will need dealing with. If you can give her tea I'll pick her up afterwards if that's okay?" Looking at each other Mary and Diane nodded and Mary said "Sounds like a plan son!" and for the first time in long time Dave tried a small smile to show his appreciation. "Thanks, I'd better get going Caroline will be finishing at 3.30 and I don't want to be late" and putting down his half finished cup of tea, he hugged him mum and then Diane, before looking at Alan and Jim and with an unexpected show of affection he extended his arms and hugged them together, and with that headed out of the house where he had grown up where all his hopes and dreams had been created, only to be crushed last night.

"Daddy!" came from a voice in among the other children, as school ended, and Caroline saw Dave standing with the other parents, none of who seemed able to look him in the eye, as word has obviously got out. Taking his hand she looked up at him and handing him her coat, she tried to keep in step as they headed for home. "Do you think mummy will like Heaven Daddy?" she said as they neared their house, and stopping for a moment to pick her up he looked at the blue eyes staring back at him, awaiting an answer and holding back a tear he replied "Darling, I know she would rather be here with us, but God will look after her, and she can watch over us!" and with no reply they made it to the Front door, before she decided on another question "Will she look after us like God looks after her, Daddy?" Stung by the innocence of youth he thought about his answer as he opened the door "I'm sure she will baby, didn't she always look in on you when you were asleep and check you were alright, even though she knew you were!" "What's for tea Daddy?" ended the conversation as he closed the door behind him to the world outside, that was far too cruel for a six year old to understand.

The Inquest took place on the 12th May 1992 and was opened and adjourned after three minutes to await the result of the post mortems. The ongoing Enquiry continued apace into the Archive Chambers fire of the 7th May 1992. Dave didn't attend, as he had already been told nothing would happen until after the Enquiry published its findings which could take up to six months, and in the meantime the wheels of bureaucracy would go through the evidence and reports, and at some time in the future would announce their findings. In the meantime life would go on, but for those involved the tortuous round of interviews, meetings and reminders kept coming, although Daniel Bruce, the only person who could answer everyone's questions, was out of hospital, but he apparently had no recollection of the events of the day.

◆ ◆ ◆

Chapter 22

5<u>th</u> August 1992 The Inquest

Sitting in the Courtroom, Dave was sat next to his mum and dad Alan and Mary, with Sandra's parents Diane and Jim, sat to his right as they sat opposite the Coroners as he opened proceedings.

"Ladies and gentlemen I am Mr Neil Flanders, the Coroner for the Kirkdale region. We are here today to conduct the Inquest into the fire of the 7th May 1992 and the subsequent deaths of Mr Sam Brown and Ms Sandra Robertson. Following a review of the evidence I will give my report.

Inquest Statements

Chief Fire Officer Darlow

"Following a substantial fire in the Kirkdale Archive Chambers on Wednesday 6th May 1992 the Kirkdale Fire Brigade attended the site at 4.08pm and once the fire was under control at 6.07pm a thorough search of the site was undertaken which resulted in the discovery of three individuals who were reported missing. Due to the heat of the fire it wasn't until the search entered what is known as the Estates Section of the Chambers, which is situated at the back of the Chambers at a right angle to the rest of the building that two bodies were found under fallen metal bookcases. Despite checking for life it was confirmed by the Medical Officer that there was no sign of life present. While completing the search for the third missing person the Officers found an unconscious body that we now know to be Mr Daniel Bruce, who had managed to fashion a shelter behind a desk which probably saved his life. It would appear that the angle of the Estates Section and the metal structures and relative newness of the bookcases in this section stopped the fire from spreading further saving Mr Bruce's life. After extensive examination of the scene it is with a level of certainty that the fire started in the legal section, where a waste bin has been identified as the potential source of the fire. A match or cigarette butt would be enough to set fire to the documents in the Archive Chambers, many of which will have been old and dry hence the rapid spread of the fire. There is no sprinkler system in the Archive Chambers but I can't say it would have put out the fire as material was extremely combustible but it might have helped. There were sufficient fire extinguishers in the Archive Chambers with two fire extinguishers in the front of the Archive Chambers which were found to be fully functioning. There was also one Fire Extinguisher that had been used in the Estates Section, by whom it is impossible to say, as it was found some 10 feet from the Estates Section and it was badly burned in the fire"

Detective Sergeant Wilson

"I attended the scene at the request of Chief Fire Officer Darlow. Following a search of the site there were many questions that needed answering. What was the source of the fire and who actually started the fire, and how did the two deceased end up under the metal filing cabinets. Following consultation with the Dr Simon Staunton I have to come to the conclusion that whoever set the fire also perished by it. Dr Staunton found a lighter and an opened pack of cigarettes in Mr Sam Brown's pocket with the possibility that he set the fire, but it got out of hand due to the age of the documents. Although I have been unable to ascertain a motive for setting the fire it would appear that Ms Robertson tried to stop him, and paid for her actions with her life. I have interviewed Mr Daniel Bruce since the fire, but unfortunately he has no memory of the events of the fire, and I can only conclude that he was already in the Estates Section when Mr Sam Brown started the fire trapping him there. Until Mr Bruce regains his memory, and indeed if he ever does, then and only then will we get the full facts"

Head of Estates and Property – Eric Normanton

"Following the Fire Alarm going off at 4.21 the building was evacuated according to the Council Fire Evacuation plan and assembled staff in the Council car park where a roll call was made. On informing Chief Fire Office Darlow that there were three people missing, I handed him a list of their names and arranged for the remaining staff to go home. The rest of the building was searched but there was no sign of any of the three missing persons. The Archive Chambers was only opened last year to cope with the expanding workload and there were plans to upgrade the Chambers in next year's budget with new metal bookcases throughout, as were used in the Estates Section which might have prevented this tragedy"

Coroner Dr Pritchard

The following statement has been provided by the Kirkdale Chief Pathologist, Dr Simon Staunton.

"Following a post mortem on the 9th May 1992 on Mr Sam Brown, and Ms Sandra Robertson I can confirm the following."

"Mr Sam Brown died as a result of smoke inhalation. The post mortem on Mr Brown found that there was a large contusion on the right side of the head, but it was impossible to ascertain what caused it due to the extensive destruction of the site. He also had bruising on his torso and legs which appeared to be as a direct result of the collapse of the metal bookcases he was found under. There were burns to the hands and feet, with the rest of the body being shielded from the fire by the metal bookcases that had collapsed. There was a lighter and opened packet of Embassy cigarettes in his pocket along with some scraps of paper that related to his work. There was some residue of extinguisher foam on the body which helped to preserve the body."

"Ms Sandra Robertson died as a result of smoke inhalation. The post mortem on Ms Robertson found bruising on her stomach and legs which again appeared to be as a result of the metal bookcases collapsing. The body was shielded in the majority from the fire by the metal bookcases that had collapsed. There was a small amount of residue of extinguisher foam which helped to preserve the body. Upon the results of the autopsy I can confirm that Ms Robertson was in the early stages of pregnancy at around 3 to 4 weeks."

As the words sank in Dave's head fell down to his knees and he felt the tears on his hands as he wondered if life can get any crueller. The hand on his back from his dad could do nothing to improve the situation, but it meant he knew he had someone to share the pain with. He heard Mary and Diane crying but didn't have the strength to look at them for fear of the emotion it would bring. Trying to think back to the weeks before she died Dave tried to work out why she hadn't told him and why he hadn't figured it out, but those moments were gone forever. Hearing the Coroner's voice he raised his head to look at him as he started on his summing up.

Coroner's Report

In light of the reports provided, and taking into account the various statements from the deceased families, it is my duty under the Coroners Act 1988 to report that the death of Mr Sam Brown and Ms Sandra Robertson were both as a result of the fire which was started by person or persons unknown. I am therefore going to report both deaths as misadventure. Should Mr Daniel Bruce regain his memory the Coroner's Office should be immediately informed, as he may have pertinent evidence that could shed light on how this tragedy occurred.

I further recommend that Kirkdale Council conduct a thorough review of their Archive and Records buildings specifically looking at the safety of their employees under the Health and Safety at Work Act 1974 to prevent a repeat of this event.

The bodies have been released to the families for burial.

That concludes my Report

Chapter 23 - The Aftermath

As the Baxter and Robertson families stood up with arms around each other the Coroner left the Courtroom and with him all their chances of closure. Sam Brown's family left immediately with the door to the Coroner's Office closed behind them, with anger rather than tears on their faces at the assassination of their son's name by Detective Sergeant Wilson. Heading out of the Court the sunlight was directly behind the small crowd of friends and relatives, and it wasn't until he was on the bottom step that Dave realised a woman was holding a microphone in front of him asking "Mr Baxter would you like to comment on the Coroner's verdict, do you think Sam Brown kill your wife?" and looking at the reporter in front of him, he almost ignored her, but for some reason he stopped at the last minute and said "The only person who knows what really happened is Daniel Bruce, why don't you ask him!" and before he could say anything else Alan took hold of his elbow and led him to his car with the words "What do you mean by that Mr Baxter" following on the air from the reporter unanswered. Sitting in the car watching as the crowd dispersed it was a few minutes before Alan turned the ignition and they set off for the Robertson household with more hurt in their hearts.

Sitting in the Lounge as Diane and Mary set about making a pot of tea, trying to find something to do, instead of something to say they eventually with red eyes, entered the room and placing the tray on the sideboard Diane looked at Dave as he sat with Alan's arm around him as everyone avoided the question that had come up at the Inquest. Taking a cup of tea Dave looked up and answering his and their question in one, he said through the pain "I didn't know she was pregnant, I wish to God I had, but I didn't! She was so good at keeping a secret, I didn't even know she was pregnant with Caroline until she was certain" Taking a sip of tea he looked around the room for a word of wisdom but it never came. The day slowly came to a conclusion, when it was time to pick Caroline up from school and with embraces all round he left Sandra's old house, and went to pick up his daughter and his only remaining link to the woman he had anticipated spending the rest of his life with.

"Hello darling!" he said as she made her way through the rest of the parents at the school gate and taking her hand they set off for the short walk home to Windy Hill as they had done every day since the fire. Chatting all the way home about her day at school Dave knew he would have to return to work himself next week and with the thought constantly on his mind he was glad of the distraction that his now 7 year old daughter gave him. Her birthday last month had been held in glorious sunshine in the back garden but had ended badly when one by one, all the children's parents came to collect their children leaving Caroline holding his hand saying "Daddy, why did God take mummy, I miss her so much! All the other children have mummies and daddies" and the tears came until it was bedtime, and he tried to explain that mummy was looking down on them, and she was helping to keep him strong so he could look after her "Do you miss her daddy?" came the words that had no answer and realising she was waiting for his reply he finally replied as he tucked her into bed on her first birthday without her mother. "Of course I miss her darling, every minute of everyday but she left me you, to look after and remember her, so every time I look at you, I see your mummy and remember the time we had together before she......" and unable to finish as the tears started he pulled her to him, and kissing her on the head he just found the strength to say goodnight, as he turned to turn the light off leaving a broken hearted Birthday Girl to dream of the mummy she would never see again, as Dave headed straight to bed and his own dreams of what would now never come true.

Monday finally came and after two months off it was with a lot of trepidation that Dave returned to work. Before entering the main door he stopped at the top of the steps to look at the empty space where the Archive Chambers had been. Deemed structurally unsafe the old building was demolished as soon as the police investigations were completed. The welcome backs that he got as he headed for the Estates Department were said with good intentions, but delivered with an awkwardness that he understood. Knocking on Eric Normanton's Office he entered without waiting, and as Eric offered him a seat with an open palm on his extended arm he knew this wasn't going to be easy for either of them. "Good to have you back Dave how have you managed since... the fire?" and sensing his unease Dave let the question hang for a moment before replying "I'm not going to lie Eric, it's been really hard, and if it wasn't for Caroline, well I don't know. But I need to get back to work and a routine so here I am!" playing with a few papers to play for time Eric replied "The whole thing was horrible, more so for you, but I can't believe Sam was responsible, but until Daniel's memory comes back we'll never know!" and for the first time in weeks Dave thought about the Coroner's Report "So I take it Daniel hasn't regained his memory?" the shake of the head saved the words being said "He's off on long term sick until October in the hope that peace and quiet will help him, but the doctors report said he may never get his memory back. So there's just the three of us until he comes back and with the review of archives and records departments to be done by the end of the year as ordered by the Coroner, so I could do with your help to get us back on track, but if it's too early let me know, as Caroline is obviously now your priority!" Seeing the slightly desperate look in Eric's face and understanding his predicament with John Marshall who had only been with them a year the only other Surveyor, he looked back at Eric and said "Sandra's mum will look after Caroline and she could do with some female company after the last couple of months, so I'm good to go, apart from this Friday when the funeral is of course!"

St Peter's Church was full as the funeral car pulled up outside with a wreath of Sandra on one side and Mummy on the other. The coffin was carried inside and as Dave held Caroline's hand they passed rows of her workmates and taking their seat at the front they listened as the Vicar gave the Eulogy which he had helped to write with the help of Diane. Her childhood and then meeting Dave were the main body of the text and when Caroline was mentioned she looked at Dave with a smile that said it was going to be alright, as she held his hand just as her mother had done a few months back. He could hear some tears from the seats behind him and fighting to hold back his own he took Caroline's hand as they stood and approached the wooden lectern.

Dave took a breath and looking down at Caroline he addressed the church "I thought I would spend the rest of my life with Sandra, but that wasn't to be, but she left me Caroline, the best present in the world, and she would like to say something to her mummy!" and lifting Caroline up to the microphone, he smiled at her as their pre-arranged plan come to fruition. Leaning into the microphone she said "Love you mummy, see you soon!" and pleased with her words she put her arms around Dave as the tears came and still carrying her he set off down the aisle as 'Blue Eyes' by Elton John came over the loudspeaker. They wall of tears as they passed each aisle intensified as they walked past, Caroline buried into Dave's neck, and it was only when they had got out into the sunlight as the last verse finished that he slowly put her down and wiping the tears from her face he said "Mummy will be so proud of you darling!" as Diane and Jim arrived behind them and with an emotional hug they were soon joined by Alan and Mary, as the church slowly emptied on the day a 7 year old broke the hearts of all who went, and would never forget.

August came and went, and with a degree of normality Diane took up her duties of looking after picking up Caroline from school and giving her tea apart, from Friday when Dave finished early, and although the plan worked well, it was a reticent Diane that said to Dave on the Thursday night, at the end of August, that it might be good for him to go out with Sid and she would have Caroline for the night. Initially he decided against it, but after a tough day and mentioning the idea to Eric Normanton who said "We all need some time to ourselves every so often Dave, and Caroline will be asleep by the time you go out anyway, so what is she going to lose out on, a bit of time with her Grandma?" Deciding it wasn't being unkind to Caroline he rang Diane to agree to her having her for the night, and would pick her up at 10.00 on Saturday morning. Putting down the phone he called Sid at work and arranged to meet in the Malt Shovel at 8pm for a couple of beers. Picking up some fish and chips for his tea he headed home, and eating them out of the paper he almost finished them before heading upstairs to get changed for his first night out alone in over 10 years. Deciding to walk and get a Taxi back, he left in good time arriving at 7.40pm ready for a drink after his 3 mile walk. Spotting Sid already at the bar he tapped him on the shoulder as he was chatting to Ian the Manager. Doubling his order Sid put his arm around Dave "Good to see you after all this time, how you coping?" taking his pint in his left hand and taking a mouthful of Lager he responded eventually "Coping is probably the best word for it, but Caroline helps!" and with the wisdom of the night dealt with, they headed to the pool room with little to say, until the alcohol loosened them up a bit.

"So what about you and Jane, still together I hear!" Dave said trying to work out how to get to the black ball that Sid had neatly snookered "Oh you know me Dave, happy as Larry then I'll blow it, but this one's a keeper and as long as I don't fall in love with someone, she seems to accept me for what I am!" "Don't look in the mirror then will you!" said Dave with a smile, hitting the white in off the black and as Sid finished the game off he shook his head and said "We're not all as lucky as you Dave, if you know what I mean!" and realising he was heading into emotional territory he quickly changed the subject "It's your round for losing anyway!" picking up their empty glasses ,he said as he set off for the bar "I know what you meant Sid and it's fine, I'll get them in, while you rack them up" and taken back a bit with his own comment, he headed for the bar suddenly aware that he was getting used to living without Sandra. The evening was spent mostly in the pool room until they got bored and went to sit in the main lounge area. "We should make this a regular meeting!" said Sid as he returned from the bar with another couple of pints. "Good job I'm getting a Taxi home" said Dave as he was handed another pint. "Lightweight!" came the quick response, followed by an even quicker, "Sorry!" as Sid tried to backtrack. "So you're back at work, how's that going?" asked Sid changing the subject. Taking a mouthful while he thought about it he eventually replied "I thought it would be harder, but we've got loads of work on, and Diane picks up Caroline in the afternoon so we have a plan that works for us. There are only three of us at the moment, but Eric has been really good and James Marshall is fitting in well so it's not too bad. Bit difficult without the archives but we seem to be getting by." Deciding now was a good time Sid took a drink and said "Didn't see you at Sam's funeral!" looking slightly unsettled Dave quickly said "It was a bit close to Sandra's .....and well I can't believe he was responsible but the Detective Wilson wasn't it, said he thought it was him so I decided not to go. Anyhow how do you know Sam?" choosing his words a little carefully he started "Well he's related to Jane so we went and although his mum is heartbroken and won't talk about it, his dad is adamant that Sam wouldn't do something like that, he had no reason he said, he got along well with Sandra he says" "Yes he did!" Dave interrupted. Deciding he had started Sid had no choice but to finish "When Sam's body was released with his belongings there was something that didn't ring true!" taking a drink "Such as?"Dave quickly asked his interest piqued by the strange way Sid had manoeuvred the conversation like it was planned. "Well according to the Coroner's Report an opened packed of Embassy cigarettes was found in his pocket with a lighter!" looking puzzled Dave said "So?" "Well, when Ann Brown, Sam's mother got his jacket and personal belongings from his locker at the Council, there was a lighter and an opened packed of Silk Cut!" taking a few seconds before answering, Dave wasn't sure what Sid was getting at until it hit him like a truck "If I've got this right what your saying is that someone else set the fire and left their cigarettes in Sam's pocket. ... Nah he probably just changed brands and had an old packet!" Finishing his pint while Dave was still halfway down his Sid said "just think about it while I get one for the road, be back in a moment" and heading off towards the bar, he left Dave trying to make sense of a situation that had massive implications as he struggled with where his mind was leading him to. Returning with fresh pints which was the last thing Dave wanted, with a conundrum going round in his head, Sid put the drinks down and sat down before saying "Makes you wonder doesn't it, two packets of different cigarettes and two lighters?" and looking at his friend Dave for once had nothing to say. "Think about it and we'll maybe make sense of it next week!" and nodding as the worst case scenario came into his mind, Dave slowly finished his pint finding it hard to put into words the reality of what Said had divulged. Getting into a Taxi, Sid said as he closed the door "Don't say anything to anyone just yet, will you Dave!" at which a hand slap on the roof told the driver to go, taking Sid and his story home while Dave waited for the next Taxi, wondering what he was going to make of Sid's story, and where it would take him in the future.

Saturday came quickly as Dave struggled with a hangover for

the first time since his birthday in September last year. Getting into the Jaguar that he had eventually agreed to buy from Alan, he set off for the Church Street like he had done hundreds of times before, but on this occasion he felt strangely alone. With a hangover and the thought of what Sid had told him running round his head, he arrived at Church Street with no memory of the journey from Windy Hill. Sitting for a second as he turned the engine off, he suddenly came to the obvious conclusion that he had tried to avoid last night. If there were two separate packets of cigarettes then there was someone missing in the equation, and unless someone had run away from the scene, the only person that could be involved had no memory of the fire, Daniel Bruce!

Stepping out of the car he paused for a second, as he locked the Jaguar, shaking his head, he headed down the garden path putting his darkest thoughts to the back of his mind, as he saw Caroline waving at him from the front window. Opening the door he was greeted as always with a hug from his daughter and taking his hand she led him into the kitchen where Diane and Jim sat having their breakfast. "I made you breakfast daddy!" and looking at the plate with two slices of toast and jam, cut almost in a diagonal, and a cup with tea just poured by Diane as Caroline went to shut the door, he sat down as Caroline took the seat next to him and said "Thank you darling just what daddy needed!" and taking a bite of the cold toast, he smiled as Jim put down his knife and fork after finishing his full English breakfast. "Didn't think you would want a full English after last night!" and finishing the first slice of toast he smiled, and shook his head grateful that he only had toast to deal with this morning. "Been a good girl for Grandma and Granddad darling?" he asked as Caroline finished her orange juice already knowing the answer which came nevertheless for a very proud Diane "She's been a dream just like her ....." and letting the sentence fade, as Jim took hold of her hand, the unspoken ending was left hanging. "So what shall we do today young lady?" Dave said after taking a sip of tea "Swimming daddy, can we go swimming?" and as his stomach did a quick somersault the words "Of course we can go swimming, good idea!" came out of his mouth before he had a chance to engage his brain and the look from Diane told him it probably wasn't a good idea, but the deal had been done, and you don't back down with a hangover, against a 7 year old.

After an hour and a half swimming it was a hungry Caroline who suggested they get chips on the way home as they got dressed, and with still wet hair they headed for the Jaguar and the short trip home via Tom's Chippy. Ordering a fish and two bags of chips, one with scraps on and a portion of peas at which Caroline held her nose, in disgust saying "Yuk!" aloud, they headed home with the day still light but their day over. Watching TV with plates on their knees it wasn't long after she had eaten her chips that Caroline snuggled up to Dave and slowly fell asleep as the news came on. Giving her time to settle down, he watched as the final story appeared on the screen as a news reporter announced that discussions had started, and were ongoing on with the Miners Union regarding the closure of more pits, and watching as a replay of film from the Miners strike of 1984 populated the screen, he slowly shook his head at the thought of another confrontation between the Miners and the Government, until the news was over and the football results were read out, before he picked a now fast asleep Caroline up and took her to bed.

Settling down to watch TV on his own after a busy day that soon got rid of his hangover, he struggled to concentrate as Beadle's About came on, and giving up he went to make a mug of tea and standing looking out of the kitchen window onto Caroline's swing as the light faded, he heard the kettle click and turning round he saw Caroline standing in the doorway "I had a nightmare daddy!" she said quietly, and as he walked to pick her up, his mind settled down and concentrated on the one important thing left in his life. "Shall I make you some hot chocolate?" he said and leaning into him she said "Yes please" as he reached for another mug and the jar of hot chocolate from the cupboard. Mixing the milk and hot chocolate powder together, he tested it to check it wasn't too hot for her, finishing his own tea he put her down and with one hand led her into the Lounge, the two mugs in his other hand, as they returned to the sofa as Match of the Day started, and they repeated teatime's routine.

Sunday came and went with a visit to his parents and Sunday lunch, which had become a regular first Sunday of the month occurrence. Despite Caroline saying she was full after her small portion of Roast Beef, carrots, mashed potato and a small Yorkshire pudding, she always had room for Ice Cream that Mary seemed to have bought in bulk for just this occasion. Sitting in the Kitchen after dinner Mary and Caroline were drawing pictures of flowers as Dave and his father went into the Front Room with their cups of coffee. "How's work going son?" Alan said breaking the silence. "Oh it was a bit strange at first, but it seems fine now, and Diane picking up Caroline is working out well so I suppose things are okay, why do you ask?" taking a sip of coffee Alan answered "Well your mother, actually both of us, were worried that you had gone back to work too soon, and what with the Coroner saying Sandra was pregnant that must have been hard to take and we haven't really had time to discuss it since the Inquest and the Funeral" putting down his coffee Dave looked at his father and with a firm look on his face he slowly told him "Dad, I've thought about what the Coroner said and it might seem a bit hard to say this, but I didn't know she was pregnant at the time and there's nothing I can do to change what happened, but I don't want it to get in the way of my memories so I've put it at the back of my mind. I feel they died together, so I'll mourn for them together, as one which is the only way I can deal with it, if that makes any sense!" Sitting taking in what Dave had said, it made complete sense to Alan and as Caro-

357

line and Mary came into the room with a picture of a bright purple flower that covered the whole paper, the conversation changed to what the week ahead would bring, how the Jaguar was running, Match of the Day and as the afternoon ran away with them it was nearly 5pm when Dave made their excuses and he and Caroline headed for Windy Hill, and the start of another week tomorrow the last day of August 1992.

Dropping off Caroline at Northfield School with her "Love you, see you soon" goodbye ringing in his heart, Dave had an easy trip into work. Entering the Estates Department he could see Eric Normanton had also just arrived, and was taking off his coat, heading over to where he was now hanging up his coat Dave waited until he turned round before asking a question that had been running through his head all weekend. "Eric, got a moment?" he said as he turned to face him "Sure what can I do for you Dave?" almost changing his mind he went ahead with his query wondering where it would lead "Well I just wondered if Sam... Sam Brown smoked that's all!" as Eric tried to find the angle that Dave was coming from he replied "It won't bring her back Dave, but yes he did, used to pop out the back door for a quick one, after I told him to stop standing infront of the building as it looked bad. Any reason you want to know out of interest?" sensing unease Dave almost let it go but as he was halfway there he added "Just trying to get some closure Eric" and realising he had a chance to get a definitive answer he finished "I hear he was an Embassy man!" without realising he was answering Dave's question, Eric said "No, said he couldn't afford them, Silk Cut was his brand although why he bothered I never understood only ever had 3 or 4 a day, just to have a break he used to say. Anyway shall we get to work unless there's something else?" "No there's nothing else Eric thanks!" and walking slowly to his desk he now had more questions running through his head than before, as he picked up the first file of the day in an attempt to stop his mind wandering, to an answer he wasn't ready to contemplate.

September flew by as Dave settled into a routine of work and home life with weekends split between the Robertson's and his own parents, and with a fortnightly agreement to meet Sid on a Friday night it was with a degree of trepidation that Dave headed for the Malt Shovel on the 11th September. Nursing another hangover on the Saturday morning he realised as he went to pick up Caroline from the Robertson house that Sam Brown had never been mentioned, as there was a pool competition on in the pub. He and Sid had entered and managed to come 2nd which gave them little chance to talk about anything but pool, and although he regretted drinking quite so much it did mean his demons had a weekend off. A rather messy Caroline was in the kitchen baking with Grandma Robertson as he arrived at Church Street and let himself in. Taking a look at his daughter as she heard him enter the kitchen his first spoken words of the day were "Is there any chocolate left for the cake darling?" as the brown smeared face looked at him she said "Don't be silly daddy this is the .....bakers treat!" and looking at Diane for confirmation she had got it right, she continued licking the palette knife. Sitting with a very welcome cup of tea, Dave waited until the cake was done and cooling on the side, and seeing that it had the full attention of his daughter he said "Diane, shall I take Caroline swimming this afternoon and then come back for a slice of cake at tea time if that's okay with you that is!" seeing the look on Caroline's face Diane replied "Seems like someone thinks that's a good idea, but why don't you come for your tea, it will save you cooking and we were going to get a Chinese as Jim is working overtime this afternoon." Turning to Caroline she added "What do you think darling?" Nodding and licking at the same time is a hard trick to manage, but Caroline managed it without saying a word and a grateful Dave mouthed "Thanks" to an even more grateful Diane who would get to spend more time with her precious Granddaughter, who everyday looked more and more like Sandra did at the same age.

Popping a very full Caroline into her car seat in the Jaguar after a mountain of Prawn Crackers and Sweet and Sour Chicken, followed by two slices of Chocolate cake, Dave turned to wave at Jim and Diane in the doorway to give them an unspoken thank you, still holding a further two pieces of Chocolate cake ostensibly for school on Monday, but he doubted they would last that long. Setting off he realised he had had an easy day after last night's excesses, and as the journey was short Caroline was still wide awake when they got home. Opening the Front door he let her in first and closing the door behind him with one hand making sure not to drop the serviette wrapped Chocolate cake he said to her "Go and wash your face darling, and put your pyjama's on and I'll make some hot chocolate and we can watch some TV together okay?" stopping at the bottom of the stairs she said "Not football daddy, okay?" and with a sideways nod of the head he agreed, already knowing she would be fast asleep well before Match of the Day started. Taking the hot chocolate and his mug of the tea into the Lounge, it was a few minutes before Caroline joined him and halfway down her hot chocolate she snuggled into him before 'Beadle's About' had finished and was asleep before the credits rolled, and well before Match of the Day started as he had anticipated.

Sunday was a bright day and taking a trip out to the nearby Northfield Reservoir they walked from Windy Hill rather than take the car with Caroline carrying what was supposed to be the remains of the loaf of bread, but was actually a half a loaf of bread. "For the birds, daddy!" she had said after being persuaded to leave two slices for her toast in the morning. Proudly walking hand in hand they arrived at the footpath around the reservoir, as the sun made a vain attempt to break through the oncoming winter clouds. Stopping at the first sign of a Seagull it wasn't long before the scene resembled Mary Poppins, as the Seagulls and Ducks sensed an easy meal and surrounded her as she ripped the bread into pieces, and threw then into the air shouting above the squawks "They're hungry daddy!" Having emptied the loaf packet, Dave took it from her and put it into a nearby bin as the birds headed off looking for another meal having spotted another child with the same idea. "They ate all of your bread, darling, they must have been hungry!" said Dave as they set off again minus the bread. "Yes daddy, but there's another little girl feeding them so they will get plenty" she replied pointing to a little girl dressed in a red coat and her parents "Oh good, it's not nice being hungry" he said alluding to the birds "I'm hungry daddy!" and looking at the girl who had toast and chocolate cake for breakfast, he smiled as the smell of the Northfield Fish and Chips shop wafted over the Reservoir and settled on his senses. "Shall we have chips for lunch? Or do you want something else?" looking up at him she pulled his hand so he had to bend down "Can I have mine in a tray with a fork please?" teasing her, he asked "Do you want peas with your chips?" the screwed up face said it all before "Yuk!" came out. Taking their place in the queue they were just leaving holding their lunch and not really look-ing at who was coming in, when a voice said "Hello you two!" and looking up trying not to spill his chips and peas on a tray, while holding Caroline's hand he stopped as he recognised the voice "Hello Jane, didn't see you there, how are you?" Dave said looking around for Sid who was nowhere to be seen. "Fine thanks just out for a walk, have you met my sister Jackie?" and looking at a younger version of Jane, Dave managed to get out "Pleased to meet you" as a nervous Jackie smiled and looked away. "Well, better get in the queue or we won't get our lunch, see you around sometime, bye Caroline" said Jane as she let Jackie infront of her as they joined the ever expanding queue. Heading towards an empty bench to sit and eat their lunch Caroline said, as she sat down "She's very pretty daddy!" pop-ping a steaming hot chip covered in peas, he had to wait as it cooled, before he replied "Who darling?" "Jackie silly!" she said before concentrating on her tray of chips, as she stabbed another chip with her pretend sword.

The 27th of September came around and with it Dave's 33rd Birthday, which almost never happened as up to the last minute he was adamant that he didn't want to celebrate. Eventually a reluctant Dave gave in to his dad Alan's persistence and a low key, family Sunday meal out at the Bedlow Arms was arranged which went off well, with Caroline's present the highlight of the day. Pretending to go to the toilet Caroline headed to the kitchen unseen by Dave and she picked up the previously delivered finely crafted chocolate cake with 33 in Smarties, and a single candle on the top. Walking behind a waiter as agreed, she made it to the table and as the waiter tapped Dave on the shoulder, he turned to see the result of his daughter's hard work of yesterday at the Robertson house. "Did you make this for me darling?" he asked, as she stood with a huge smile on her face "Grandma Diane and me made it yesterday, I ate all the rest of the Smarties!" Taking the cake from her he placed it on the table, and making a wish that would never come true, he blew out the single candle before looking at a now seated Caroline "Would you like some of daddy's Birthday cake?" and the shake of her head said it for her, as Dave started to cut the cake up. Handing the first piece to his eagerly awaiting daughter, he looked up before cutting the rest and said "Thanks everyone for this it was just what I needed, although I don't know how Caroline managed to keep the cake a secret" "I had to bribe her with Smarties!" laughed Diane as she remembered yesterday's baking. "I like Smarties daddy!" said a chocolate lipped Caroline "I know darling, mummy did as well!"

October duly arrived and with it the first hints of a bad winter as the winds came from the Arctic and dropped off the moors, losing none of their strength. Daniel Bruce finally arrived back at work on the 4th October after 5 months off work. His appearance shocked Dave as he entered the Estates Department, as it looked like he had just returned from holiday with a suntan and a sunny disposition to go with it. Eric

Normanton came out of his office and shaking Daniel's hand he welcomed him back and waving at John Marshall to come over the four of them stood outside Eric Normanton's Office, as he put his hand up for silence which was already present. "Dave, John, Daniel has decided to return to work a month early, as he is feeling a lot better, obviously the sun in Spain has worked it's magic, and I'm sure you will both welcome him back with the workload we have at present. So welcome back Daniel and let's get stuck into the backlog, with a bit of luck we can get on top of things before Christmas!" "Well it's great to be back!" Daniel said, before adding "Like I've never been away!" at which Eric said "If you could come into my office Daniel, we'll sort out a schedule to get you up to speed with what's happened in your absence" as the pair headed into Eric Normanton's Office John Marshall looked at Dave and said "He doesn't mean anything by it Dave, he's always been insensitive, take no notice" and sitting down to start his work Dave could feel the stirrings of the demons that had been hiding since Sid's revelation about Sam Brown, and looking across at Eric Normanton's Office where he could see Daniel listening to Eric's instructions, he felt the question coming into his consciousness 'What if?' as he tried to concentrate on his workload and failed miserably, as Daniel Bruce walked out of the office with a smug smile on his face.

October passed slowly as the tension in the Estates Department increased since the return of Daniel Bruce, and keeping out of his way as much as possible, he went about his work very much on auto pilot until the day of the 14th which was very much different to the first two days of the week. Daniel came into the office an even more smug attitude, and heading straight into Eric Normanton's Office, without so much as a good morning he shut the door after him, leaving Dave and John Marshall in the dark as to the reason for his demeanour. After half an hour Daniel opened the door and said as he headed for the exit "I'm off to a meeting, won't be back" and with that he was gone as Dave looked at John Marshall for some kind of answer, that he knew he couldn't provide. As the door closed behind Daniel, Eric came out of his office and addressed them both "You will have seen the news yesterday regarding the Pit Closure Act that effectively means the Government is closing a tranche of pits, and while it won't have a major impact on Kirkdale, it will mean that the knock on effect will lead to the early closure of the Manchester Road Power Station, as the country goes away from coal fired Power Stations. Daniel has gone to a meeting with our legal team to see what effect the Act will have as the site provides Kirkdale Council with major funding through rates, as well as through employment of course. The major problem we have is that all our Archive records were destroyed in the fire, so we need to find out what the Legal team have in terms of documentation and that's where Daniel is starting. Daniel thinks that there could be a benefit longer term and I have allowed him to take some time to review, and report back to me in due course. Any questions?" Taking a few seconds to gather his thoughts as John Marshall shook his head to indicate he had none, Dave said "With the greatest respect Eric, some of us lost a lot more than a few records in the fire, and what's more Daniel may be Assistant Chief Surveyor, but surely the Legal Department can manage a review of their documents without his help. We have more than enough work without losing Daniel again!" realising his error Eric quickly replied "I apologise Dave, I didn't put that very well, of course Sandra was a great loss, not just to you, but the Council as well. But I have made a decision for the good of the Council as a whole, and when Daniel has completed his review I will make sure it is shared with you!" and turning to go back to his office, he missed the look of thunder on Dave's face as the demons reappeared in his mind about Daniel Bruce.

After seven working days missing, Daniel Bruce finally submitted his report to Eric Normanton on Friday the 23rd of October, and having read it with Daniel sitting in his office awaiting his comments Eric called Dave and John Marshall into his office after lunch. Daniel sat at the side of Eric with a look of triumph on his face as Eric started to explain the results of Daniel's seven day absence. "Daniel's review is very thorough, but was hampered by the lack of legal documents available as a result of the destruction of the Archives in the fire. However following extensive searching it has been possible to come to the conclusion that should the Manchester Road Power Station close, the land would revert to the Council, in the absence of any other legal claim, or rights to the land. The anticipated timescale for the closure of the Manchester Road Power Station as adjudged by Daniel is between 3 and 10 years, at which time the Council will put forward a plan to redevelop the land according to the requirements at the time. It is no secret that there is a lack of flat land in Kirkdale so it may be used for industrial usage, but it could be a mixed use, but that is just conjecture at the current time. The review will go to the next full Council meeting in November for consideration. So unless you have any comments gentlemen we should get back to work." Standing up Daniel was halted in his tracks as John Marshall said "Are there really no documents left after the fire surely there must be some, or someone can remember something about the site that might help. It just seems odd that such a big site, has no documents at all!" grasping the mantel, Daniel replied "I did extensive research, and I could find no documents that could link the land with anyone, and as you know John, without documents we are helpless!" and as John could think of nothing else to say Daniel made to set off towards the door only to be halted once again as Dave suddenly had a thought and said "What about the Micofiche system that we had as backup before we went onto computers?" Looking like he had been found with his fingers in the till Daniel blustered "I did as part of my research have a look but I found nothing relating to the site in any files that had been copied onto Microfiche" seeing the disappointment on Dave's face Daniel finally got to the door and left without another word trusting that his lie about the Microfiche wouldn't be remembered as he himself hadn't checked it during his research.

With the Friday evening set for a meeting with Sid, Dave settled for pie, chips and peas from Tom's Chippy on the way home to soak up some of the drink he had when out with Sid. Putting them on a plate with a slice of bread he couldn't get Daniel's attitude out of his head. It was like he was already running the Estates Department even though Eric Normanton was Chief Surveyor. Cutting into the pie he picked up a piece on his fork and blowing on it before he put it into his mouth he sat chewing, as his mind went back to his Trust Fund meeting with Mr Ramsdale of McParland and Co. "Do some research" he had said at the time, but he never had, and now after the Archive fire he never would be able to. Daniel had said the Microfiche copy had nothing, so that wouldn't help he thought as he put a few chips on the end of his fork and popped them in his mouth. Pondering on several questions that he couldn't answer, it was nearly 7pm when he finished his tea and putting the plate and fork on the drainer to be dealt with he went upstairs to get changed for his regular fortnightly night out with Sid at the Malt Shovel, which tonight had no appeal at all.

"Come on partner let's go and see if your pool has got any better!" said Sid holding two pints of Lager infront of him as he made for the pool room. The evening played out its usual format of too many games of pool and too many pints, but when Ian the Manager said "Time please, ladies and gentlemen, haven't you lot got any homes to go to?" he winked at Sid and Dave to say they could stay for another and when the last straggler left Ian pulled them a couple of pints and as Sid and Dave sat on a bar stool each, it was evident that Ian had something to say "Gentlemen I don't really know how to say this but I've got to get it off my chest. Had that Daniel Bruce and his mate Steve Parker in here last Wednesday, they've been coming in quite a lot recently but this was during the day, and they met this guy that Brian, one of the regulars knows, called Michael Anderson from Anderson Developments and well, after a couple of drinks this Michael Anderson leaves, but on his way out he says to me here's £50 for a tab for Daniel and Steve. So thank you very much I thought, and obviously the guys got stuck in and they finally left around 9pm. I ordered them a Taxi into Town to the Punjab for a curry. The thing is while they were waiting outside for the Taxi I was having a fag and when they left they were very drunk, but I'm sure Steve said "You sure they'll never pin the fire on you Daniel?" and Daniel put his finger to his mouth before they got into the Taxi and left. I wouldn't have thought anything of it but I don't like that Daniel Bruce at all, especially not after that attack on you, Dave!" Suddenly, like he had just woken up, Dave looked at Ian and quickly said "I don't get you. What has Daniel got to do with the attack on me, that was years ago!" Ian looked at Sid, and sensing now was the time to tell Dave, he told him a secret that he had meant to tell him years ago but had never found the right time for. "Well" said Sid finally willing and somewhat forced to tell his story "I asked Ian if he could ask around after your attack and see if there was anyone who was bragging, but there wasn't. However Daniel Bruce and his mate Steve were in the pub on the night you got attacked and according to Ian they left right after us" taking a drink Dave thought about what Sid had said before replying "I can't see it why would he attack me we hardly knew each other at the time!" Sid took the look from Ian and finished the story off "Well you know Daniel and Sandra went out together before you met her obviously, well do you remember the Council Christmas Party where you pulled her?" "Yes of course" replied Dave wondering where this was going "Well didn't we cut Daniel off at the bar as he went to buy drinks for Sandra and Marion?" looking even more confused Dave replied "So what, it was just a drink he wouldn't attack me for that surely, I think you're putting two and two together etc" and taking another drink he was almost on the point of dismissing it completely when a thought hit him and he said "If he was responsible for the attack, and the fire is the fire at the Archive, then what's the link?" Sid and Ian looked at each other and as one said "Sandra!"

Over the next hour no matter how hard they tried, they couldn't think of any more information between them as the alcohol flowed, that would help them put the pieces together. As 2am approached, Ian ordered a Taxi for Dave and Sid. Seeing them get into the Taxi, Ian watched as its lights disappeared and putting his cigarette out he muttered as he closed the door behind him "Should have kept my mouth shut!"

Saturday morning got off to a bad start as Dave slept in, and despite a 30 second shower he didn't arrive at the Robertson house to pick up Caroline until nearly 11am. Opening the door he could see her and Diane in the kitchen, where the table was strewn with pictures with scrawls of colour and hearing the door shut behind him Diane got up to put the kettle on as he made his way into the kitchen. "We've been colouring daddy!" Caroline said as he bent down to give her a kiss on the head "Tea Dave?" Diane said and a nod was accepted as a yes "So darling what have you been colouring?" he said trying to work out exactly what it was he was looking at and failing miserably as last night's alcohol slowly made its way out of his body. "It's a family of butterflies on a day out daddy!" she answered wondering why he hadn't guessed "Of course it is darling" he said as he took a mug of tea from Diane who asked already knowing the answer "Long night?" "In more ways than one!" he replied automatically before taking a sip of tea that was infinitely better than last night Lager. "What are we going to do today darling?" he said hoping it wasn't swimming. But as payment for his excesses of last night the words "Swimming daddy" were out of her mouth before knew it, and with a rueful look from Diane his fate for the day was sealed.

As Caroline went upstairs to get her overnight bag Dave finished off his tea and placing it on the kitchen table he asked as Diane tidied the pictures and pencils up "Diane this might seem a bit strange but before Sandra and I got together she went out with Daniel. Did she finish it or did he?" Leaving her tidying up she looked at Dave and replied "Whatever made you ask that after all these years?" seeing the reticence in her face he persevered "Just something Sid said last night in the pub that's all" "Well not that it matters, because it was you she loved, but she finished it" and hearing the thud as Caroline jumped off the bottom step and into the kitchen he said "Thanks for looking after Caroline, I, sorry we, do appreciate it don't we darling. Forget about that other thing just beer talk. Right swimming for you and me young lady, say thank you to Grandma" and as Caroline gave Diane a hug and a kiss Dave looked in his mind for another piece of a jigsaw that was slowly being completed in his head.

The swimming cleared his head and standing in the Foyer choosing a chocolate bar for Caroline, Dave decided she would be his priority this weekend, and work and all its growing implications could wait until Monday. "There you go" said Dave as the Dairy Milk bar dropped from its perch, and into the opening for Caroline to get and as she started to peel the wrapper off he added "What do you think about going to the pictures this afternoon Tom and Jerry, is on or Aladdin?" with a look that said 'More sweeties' Caroline thought for a moment and answered "Tom and Jerry and popcorn daddy, and a drink please" and as the thought of an hour in a Cinema with noisy children finally hit him, he made a mental note to curtail his fortnightly evenings out with Sid for a while.

Sunday dragged until lunchtime as the weather finally improved, and taking their chance they got into the Jaguar and headed for the newly opened Asda supermarket, to do some shopping. An hour later and with a bulging shopping trolley they bumped into John Marshall and his wife on the way to the tills. "Gone a bit over the top there Dave" said John as he realised who it was with the overloaded shopping trolley. "Oh hi John, not really we haven't done a decent shop for weeks. Looks like half of Kirkdale are in here today, what with the weather being crap!" "Yes, it's on the wrong side of Town for us but it's new and the prices are good, there's nothing else to do in Kirkdale on a Sunday afternoon so that's why we are here. Have you met my wife Rachel?" and smiling, as he said "No I haven't, nice to meet you, this is my daughter Caroline, say hello to Rachel darling!" and looking up Caroline said "Pleased to meet you" before returning to her job of guarding the shopping trolley that contained her Sugar Puffs. "Nice to meet you Caroline" Rachel said before adding as she looked back at Dave "I was so sorry to hear about Sandra, we were at school together, Caroline looks just like her mother" she said adding "You must miss her!" and with a nod from Dave, she required no real answer. "Well back to the grindstone for us tomorrow, wonder if Daniel will honour us with his presence" said John trying to change the conversation but not realising he had steered it in the wrong direction completely "I can't believe you have to work under Daniel Bruce, he's a bully and a liar and the sooner John get's a new job the better" said an obviously upset Rachel "Rachel went out with him at school, and let's just say she doesn't have a very high opinion of him" said an apologetic John, pushing their trolley into the newly created gap at the checkout. "You'll get out too if you've got any sense, Daniel got Headboy at school by lying about Andrew Smith who was supposed to be Headboy, but Andrew got accused of stealing some money from Steve Parker, who just happened to be, and still is as far as I'm aware, Daniel's best friend." Pausing for a moment Rachel added "Sorry about that but Daniel is rotten to the core and I should know" Rachel joined and apologetic looking John at the checkout, leaving Dave and Caroline looking at each other as the queue infront of them moved nearer the checkout. "Spaghetti for tea?" he said to a thumb up from Caroline as they both wondered what had got Rachel so angry in their own way, as yet another piece of the jigsaw fell into place.

Arriving after the short walk from home, at Northfield School after a hearty breakfast of two bowls of Sugar Puffs, he kissed her on the head at the school gates and said "See you tonight" and as ever she replied "Love you, see you soon" and she was gone into the playground leaving him standing with all the other parents watching their hopes and dreams, stream into the playground. Setting off on the walk home to get his car the wind blew into his face as he headed down the aptly named Windy Hill Street. Taking his car keys out of his pocket as he approached his car, he unlocked the Jaguar and sitting with the key in the ignition he paused for a second before turning the key, as he did so he said out loud to no one, "Jigsaw time" as the engine sparked into life.

Finding a space in the Council car park there was no sign of Daniel's Mercedes, and a little relieved, Dave headed into work to find John Marshall already at his desk. After the usual good morning and comments about the weather it was only a few minutes later that John approached Dave's desk. "Sorry about Rachel yesterday Dave, she hates Daniel from school, she's always telling me to get another job, but I like my role here, and to be fair Daniel is hardly ever here, even before the fire!" putting him at ease, Dave quickly replied "Honestly John don't worry about it, Daniel is only out for himself, he's so far out of his depth in his role, but Eric seems to have high hopes for him for some reason which is beyond me" seeing his apology accepted, John added "Rachel says he'll get to the top, but heaven help anyone who gets in the way, so watch your step Dave!" wondering if John could read his mind he replied "I'm more than aware of what Daniel is capable of John, you take care to look out for yourself!" and with that they both set about the day's workload with Daniel still to make an appearance.

The morning ran its course and as lunchtime came Dave was pondering with his quandary of what to do if, and when, Daniel turned up, his early morning decision to challenge Daniel abating as he headed out to get a pasty and coke. Returning from lunch he saw Daniel's Mercedes in the Council car park and his resolve strengthened, but he was disappointed to find Daniel already in Eric Normanton's Office with the door shut. Taking his time to finish his pasty, he was about to get back to work when Daniel left Eric's Office without a word of greeting, and headed out of the office with a smile on his face that made up Dave's mind. Dropping the remains of his pasty in the bin as he left his desk, he headed out of the office in pursuit of Daniel and was just in time to see him enter the Toilets at the end of the corridor. Taking his time to catch up Dave opened the door to find Daniel zipping up his trousers, and as he went to wash his hands Dave shut the door behind him. Seeing Dave stood in the doorway, but not making any attempt to move away from the door, Daniel started washing his hands and said "You look like you've got something on your mind Dave?" with his foot against the door stopping any intrusions, he waited until Daniel had finished washing his hands before saying "Got your memory back yet Daniel?" looking confused as to where Dave was going with this Daniel quickly said "No, nothing" collecting the various bits of his minds Jigsaw conundrum Dave said "But you can remember before the fire I take it?" now concerned where this was going Daniel automatically said "Of course I can" before adding to counter Dave "It's just the trauma of the fire that's a blank" seeing the picture better Dave countered with "So you don't remember starting the fire Daniel!" and with a sinking feeling Daniel moved towards the door where Dave had remained saying "What are you on about, I didn't start the fire, I'm sorry Sandra died in the fire, but why would I start a fire?" and as Daniel finished his sentence, Dave still couldn't fit together why Daniel had started the fire into his jigsaw. With a growing anger at his inability to get the pieces together, he moved away from the door towards Daniel. As he backed away from Dave, the fateful words he spoke, put the pieces back into place "Stay away from......" and unable to finish the sentence, as he suddenly felt the wall hit his back Daniel turned to see if there was anywhere else to go, already knowing the answer. "It ...was... you, all those years ago that attacked me!" as Dave remembered the words his attacker had used word for word, and the same voice, how had he not put it together before now! Gathering his response Daniel smug as ever, changed tack and went on the offensive. "So what are you going to do about it Dave, you've got no evidence, I was at home which I can prove!" looking more confident Daniel lent back against the wall and awaited Dave's response "I suppose it's Steve Parker that can back you up, is it Daniel?" Upon hearing Steve's name Daniel was struggling to figure out how Dave had guessed his alibi, when Dave put forward his information from Friday at the Malt Shovel to go with it "The same Steve Parker who was heard last to say last Wednesday 'You sure they'll never pin the fire on you Daniel?'"

The silence stood for a minute as they looked at each other before Daniel did what Daniel does and stood all over Dave's Jigsaw, by saying as he moved towards him with a triumphant look on his face "There's no evidence Daniel, it will be your word against mine, and well, what with my memory playing somersaults, and you being jealous of my success, plus with you still mourning over Sandra, did you know I had her before you? I think you need some time off Dave. No-one would begrudge you some time to look after what's her name Caro...." but he never finished Caroline's name as Dave took a step forward, and launched a fist that connected with Daniel's temple which propelled him backwards against the wall. As he slid down the wall to lie in a crumpled heap on the toilet floor John Marshall came into the Toilet, and seeing Daniel lying on the toilet floor he looked at Dave who quietly said "Daniel must have slipped, you'd better ring for an Ambulance" and taking hold of John's arm stopping him leaving he added "In a few minutes John, let's enjoy the moment!" standing watching

Daniel, it was the entrance of Eric Normanton that broke the moment. Seeing Daniel lying on the toilet floor he "What happened" and as Dave and John looked at each other Dave said "We found him like that!" and as John nodded in agreement, Eric went to ring for an Ambulance leaving them to silently agree a pact that would never be broken.

Once the Ambulance had taken Daniel to Kirkdale Infirmary, Eric asked Dave and John into his office and despite his best endeavours, the story remained the same that Dave and John had found Daniel collapsed in the Toilet, their pact solid as the afternoon settled back into its routine. It was the following week that Daniel returned to work, and immediately he went into Eric Normanton's Office only to come out in less than a minute followed by Eric who standing next to Daniel said "Dave can I have a minute please?" As Dave headed into Eric's Office, he took a quick glance at John Marshall's desk which was met with a thumb up, unseen by Daniel and Eric it boosted his resolve.

"Dave, Eric has made a serious accusation against you that you hit him in the Toilets knocking him out, he has informed the Police so before this goes any further I'd like to hear your side of the story!" still standing Dave looked at Eric and despite his previous high regard for him, his faith in Daniel had erased it to such an extent, that he no longer felt he could trust him. Looking at Daniel who appeared to think he had all the answers with a look of superiority on his face Dave finally answered "We found Daniel slumped on the toilet floor Eric, just before you came in, sorry there's nothing more I can add!" as Daniel took a step forward towards him, Eric said "Just a minute Daniel" and leaning out of the door he summoned John Marshall into the office, and he continued as John stood next to Dave. "John, Daniel has made a serious accusation against Dave regarding the incident in the Toilet last Monday, what have you to say for yourself?" looking Daniel in the eye John replied "We found Daniel on the toilet floor just before you came in Eric, that's it" as Daniel looked at Eric for help John mouthed "Where you belong" unheard but seen by Dave who just managed not to smile. As Eric realised he would be unable to elicit any further information from them, he reluctantly under Daniel's now furious look said "Thank you if there is anything else I'll let you know!" at which Daniel lost control "You hit me Dave Baxter and I'll get you if it's the last thing I do!" seizing the moment Dave took a step nearer Daniel and said calmly "That's a threat Daniel, infront of witnesses. It's a shame there were no witnesses in the Toilet when you slipped, do please tell me your memory coming back!" and taking a step back he followed John out of Eric's Office leaving a seething Daniel being calmed down by Eric. Sitting down at their desks it wasn't long before Daniel left Eric's Office, slamming the door behind him and headed out of the Estates Department door. "I don't know what Daniel has got on Eric, and we probably will never know, but I think we might be wise to look for a new job, he's not going to let this go" said Dave looking at John who replied almost like he had the answer ready "We're just pawns in his game Dave, he wants to get to the top and probably will, we, rather that is you, won this little battle but it's a long war!"

Despite the awkwardness in the Estates Department, Eric did his best to keep a lid on emotions as the weeks went past and with invites for the Council Christmas Party, to be held as usual in the first week of December, landing on his desk at the end of the first week in November, Dave barely looked at his invite before adding it to the recycling bin. Daniel was as cold as he could be, his hoped for Police investigation of his attack in the Toilets stalled due to lack of witnesses, which Dave had anticipated. But Daniel had to use the abilities of Dave and John on a daily basis, so it became a functional office where all involved did their job, and went home hardly speaking. Despite winning his battle with Daniel it was a still frustrated Dave who couldn't finish the ongoing Jigsaw in his head, as there were too many missing pieces, and despite being convinced Daniel had something to do with the fire there was no evidence to link him with it, apart from a barman who may have overheard a conversation between Steve Parker and Daniel. Doodling while eating his lunch one day at work Dave slowly started to put together a physical Jigsaw on paper, of meeting Sandra at the Council Christmas Party followed by the attack at Christmas 1984. There was a huge gap to May 1992 and the Archive Fire which didn't make sense at the time and still didn't. Writing Sam Brown next to Sandra's name he was stuck, until he doodled an oblong box round Sam's name and a comment from months ago came back to him as he wrote Silk Cut on the box, and added Embassy to another box he hastily drew next to it. Sitting back he got no further and as the day went on, with Daniel thankfully away today it wasn't until he passed Daniel's desk on the way to the door at the end of the day that he saw a small bundled of envelopes on his desk. Flicking through them to check for any urgent looking letters, he saw the Council Christmas Party invite, underneath an envelope stamped Anderson Developments Ltd which when held up to the light was obviously another Christmas Party invite. For no apparent reason Dave headed back to his desk and taking his newly started paper Jigsaw out of a draw he added at the bottom of the page, Anderson Developments Ltd and Malt Shovel next to it with a question mark, before heading to the photocopier and running a couple of copies off, he put them in his desk and placed the original in his briefcase, unsure if he would ever add to it and if he did would it help to complete his Jigsaw. He picked up his coat on the way out of the office and headed through the rain to his waiting Jaguar and best part of his day, the trip to pick up Caroline from Diane and Jim's house on Church Street.

The weeks running up to Christmas 1992 ran like clockwork as the workload at Kirkdale Council dropped away, with Caroline finishing school on the 20th of December, a full week before Christmas Dave booked some days off and with the addition of Bank Holiday he looked forward to spending two weeks with his daughter before he went back to work in the New Year. Despite being a bit lost at first Dave developed a routine for them with regular visits to his, and Sandra's parents and taking time to himself as his mum Mary had Caroline, he went hunting for a present for a 7 year old who had set her heart on a pink bike. Despite the crowds out in the freezing cold dark winter afternoons that had arrived at the weekend with a vengeance from the Arctic , Dave was pleased with his purchase as he loaded it into the Jaguar's boot and locked it. Looking around he saw a HMV record shop and with the afternoon to himself he spent an hour browsing before buying "Unplugged" by Eric Clapton and "Change Everything" by Del Amitri. Taking his choices to the till he picked up a VHS of Aladdin for Caroline, and handing them to the girl behind the till it wasn't until he was getting his change, that he looked up at her. Taking his carrier bag he said "Thanks Jackie!" and as she replied with a slightly nervous smile "You're welcome have a nice Christmas!" as he left the shop he tried to think where he knew her from but it wasn't until he had put the carrier bag on top of the large box containing Caroline's pink bike in the boot and locked it, that it came to him as he got into his seat realised it was Jane's sister. Sitting as the engine blew the air to clear the window screen he tried to remember what Caroline said and it finally hit him as the screen cleared "She's very pretty daddy" she had said and with a smile growing on his face, he said to the now clear window screen "Yes she is!" as he drove out of Town and headed to Albion Street, where he was sure his mother had spoiled the, oh so wise Caroline.

Christmas 1992 came and went with the freezing weather remaining and despite the concern about going back to an equally chilly atmosphere at work January, was halfway through when at the age of 60 Eric Normanton announced his intention to retire from the position of Chief Surveyor at

Kirkdale Council at the end of April 1993, and to no-one's surprise Daniel Bruce at the age of 35, was duly invited to replace him, despite two rounds of external interviews from more experienced candidates, who should have known better than to waste their time if they had done their homework. The Estates Department expanded under Daniel's leadership and with two additional members of staff, the workload eased enough for Dave and John Marshall to actually begin to enjoy their jobs again, but always aware that Daniel saw them as enemies and was only keeping them close until he could replace them, unknown to the new arrivals in the Estates Department. On the 4th February 1993 it was agreed at a Kirkdale Council meeting at the behest of Eric Normanton that the Archive Chambers be rebuilt and the motion was passed with a provisional start date of May 1993 in the next financial year.

As the year moved ever onwards it was becoming apparent to Dave that he needed to move on from Kirkdale Council as Daniel slowly wielded his power, and a month after Eric Normanton had retired Dave asked John for a drink after work on the last Friday in May. After getting served in the nearby Cross Keys, Dave could see John had probably guessed why he had asked him for a drink as he handed him a pint of Lager. Finding a table away from the bar he held his glass up to John who reciprocated, and after they clashed glasses John took a drink and let Dave have his say. "John I wanted you to be the first to know, I've decided to hand my notice in on Monday. I can't work anymore under Daniel, now he's the boss, I haven't enjoyed the last year for obvious reason so I'm going to have some time over the summer with Caroline and see what comes up. I hate to leave you on your own but I've had enough" as a smile Dave hadn't anticipated appeared on John's face he replied "Going to be a busy Monday then, I've already written my resignation letter out at home. I've got a job at Ramsdens Construction, so here's to us!" and clashing glasses again Dave took a moment before saying "I'm so pleased for you, I felt so guilty leaving you with Daniel!" shaking his head John took a drink and replied "I've been looking ever since that day ....we found Daniel in the Toilet. To be honest I wish it had been me that...." with a smile on his own face Dave finished the sentence "Wiped the smile off his face?" and taking a chance no one would hear John added checking no one was listening nearby "You mean wiped the Toilet floor with him!" and as they sat with their own memories of that day, the pact stayed secure, as always. After they finished their drinks and headed back to the Council Car Park to get their cars John said "Thanks for everything Dave and if you ever want a job I would recommend you to Ramsdens, I'm sure they would bite your hand off!" and shaking his hand Dave nodded before adding "Something will turn up I'm sure, say hi to Rachel for me, I guess she'll be happy you got out from under Daniel's clutches!" still holding his hand John swiftly said "She's delighted, one day I'm sure he'll get his, I just hope I'm around to see it, you take care, and when you're settled give me a ring" letting go of his hand John headed for his car leaving Dave standing beside his Jaguar, suddenly aware that at the end of June he would be a single parent and unemployed.

Chapter 24 – July 1993 - A new start

"The world doesn't stop turning just because I step off mum" said Dave as he sat nursing a cup of coffee at his parent's house with Caroline playing in the garden as they awaited Alan's return from work before they were due to go out for tea when he got home. "I know dear but you have Caroline to think about, and with no income how are you going to manage, and for how long, you had a good job at the Council, what were you thinking?" taking a sip of coffee he had hoped his dad would have explained it all before now and he probably had he thought, but she wanted to hear it directly from him obviously "Well the job was fine, but the new boss and I, well we didn't get on, so that was an easy decision. As for money, well thankfully Granddad Carey has taken care of that, I paid off the mortgage and there's a Trust Fund for Caroline, but there's still a decent amount left even after Black Friday and the reduced interest rates and then there's ......Sandra's Life Insurance and Death in Service payment, so we're fine mum honestly!" and standing up her moved and gave her a hug as Alan walked through the door. "God I'm hungry where are we going to eat tonight?" and looking for a response he heard Dave say "Mum doesn't think I have enough money to go out, so we're getting a portion of fish and chips and scraps of course, to share between us all" and as he felt a slap on his arm Mary said "That's not what I said David, and you know it, I'm just worried about you and Caroline that's all!" as the penny dropped Alan said putting down his briefcase by the door "They're fine Mary, really they are. Now shall we go to the Tavern or into Town, and a Chinese?" and as a voice from the direction of the garden, followed by a physical presence in the kitchen said "Chinese Granddad!" the decision was made and wasn't contested."Right Caroline, let's wash those hands and make you pretty and then we can get some tea, who said they were hungry?" said Mary taking charge, leaving Alan to talk to Dave as she had planned. "Your mum is worried because you're not working that's all, she probably has an idea of how much you have but I bet it's a mile off. It's been what 8 years since you got the money and although it's only been getting around 11% interest until Black Friday that is, you didn't go on a spending spree apart from the Jaguar obviously, and I gave you a good deal on that, so I reckon you will have built the pot back up over £100k which should see you good for whatever you have in mind." Having worked out that what his dad had worked out was on the low side, he let it go as Mary and Caroline came downstairs into the kitchen, ready for the trip to the Chinese. "I'll drive dad and you can have a beer or two, as I've got no money!" and a look from his mother told he had pushed it a bit too far as he opened the door and took Caroline's hand as they headed for the Jaguar.

As Caroline's 8th birthday loomed up Dave was caught between taking her on holiday and staying at home so they could have a party, and sat watching TV one night with Caroline safely asleep upstairs he switched TV Channels and on ITV watched "Wish you were here" During the program he watched as Judith Chalmers meandered around Edinburgh, and with an idea in his head he determined to spend a little of the money his mum said he didn't have. The days went by and with Caroline now finished school, Dave set their routine of breakfast and a walk to get a paper before she watched the morning's children's TV, as he read through the depressing news of yesterday. Lunch could be anything in the fridge, and the afternoon would be a walk or drive somewhere with the obligatory Ice Cream before heading home for tea and a bath, and a book which Dave had already read. So one day they joined the local Northfield Library and Dave didn't have to read anymore as Caroline's interest kept her attention before a cuddle on the sofa infront of the TV, where on many occasions she fell asleep and had to be put to bed.

The World outside of 15 Windy Hill Street passed them by and on the 27th July Caroline had her 8th Birthday Party in the garden with all her friends from school invited, and as Diane and Mary tried to guess how many mini sandwiches, sausage rolls and hot dogs to make and Dave left them to it and went inside to make a phone call. With 1pm almost on them and most of the children already arrived, it was a bright yellow van that pulled up outside Number 15 and at precisely 1.15pm as agreed on the phone, the party took off as 'Mr Mustard the Entertainer' dressed in a bright yellow suit and a red top hat, walked into the garden blowing a trumpet to make sure everyone noticed. The shrieks of shock and laughter mixed with clapping and shouting, would prove to be just the beginning as he set down a portable tape player and started the afternoon off with "Yellow Submarine" swiftly followed by a vast array of children's tunes and a seemingly endless supply of balloons with which to make animals, and it wasn't until nearly an hour later that Dave announced "Mr Mustard is having a break for a short time so all you children can have their sandwiches, drinks and crisps which are in the kitchen, so can we have a big hand for Mr Mustard children, and we'll see him in a short while!" the clapping was loud but short lived as the children whose attention had previously been captured by Mr Mustard, set about the mountains of small sandwiches, plates of sausage rolls and bowls of crisps. Bolstered by the sugar rush of the food and drinks the children, and some adults who had remained clapped, as Mr Mustard made his second appearance and with some games and even more balloons, the afternoon went better than Dave had hoped culminating in Birthday Girl Caroline getting a balloon dog made by Mr Mustard, and while he would never divulge how much Mr Mustard had cost to Mary, Dave thought it was worth every penny to see Caroline's face smile all day. "It was a small price to pay mum!" Dave said as Mary and Alan were leaving and as Mary kissed Caroline goodbye, she looked at Dave and nodded, before heading to their car. After the last of the children and adults had gone Dave and Caroline moved all the presents inside to the Lounge and sitting on the floor Dave sat and watched, as each present was unwrapped and put to one side and the wrappings left in a separate pile, and once all the presents were opened Caroline sat quietly for a second and for the first time in months said "Daddy I miss mummy, I wish she was here today!" lost for words, as he was thinking exactly the same, that Sandra would be so proud of her daughter, he picked her up and with her arms around his neck he added "Mummy is always looking after us darling, I'm sure she would have liked Mr Mustard!" and with the moment gone Caroline went to get her multi coloured balloon dog from the kitchen. As she returned holding the balloon dog upside down she looked at Dave and said "Daddy can we get a dog like this?" and realising it was upside down she turned it upright and added "But not with green legs of course".

With the start of the new school year Dave decided it was time to look for employment, but after a few interviews he decided that the time was right to start working for himself. With a few recommendations and contacts, he set up as a freelance Building Surveyor much to the annoyance of him mum. "You wanted me to go back to work and that's what I have done" he said over a cup of coffee not long after he had started working for himself "That's not what I meant and you know it David" she swiftly replied. "Well it's done now and if it works out I'll start a Property Surveying Practice next year as there is a shortage, so let's just see how it goes mum okay?" and defeated, Mary said in a final response "You just make sure Caroline is looked after, that's all I ask!" Taking her hand for the first time since he was a little boy, Dave quietly replied "Mum, if I had to, I'd go back to the Council if things don't work out okay!" and appeased, Mary squeezed his hand and got up to put the kettle on again, leaving Dave to ponder lying to his mum for the first time in his life.

As a new routine started with Dave walking Caroline to school, then driving to his rented office on the outskirts of Town where rents were affordable, Dave soon picked up some clients and with a recommendation from John Marshall, it wasn't long before he was working four full days and a half day on a Friday which fitted in well with his plan to get the business on its feet, and build a Surveying Practice in the second year. The fortnightly Friday nights with Sid had stretched out as Dave left Kirkdale Council to a month, and sometimes two months as time had passed. Feeling it was about time to get back in touch Dave picked up the phone and arranged to meet Sid on the last Friday in August at the Malt Shovel. Diane had said the previous week that she missed having Caroline on a regular basis, so it was an ideal opportunity, and as he finished early on the Friday he took the chance to get his hair cut and do some shopping, before he met Sid, as Diane was picking up Caroline from school. Entering Brian the Barber's Dave saw that he had two customers already waiting but with time on his hands he sat down and waited his turn. Picking up the Kirkdale Times left by a previous customer, the lead story was about increasing parking charges, but as he didn't go into Town anymore unless on a special occasion to eat, he skipped the story and finding the Business Section his attention was caught by an article on Anderson Developments Ltd.

'Anderson Developments Ltd has announced that following prolonged discussions with Kirkdale Council, it will be working closely with the Kirkdale Estates Department to create a long term plan for the future use of land owned by Kirkdale Council to maximise revenue streams to benefit the rate payers of Kirkdale'

'Pictured in front of the new Kirkdale Archive Centre, due to open in June 1994 are Michael Anderson, MD of Anderson Developments Ltd, and Daniel Bruce Head of Kirkdale Estates Department'

Managing to not rip the paper to bits, Dave read the rest of the page of Business News and with nothing further of interest he heard "Next" called out, and realising it was him, he put the paper down, stood up and hung his coat up, as the previous customer picked his coat off the next hook and tried to brush stray hairs from his neck failing miserably as Dave took the now empty seat. While the Barber sorted his hair out Dave had time to think about the article he had just read. "Didn't waste any time there Daniel" he thought, indeed he was so quick off the mark Dave was wondering how it had all been done so quickly, which wasn't the Kirkdale Council that he remembered. Might be one for his Jigsaw he was considering, until the Barber regained his attention "I hear they're going to close the Power Station, that's going to lead to a lot of job losses!" trying to figure out where a Barber would get this sort of information he was about to comment when he thought better of it and just said "That's a shame" at which the well informed Brian added "I hear they're going to build a Leisure Centre, when it's all demolished that is!" "Really!" said Dave astonished at the amount of information coming out from what he considered a humble Barber "Yeah, I had that Daniel Bruce from the Council in here earlier this week getting his hair done for a presentation, likes to look smart does Daniel!" and suddenly the part forgotten Jigsaw in his mind added another piece.

"So what's it like, working for yourself?" Sid asked Dave as they waited for Ian to pull their first drinks of the night at the Malt Shovel. Leaning on the bar Dave took a few seconds and as the drinks were put infront of them he said "Just the same, but without the pain of having a Boss!" taking his first mouthful a wry smile came across Sid's face "But you're your Boss!" and waiting for it to sink in Sid headed as usual for the pool room leaving Dave to follow. "That's just a play on words Sid!" he said as he joined him in the pool room "I know, just wondered if you've told yourself off, yet!" "What are you on about?" Dave responded taking a drink "Relax, just shop floor humour, get them set up, and then we'll see who's Boss!" and lost at where Sid had got his humour from, Dave the Boss did as he was told and set the balls up. Picking up a cue he was about to break when Sid put his hand on the table "Hold on who said you could break" he said stopping Dave in his tracks. "Shall we toss to see who breaks?" he added pulling a 50p out of his pocket "Heads or Tails" he said flicking the coin in the air. As it landed on the pool table Dave called "Heads" and Sid with a huge grin on his face said "Nope Tails, that's another bad decision Boss!" Completely baffled by Sid's behaviour Dave waited until Sid had broken and potted a couple of balls before he got it. "Been watching Spitting Image by any chance Sid?" realising Dave had worked it out, he replied "No I haven't, who said I have, bring me his head!" and breaking into a guttural laughter he mishit the white ball, and watched as it slowly made its way into the far pocket and effectively the game was open for Dave to win but not ready to give up on his new found humour Sid added "You Bosses always come out on top!" as Dave cleared the remaining balls on the table, but purposely missed an easy black, he turned to Sid and after much thought said "Not all Bosses are the same Sid!" and leaving the table to go to the bar for another round, he left Sid to pot the black and take a small victory even if it was handed to him by a Boss.

Despite Mary and Diane trying to organise a party for Dave's 34th Birthday on the 25th September, he managed, after agreeing to a family meal out, to almost get his way and they all headed to the Casa Italian Restaurant with Tony and Gill who returned from Sunderland in January, invited. Gill's mother Angela had their one year old Matthew for the evening, so with a table for 8 booked for 6pm on Saturday, the day of Dave's birthday, they arrived in two cars to find an already busy restaurant. After being seated the usual small talk went round the table until the waiter returned to take their order.

As the conversation started up again Dave was sat next to Tony with Caroline on his other side being spoiled by Diane. "So how are you settling in now your back from Sunderland Tony?" Dave asked before taking a sip of his drink. "Well it's been easier than I thought" Tony quickly replied before adding "I suppose dad has made it that way, but I don't see him much at work and we're so busy that it's been non-stop since we returned!" seeing Caroline devour another breadstick Dave caught part of the next comment, but had to ask him to repeat it "Sorry Tony I missed that what did you say?" "We got a large order from Anderson Developments last month which will keep us busy until Christmas" he repeated and seeing a quizzical look come across Dave's face Tony answered the question Dave was about to ask "It's the brochures and plans for the new Leisure Centre on the Power Station site" Picking up a breadstick and breaking it in half to give a piece to Caroline, Dave turned back to face Tony and giving nothing away said "That's great news Tony I'm pleased it's all working out for you. How is Matthew doing?" and leading Tony back to a conversation about his little boy, Dave put the information to the back of his mind until another time as the first meals arrived and the conversations were cut short as they all started to eat.

In the lead up to Christmas it was on a rare Saturday night that Sid and Dave went into Town and after quite a few pints they were stood in the George nursing their drinks, trying to decide whether to have a curry, or another pint and then home, when Jane and her younger sister Jackie came into the pub. "Buy a girl a drink mister" Jane said as she approached Sid from behind. Realising who it was he promptly replied "What's in it for me?" at which Jane brazenly said "Whatever your heart desires!" and awaiting his reply she wasn't at all surprised when he finally said "Nah I'll pass!" without a seconds thought. Jane said looking at her sister "See Jackie, I told you he didn't have a heart, we'll get our own drinks" As Jane went to move around Sid, Dave put his hand out and said "I'll get these Jane, some of us still have manners. Lager is it and for you Jackie?" A nod said yes, as Jane thumped Sid in the back. After getting served Dave handed each of them their drinks and looking behind Sid he saw an empty table, motioning with his free hand, he loudly said "Shall we sit down, before Sid falls down" To the sound of "How dare you I'm not drunk!" from Sid, they sat down with a slightly awkward silence between Dave and Jackie, as Jane and Sid argued about something and nothing which wasn't unusual. "Thanks for the drink!" Jackie finally said smiling at Dave who had a sudden memory "She's very pretty daddy!" and as the memory returned to its hiding place he replied "Your welcome Jackie" using her name as if he wanted to get used to saying it he said, adding "Are you still working at HMV?" and trying to keep the conversation going said "I bought some albums at Christmas and you were working, not that you'll remember it being so long ago!" The look on her face said she did, but she didn't let on but said "It was just a temporary role between jobs. I work at Ramsden Construction now, do you know them?" "I know John Marshall very well" Dave immediately replied, and with that they found a common ground to talk about until the "Time please" voice called an end to the evening. As they headed for the Taxi rank with Sid and Jane now arms around each other, Dave and Jackie were a few steps behind them still chatting when Jackie said "Don't you have a little girl?" and Dave automatically said "Yes, Caroline, she's 8 now! She's at her Grandma's tonight" "She's very pretty!" came an immediate reply which Dave didn't get a chance to reply to as Sid got into a Taxi and Jane said "Jackie, come on Taxi's waiting" as she got into the back seat of the waiting Taxi. "Thanks for the .....chat it's been really nice, maybe see you around" and with that she got in next to Jane and the Taxi pulled away leaving Dave waiting for the next Taxi, and perhaps a lot more.

The second Christmas without Sandra came and went and with the beginning of January, Caroline returned to Northfield school and after the excesses of the extended Christmas period Dave was glad to get back to work having put on a couple of pounds, as he spoiled Caroline and himself not necessarily in that order. The routine of finishing early on a Friday was now so well established that Dave found himself looking forward to his 'Me time' more and more. Making a decision to walk to the Bedlow Arms for tea, with Caroline due at Diane's for the night, he left his Jaguar at home on the last Friday in January and wrapped up well against the weather he put on his old flat cap and set off for the Moorland trail and a healthy 6 mile circular walk. Not in a hurry he stopped at the far corner of Bedlow Moor, and through the mist he could just see the Manchester Road Power Station which normally would be lit up against the dark January sky, but it was now just a few street lights on the access road that he could see with the main plant and towers in darkness. Progress he thought to himself and although he had added some information to his paper rather than mental jigsaw over the months, he still couldn't figure out where it was leading as he set off in the direction of the far off Bedlow Arms and a well deserved tea.

Damp rather than drowned it was a grateful Dave who finally arrived at the Bedlow Arms just after 5pm. Heading to the bar after taking of his coat and old flat cap and hanging them up he was trying to get served, but when he finally attracted the attention of the barman and ordered a Pint of Lager he heard a voice behind him say "Put that on my tab please George!" Turning round to see John Marshall standing there holding out his hand, he shook it and at the same time said "What are you doing here?" but before he could answer, George placed his drink on the bar saying "There you are sir" Finally John said "We're having a little Birthday drink, come and join us Dave" "Are you sure John?" a slightly hesitant Dave replied as John headed towards a hidden alcove saying "Come on, it's fine" and following John he saw the balloons first and Jackie second.

"Everyone this is a good friend of mine Dave Baxter, Dave it's Jackie's birthday today and we always go for a drink, so do come and join us, just don't ask how old Jackie is!" Dave took a seat next to John and after introductions had been completed all round, they caught up on what they had each been doing since leaving Kirkdale Council. It was only as he got to the bottom of his glass that he took an opportunity as the conversation between him and John was interrupted by John's colleague Peter, sitting to Johns right. "I'll just get a drink John" he said standing up, with the words from John "Get George to put it on the tab Dave" before he returned to his conversation with Peter. Returning with his second 'free pint' Dave was brought into the conversation with John and Peter with the words "Dave, what do you think will happen to the Manchester Road Power Station?" from John and from nowhere Dave immediately replied "I have it on good authority that it's going to be a new Leisure Centre!" Taking a drink as John and Peter took in his comment, no doubt wondering who this good authority was, but not willing to ask. Peter said to Adrian next to him "What do you think Adrian, a new Leisure Centre?" taking a second to put together his response Adrian Ramsden said "It's the last really big site in Kirkdale, and it should be industrial and housing, but nothing Kirkdale Council is doing at the moment would surprise me. I would be interested in finding out who, your good authority is Dave!" and with a shake of his head Dave answered "Couldn't possibly say Adrian, it was told to me in good faith!" leaving out that it was Brian the Barber while he was getting his hair cut, but automatically going up in Adrian Ramsden's esteem.

As a few of the 12 strong Birthday drink party left, citing the need to take their car home it wasn't long before a gap appeared next to Jackie and leaving John and Adrian to their discussion he stood up to go to the bar and holding his empty glass up he mouthed "Can I get you a drink" to Jackie as she caught his movement. With a nod she indicated she would and as there was a space next to her on his return he sat down, and handing her a half of Lager said "Happy Birthday Jackie, don't worry I won't ask your age" taking a drink she smiled and replied "The Big 30!, so now you know" and putting down her drink she asked him what he was doing at the Bedlow Arms, and as he explained about his routine and how he liked to get out they were both unaware that there were now only 4 sat down, until John caught his attention as he said "Dave, Jackie, Adrian and I are getting a Taxi, do either of you want a lift?" and without looking at him Jackie said "No we'll be fine thanks for asking, and thanks for my Birthday drinks" Returning to their conversation neither of them saw John and Adrian leave, as a Taxi horn sounded and they headed outside into the January rain.

Can I buy you a Birthday meal Dave said realising after three pints that he was starving after his walk and despite initially thinking no, Jackie eventually said yes as she had no plans for the rest of the night other than meeting her sister and Sid, and a few old friends that may or may not show up at the Malt Shovel. After moving to a smaller table they ordered food and continued filling each other in on their history. Jackie obviously knew about Sandra's death not just from her sister, but it had also been in all the papers, but rather than ignore or skirt around the topic, she asked him about Sandra and how he was coping. Surprising even himself, Dave outlined that while he obviously missed her enormously, Caroline was a joy and made his life have a purpose for which he was grateful. The initial anger had subsided he explained, but there were still lots of questions that he knew he would never have the answer to but it was getting easier. As their meals arrived, the conversation didn't come to a complete halt but was certainly more about day to day life, the news and generally finding things they had in common. Deciding not to bother with a pudding they moved to a window seat and continued to find their mutual interests and it wasn't until "Last orders please Ladies and Gentlemen" was announced by George that they realised it was time to go. Ordering a Taxi to share, they finished their drink just in time to see the headlights of a Taxi approaching, and sitting together in the back of the Taxi having given the driver Jackie's address first, and then onto Northfield it was a slightly drunk Dave who felt Jackie's hand hold his, as they headed for her house. "Thanks for a lovely evening, we should do it again" and with a kiss on the Dave's cheek she left the Taxi and made for her door, stopping to turn as the Taxi did a U Turn to go down the cul-de-sac, and with her hand held out imitating the shape of a telephone she hoped Dave had seen, as she smiled her way at the end of a very interesting 30th Birthday, to the Front door.

Saturday morning came quickly and suffering slightly from a hangover, Dave made his way to Church Street to pick up Caroline. He didn't really have time to think about the consequences of last night's impromptu evening out as he pulled up outside No 9. Sitting in his car as he gathered his thoughts he eventually got out of the car and after locking it, he made his way as ever without knocking into the Robertson house where from the sound of the squeals, his daughter was having a ball. Walking into the kitchen where the noises had come from it was no surprise that Diane and Caroline were baking again, but this time they were making biscuits in the shape of animals. Seeing Dave arrive Caroline abandoned her baking and ran to give him a hug, leaving flour everywhere "Daddy we're making animal biscuits for school and I'm making an Elephant with Smartie eyes, come and look!" and looking at the animals on the baking sheet that looked more like a T Rex, he smiled and said "They're brilliant, do they have names?" "Don't be silly daddy!" came the immediate reply just before "They're just Mr and Mrs Elephant" and popping a Smartie in her mouth, she added once she had finished it "I like Smarties daddy!" and just for a second Dave wondered if Jackie did as well. Saturday routine was maintained as they went swimming, but with his mind on last night he didn't really enjoy the hour they had had, and having already done some shopping on Friday before his walk to the Bedlow Arms they were home by 3pm and with an early tea, Saturday slowly went past as Dave struggled with the events of Friday night.

Sunday came and with a break in the weather they set of for a late morning walk round Northfield Reservoir and a stop for Ice Cream on the way. As they went into the busy Ice Cream shop and joined the queue, Dave saw Sid and Jane two places infront of them in the queue. Unsure what to do, his escape was blocked as another couple joined the queue behind them. As Caroline looked at the pictures on the Ice Cream posters Sid and Jane got and paid for their 99 Ice Creams and turning to squeeze their way out they saw Dave and Caroline, who by now had chosen a Fab Ice-Lolly. "Hello you two" said Sid trying eat his Flake without spilling it and speaking at the same time. "Hello you two, too" replied Dave and moving a step forward, he got out his money ready to pay as they were next in line. "What are you having Caroline?" Jane asked as her 99 Ice Cream slowly started to melt "I'm having a Fab!" she replied and seeing a place at the counter her conversation was done as her Fab Ice-Lolly appeared on the counter. Taking the wrapper off, Dave handed the Fab Ice-Lolly to Caroline which she eagerly took. Handing over his money and taking his own 99 Ice Cream they headed out of the shop to where Sid and Jane were waiting for them. Looking around Sid said "We're going to the Hobbit Inn at teatime for a Sunday Roast, you're more than welcome to join us!" despite thinking it was a good idea and it would save him making tea, he was about to say no when Jane, out of earshot of Sid, said quietly to Dave, as Caroline concentrated on her Fab Ice-Lolly "Jackie will be there" and his decision was made.

The hastily arranged change of plan was duly settled with a meeting time of 4.30pm at the Hobbit Inn and as Dave and Caroline left Northfield Reservoir he explained their new arrangements which delighted Caroline, who was now halfway down her Fab Ice-Lolly, as there was a chance for more Ice Cream. Choosing a bright yellow dress he left her to brush her hair and choose a hair band, as he put on a shirt on a Sunday for the first time in ages, and when she came downstairs she stood on the last step at the bottom of the stairs and waited for the compliment that she knew was coming."Very pretty darling, let's get your coat and shoes, and we can go" With a smile she jumped down the last step onto the floor and putting on her coat and shoes she took his hand as they made their way to the Jaguar, both really unaware of what lay ahead.

Arriving at the Hobbit Inn it was a strangely nervous Dave, who spotted Sid and Jane already sat at a table. Not seeing Jackie he wondered if the decision had been a mistake until he saw her coming back from the bar with a tray of drinks. After introducing Caroline to Jackie they sat down at the table as Jackie said "I got you a Pint of Lager and a coke for Caroline I hope that's okay?" The "Thank you" from Caroline beat Dave to the response, and taking hold of the straw she settled next to Dave separating Dave and Jackie, as Sid looked on clueless as to what was happening infront of him. With a few comments about this morning's walk out of the way the waiter came and took their order. Usually Dave would organise Caroline, but she was already in discussion with Jackie by the time Dave had finished talking to Sid. "Two Roast Beef dinners for me and Jane please, what do you lot want?" said Sid unknowingly already considering Dave, Jackie and Caroline as one lot. "I'll have a Roast Beef dinner as well what do....." but he never finished his sentence as Jackie interrupted "Caroline and I have decided to have the Turkey dinner, and then we can pretend that it's Christmas!" Looking at a beaming daughter with thoughts of Christmas in her mind, he was about to say "Good choice" when Caroline tugged at his elbow and said a little too loudly "It's not really Christmas daddy!" at which he looked at Jackie, who had heard the comment and her smile said today was definitely going to be one of his better decisions. The time flew by as Caroline entertained Jackie with stories from school and as Caroline finished her story of Mr Mustard from her birthday Jackie said "Oh I wish I had been there to see that!" which brought an immediate response from Caroline as she tugged his elbow again "Daddy can Jackie come to my next Birthday Party?" and with a slightly confused look Dave answered "Darling your birthday isn't until July, what if Jackie is busy" "You're not going to be busy are you Jackie" came back immediately from Caroline "Well I don't know Caroline perhaps if your dad were to ask me, then I would definitely come" Jackie replied looking directly at Dave. Taking a chance, Dave asked a question that he hoped he already knew the answer to "Well I can't just ask someone I hardly know to your Birthday Party darling, but if I get to know Jackie better, then I'm sure she can come. That's if she wants to of course!" and with a smile that said she had understood his comment she replied "I would love to get to know your dad better!" and the deal was done as the Chocolate Ice Cream arrived for Caroline, whose attention moved onwards, and whose world had just got a lot better in more ways than one, as Sid got stuck into his Apple Crumble, missing the first good news his best friend had had for a long time, but not unseen by Jane.

The next few months passed and as the Friday nights with Sid, became the Friday nights with Jackie, it was on the first Saturday in April that Dave headed to Church Street to pick up Caroline, with a feeling of guilt and emotion, dropping Jackie off at her house on the way. Sitting in the Jaguar he tried to set up a few sentences in his mind, but the words just didn't seem to fit. Locking the car door he made it to the Front door of No 9 without changing his mind. Closing the Front door behind him he found Caroline and Diane in the kitchen as always, with Caroline doing a painting by numbers picture of a sunflower. "Hello daddy" she said and promptly returned to her painting leaving a smiling Diane looking up at a very nervous

Dave. "Can I have a word Diane" he said adding "In the Lounge would be best" and figuring that this wasn't for the ears of an 8 year old, Diane said to Caroline "Just going into the Lounge for a moment darling, you carry on" and with a smile and a nod she returned to her painting, as Dave and Diane headed for the Lounge. Sitting opposite each other Dave eventually explained "I've met someone and I want to bring her into Caroline's life but I wanted you to know and … well, see if it is okay with you!" "So when are we going to meet Jackie then Dave?" came the immediate reply. Sitting with nothing to say Diane put him at ease. "Caroline told us months ago that she went to dinner with a very pretty lady, and she was coming to her Birthday Party. Honestly Dave you didn't need to keep her hidden, we'd love to meet her. It's been almost two years since Sandra died, and I know you loved her dearly, but Caroline will need a woman in her life, and so do you. So bring her round whenever you want, and we'll welcome her with open arms. Although I think she will have to be special, to match up to Caroline's comments. Now give me a hug you big softie" With that, the trepidation and fear that Dave had nurtured all morning went away, and after giving Diane a hug they returned to the kitchen where Caroline had happily painted her sunflower Red!

With Jackie spending more time with Dave, Caroline was introduced to Jackie formally on the last Saturday in April, just a week before the second anniversary of Sandra's death. Leaving Jackie in bed after their night out Dave had a shower and returning to the bedroom as he dried himself, he felt for sure, as they discussed last night that today would be a good day to let Caroline know what will be changing in her life. "I'll be about an hour getting her" he said as Jackie propped herself up in bed watching him get dressed. "I'll have a shower and tidy up and be here waiting, when you get back, do you still want me to stay tonight?" she added. Putting on a polo shirt he looked back at the bed and replied with a smile "Yes, I like waking up next to a naked body!" and as he left to go down-stairs he missed the quiet response of "Me too!" as Jackie got out of bed and headed for a shower, all thoughts of Caroline temporarily gone as she remembered last night.

Pre-warning Diane the previous week, that he was going to bring Jackie in to Caroline's life this weekend, he set off for Church Street and without a moment's hesitation he let him-self into the house on his arrival. With no sound from the kitchen he looked out of the window to see Diane and Caro-line picking flowers in the garden, and opening the back door he announced his arrival "Hello you two" and immediately Caroline turned round to show him her collection of flowers "Daddy look we've been picking flowers, and I'm going to pick some more for mummy next week!" and with a sudden pang of guilt, he looked at Diane for reassurance and it was there as always as she said "I think it's time your friend became part of the family not just .....well you know!" and picking up the flowers she had picked for herself, she headed past Dave quietly saying "There would never be a good time for anyone to take Sandra's place, but Jackie seemed really nice when we met last week and you can see she cares about you, so it's a good start, cup of tea?" and she was gone leaving Dave and Caroline in the garden where her mother had spent her child-hood. "Come on darling let get a drink and then we can go home. Taking her spare hand with the other squeezed around the flowers she had picked, they headed inside where the sound of cups and glasses could be heard as they stepped into the kitchen. "Doing anything special today you two?" Diane asked pouring out two mugs of tea, handing one to Dave she waited for his answer as she handed Caroline a glass of orange juice and took her flowers to wrap up in the Kirkdale Times. Fi-nally Dave got his answer out "Well I don't know, I think we'll just take the day as it comes, but it may have a few surprises!" Looking up from the rather industrial bouquet, handed to her by Diane Caroline said "Not scary surprises daddy?" and with a smile he quickly said with a memory of last night in his mind "No darling, not scary at all!" and taking a drink of his tea he caught Diane also with a smile on her face, as she understood his innuendo.

With Caroline safely in the Jaguar holding her bouquet of flowers, Dave gave Diane a hug and said "Thanks for looking after her, and for the flowers" and as they parted Diane replied "You're welcome, as always Dave, now off you go, I'm sure Jackie will love the flowers!" and as it suddenly dawned on Dave what Diane had done, he smiled and mouthed 'Thanks' as he opened the car door. Standing for a second he looked at the house where Sandra had lived and been brought up until she came into his life. Getting in the car and setting off for home he looked in the mirror to check on Caroline, seeing Diane headed down the garden path, and closing the Front door behind her as life moved on.

Holding Caroline's spare hand as she held her bouquet of flowers, Dave opened the unlocked door of 15 Windy Hill Street and stopping to take her jacket off at the door, he handed her back her flowers and said "There's a surprise in the kitchen darling!" and without a seconds thought she went into the kitchen to find Jackie nursing a cup of tea. Looking back at Dave, Caroline turned back to Jackie who was now nervously looking at Dave. "Do you like my flowers Jackie?" and bending down she replied "Very much, they're very pretty, shall we put them in some water?" and with a nodded yes Jackie looked around for a vase to put them in, but was beaten to it by Dave who handed her a short vase from the cupboard behind him. "Let's put your flowers on the table, and then we can arrange them in the vase" she added filling the vase halfway with water from the tap and placing it on the table. Taking a seat Jackie was a little surprised to see Caroline immediately move a chair and put it next to her. Sitting next to Jackie, Caroline smiled at her before concentrating on undoing the now soggy Kirkdale Times to release her newly picked flowers. Watching as the trainee flower arrangers spent 5 minutes filling the vase, Dave stayed watching with his back to a cupboard as finally the job was done, and Jackie moving the vase into the centre of the table, wrapped the soggy mess that remained and stood up to put it in the bin. Looking up at Dave, a happy looking Caroline said "Look what me and Jackie have made daddy!"

The day had got off to a good start and despite a degree of nervousness, the plan for the day had been to keep to something of the routine Dave and Caroline had got used to. So with a walk in mind and the late April sun shining, it was just after 1pm when they set off for the Northfield Reservoir walk with Caroline holding Dave's hand walking between him and Jackie. After they had turned left at the end of Windy Hill Street, Caroline took hold of Jackie's hand and checking it was alright by looking up as Jackie looked down, they smiled at each other and a long forgotten memory jumped into Caroline's mind as they headed for the path to Northfield Reservoir. Almost silently they made it onto the circular path around Northfield Reservoir and seeing the newly installed playground where the swings were empty, Caroline let go of both hands and set off to try them out missing Jackie and Dave catching a kiss, and with no Caroline, they held hands as they followed her to the sparsely occupied playground where she was already on a swing but struggling to get moving. "Daddy, push me!" came the call and as his parental duties kicked in, he let go of Jackie's hand when they arrived behind Caroline. Giving Jackie another quick kiss behind Caroline's back, he pushed her until she said "Enough daddy!" and watching his daughter go back and forward on the swing, like his life since Sandra died, he took Jackie's hand, and stood watching Caroline as his life returned to some sort of normality after two years.

The afternoon continued with a bit of routine as Caroline got her Ice Cream on the walk round Northfield Reservoir and finally making it home after 3pm it was time for Dave to have a chat with Caroline about Jackie, having made drinks they sat at the kitchen table as Caroline admired her flowers in the vase in the centre of the table. "Caroline, I want to tell you about Jackie being here today, and well, what it means for the future" seeing he had her attention he continued "Jackie and I like each other.... a lot, and we're going to be seeing each other, so I wanted you to know that. You do like Jackie don't you?" after a moment's hesitation she replied "Is Jackie going to be your girlfriend daddy?" Looking at Jackie for a second he turned back to reply "Yes darling she is my girlfriend!" and as she started giggling she said "Daddy's got a girlfriend, daddy's got a girlfriend" in rhyme, and as Jackie burst out laughing, it was a few seconds before Dave caught up and joined in, pointing his finger at his cheeky daughter in admonishment, but giving up almost immediately as he knew she was right, he did indeed have a girlfriend.

Teatime came around and with a Chinese ordered Dave went to collect it, to leaving Caroline and Jackie alone to set the table for tea. As Caroline got the knives and forks and Jackie found the plate cupboard the table was soon set, with the vase of flowers still taking pride of place in the centre. "Shall we have some serviettes Caroline?" Jackie said as she found an un-opened pack in the plate cupboard adding "I'll show you how to fold them into shapes if you like!" With a smile Caroline stood next to Jackie and after a few attempts at folding, on the fourth go Jackie managed to help to get Caroline to make a fan shape that with a bit of luck would last until Dave got back with the Chinese, to go with the two that she had man-aged to make herself. Placing them on the plates it wasn't long before Jackie heard the door of the Jaguar close, and quickly she said to Caroline "Let's sit down so we are ready!" taking her instruction from Jackie they were both seated as Dave came into the kitchen with a bag full of Chinese takeaway. Seeing the table set and the serviettes he said "You've been busy, the table looks beautiful, wow serviettes as well, who's for Chinese?" putting the bag on the drainer and taking out the containers, he missed the look between Caroline and Jackie that said so much without words. The evening slid into the night and at 9.30 Dave said it was time for bed and with a slight look of disappointment Caroline got off the sofa where she had been sat between Dave and Jackie, kissing Dave on the lips with her arms around his neck she was halfway to the door when she turned back and did the same to a slightly shocked Jackie, and as Jackie recovered she managed to say "Goodnight Caroline, see you in the morning!" and with that Caroline went up the stairs to bed, leaving Dave and Jackie to fill the little gap on the sofa between them, as their first day as a family ended successfully.

Dave was in the shower on Sunday morning and as he returned to the bedroom with a towel around his waist, he was stopped in his tracks as he entered the bedroom where he had left a sleeping Jackie. Propped up in his place with Jackie's arm around her was a beaming Caroline "Good morning daddy!" she said before bursting out in laughter nuzzling closer to Jackie, as she looked at Dave with an 8 year old still laughing at her own sense of humour under her arm. "I thought it was you, but found this little lady getting into bed instead. So as you are up can you put the kettle on, and shall we have some toast Caroline?" with a nod from a half covered head she added "Yes we'll have some toast and jam as well please!" As Dave knew he had lost this battle, he quickly put on some clothes, making his way down the stairs, he shook his head at the ease with which Jackie had fallen into his and Caroline's life, until his feet hit the cold kitchen floor and he set about his instructions putting together a tray as the kettle boiled. Loading the tray with two mugs of tea and a glass of orange juice he waited until the toaster popped up. Buttering and then spreading Strawberry Jam on the toast he cut them into diagonals and placed them on a plate already on the tray. Picking up the tray, as his feet grew used to the cold, he carefully made his way back up the stairs to his bedroom where he found Jackie reading Caroline a story as he entered the bedroom "Room service!" Dave announced putting the tray down on the side cabinet next to Caroline. Handing Caroline her drink of orange juice with an obligatory "Be careful!" he placed the plate of toast on top of Jackie's legs before placing a mug of tea on the side cabinet next to Jackie, saying quietly so that Caroline wouldn't hear "Not what I had in mind for this morning!" Looking at Caroline who had her glass of orange in one hand and a slice of toast in the other, Jackie looked back at Dave and replied "Well boyfriend, I think this is just perfect!" Standing watching he took a drink of his tea and had to agree as the women in his life demolished his toast and jam without another word, but an occasional look at each other, just as Sandra had once done.

The week leading up to the second anniversary of the Archive Chambers fire, and the death of Sandra and Sam Brown was no different as far as Dave was concerned, he had his routine and it wasn't until Jackie knocked on his door on Wednesday night that it really hit him. Opening the door at 9pm he was a little surprised to see Jackie standing there, but quickly he said "Come in, this is a nice surprise" as Jackie went past him without a kiss, he was no longer sure, but closing the door and following her into the Lounge he sat down next to her on the sofa. Taking her hand he looked at her face that was giving nothing away until she said "I'm not sure I can go to the Memorial on Friday for Sandra, it just feels like I am trying to take her place and Caroline will be thinking of her mum .... and I'm not her mum!" sitting back, Dave took a few seconds before he could think of the words to say which he hoped were the right ones. "I can understand what you are saying, but I would really like you to come, and I'm sure Caroline would as well, but as it's two days away why don't you sleep on it and if you still feel the same on Friday ring me in the morning. What do you say?" squeezing his hand she nodded and standing up said "Okay let me sleep on it! I'd better go, I just wanted to tell you rather than ring you" heading towards the door with Dave following, she opened it and turned to face Dave and kissing him tenderly on the lips she said "Are we okay boyfriend?" as she held the door open. "Yes we are okay girlfriend. Sometimes life just throws a spanner in the works and gets in the way!" Leaving the door open she headed for her car leaving Dave to close the door wondering what more life could throw at him.

Friday the 6th May came and by lunchtime Dave hadn't heard from Jackie and picking up Caroline from Northfield School after lunchtime, he decided to give life a chance and trusting in his own judgement he didn't call Jackie at work, but concentrated on getting Caroline dressed up, as much as you can for an 8 year old to attend her mum's Memorial. With her hair brushed and a dark coat on Dave was just polishing her black shoes when there was a knock on the door. "I'll get it daddy" said the shoeless Caroline as she headed for the door. Opening the door she found Jackie stood looking at her "Wow, daddy has been busy, you look very smart young lady!" Delighted at the complement and the sight of Jackie, Caroline turned to tell her dad, but Dave was already stood in the hallway with a polish brush in one hand and a shoe on the other. As he smiled at her she said "I slept on it, now give me those and go and get yourself ready, while I deal with this very pretty young lady!" Without a spanner in the works, Dave headed upstairs to put on his suit and happy with his appearance, he found two very pretty young ladies chatting in the kitchen on his return. "Ready" he announced and picking up his car keys, he opened the Front door and let Caroline go first before Jackie joined him at the door, where he quickly gave her a kiss which wasn't spoiled in the least by the "Yuk!" from Caroline as she spotted them. Jackie put her arm in Dave's as they made the short walk to Northfield Cemetery with Caroline holding Dave's hand on the other side.

The Memorial Service went as well as could be expected and

despite many tears the pain of the first Memorial Service weren't repeated. As it was a joint service Sam Brown's parents were there with their small family, and as they filtered out of the service Jackie went over and gave Sam's mother Ann Brown a hug, after a few words they parted and she returned to where a slightly confused Dave stood and seeing the puzzled look she said "I went to school with Sam, he was a nice boy, used to get into trouble for smoking, Silky we used to nickname him! His mum still can't believe he had anything.... well you know?" after they had made their way out of the cemetery the Robertson and Baxter families stopped for a drink at The Murg, but after a couple of drinks the general consensus was that it was time to go home at 5pm and with hugs and handshakes all round the two families left Dave, Jackie and Caroline to their own devices, with a promise to meet up next weekend. Finishing their drinks Jackie took Caroline to the toilet as Dave pondered what to have for tea. "How about fish and chips for tea" he said as they returned to a scowl from both. "Pizza and chips for us, and chicken and chips for Caroline" Jackie said, and not really bothered he shrugged his shoulders and said "Fine by me girls!" Taking Caroline's hand, Dave looked at Jackie and said quietly "Thanks for today, it meant a lot!" Taking his spare hand they walked to the local Pizza Takeaway and ordering their choices and with a couple of cans of coke thrown in, they sat waiting for the meal to be cooked and Dave asked Jackie about something that had been bugging him since the service, as Caroline tried to read the large menu board "Why did they call Sam Silky?" "Because he always smoked Silk Cut, silly!" and suddenly, in a Pizza Takeaway in Northfield, finally the Jigsaw fitted.

When the meals were ready Dave paid, and they walked home with Dave holding the meals and Jackie holding Caroline's hand, listening to her say she wanted a Margaret Pizza next time which kept them both amused, as Jackie tried to explain her accidental joke. While Dave put the food on plates

Jackie and Caroline went upstairs. As a pyjama clad Caroline came downstairs, Dave was stood looking out of the kitchen window with the food on the table, and choosing her chicken and chips, she sat down and started to fill her empty stomach. Realising he was no longer alone, he turned and asked "Where's Jackie darling?" and before she could answer Jackie came into the kitchen with a holdall from her car "I packed a few things for the weekend. I thought you might like the company!" Seeing the look on her face, his old humour resurfaced from nowhere "But where are you going to sleep?" he asked "Silly daddy!" came the sudden interruption from Caroline, "Jackie can sleep in your bed!" before returning to her chicken and chips. Jackie looked at Dave and said "Is that alright?" Jackie questioned "Only, if you eat all your tea!" he replied with a look, his humour let loose. Sitting down she set about the Pepperoni Pizza taking a slice with a smile, and reaching for Dave's hand under the table, as he sat down next to her. With the meals finished and the table cleared they made their way into the Lounge, and turning on the TV they settled down for a night of average TV on a very un-average day as Caroline slowly fell asleep between them.

Waking up next to Dave was now almost accepted on a Saturday morning, but Jackie was surprised to find him already up at just after 7am. Putting on a pink nightie, she went downstairs to find him sat at the kitchen table, with an odd looking piece of paper infront of him, a mug of tea in his left hand and a pencil in his right hand. "Morning!" she said as she came into the kitchen. As he looked up, he said "You look beautiful in that!" "You should see me out of it!" she speedily replied, but realising his heart wasn't in it, she changed tack "Is something wrong Dave?" as he said "It was something you said last night!" suddenly realising she might misconstrue his comment he immediately added "Sorry, it was what you said about Sam Brown and his nickname" Moving a chair next to him she sat down and looked at the paper infront of him, seeing various doodles and dates and boxes she asked the question that up until last night he wouldn't have been able to answer, but now felt he could. "What does it all mean?" taking a few seconds to finish his tea he answered without looking at her as he stared at paper Jigsaw and the truth. "It means Sandra.........and Sam were murdered by Daniel Bruce, and there's absolutely nothing I can do about it!"

♦ ♦ ♦

Chapter 25 - The Jigsaw

"You can't be serious!" Jackie said staring at the paper adding "Murdered! Daniel Bruce!" shaking his head Dave replied "There's no other explanation. It all fits together, I know it seems farfetched, but when I tell you what I know it will make sense, the problem is what to do next!" returning to the paper Jigsaw, he sat for a few minutes as he tried and failed to find a flaw in his Jigsaw as Jackie made another two mugs of tea, and sat down to look at the paper again. "I just can't....." Jackie was halfway through saying, when a half awake Caroline came into the kitchen "I heard voices" she said and as Jackie automatically picked her up and put her on her knee, she said "Do you want toast or Sugar Puffs?" with "Puffs" the one word answer, Jackie put Caroline on her seat and went to get a bowl of Sugar Puffs, adding milk, she placed them with a spoon infront of a now more wide awake Caroline, she then returned her gaze on the paper Jigsaw, as silence returned to the kitchen. "Can I have some orange juice please?" broke the silence as Caroline finished her Sugar Puffs, and as Jackie went to the fridge she picked up 3 glasses, and placing them all on the table Dave just managed to pick up his Jigsaw paper, as Caroline spilt some orange juice. Taking it as a sign Dave said "I'll put this away, maybe we can discuss it tonight, you're staying tonight aren't you?" with a quick look at Caroline she replied "Yes, I wouldn't want to miss breakfast in bed with this one!" and kissing Caroline's head just like Sandra used to do, the new routine was set as Jackie went to get a shower to try to clear her mind of the thoughts going round her head, not quite the early morning awakening she was expecting.

Sitting in the kitchen, Jackie was daydreaming when Dave and

Caroline came downstairs. Hearing the noise of feet, she felt the arms of Caroline around her waist and turning she saw a fully dressed young lady. "Well someone is ready for a day out, where are you ....." and seeing the look of disappointment on Caroline's face she smiled, and added "Just teasing, where are we going?" and with a big smile, she shouted "Seaside!" and Saturday was settled and the Jigsaw paper on the sideboard, forgotten for the time being. With a towel, blanket and a wind break in the boot, they set off for Scarborough as the sun broke through the clouds as they left Kirkdale. Jackie had decided to sit in the back of the Jaguar to keep Caroline company, and as Dave was now relegated to the role of Chauffer he steered the car towards the York bypass, with the radio drowning out the chatter from the backseats. Despite leaving the paper Jigsaw at home, it was implanted on his mind, as they cruised towards their destination. By the time they arrived in Scarborough he had got no further in his quest to make a decision on his Jigsaw and finding a parking space in the North Shore car park he turned the engine off, and with it his attention turned to the passengers, who hadn't stopped talking all the way from home.

Dave as always had a plan, leaving the car they made for Peasome Park, and the boating lake. Choosing a boat that resembled a swan with a long neck at the front, Dave took control of the oars and with his passengers on board, the ticket seller pushed them off and they made their way out onto the water. Sitting facing Caroline and Jackie he pulled at the oars as he steered a course around the island, his mind wondering at how easy Jackie was with Caroline, even though it had only been 3 months since they had got together after a chance meeting on her 30th Birthday, he felt she was filling a huge gap in his, and now Caroline's life. Would it be too soon to ask her to move in, he was thinking until a shout of "Daddy!" cut through his thoughts as they were headed directly for the island, his attention momentarily elsewhere. Firmly hitting the shore, Dave said "Sorry about that", he managed to push the boat off the island with an oar, and as they drifted backwards into the lake Jackie said with a hint of humour "Do you want me to have a go?" taking a few seconds to settle the boat, he replied "Yes, feel free!" and carefully swapping seats he sat next to Caroline and put his arm around her, as Jackie took up the oars and with ease steered them around the rest of the island and into free water. "Very impressive Captain Jackie" Dave said, as Caroline started giggling and they slowly made a full circuit of the lake, until they came back to the dock. Getting off the boat first, Dave helped Caroline out of the boat, and reached out for Jackie's hand as she stepped off the boat. Stumbling a little as another boat knocked their swan boat, she fell into Dave and taking his chance he kissed her for the first time today, to the sound of "Yuk!" as Caroline watched from the safety of the pier. Turning to see Caroline with a grimace on her face, they looked at each other and with an uncanny, unspoken agreement, they both set off to chase her towards the exit catching up with her in only a few steps, as she shrieked before finding herself in mid air, as they took a hand each and swung her between them. Taking the footpath to the beach, Dave left Jackie with Caroline eagerly looking at the Ice Cream Kiosk, as he went back to the Jaguar and got the blanket, towel and windbreak. Returning with them under each arm, he saw Jackie had bought Caroline a 99 Ice Cream with red sauce and was holding two more. "I wasn't sure what to get you, but everyone likes a 99!" with both his hands spoken for, she gently took one of the 99's and dabbed it on his nose, leaving a white smear of Ice Cream, which seemed to be the funniest thing Caroline had ever seen, as she shrieked even louder than before. Dropping the towel, blanket and windbreaker on the beach he took the offending 99 from her and wiping his now cold nose he responded "I'll make you pay for that!" with a wicked smile that he was getting used to, she replied out of the earshot of Caroline "Promises, promises!" Spreading out the blanket, and putting up the windbreaker they settled down to enjoy their ice creams as the May sun finally caught up from Kirkdale.

With their Ice Creams finished Dave and Jackie lay back on the blanket and watched as Caroline took of her shoes and socks and after jumping around, she made her way to the sea as Dave sat up on his elbow and watched her run towards the incoming waves, and then run even faster back as the cold water touched her toes. "She's going to break someone's heart when she grows up!" Jackie said, seeing Dave sat up watching his daughter. "You may be right there, but he'll probably deserve it!" and turning to look at Jackie, he gently leaned down to kiss her to which she responded, but after a few seconds he returned to watch Caroline at the seashore saying "That was nice girlfriend, I bet you've broken a few hearts!" after a little silence, she replied "That's history, I'm only interested in mending hearts now!" Taking his hand, she kissed it tenderly, and linking fingers they sat in silence until Caroline, who after 20 minutes, had finally had enough of chasing, and being chased by waves, landed between them with a smile, before being picked up by Dave and sitting her on his knee, he dried her feet as best he could, before putting on her socks and shoes. "Who's for some lunch then?" he said squeezing Caroline until she wriggled free, and took Jackie's hand. Standing looking at them for a second for no apparent reason saving the memory, he snapped out of his thoughts and gathered up their bits and pieces. Reaching the Jaguar he put their stuff in the boot, and locking the car they set off for the long walk along the promenade to the centre and lunch. Choosing a little cafe on a back street they ordered cheese toasties and chips for their lunch, and sitting back they awaited their meals as their drinks arrived. With a Strawberry milkshake in front of her Caroline's attention was taken as Dave took Jackie's hand under the table and said "Enjoying yourself girlfriend?" looking directly at him she replied "I could get used to this......boyfriend!" and squeezing his hand, she leant in to give him a kiss not unseen by Caroline, but not commented upon this time, as she tackled her Strawberry milkshake which was far more important.

With an obligatory visit to the slot machines and after buying some rock for Granddad Baxter, the small fun fair by the harbour gave Caroline time to enjoy herself before the journey home. After three rides, it was a smiling Caroline who came hurtling down the Helter Skelter, and into the arms of Dave, as Jackie stood watching quietly, wondering just where this was going. Feeling a tug on her hand, she looked down to see Caroline intimating she needed to speak to her. Bending down to hear what she had to say, it came as no surprise when she said "I need to go to the Toilet" straightening up, she kept hold of her hand, and quickly said "Excuse us, girl time!" as they headed across the road to the Toilet. Dave stood watching as they disappeared inside, as a decision slowly formed under the squawk of the seagulls overhead. Sitting Caroline in the back on her own for the journey home with a stick of Candyfloss to keep her amused, Jackie sat watching the road as the Jaguar smoothly ate up the miles to home. Looking behind her to find Caroline asleep with half the stick of Candyfloss stuck to her jumper, Jackie leaned back and took the sticky mess from her and managed to wrap it in a tissue without making too much mess, and without waking her. Seeing his daughter asleep Dave quietly said "Do you want to talk or snooze?" wondering where he was going with the question, despite feeling a bit sleepy, she said "I'm fine, we can talk, what's on your mind?" taking his left hand off the steering wheel for a second he felt for and found her hand. "Let me finish, and then feel free to ask away!" Putting his hand back on the steering wheel he started, as once he had done before, to outline a plan that he hoped Jackie would understand. "Thanks for coming to the Memorial Services, I know it can't have been easy but I do appreciate it, and thanks for staying over, it meant a lot. It's been two years since Sandra died and although I could never replace her, when I met you on your

Birthday, and we got along, and well over the last three months I feel we have got a lot closer, and I know the next step will be a big one, but I wanted you to at least think about it as we have some time, but with the way you get on with Sleeping Beauty in the back and the way she has taken to you. Well what I am trying to say is that when you first met her, she invited you to her next Birthday Party, which incidentally is on the 27th July and I thought it would be nice if you moved in with me ....I mean us before then. So what do you think?" with the evening turning dark he waited as the headlights caught the road for her reply. "So basically after all that, what you're asking is will I move in with you? Is that it?" slightly hurt by her abrupt reply he said rather timidly "Well yes!" "But where will I sleep?" she rapidly answered, with a fake questioning look on her face, that he caught in the streetlights, and he got his answer without a word as they neared Kirkdale and home.

"I'll get Caroline" said Jackie as they pulled up outside 15, Windy Hill Street. Opening the back door she managed to get her out of the car without waking her, and following Dave down the garden path, she went past him as he opened the door and took her straight upstairs to her bed, only returning downstairs when she was happy that she had settled." I thought you had gone to bed" said Dave, as she joined him on the sofa in the Lounge, "Well if you ask nicely!" she quickly replied, with that wicked smile that she could turn on in an instant. Putting his arm around her he pulled her closer, and she settled next to him before quietly saying "You sure about me moving in, it's not like there's just us, there's Sleeping Beauty to think of as well. What if it doesn't work out, I'd really miss her!" Moving his head he kissed her tenderly on the lips, with his face a few inches from hers he replied "When you get to know me better you'll find that if I put my mind to something I usually succeed" pulling her close until their lips met, he kissed her more passionately until after a few minutes, he pulled away from her and stood up, as he said with a smile "It's been a long day I think we should have an early night!" and as he took her hand to help her up she relied "And early morning!" with her wicked smile.

Sunday came and went, and on a walk around Northfield Reservoir, Jackie said out of nowhere, as Caroline played on the swings "I've thought about what you said about Daniel Bruce and the fire and I think you should either get onto the Police, or maybe get a Private Detective to see if there is a link, you're a Surveyor, not a Detective, let the professionals deal with it!" Looking quizzically at her, he thought for a second or two, and replied squeezing her hand "Not just a pretty face then!" After Jackie had left and gone home after tea, with lots of hugs and kisses from Caroline, and a slap on the bottom from Dave, he was left alone once Caroline was tucked up in bed, with the Jigsaw paper he had been avoiding. Sitting in the Lounge with a bottle of Lager it made complete sense. Daniel had attacked him at Christmas 1982 in revenge for him and Sandra getting together at the Council Christmas Party, of that he was sure. The Archive Chambers fire has a conversation that Ian the Malt Shovel Manager's overheard about Daniel not getting caught. The packet of Embassy cigarettes in Sam Brown's pocket, but Silk Cut cigarettes in his locker, and his nickname Silky, it could be that he had just bought another packet, but smokers as far as he knew from people that did smoke, never changed their brand. All of that he could be reasonably sure of, but if Daniel Bruce did start the fire the big question remained why. That only left Anderson Developments and the meeting in the Malt Shovel with Steve Parker, when Daniel was supposed to be off work. Michael Anderson of Anderson Developments paid for their tab. Brian the Barber, and his Leisure Center comments, and then Tony saying that they were printing brochures and documents for Anderson Developments. The Archive Chambers rebuild which was due to be finished this month was done by Anderson Developments. The report on the Manchester Road Power Station that took Daniel weeks to produce, and was done at a time when the Malt Shovel meeting with Michael Anderson took place. Sitting back to take another swig from his bottle it jumped out of the page and taking his pen he drew a circle round every Anderson Developments mention and with 5 circles, he added Anderson Developments working with Kirkdale Council and circled it making 6 circles. Looking at the paper he knew there was something else but couldn't manage to reach it in his mind, so getting another bottle of Lager he sat down and started at the beginning and had got to Sam Brown the second time around, when he suddenly remembered the suspension of Daniel because Sam had allowed a file hidden by Daniel be accidentally found by Eric Normanton "Oh shit!" Dave said out loud, as he wrote down the subject of the suspension, Manchester Road Power Station, adding Anderson Developments and circling it he added the number 7, before putting the paper Jigsaw down and taking a long drink.

So that was it, he thought. It's all about money. Daniel and Michael Anderson must be working together. They seemed to be getting more than their fair share on contracts with Kirkdale Council, and if they got the Manchester Road site it would be worth tens of millions. Daniel would get his own back on Sam for the accidental folder suspension, but what the hell did Sandra have to do with it? Stuck with a question unanswered, Dave finally gave up and went to bed, alone for the first time since Thursday night, and despite a difficult night's sleep, he woke early with a nagging feeling he was missing something as he got Caroline ready for school. "Did you have a nice weekend darling?" he asked as she finished off her toast and jam "Yes daddy, I like Jackie she's nice" almost ignoring her comment he took her plate and said "So you wouldn't mind if she spent more time here, and maybe even moved in sometime in the future?" sensing this was an important conversation, she replied "Will she be my new mummy?" kneeling down next to her he took her hand and looking straight at her he replied "Sandra will always be your mummy darling, Jackie can never replace her, but she would like to get to know you better, and living here would make that easier, maybe in time you could call her mummy but that will be up to you" a silence came over the kitchen as she took it all in, before answering "Okay daddy" adding "Will it make you happy if she lives here?" wondering where she was going with her question, he replied quickly "Yes darling, it would make me happy!" and putting her arms around his neck, he heard her quietly say "Love you daddy!" and a little tear came down his cheek as he held the worldly wise 8 year old, that Sandra left to look after him.

With the emotional breakfast over, Dave walked Caroline to Northfield School and as his thoughts returned to the problem of the paper Jigsaw on the walk home, he let himself into the house and putting the kettle on, he took out the piece of paper the school had given him this morning with dates for the next month of school activities, he realised he hoped Jackie would move in sooner, rather than later. Taking a pen he went to the 5 year Calendar on the wall and as he put the first activity in a week's time on Tuesday 17th May, the Calendar finally fell off the nail that had been hanging there for the last three years. Picking up the Calendar as the kettle clicked off, it had fallen open on May 1992, and there in Sandra's writing was 'Research Manchester Road PS' on the 5th May 1992 circled in Red. The tears ran down his face, as he finally had the key to the Jigsaw. The key was their research into Manchester Road Power Station, with Daniel Bruce sat in Eric Normanton's Office listening as he asked for permission. Slamming his hand down hard on the table he couldn't believe he hadn't seen it before "Idiot, Idiot, Idiot" he said to himself, over and over until the anger inside him reached out, and buried his previous guilt. Leaving the Calendar on the table he went to his briefcase in the Lounge and taking out his diary he looked back to May 4th 1992 and there it was 'Ok from Eric re Research MRPS'. Replacing the diary he looked around the room and seeing the family picture on the wall, he mouthed "Sorry" and turning, he picked his briefcase up and left the Lounge, stopping to pick up his completed paper Jigsaw from the kitchen, he took his coat from the rack as he headed out of the door and pulling the door closed, he locked it, and slowly and deliberately he set off up the garden path to where his Jaguar was parked. Unlocking the car door and settling into the drivers east he turned the ignition key and slowly made his way to his office, and by the time he had arrived he had another very serious plan forming in his mind.

On arriving at his office, he placed all his information on his desk, before scribbling a few notes on a separate piece of paper. Picking up the local Phone Directory he found Sam Brown's parents phone number and adding it to the paper he rang and after four rings Ann Brown answered. After a few difficult pleasantries, he got to the point of his call and asked the question that if the answer was no, his whole plan would fall at the first hurdle. "I know I still keep certain things of Sandra's and I wondered if you kept any of Sam's things after the fire?" he asked hoping he crossed his fingers as he waited for her answer "Yes I kept everything of Sam's, it's all in the attic, why do you ask?" as the question he knew off by heart entered his mind he asked "Including his cigarettes?" after a moments silence he heard the reply he wanted "Everything, I still believe he didn't do it, but no one else seems to think the same. He was a good boy was Sam. Why are you asking now after two years?" Lost for what to say as his emotions took over he replied "I just think something is wrong, but there's no evidence according to the Police, so I thought I would look into it myself that's all" before he could say anything else, he heard her say "If you need to look at Sam's stuff you just give me a call. I never liked that Detective Sergeant Wilson, he was too quick to make a decision for my liking, he never looked at any of Sam's stuff, had him guilty before he was buried, even though the Coroner Dr. Pritchard gave a Misadventure verdict. You let me know how you get on Mr Baxter!" and she hung up. Sitting back he was amazed she had remember everyone's name, he certainly couldn't remember Detective Sergeant Wilson. Twiddling with his pen he scribbled a few additional notes and stuck for where to go next, he picked up the Phone Directory and looking under the heading Private Investigators, he ran down the small list with his pen, settling on Stirling Investigations in nearby Huddersfield. Picking up the phone he explained he would like to meet to discuss a case and with an appointment set up for Wednesday with Mr Williams, he set about his workload for the day and week ahead, adding the appointment in his diary out of habit.

Wednesday soon came and armed will copies of all his evidence, as well as a summary of why he thought there was a case for investigation he parked on a side street, and finding the Offices of Sterling Investigations he was shown into a small office by a pleasant Receptionist where Mr Williams sat looking at some files on his desk as Dave was announced, Mr Baxter, Mr Williams. Starting with the Archive Chambers fire, Dave worked backwards and forwards, until he was sure he had covered everything. Taking a few minutes to study the papers Dave had brought, Mr Williams eventually sat back and said "So Mr Baxter you think the deaths of your wife Sandra and Mr Sam Brown are connected with this Daniel Bruce, and he is connected to Anderson Developments?" Hoping he had got a good grasp of the situation he answered "Yes basically that's right!" and after a few seconds Mr Williams added "Well it's a little tenuous and circumstantial, but if you want us to investigate, it we will. But it could take some time and some money. The first part is to investigate the actual deaths and get the Police to reopen the case. That may be possible with the cigarette scenario, hard to believe the Police didn't look into that. The difficulty will be the hearsay evidence and linking Daniel Bruce to not only to the fire, but also his motive, which you are sure is linked to Anderson Development Ltd and Michael Anderson" nodding his head Dave said "Yes that's how I see it" pausing for a few second Mr Williams stood up and shook Dave's hand and said "If you could sign our Terms of Business, I will get onto it this week. It's a shame there are no records, but then if it wasn't for the fire, there'd be no deaths" he added answering his own question. "Will weekly reporting, be sufficient to go on with?" he finished, and as Dave signed the Terms of Business that would take a chunk of his money, he walked out of the Offices of Sterling Investigations, to get on with his life.

May soon petered out and with the weekly reports from Sterling Investigations basically going over the ground Dave had already covered, he wondered where his money was going, but Jackie always said that if they rush, they might miss something, like she knew what she was talking about. With the weather improving the weekends became a happy time for them, and with trips to various parks as well as their regular walk around Northfield Reservoir where on Saturday the 18th of June, Dave broached the subject that he hoped Jackie would have mentioned before now as they approached the Ice Cream shop. Letting Caroline go to the shop with a £1 coin, they waited outside to see what Ice Cream she would choose "Jackie, have you changed your mind about moving in?" he asked with an element of concern. "Not a chance boyfriend, the lease on my house is up on the 30th so I'm all yours from two weeks on Friday, if you still want me that is!" she replied. With a smile appearing on his face he managed to say "I think I proved that this morning!" just as Caroline came out of the Ice Cream shop with a Rocket Ice Lolly. Bending down to take the wrapper off for her, Jackie looked at Dave as she stood up and replied "No complaints here!" and giving him a kiss as Caroline concentrated on her Rocket Ice Lolly she added "Looking forward to waking up next to you everyday .....boyfriend!" and with her hand in his, she took Caroline's spare hand as her tongue turned orange, and they set off for home and their new life together.

Moving in day came, and with some help from Sid and Jane, they were all done by mid afternoon and deserving of some reward for their endeavours they went to the Bedlow Arms for tea, with a very happy Dave offering to pay the bill for his 'Labourers' which after changing the title to 'Relocation Assistants' they accepted. Sitting down and choosing from the menu, which they knew almost off by heart, Jackie was asking Caroline what she wanted, when she heard a voice from work "Hello Jackie!" she heard as her boss Adrian and his wife stopped by their table "Adrian hi, let me introduce you, this is my sister Jane and her boyfriend Sid, and this beautiful young lady is Dave's daughter Caroline. What brings you here today?" Dave stood up, and shook Adrian's hand after Adrian had introduced his wife Angela. Saying to his wife "Angela, can you get our table and I'll be with you in a moment, I'd just like a quick word with Dave here!" as she left to find their table, Adrian took Dave to one side and out of hearing of the others said "Dave, I wonder if you can come in and see me next week, I have something that has been bugging me, and I'd like your input and advice, does Tuesday morning suit?" with a seconds thought Dave replied "Would 10.30 suit?" quickly Adrian replied "Fine, see you Tuesday then, must find Angela, said I wouldn't mention business, thanks" and he left to find Angela, sitting slightly annoyed at a far table As Dave sat down with the waiter leaving, the others having already ordered "I ordered you the Meat Pie and Chips, is that okay?" Jackie said as he sat down "Perfect!" he said taking a second to wonder what Adrian could possibly want.

With Caroline sat between them eating her sausage and mash, it was only after they had finished their meals that Jackie got a chance to ask Dave what Adrian wanted as Caroline went to the Toilet "To be honest I don't know, he just wants to meet about something that's been bugging him so I'm seeing him on

Tuesday" and a Caroline returned just in time to see her Chocolate Ice Cream arrive, the conversation switched to general chat between Sid and Dave, and Jane and Jackie as they caught up on their personal lives over pudding. Once the plates had been taken away they finished off their drinks, and with hugs and back slaps they parted, heading back to Jackie's new home at 15 Windy Hill with Jackie sat next to Caroline in the back of the Jaguar, they pulled up next to Jackie's Peugot. Getting out first, Jackie helped Caroline out of the car, but as soon as she was on the ground she went and took Dave's hand leaving Jackie a little confused. A few seconds later, Caroline returned and took Jackie's hand and a little confused and unaware of what was happening, they made their way to the Front door of No 15 where they waited for Dave to finish locking the Jaguar and let them in. A tug on her hand made Jackie look down to Caroline who had a huge grin on her face and was holding up a key in her other hand. "We got this for you!" and taking the key from her hand, with a fob that had "Home" printed on it, she opened the door of 15 Windy Hill Street for the first time.

The weekend went fast as Jackie settled in, and she and Caroline got to know each other even more. After managing the first Monday at work from her new home, Jackie got home to find Caroline and Dave had made a tea of chicken and chips. Once tea had been finished Dave started to put the dishes on the drainer when Jackie interrupted "Let me, you deal with Caroline and I'll get these done" With the plates washed and on the drainer, Jackie looked around the kitchen and with an idea in her head, she dried her hands and went to sit in the Lounge to await Dave and Caroline joining her, after Caroline's bath. "Hello gorgeous, you smell nice!" she said as Caroline sat next to her on the sofa. Picking up the first book from the pile on the coffee table, she opened the book and listened as Caroline tried to read it, and with a little help from Jackie, they finished 'The Thing in the Sink', before Jackie took her to bed and after reading 'Jolly Snow', she kissed her goodnight, tucked her in, and went to join Dave in the Lounge. Finding him listening to Eric Clapton's Unplugged, she settled down next to him on the sofa and taking his hand said "She'll be asleep in a bit" changing the subject completely she added "What do you think about getting a dishwasher?" just a 'Rollin' and Tumblin' finished. "Beg your pardon!" he responded having missed the beginning of the sentence "I said, what do you think about getting a dishwasher, you don't want me to ruin my soft hands, do you!" she repeated stroking his arm with her free hand. "Oh no, we don't want to ruin your soft hands!" he replied, as he kissed the palm of her free hand "But you also need plenty of sleep to keep your hands soft, and standing up he pulled her up from the sofa to stand next to him. Letting go of her hand he put both his hands on her bottom and pulling her into him, he kissed her passionately and squeezing her bottom he said into her ear "Let's see who's got the softest hands!" Leading her upstairs, past the now sleeping Caroline's bedroom, he quietly closed the bedroom door behind them, as they found a better use for Monday night than Panorama.

Tuesday came, and after dropping off Caroline at Northfield School, Dave took the route that Jackie had taken an hour before, as he headed for Ramsden Construction, on the outskirts of Town. Arriving early he found a cafe nearby and sitting sipping a mug of coffee, he tried to figure out what Adrian wanted to see him about. Without getting anywhere, he took the Monday morning post he had been given by the Postman that he had crossed paths with, on his way home this morning to pick up the Jaguar, out of his pocket and seeing the envelope franked with a Huddersfield stamp, he knew its sender and taking out the 4th report from Sterling Investigation he was a little disappointed to find that there was no progress on the cigarette packet issue, as Detective Sergeant Wilson had responded to their request to reopen the case with a short response that there wasn't enough to reopen the case based on their findings. The research into the connection of Daniel

Bruce and Anderson Developments Ltd was ongoing, but they hadn't found anything to link the two as yet, but would persevere and send the next report with hopefully some improvement. Mr Williams had also kindly enclosed the Invoice for Services for £800 plus VAT. Sitting looking at his money going down the drain, he finished his coffee and took the short journey to Ramsden Construction Offices and parked in the Visitor signed parking spot a few rows away from Jackie's old Peugot.

After signing in he was met at Reception by Adrian and after shaking hands, he led him towards his office, as he saw out of the corner of his eye Jackie hold her hand up, and raising his hand he mouthed 'Hi' before following Adrian into his office. Shutting the door after him Adrian immediately said "Take a seat Dave this has been bugging me for a long time and I need to get it off my chest. So if you are ready I'll start. For several years now we have been competing against Anderson Developments Ltd and while we won some and lost some, we got our fair share of work against them and some we didn't want anyway because we wouldn't have made any money. But over the last two years every time we have put in a Bid for work at Kirkdale Council, we have lost out to them. Sometimes, even though we were cheaper than them, for example the rebuilding of the Archive Chambers. So we did some investigation work and although it is hard to be 100% sure it looks like someone in Kirkdale Council is making sure that they win the Bids" with a gut feeling that he knew where this was going Dave let Adrian continue. "You presumably, will have heard that the Manchester Road Power Station site is due to close and be demolished as we go away from coal fired Power Stations. We have clients that are very interested in that site, as it is the last large site left in the Kirkdale area. The problems is that Kirkdale Council seems hell bent on a Leisure Centre being built there which will only take a small part of the site, and the work will go to Andersons which leaves a big question of what are they going to do with the rest of the site, and will

Andersons get the rest of the work?" taking a moment to have a drink Adrian realised he was so intent of having his say that he hadn't asked Dave if he wanted a drink. "Sorry, needed to get that off my chest Dave. Do you want a drink?"

Needing some time to collect his thoughts he replied "Just a glass of water would be fine" and as Adrian rang to get Reception to bring two glasses of water, Dave wondered where he was going to go with his response. "Interesting Adrian, I can see you think it looks strange that Andersons keep winning the Bids, but when you say you had some investigation work could you elaborate?" As the door opened and the Receptionist brought in two tall glasses of water she placed then on the desk and left without a word, closing the door behind her as Adrian said "We spent a small fortune on going through the Bids we had lost, and when there were any amendments to a project we put in a revised bid which was based on current industry costs, but every time we were undercut by exactly £1000.00 which looked suspicious, but we could never get a paper trail that proved it until we put in a ridiculous over the top bid for work on the Archive Chamber. Exactly a day after we put in a bid for £2.2 million Andersons came in with a £2,199,000 bid which was accepted. The fact that it was exactly £1,000 below our Bid, and our Bid was £100,000 over what it should have been, raised a red flag for us, and we have been trying to get to the bottom of it since then. I know this may be a bit close to the bone with the Archive Chambers and Sandra, but I thought you may be able to help!"

Sitting back in his chair Dave took a drink of water, and picking up his briefcase he took out his Diary and going back to 1993, he asked a question that he had a feeling he already had the answer to. "Adrian I can understand where you are coming from, but can I ask a couple of questions first?" seeing a glimmer of hope Adrian immediately said "Yes, please ask away!" and looking down at his Diary, Dave replied "What date was it when you put your Bid in for the Archive Chamber?"

Opening his desk diary Adrian replied "Dave, all bids had to be in by 12.00 on Thursday 4ᵗʰ February 1993 we sent ours in on the 4th" "And you got a stamped receipt?" Dave immediately asked, Adrian stopped for a second and picking up the phone he called Reception and asked for the Bid Receipt book for February 1993 "Do you think you've found something Dave?" Adrian asked as they waited for the Receptionist to appear "I don't know yet, but maybe. I did have 10 years at Kirkdale Council until ......" and letting the sentence hang a nagging question from years back came to the forefront of his thoughts. "I thought that the Manchester Road Power Station site would revert to its previous owners when the 50 year lease was up?" "Wow your well informed" Adrian immediately replied before adding "But according to my sources Kirkdale Council will inherit it at the end of the 50 years, or when the site is closed, whichever is the soonest. Apparently the previous ownership is impossible to trace after the Archive Fire" As the Receptionist made her second visit to the office she handed Adrian the Bid Receipt Book. "Thank you Debbie" Adrian said as she left and turning to February 1993 he looked at the attached receipts, and handing Dave the book he saw the Receipt signed by Daniel Bruce in his usual scrawl on the 4ᵗʰ February at 11.30 Unable to make out the counter signature, he handed it back to Adrian and said "I can't make out your company signatory, can you?" Looking at the Ramsden Construction signature Adrian immediately said "Steve Parker, he works in our Bid Team" Finishing his drink of water, he put down the glass on Adrian's desk without saying a word, as the final piece of the Jigsaw that he didn't know he needed, sat infront of him.

"Can I have a few minutes to collect my thoughts Adrian, preferably outside, oh and can I borrow Jackie at the same time?" Stumped as to what Dave was up to, he said "Yes, of course!" without really knowing what he was agreeing to, he picked up the phone and called Jackie's extension and asked her into his office. As she got to the office door, Adrian cut her off before she could enter the office" Dave would like a few minutes of your time" taking her hand he led her out into the car park with a look on his face that she had only glimpsed once before, when he explained about Daniel Bruce and his theory that he had murdered Sandra and Sam. Opening the door to the Jaguar he got into the driver's seat, but made no attempt start the car as Jackie got into the passenger seat, and waited for an explanation. Dave banged the steering wheel twice with his hands as Jackie looked at him, still waiting for him to let her know what was going on. "The Jigsaw! Jackie! I've finished the Jigsaw!" and leaning into kiss her he said "I couldn't have done it without you!" Completely confused she waited until he had sat back in his seat "Dave you're not making any sense!" Shaking his head he said "Sorry, let me ask you a couple of things first. You all have to sign in and out of work?" "Yes everyone, Health and Safety and in case of fire they use it as a roll call" looking quizzically she was even more confused by the next question "Can anyone use the photocopiers?" with no idea why he was asking she answered "Each department has its own codes, so the cost gets charged to the correct department" Banging the steering wheel again he turned to face her, and asked one final question, "Shall we go away this weekend?"

Walking back into the Ramsden Construction Offices holding Jackie's hand, Dave had a determined look on his face as they entered Adrian's Office. Closing the door behind them, Dave pulled a spare seat next to his for Jackie, as Adrian looked on waiting for the explanation for Dave's strange behaviour. Sitting down next to Jackie he said "Adrian, you have a legal department, is your Head of Department able to take sworn statements?" completely lost he could only say "Yes, Alistair Clark is our Head of Legal and can take and sign off statements. I take it you would like him to join us?" and picking up the phone he was about to dial his extension, when Dave put his hand on the phone stopping him. Looking at a shocked Adrian Dave said "Is he related to Steve Parker?" unable to follow Dave's path of thought Adrian said "No he joined us last year from McAllisters in Glasgow" taking his hand off Adrian's he said "Sorry about that, can you ask him to join us, please" Sitting waiting for Alistair to join them Adrian looked at Dave and Jackie sat next to each other, and wondered what he had got himself into, as a knock on the door followed by a 6ft tall Alistair Clark as he entered the office "You wanted something Adrian?" "Yes Alistair, well actually not me, Dave here, would like you to take a statement and.... well anything else Dave?" he added hoping the answers would be worth the upheaval. "Just one more thing Adrian" at which Adrian held up his open hand to imply whatever you want "Can you make sure Steve Parker doesn't leave the office today!" "Can't Dave, he's on holiday this week" with a smile that Adrian couldn't read, Dave replied "Even better, right let me begin, you ready Alistair?"

As Dave outlined his Jigsaw theory now backed up by facts, the looks on the faces of Jackie, Adrian and Alistair slowly went from sorrow, to astonishment and finally anger, as Dave tied all the pieces of his Jigsaw together. "I couldn't understand how or why Sandra had died, and slowly over the next two years things came out of the woodwork. First there was the attack on me that I couldn't prove, but which I now believe to be by Daniel Bruce as payment for going out with Sandra. Steve Parker who worked at the Council and now works for you, was his alibi when I eventually challenged Daniel about it. Then there was the overheard story of Steve Parker saying to Daniel Bruce about getting away with the fire. Both of these are hearsay, but the cigarette packets of Silk Cut in Sam Brown's locker, and the fact that he was known as Silky and a packet of Embassy cigarettes found on him after the fire, which I am sure is Daniel's chosen brand. It would be interesting to get the packet of Embassy cigarettes finger printed. It all kind of made sense but I couldn't link it to anything that made sense until now. Steve Parker is Daniel Bruce's best friend, and the signature on the Bid for the Archive Chambers contract you showed me is countersigned by Steve Parker and Daniel Bruce, the day the bids had to go in so how did they manage to undercut you, and why always a £1,000 was that a sign that Daniel had dealt with it. It then occurred to me that the link was nothing to do with Sandra and Sam, but just pure old fashioned greed. The Leisure Centre on the Manchester Road site doesn't make any sense to me financially, but the day before the fire, I asked Eric Normanton if Sandra and I could do some research into the Manchester Road site, as a relative of mine used to work there and left me a trust fund that it seems had something to do with the site, from when the Ramsbottoms owned it. That bit I can go into later, and there were rumours that it would be closing after the move away from coal fired power stations, and Daniel Bruce was in the office when I asked Eric Normanton about the research. So knowing we would be searching the records relating to Manchester Road, Daniel needed to get rid of the records, so Andersons can get hold of the site when it closes. I bet Daniel has a few of the records tucked away somewhere, he must have caught Sandra and Sam looking and probably not finding any records, and the rest is history. You'll need to get the Kirkdale Council records for 4th Feb 1993 but there is no way that Andersons could change their bid after you had lodged yours, unless someone from the inside had done it. Then you need to check any other bids you lost. The Police need to be persuaded to re-open the case on the fire, and finally although I hate to say it, it might be worth investigating Eric Normanton, I can't believe he didn't know anything, the way Daniel treated him was awful."

As Alistair finished his shorthand writing that looked like spaghetti, Adrian was the first to act. Picking up the phone he dialled a number he seemed to know off by heart and when his call was answered he said "Chief Inspector Adams please, tell him Adrian Ramsden is calling" after a few seconds. Adrian was having a conversation with his old friend and agreeing to meet for a drink after work he put the phone down. "Alistair. can you have that typed up and copied as soon as please!" and leaving the office he stopped before opening the door "Some story Dave!" and turning the door handle, he left Adrian sitting staring at Dave, and Jackie, who hadn't said a word in 20 minutes. "Some story Dave, as Alistair said, the difficult part will be getting Daniel Bruce to admit anything. Steve Parker will cough for sure. Eric Normanton, well it will be a shame to spoil his good name but as you say he must have know, or be complicit with what was going on. I'm going to speak to Francis tonight, that's Chief Inspector Adams to you, about re-opening the case. Not going to be easy but we have a paper trail to go at with the bids, and that might lead to an investigation of Andersons. It's just a shame there are no records of Manchester Road after the fire so we can keep Andersons and Kirkdale Council away. Apologies, but back to Money Dave"

For the first time in almost 30 minutes Jackie found her voice "But there are records!" at which both Dave and Adrian looked at the previously quiet Jackie, with Adrian getting in first "What do you mean Jackie?" taking a second she said "When I was between jobs a few years ago I got a temporary role through erm... Facilities Recruitment, and they placed me at Kirkdale Council in the Archive Department for 6 months" "When was this Jackie?" Adrian interrupted as Dave sat wondering what this had to do with what they had been discussing. "Well" she continued from memory "I think it was just before Christmas 1990 to summer 1991, it was supposed to be for a month, but they kept extending it as they were so far behind" desperate for some clarity, Dave cut in before she had a chance to finish "So what were you doing for 6 months Jackie?" "Copying files and plans onto Microfiche, we only got as far as the end of the Estates section before they called a halt, something to do with budgets, and I left to get another job"

As Jackie finished, a silence fell until Dave said "Microfiche, Christ I'd forgotten about that, more to the point I bet Daniel has as well. Every record is scanned and copied, date stamped electronically, and can be cross referenced with who last used them. Unbelievable!" Lost in his own world, Dave sat smiling to himself as Adrian said "I'll give you two a few minutes!" as he left his office closing the door behind him, with a smile of triumph on his face. Picking up the phone, Dave dialled Sterling Investigations and after being put through to Mr Williams, he said with a smile as he looked at Jackie "Mr Williams, I would like to cancel your services, I won't be needing them now, send me your final bill and the work you have done so far. Thank you" and putting down the phone he took Jackie's hand, and said "Let that be an end to it all!"

◆ ◆ ◆

Chapter 26 -The Reckoning

The following day the Offices of Anderson Developments Ltd were raided by the Police Fraud Squad team and the Kirkdale Council Estates Department was closed while forensic tests were carried out. The Microfiche section was taken away to be investigated. Daniel Bruce was arrested and released on bail pending further enquires, and Steve Parker was arrested upon his return from Benidorm, and also released on bail, with a condition that he not communicate, or contact Daniel Bruce until the trial.

Although it took some months the Police finally found enough evidence to charge Daniel Bruce, Steve Parker and Eric Normanton with a series of offences including 72 cases of Theft, 42 cases of Conspiracy to Defraud, 64 Counts of Breaking the Data Protection Act.

Eric Normanton gave evidence against both Daniel Bruce and Steve Parker, as it turned out Daniel had coerced Eric into initially turning a blind eye and later full complicity, all due to his desire for a classic Jaguar Mark II car for his retirement.

In June 1995 after a trial lasting 8 weeks at Leeds County Court, Judge Wilson asked the Jury Forewoman if they had reached a decision. The words Dave wanted to hear as he sat holding Jackie's hand in the Gallery came slowly, but clearly. "We have you Honour, we find the Defendants guilty"

Daniel Bruce was convicted, and sentenced to 5 years imprisonment.
Michael Anderson was convicted, and sentenced to 5 years imprisonment.
Steve Parker was convicted, and sentenced to 2 years impris-

onment.

Eric Normanton was convicted, and sentenced to 2 years imprisonment, suspended for two years.

As Daniel Bruce was led away from the dock he looked at where Dave was sat and although he couldn't be sure, he thought he heard him say "This isn't over!" but for Dave as he held Jackie's hand, it was.

Although the Police tried their best under the direction of Chief Constable Adams, there was still insufficient evidence to convict Daniel of starting the Archive Chambers fire. The fingerprints on the packet of Embassy cigarettes were inconclusive, due to too many people handling the packet and blurring the fingerprints, not only at the site, but subsequently either by the Police when in their evidence locker, or by the family of Sam Brown. His QC argued successfully that there are millions of packets of cigarettes in use every day, and one particular packet could easily have change on the day, should the shop Sam usually bought from have only Embassy cigarettes in stock. It was impossible to confirm which day the Embassy and Silk Cut cigarettes were purchased. Subsequently, the case of Murder was unproven against Daniel Bruce, but left on file.

Anderson Development Ltd was purchased out of Administration by Ramsden Construction Ltd in April 1995.

In July of 1995 Sid and Jane finally got engaged, just before the arrival of Samantha Clough in September 1995.

Dave and Jackie lived together at 15 Windy Hill, with a now 9 year old Caroline who every day looked more and more like her mother, according to Grandma Diane. When the Manchester Road Power Station file resurfaced as a result of the police work, when it was found at Daniel Bruce's house in the attic, and finally returned to Kirkdale Council following the trial, Dave was finally able to complete some research. It was with the aid of the Legal department of Kirkdale Council, following the release of the Microfiche files at the completion of the trial, that Dave set about finding the research that Mr Ramsdale of McParland and Co. had suggested in 1984. Hardly had he got through a week's worth of research, than the Manchester Road Power Station Company Limited wrote to McParland and Co on the 29th September 1995, and on Tuesday the 3rd of October, a letter arrived for Dave with the McParland and Co. name printed on the top left corner of the envelope. Arriving back at home after dropping off Caroline at Northfield School, he was just getting into the Jaguar, when the postman handed him two envelopes as he went past on his round, punctual as always. Deciding to read the contents at work he set off for his new Offices at Ramsden Construction Ltd, where he was, and had been Chief Surveyor for the last 6 months. Sitting at his desk, he opened the first envelope which was unmarked, seeing it was a dental appointment, he took out his diary and added it to next month's page. Picking up the second letter, he noted the printed name at the top of the envelope McParland and Co. and he wondered for a second, if they wanted the money back, before he opened it with his very nice, new letter opener that Jackie had bought him for his birthday. Taking the letter out he saw the usual giving nothing away letter that he had seen years before, this time signed on behalf of Mr Pearce.

2nd October 1995

Dear Mr Baxter,

We would be grateful if you could make an appointment with our Senior Partner, Mr Pearce at your earliest convenience to arrange and inspect some relevant legal document that are pertinent to yourself.

I look forward to your response

Mrs G. Sands (PA to Mr Pearce)

Picking up the phone, he dialled the number given and with

some gaps in his diary, he managed to squeeze in 4pm today with Mr Pearce, and dialling extension 52, he heard a voice he knew so well and said "Can you pick up Caroline tonight, I've got a meeting?" as he heard the words "Yes Mr Baxter" he knew she was with someone, and settling down to his work he wondered what McParland and Co. had got up their sleeve. Setting off early he managed to find a parking space in the small car park by the Offices of McParland and Co. Entering the offices, he introduced himself to the girl on Reception and took a seat, but hardly had he sat down than Mr Pearce was heading his way with a look that said 'Good news' . "Mr Baxter do come this way, Melanie, no calls please" and following Mr Pearce into the back of the offices, he found himself in the same room as some 10 years ago, which obviously hadn't see a decorator in all that time. "Take a seat Mr Baxter, well this is an auspicious day" he added sitting behind the desk that Mr Ramsdale has used all those years ago. Taking a letter out of the folder, he handed it to Dave and as he looked at it, saw it was from the Manchester Road Power Station Company Limited, but with a London address. He read the contents and not sure that what he had just read was what his mind was telling him, he read it again before sitting back and looking up from the letter quietly said "Does this mean what I think it means?"

Smiling like a man that has won the Lottery, Mr Pearce said "Yes Mr Baxter. Your Grandfather Windsor Carey must have been quite a man. I have had it confirmed by the Ramsbottom family solicitors, that all is above board and legal. You, Sir, are now the owner of the Manchester Road site. May I be the first to congratulate you!" seeing the colour go from Dave's face, he added "Shall I get you a glass of water, or perhaps something stronger!"

Walking back to his car he sat in the driver's seat for a few minutes and taking the letter from his pocket he read it again, before putting it back in his pocket. Driving home more than a little distracted, he stopped for some petrol when the gauge symbol flashed, for no apparent reason he picked up some flowers from the display before he went inside to pay. Picking up some Smarties for Caroline at the till, he paid and turned to headed back to his car "Your flowers Sir!" a voice said and smiling at the cashier, he reached and got the flowers from the counter and made it to the car, checking he had the Smarties in his pocket before he opened the door.

Parking behind Jackie's Peugeot, he locked the Jaguar and went down the garden path before opening the Front door awkwardly, with one hand trying to keep the flowers hidden behind his back. "I'm home" he called and Caroline ran as always with a smile, from the Lounge to greet him "Daddy" and handing over the Smarties she wasn't expecting, he took her hand and led her back to the Lounge, where Jackie was sat on the sofa "These are for you" he said handing her the flowers, as he saw Caroline popping a Smartie in her mouth. "Good meeting?" she asked, looking at the obvious petrol station flowers "Yes, have I got news for you!" he said with a sense of purpose "Well you'd better sit down Dave, because I've got some news for you, haven't we Caroline!" Jackie said with trepidation in her voice, and as Caroline jumped around, she shouted "Jackie's having a baby!" and with that, he knew his news could wait as he sat down next to Jackie, putting his around her he said "I think girlfriend, it's time I made an honest woman of you!" and kissing her softly, he realised it was something that he had meant to say to Sandra but never did, until she was gone and it was too late.

"I believe for every heart that's broken, there's a stranger's smile who can put it on the mend"

Jennifer Warnes/Restless

References:

Cover picture by: Ekaterina Chernenko

Books:

'The Thing in the Sink' by Frieda Hughes

'Jolly Snow' by Jane Hissey [i]

[i]Copyright : DG Leach 11/09/2020

ABOUT THE AUTHOR

D G Leach

The first of hopefully many books by this new Author proving that there is a book in everyone. Enjoy!

Printed in Great Britain
by Amazon

54012886R00249